The Midlander

Booth Tarkington

The Midlander

Copyright © 2020 Bibliotech Press
All rights reserved

The present edition is a reproduction of previous publication of this classic work. Minor typographical errors may have been corrected without note; however, for an authentic reading experience the spelling, punctuation, and capitalization have been retained from the original text.

ISBN: 978-1-64799-890-5

DEDICATED
TO
S. K. T.

CONTENTS

CHAPTER

I	1
II	11
III	20
IV	26
V	38
VI	46
VII	58
VIII	66
IX	71
X	84
XI	91
XII	98
XIII	106
XIV	112
XV	118
XVI	127
XVII	135
XVIII	145
XIX	151
XX	159
XXI	165
XXII	173
XXIII	177
XXIV	182
XXV	189
XXVI	194
XXVII	201
XXVIII	207
XXIX	208
XXX	220

CHAPTER I

PEOPLE used to say of the two Oliphant brothers that Harlan Oliphant looked as if he lived in the Oliphants' house, but Dan didn't. This was a poor sort of information to any one who had never seen the house, but of course the supposition was that everybody had seen it and was familiar with its significance. It stood in a great, fine yard, in that row of great, fine yards at the upper end of National Avenue, before the avenue swung off obliquely and changed its name to Amberson Boulevard. The houses in the long row were such houses as are built no more; bricklayers worked for a dollar a day and the workman's day was ten hours long when National Avenue grew into its glory. Those houses were of a big-walled solidity to withstand time, fire, and tornado, but they found another assailant not to be resisted by anything: this conqueror, called Progress, being the growth of the city. Until the growth came they were indomitable and fit for the centuries.

Moreover, they were of a dignified spaciousness not now to be accomplished except by millionaires with wives content to spend their days getting new servants. The New Yorker, admitted to these interiors upon a visit westward, discovered an amplitude with which he had little familiarity at home, where the brownstone fronts and squeezed apartments showed him no such suites of big rooms; for, of all the million people in New York, only a dozen families could have houses comparable in size or stateliness. "Stately" was the word, though here some little care must be taken, of course, with an eye to those who will not admit that anything short of Blenheim or the Luxembourg is stately. The stateliness of the Oliphants' house was precisely the point in that popular discrimination between the two young men who lived there: Harlan Oliphant, like the house, was supposed to partake of this high quality, but stateliness was the last thing any one ever thought of in connection with Dan.

The youth of the brothers, in the happy and comfortable nineties of the last century, is well remembered in their city, where the Christmas holidays could never be thought really begun till the two Oliphants had arrived from college and their broad-shouldered, long-tailed coats and incredibly high white collars were seen officially moving in the figures of a cotillion. They usually arrived on the same day, though often not by the same train; but this was the mark of no disagreement or avoidance of each other, yet bore some significance upon the difference between them. It was the fashion to say of them that never were two brothers so alike yet so unlike; and

1

although both were tall, with blue eyes, brown hair, and features of pleasant contour decisively outlined in what is called a family likeness, people who knew them well found it a satisfying and insoluble puzzle that they were the offspring of the same father and mother.

The contrast appeared in childhood and was manifest to even the casual onlooker when Dan Oliphant was eleven or twelve years old and Harlan ten or eleven. At that age Harlan was already an aristocrat, and, what is more remarkable, kept himself always immaculate. If his collar rumpled or was soiled he went immediately to his room and got a fresh one; he washed his hands three or four times a day without parental suggestion and he brushed his hair almost every time he washed his hands. He was fastidious in his choice of companions, had no taste for chance acquaintances, and on a school holiday could most frequently be found in the library at home, reading a book beyond his years. The lively Daniel, on the contrary, disported himself about the neighbourhood—or about other neighbourhoods, for that matter— in whatever society offered him any prospect of gayety. He played marbles "for keeps" with ragtag and bobtail on every vacant lot in town; he never washed his hands or face, or brushed his hair, except upon repeated command, yet loved water well enough to "run off swimming" and dive through a film of ice upon an early Saturday in March. He regaled himself with horseplay up and down the alleys and had long talks with negro coachmen in their stables, acquiring strange wisdom of them; he learned how to swear with some intricacy, how to smoke almost anything not fireproof, how to "inhale," how to gamble with implements more sophisticated than marbles, and how to keep all these accomplishments from the knowledge of his parents. He kept them from Harlan's knowledge, also, though not out of any fear that Harlan would "tell."

At some time in their early childhood the brothers had made the discovery that they were uncongenial. This is not to say that they were unamiable together, but that they had assumed a relation not wholly unknown among brothers. They spoke to each other when it was necessary; but usually, if they happened to find themselves together, they were silent, each apparently unconscious of the other's presence. Sometimes, though rarely, they had a short argument, seldom upon a subject of great importance; and only once did a difference between them attain the dimensions of a quarrel.

This was on a summer day of feverish temperature, and the heat may have had something to do with the emotion displayed by young Daniel, then aged twelve. He was engaged, that afternoon,

2

with a business friend, Master Sam Kohn, and they were importantly busy in a latticed summer-house, an ornament of the commodious lawn. They had entered into a partnership for the sale of "Fancy Brackets and Fittings," which they manufactured out of old cigar boxes, with the aid of glue, a jig-saw, and blue paint. The computed profits were already enormous, though no sales had been attempted, since the glue was slow to harden on such a hot day; and the partners worked diligently, glad to shed their perspiration for the steadily increasing means to obtain riches.

At five o'clock Harlan dropped lightly from the big stone-trimmed bay window of the library, crossed the lawn, where the grass was being gilded now by the westering sun, and halted before the entrance of the summer-house. He was the picture of a cool young gentleman, perfect in white linen; his coat and trousers of this pleasant material were unflawed by wrinkle or stain; his patent-leather pumps, unmarred by the slightest crack, glittered among the short green blades of grass; his small black satin tie was as smooth as his brown hair.

To this perfection the busy partners within the summer-house were a sufficient contrast. Soiled blue upon every available surface, they continued their labours, paying no visible attention to the cold-eyed young observer, but consulting each other perhaps the more importantly because of the presence of an audience, however skeptical. Master Kohn, swarthy, bow-legged, and somewhat undersized for his thirteen years, was in fact pleased to be associated with the superior Harlan, even so tenuously. He was pleased, also, to be a partner of Dan's, though this was no great distinction, because Dan, as the boys' world knew, would willingly be friendly (or even intimate) with anybody, and consequently no social advancement was to be obtained through him. That commodity is to be had of only those who decline to deal in it, and thus Sam Kohn felt that he was becoming imbued with a certain amount of superiority because Harlan Oliphant had come to look on at the work.

Sam decided to make a suggestion. "Look at your brother," he said to Dan. "Maybe he'd like to git into our partnership. We could give him a share, if he starts in fresh and works hard."

"Thanks!" Harlan said with cold sarcasm, and addressed his brother: "Do you know what time it is and what the family is supposed to do this evening?"

"Yes," Dan answered, not looking up from his jig-saw. "We're goin' to dinner at grandma Savage's."

"Mother sent me to tell you it's time for you to come in and wash yourself and dress up," said Harlan. "The mess you've got

3

yourself in, it'll take you till after six o'clock, and we're supposed to be there then."

"Sam and I got some pretty important jobs to finish," Dan returned carelessly. "I got plenty time to change my clo'es and get washed up."

"No, you haven't. You quit playing with that boy and those dirty things and go in the house."

Upon this, Dan stopped the operation of the jig-saw and looked at his brother in a puzzled way. "What you mean callin' our brackets and fittin's 'dirty things?'" he inquired. "I expect you don't hardly realize Sam Kohn and I got a regular factory here, Harlan."

"A 'factory,' is it?" said Harlan, and laughed in the manner of a contemptuous adult. "Well, you close up your old factory and come in the house and get ready."

"I can't for a while," Dan returned, beginning his work with the jig-saw again. "I told you we got lots to do before we quit to-night."

"You stop playing with that silly little saw," Harlan said sharply, for he had begun to feel some irritation. "You come in the house right this instant."

"No; I can't yet, Harlan. Sam and I got to—"

"Never mind!" Harlan interrupted. "You come in the house and let this boy go home."

There was a frosty sharpness in his way of saying "let this boy go home" that caused Dan to stop his work again and stare at his brother challengingly. "Here!" he exclaimed. "This is as much my father and mother's yard as it is yours, and you got no business hintin' at any friend of mine to go home."

"Haven't I?" Harlan inquired, adopting a light mockery. "So this is a friend of yours, is it?"

"Yes, it is."

"Oh, a friend?" Harlan mocked. "Oh, excuse me! I didn't understand!"

This proved to be intolerably provocative;—Dan abandoned the jig-saw and stepped out of the summer-house to confront his brother frowningly. "You shut up, Harlan Oliphant," he said. "This is Sam Kohn's and my factory, and he's got a right here. You quit your talkin' so much around here."

"You quit your own talking," Harlan retorted. "You do what mother sent me to tell you to, and let that dirty little Jew go home!"

"What?" Dan cried.

"You better!" Harlan said, standing his ground, though Dan lifted his hand threateningly. "We don't want any dirty little Jews on our premises."

4

Dan gulped. "It isn't his fault he's a Jew. You take that back!"

"I won't," said Harlan. "He is little and he is dirty and he's a Jew. How you going to deny it?"

Flushed with anger and greatly perplexed, Dan glanced over his shoulder at Master Kohn, who looked on with an inscrutable expression. "Well, what if I can't?" Dan said desperately, after this glance at his guest and partner. "You got no right to insult him."

"It isn't an insult if it's true, is it?"

"Yes, it is; and you ought to be ashamed of yourself. I got a notion—I got a notion—"

"What notion have you got?" Harlan asked scornfully, as his brother paused, swallowing heavily.

"I got a notion to make you ashamed!"

"How would you do it?"

" 'How?' I'll show you how!" And again Dan's clenched right hand lowered threateningly. The brothers stood eye to eye, and both faces were red.

"Go on," said Harlan. "Hit me!"

Dan's fist, like his expression, wavered for a moment, then he said: "Well, I wish you weren't my brother; but you are, and I won't hit you."

"I thought you wouldn't," Harlan retorted, turning toward the house. "I guess I'll have to tell mother you won't wash yourself and dress until she comes and sends this dirty little Jew out of our yard."

Thus, having discovered the tender spot in his opponent's sensibilities, he avenged himself for the threat, and went on. His brother moved impulsively, as if to follow and punish, but Mrs. Oliphant had long ago impressed her sons heavily with the story of Cain and Abel, and he halted, while Harlan went on coolly and disappeared into the house by a side entrance.

"Doggone you!" Dan muttered; then turned back to the factory, where Master Kohn, his head down and his hands in his pockets, was scuffing sawdust meditatively with the soles of his shoes. Dan likewise scuffed sawdust for a time.

"Well," Sam Kohn said finally, "I guess I better go on home before your mamma comes to turn me out."

"I don't guess she would," Dan said, not looking at him, but keeping his gaze upon his own scuffing shoe. "She's got a good deal o' politeness about her, and I don't guess she would. You got a right to stay here long as you want, Sammy. It's half your factory."

"Not if your family puts me out, it ain't."

"He had no business to call you that, Sammy."

"To call me which?"

"A—a Jew," said Dan, still keeping his eyes upon the ground.

5

"Why, I am a Jew."

"Well, maybe; but—" Dan paused uncomfortably, then continued: "Well, he didn't have any right to call you one."

"Yes, he had," Sam returned, to his friend's surprise. "He could call me a Jew just the same I could call you English."

"English? I'm not English."

"Well, you're from English."

"No," Dan protested mildly. "Not for a couple o' hundred years, anyway."

"Well, I ain't from Jews a couple thousand years, maybe."

"But I'm full-blooded American," said Dan.

"So'm I," Sam insisted. "You're American from English, and I'm American from Jews. He's got a right to call me a Jew."

Dan stared at him incredulously. "Don't you mind it?"

"Yes," Sam admitted, "I do when he says it for a insult. He's got a right to call me a Jew, but he hasn't got no right to call me a Jew for a insult."

"Well, he did," Dan remarked gloomily. "He meant it the way you might call somebody 'Irish' or 'Dutchy' or 'Nigger.' "

"I know it. He called me dirty and little, too. Well, I am little, but I ain't no dirtier than what you are, Dan, and you're his own brother."

"Well, then, you oughtn't to mind his callin' you dirty, Sam."

"He wouldn't call you dirty the same way he would me," Sam returned shrewdly; and then, after a momentary pause, he sighed and turned to go.

But that sigh of his, which had in it the quality of patience, strongly affected Dan's sympathies, for a reason he could not have explained. "Don't go, Sammy," he said. "You don't have to go just because he—"

"Yeh, I better," Sam said, not looking back, but continuing to move toward the distant gate. "I better go before your mamma comes to put me out."

Dan protested again, but Sam shook his head and went on across the lawn, his hands in his pockets, his head down. The high iron fence, painted white, culminated in an elaborate gateway, and, when Sam passed out to the sidewalk there, the iron gateposts rose far above him. Plodding out between these high white posts, the shabby little figure did not lack pathos; nor was pathos absent from it as it went doggedly down the street in the thinning gold of the late afternoon sunshine. Sam looked back not once; but Dan watched him until he was out of sight, then returned to the interior of the summer-house, sat down, and stared broodingly at the littered floor. The floor was not what he saw, however, for his actual eyes were without vision just then, and it was his mind's eye that was busy. It dwelt upon the picture of the exiled Sam Kohn departing forlornly, and the longer it thus dwelt the warmer and more threatening grew a painful feeling that seemed to locate itself in Dan's upper chest, not far below his collar bone.

This feeling remained there while he dressed; and it was still there when he sat down at his grandmother's table for dinner. In fact, it so increased in poignancy that he could not eat with his customary heartiness; and his lack of appetite, though he made play with seemingly busy fork and spoon to cover it, fell under the sharp eye of the lady at the head of the table. She was a handsome, dominant old woman, with high colour in her cheeks at seventy-eight, and thick hair, darker than it was gray, under her lace cap. She sat straight upright in her stiff chair, for she detested easy-chairs and had never in all her life lounged in one or sat with her knees crossed; such things were done not by ladies, but by hoodlums, she said. Her husband, a gentle, submissive old man, was frail and bent with his years, though they had brought him great worldly prosperity; and the grandchildren of this couple never spoke of the house as "Grandpa Savage's," but always as "Grandma Savage's," an intuitive discrimination that revealed the rulership. Mrs. Savage ruled by means of a talent she had for destructive criticism, which several times prevented her optimistic husband from venturing into ruin, and had established her as the voice of wisdom.

"Daniel," she said presently;—"you're not eating."

"Yes, I am, grandma."

"No. Ever since you came to the table, you've been sitting there with your head bent down like that and moving your hands to pretend you're eating, but not eating. What's the matter with you?"

"Nothin'," he muttered, not lifting his head. "I'm all right."

"Adelaide," Mrs. Savage said to his mother;—"has his appetite been failing lately?"

"Why, no, mamma," Mrs. Oliphant answered. She was a pretty woman, quietly cheerful and little given to alarms or anxieties. "Not seriously," she added, smiling. "He did very well at lunch, at least."

"He looks sickish," said Mrs. Savage grimly. "He looks as if he were beginning a serious illness. Well people don't sit with their heads down like that. What is the matter with you, Daniel?"

"Nothin'," he said. "I told you I'm all right."

"He isn't though," Mrs. Savage insisted, addressing the others. "Do you know what's the matter with him, Harlan?"

"Too much glue, I expect."

7

"What?"

"Too much glue," Harlan repeated. "He was playing with a lot of nasty glue and paint all afternoon, and I expect the smell's made him sick. Too much glue and too much Jew."

"Jew?" his grandmother inquired. "What do you mean by 'too much Jew,' Harlan?"

"He had a dirty little bow-legged Jew playing with him."

"See here!" Dan said huskily, but he did not look up. "You be careful!"

"Careful of what?" Harlan inquired scornfully.

"Careful of what you say."

"Daniel, were you playing with a Jew?" his grandmother asked.

"Yes, I was."

He still did not look up, but his voice had a tone, plaintive and badgered, that attracted the attention of his grandfather, and the old gentleman interposed soothingly: "Don't let 'em fret you, Dannie. It wasn't particularly wicked of you to play with a Jew, I expect."

"No," said Dan's father. "I don't believe I'd let myself be much worried over that, if I were you, Dan."

"No?" said Mrs. Savage, and inquired further, somewhat formidably: "You don't prefer your sons to choose companions from their own circle, Henry Oliphant?"

"Oh, yes, I do, ma'am," he returned amiably. "As a general thing I believe it's better for them to be intimate with the children of their mother's and father's old family friends; but at the same time I hope Dan and Harlan won't forget that we live in a country founded on democratic principles. The population seems to me to begin to show signs of altering with emigration from Europe; and it's no harm for the boys to know something of the new elements, though for that matter we've always had Jews, and they're certainly not bad citizens. I don't see any great harm in Dan's playing a little with a Jewish boy, if he wants to."

"I wasn't playin'," Dan said.

"Weren't you?" his father asked. "What were you doing?"

"We were—we were manufacturing. We were manufacturing useful articles."

"What were they?"

"Ornamental brackets to nail on walls and put things on. We were goin' to make good money out of it."

"Well, that was all right," Mr. Oliphant said genially. "Not a bad idea at all. You're all right, Dannie."

Unfortunately, a word of sympathy often undermines the

8

composure of the recipient; and upon this Dan's lower lip began to quiver, though he inclined his head still farther to conceal the new tokens of his agitation.

He was not aided by his coolly observant young brother. "Going to cry about it?" Harlan asked, quietly amused.

"You let Dannie alone," said the grandfather; whereupon Harlan laughed. "You ought to see what he and his little Jew partner called brackets!" he said. "Dan's always thinking he's making something, and it's always something just awful. What he and that Sam Kohn were really making to-day was a horrible mess of our summer-house. It'll take a week's work for somebody to get it cleaned up, and he got mad at me and was going to hit me because mamma sent me to tell him to come in the house and get ready for dinner."

"I did not," Dan muttered.

"You didn't? Didn't you act like you were going to hit me?"

"Yes," Dan said. "But it wasn't because what you say. It was because you called Sam names."

"I didn't."

"You did!" And now Dan looked up, showing eyes that glistened along the lower lids. "You—you hurt his feelings."

Harlan had the air of a self-contained person who begins to be exasperated by a persistent injustice, and he appealed to the company. "I told him time and again mamma wanted him to come in and get ready to come here for dinner, and he simply wouldn't do it."

Mrs. Savage shook her head. "I've always told you," she said to her daughter, "you'll repent bitterly some day for your lack of discipline with your children. You're not raising them the way I raised mine, and some day—"

But Harlan had not finished his explanation. "So, after I waited and waited," he continued, "and they just went on messing up our summer-house, I told him he'd better come in and let the dirty little Jew boy go home. That's all I said, and he was going to hit me for it."

"You—you hurt his fuf-feelings," Dan stammered, as his emotion increased. "I told you, you hurt his feelings!"

"Pooh!" Harlan returned lightly. "What feelings has he got? He wouldn't be around where he doesn't belong if he had any."

"I asked him there," Dan said, the tears in his eyes overflowing as he spoke; and he began to grope hurriedly through his various pockets for a handkerchief. "He had a right to be where he was invited, didn't he? You—you called him—"

9

"I said he was just exactly what he is, and if he ever comes around our yard again, I'll say it again."

"No, you won't!"

"Oh, yes, I will," Harlan said with perfect composure; and this evidence that he believed himself in the right and would certainly carry out his promise was too much for the suffering Dan, who startled his relatives by unexpectedly sobbing aloud.

"You dog-gone old thing!" he cried, his shoulders heaving and his voice choked with the half-swallowed tears in his throat. "I will hit you now!" He rose, making blind sweeps with both arms in the direction of Harlan, and, in a kind of anguish, gurgling out imprecations and epithets that shocked his family; but Mr. Oliphant caught the flailing hands, took the boy by the shoulders and impelled him from the room, going with him. A moment or two later the passionate voice ceased to be coherent; plaintive sounds were heard, growing fainter with increasing distance; and Mr. Oliphant, slightly flushed, returned to finish his dinner.

"I sent him home," he explained. "He'll probably feel better, out in the dark alone."

"And may I inquire, Henry Oliphant," said the old lady at the head of the table;—"is that all you intend to do about it?"

"Well, I might talk to him after he cools off a little."

"Yes, I suppose that will be all!" Mrs. Savage returned with a short laugh, emphatically one of disapproval. "It's a fine generation you modern people are raising. When I was fifteen I was supposed to be a woman, but my father whipped me for a slight expression of irreverence on Sunday."

"I'm sorry to hear it, ma'am," her son-in-law said genially.

"I'm not sorry it happened," she informed him, not relaxing. "Such things were part of a discipline that made a strong people."

"Yes, ma'am; I've no doubt it's to your generation we owe what the country is to-day."

"And it's your generation that's going to let it go to the dogs!" the old lady retorted sharply. "May I ask what you intend to do to protect Harlan when you go home and his brother attacks him?"

But at this Oliphant laughed. "Dan won't attack him. By the time we get home Dan will probably be in bed."

"Then he'll attack Harlan to-morrow."

"No, he won't, ma'am. I don't say Dan won't sleep on a damp pillow to-night, the way he was going on, but by to-morrow he'll have forgotten all about it."

"He won't," she declared. "A child can't have a passion like that, with its parents doing nothing to discipline it, and then just forget. Harlan only did his duty, but Dan will attack him again the first chance he gets. You'll see!"

Oliphant was content to let her have the last word—perhaps because he knew she would have it in any event—so he laughed again, placatively, and began to talk with his father-in-law of Mr. Blaine's chances at the approaching national convention; while Mrs. Savage shook her gloomy, handsome head and made evident her strong opinion that the episode was anything but closed. There would always henceforth be hatred between the two brothers, she declared to her daughter, whom she succeeded in somewhat depressing.

But as a prophet she appeared before long to have failed, at least in regard to the predicted feeling between her two grandsons. Dan may have slept on his wrath, but he did not cherish it; and the next day his relations with Harlan were as usual. The unarmed neutrality, which was not precisely a mutual ignoring, was resumed and continued. It continued, indeed, throughout the youth of the brothers; and prevailed with them during their attendance at the university at New Haven, whither they went in imitation of their father before them. The studious Harlan matriculated in company with his older brother; they were classmates, though not roommates; and peace was still prevalent between them when they graduated. Nevertheless, in considering and comprehending the career of a man like Daniel Oliphant, certain boyhood episodes appear to shed a light, and the conflict over little Sammy Kohn bears some significance.

CHAPTER II

IT WAS not altogether without difficulty that the older of the brothers graduated. Harlan obtained a diploma inscribed with a special bit of classic praise, for he was an "Honour Man"; but Daniel trod the primrose way a little too gayly as a junior and as a senior. Anxiety had sometimes been felt at home, though knowledge of this was kept from old Mrs. Savage; and Mr. and Mrs. Oliphant were relieved of a strain when Dan was granted his degree at a most reluctant eleventh hour, and telegraphed them:

Last prof to hold out gave up after I talked to him all afternoon and said I could have diploma, if I would quit arguing.

Thus the two young bachelors of arts came forth together into a pleasant world, of which they already knew somewhat less than they supposed they did.

The world for them, in that day, which the newspapers were beginning to call fin de siècle, included rather sketchily London, Paris, Florence, and a part of the Alps, for they had spent two vacations abroad with their parents; but in the main the field of action to which they emerged from the campus consisted of their own city and New York. No sooner were they out of the university than they began the series of returns eastward that was part of the life of every affluent young midland graduate. They went back for the football games, for class dinners, for baseball and boat races, and commencement. New York was their playground as they went and came; and they remained there to play for months at a time.

It was a pleasanter playground in those days than it is now, when even the honeycombed ground under foot has its massacres, and the roaring surface congests with multitude on multitude till fires must burn and patients must die, since neither firemen nor doctors may pass. For the growth came upon New York as it came upon the midland cities, and it produced a glutted monster, able to roar and heave and mangle, but not to digest or even to swallow the swarms that came begging to be devoured. In the change there perished something romantic and charming, something that a true poet used to call Bagdad.

So far as it concerned Mr. Daniel Oliphant, aged twenty-six, New York was romantic Bagdad enough when the jingling harness began to glitter in the park and on the Avenue in the afternoon, and he would go out from the Holland House to see the pretty women, all beautifully dressed, he thought, and wearing clumps of violets, or orchids, as they reclined in their victorias drawn by high-stepping horses. Dan liked to watch, too, the handsome grooms and coachmen in their liveries, with cockaded silk hats, white breeches, top boots, and blue coats; for they were the best-dressed men in the town, he thought, and he often wished he knew whether they were really as haughty as the horses they drove or only affected to be so proud professionally.

In New York, this Daniel took some thought to his own tailoring and haberdashing; he would even add a camellia to the lapel of his frock coat when he strolled down to lounge in the doorway of the great Fifth Avenue Hotel and stare at the procession of lovely girls from everywhere in the country, their faces rosy in the wind, as they walked up Broadway after an autumn matinée. Then he would join the procession, a friend accoutred like himself being usually with him, and they would accompany the procession

12

sedately in its swing up the Avenue; sometimes leaving it, however, at the magnificent new Waldorf, where the men's café offered them refreshment among lively companions. In truth, this congenial resort had too great an attraction for the amiable Dan, and so did the room with the big mirror behind the office at the Holland House. Moreover, when he spoke of Daly's, he did not always mean Mr. Augustin Daly's theatre, though he preferred it to the other theatres; sometimes he meant a Daly's where adventure was to be obtained by any one who cared to bet he could guess when a marble would stop rolling upon a painted disk.

Of course he made excursions into the Bowery, waltzed and two-stepped at the Haymarket after long dinners at clubs, fell asleep in hansom cabs at sunrise, and conducted himself in general about as did any other "rather wild young man," native or alien, in the metropolis. There were droves of such young men, and, like most of the others, Dan frequently became respectable, and went to a dinner or a dance at the house of a classmate; he was even seen at church in the pew of a Madison Avenue family of known severity. However, no one was puzzled by this act of devotion, for Lena McMillan, the daughter of the severe house, was pretty enough to be the explanation for anything.

Her brother George, lacking the severity of other McMillans, and as unobtrusive as possible in advertising that lack, was one of Dan's chance acquaintances during a Bagdadian night. At the conclusion of many festivities, the chance acquaintance murmured his address, but Dan comprehended the unwisdom of a sunrise return of so flaccid a young gentleman into a house as formidable as the McMillans' appeared to be, when the night-hawk hansom stopped before it; and the driver was instructed to go on to the Holland House. Young McMillan woke at noon in Dan's room there; shuddered to think that but for a Good Samaritan this waking might have taken place at home, and proved himself first grateful, then devoted. It was the beginning of a lifelong friendship; and he took Dan to tea in Madison Avenue that afternoon.

Something withholding about the McMillans reminded their guest of his brother Harlan; and probably Dan would have defined this as "an air of reserve"; but it was more than reserve, deeper than reserve, as in time he discovered. George McMillan alone seemed to have none of it; on the contrary, his air was habitually friendly and apologetic—possibly because of what he knew about himself and what his family didn't. Mrs. McMillan and her daughters found it unnecessary either to smile or offer their hands when George presented the good-looking young Midlander, nor did they seem to believe themselves committed to any effort to make the stranger feel at home in their long, dark drawing-room.

They gave him a cup of tea and a bit of toast, and that appeared to be the end of their obligation to a stray guest, for they at once continued a conversation begun before his arrival, not addressing themselves to him or even looking at him. Mrs. McMillan's cousin's husband, named Oliver, he gathered, was about to be offered a position in the cabinet at Washington, and Mrs. McMillan hoped Oliver wouldn't accept, because Milly and Anna and Charlotte, persons unknown to Dan, would have to give up so much if they went to live in Washington instead of Boston. If it were an ambassadorship the President wanted Oliver for, that would be better, especially on Charlotte's account.

The guest began to have an uncomfortable feeling that he must be invisible;—no one seemed to know that he was present, not even the grateful George, who was feeble that afternoon and looked distrustfully at his tea, of which he partook with an air of foreboding. Dan could not help meditating upon what a difference there would have been if the position were reversed, with George as the guest and himself as the host. Dan thought of it: how heartily his mother and father would have shaken hands with the young Easterner, welcoming him, doing every reassuring thing they could to make him feel at home, talking cordial generalities until they could get better acquainted and find what interested him. But although Dan felt awkward and even a little resentful, it was not the first time he had been exposed to this type of hospitality, and he was able to accept it as the custom of the country. He made the best of it and was philosophic, thinking that the McMillans had given tea to a great many stray young men of whom they knew nothing, and saw once but usually never again. Also, it was a pleasure to look at Lena McMillan, even though she was so genuinely unaware of him.

Outwardly, at least, she was unlike her mother and older sister. Mrs. McMillan was a large woman, shapely, but rather stony—or so she appeared to Dan—and her hair rose above her broad pink forehead as a small dome of trim gray curls, not to be imagined as ever being disarranged or uncurled or otherwise than as they were. She and her older daughter, who resembled her, both wore black of an austere fashionableness; but the younger Miss McMillan had alleviated her own dark gown with touches of blue—not an impertinent blue, but a blue darkly effective; and, with what seemed almost levity in this heavy old drawing-room, she wore Italian earrings of gold and lapis lazuli. Her mother did not approve of these; no one except opera singers wore earrings, Mrs. McMillan had told her before the arrival of the two young men.

Lena was sometimes defined as a "petite brunette," and sometimes as a "perfectly beautiful French doll"; for she had to perfection a doll's complexion and eyelashes; but beyond this point the latter definition was unfair, since dolls are usually thought wanting in animation, a quality she indeed possessed. Dan Oliphant, watching her, thought he had never before met so sparkling a creature; and a glamour stole over him. He began to think she was the most beautiful girl he had ever seen.

Possibly she became aware of the favour with which he was regarding her, for although her shoulder and profile were toward him, and for twenty minutes and more she seemed to be as unconscious of his presence as her mother and older sister really were, she finally gave him a glance and spoke to him. "George tells me you're from the West," she said.

"No. Not very," he returned.

"Not very west?"

"I mean not from the Far West," Dan explained. "Out there they'd call me an Easterner, of course."

"Gracious!" she cried incredulously. "Would they, really?"

Already he thought her a wonderful being, but at this he showed some spirit. "I'm afraid so," he said.

She laughed, not offended, and exclaimed: "Oh, so you don't mind being a Westerner! I only meant you people are so funny about rubbing in the letter R and overdoing the short A that no one can ever make a mistake about which of the provinces you belong in. I've been in the West, myself—rather west, that is. I didn't care for it much."

"Where was it?"

"Rochester. I believe you're from farther out, aren't you? Perhaps you can tell me if it's true, what we hear things are like beyond Rochester."

"Things beyond Rochester?" he asked, mystified. "What sort of things do you mean?"

"All sorts," she answered. "I've always heard that when you get west of Rochester every house has a room you people call a 'sitting-room', and you always keep a sewing-machine in it and apples on a centre table, and all the men keep tobacco in their cheeks and say, 'Wa'al, no, ma'am,' and 'Why, certainly, ma'am,' and 'Yes, ma'am!' Isn't that what it's like?"

"Who told you so?"

"Oh, I had a cousin who used to visit people out there. She said it was funny but dreadful. Isn't it?"

"I wish you'd come and see," he said earnestly. "I wish you and your brother'd come and let me show you."

15

"Good heavens," she cried;—"but you're hospitable! Do you always ask everybody to visit you after they've said two words to you?"

"No, not everybody," he returned, and on the impulse continued: "I'd ask you, though, after you'd said one word to me." And because he meant it, he instantly became red.

"Good heavens!" she cried again, and stared at him thoughtfully, perceiving without difficulty his heightened colour. "Is that the way they talk in the West, Mr.—uh—"

"Oliphant," he said.

"What?"

"My name's Oliphant," he informed her apologetically. "You called me Mister Uh."

"I see," she said, and as her attention was caught just then by something her sister was saying about Milly and Anna and Charlotte and Oliver, she turned from him to say something more, herself, about Milly and Anna and Charlotte and Oliver. Then, having turned away from him, she turned not back again, but seemed to have forgotten him.

The son of the house presently took him away, the mother and her older daughter murmuring carelessly as the two young men rose to go, while Lena said more distinctly, "Good afternoon, Mister Uh." But the unfortunate Daniel carried with him a picture that remained tauntingly before his mind's eye; and he decided to stay in New York a little longer, though he had written his father that he would leave for home the next day. He had been stricken at first sight.

He could not flatter himself that she had bestowed a thought upon him. On the contrary, he told himself that his impetuosity had made headway backwards; and he was as greatly astonished as he was delighted when George McMillan came to see him two afternoons later, at the Holland House, and brought him a card for a charity ball at the Metropolitan. "We had some extra ones," George said. "Lena thought you might like to come."

"She did? Why, I—I—" Dan was breathless at once.

"What?"

"Why, I didn't think she noticed I was on earth. This is perfectly beautiful of her!"

"Why, no," George assured him; "it's nothing at all. We had four or five cards we really didn't know what to do with. There'll be an awful crowd there, all kinds of people."

"Yes, I know; but it was just beautiful of her to think of me." And Dan added solemnly: "That sister of yours reminds me of a flower."

"She does?" George said, visibly surprised. "You mean Lena?"

16

"Yes, I do. She's like the most perfect flower that ever blossomed."

"That's strange news to me," said George. "Then maybe you'd be willing to come to the house to dinner and go to this show with the family. Heaven knows I'd like to have you; it might help me to sneak out after we get 'em there. You sure you could stand it?"

"I should consider it the greatest privilege of my life," said Dan.

"Heavens, but you're solemn!" his caller exclaimed. "You make me feel at home—I mean, as if I were at home with my solemn family. Wait till you meet some of the others—and my father. He's the solemnest. In fact, they're all solemn except Lena. There's only one trouble with Lena."

"What is it?"

"The poor thing hasn't got any sense," Lena's brother said lightly. "Never did. Never will have. Otherwise she's charming—when she's in a mood to be!"

Evidently Lena was in a mood to be charming that night; she sat next to Dan at the solemn dinner and chattered to him gayly, though in a lowered voice, for George had not exaggerated when he spoke of his father. If she was a French doll, she was at least a radiant one in her ball gown of heavy ivory silk, and it was a thrilled young Midlander indeed who took her lightly in his arms for a two-step when they came out upon the dancing floor that had been laid over the chairs at the opera house. "It was nice of you to send me these flowers," she said, as he dexterously moved her through the crowd of other two-steppers. "They'd tell anybody you're Western, if nothing else would. Western men always send orchids. But then, of course, nobody'd need to be told you're from out there. You tell them yourself."

"You mean I always mention it?"

"No," she laughed;—"your dialect does. The way you pronounce R and A, and slide your words together."

"I've got a brother that doesn't," said Dan. "He talks the way you and your family do; he says 'lahst' and 'fahst' and calls father 'fathuh' and New York 'New Yawk,' and keeps all his words separated. He began it when he was about fifteen and he's stuck to it ever since. Says he doesn't do it to be English, but because it's correct pronunciation. I expect you'd like him."

At that she looked up at him suddenly, and he was shown an inscrutable depth of dark blue glance that shook his heart. "I like you!" she said.

"Do you?" he gasped. "You didn't seem to, that day I met you."

She laughed. "I didn't decide I liked you till after you'd gone.

You aren't quite cut to the pattern of most of the men I know. There's something hearty about your looks; and I like your broad shoulders and your not seeming to have put a sleek surface over you. At least it's pleasant for a change."

"Is that all?" he asked, a little disappointed. "Just for a change?"

"Never mind. Is there anybody else in your family besides your brother?"

"Heavens, yes! To begin with, I've got a grand old grandmother; she's over ninety, but she's the head of the family all right! Then there's my father and mother—"

"What are they like?"

"My mother's beautiful," Dan said. "She's just the loveliest, kindest person in the world, and so's my father. He's a lawyer."

"What are you?"

"I'm nothin' at all yet. So far, I've just been helpin' my grandmother settle up my grandfather's estate. Somebody had to, and my brother's in my father's office."

"And do your grandmother and your mother have sitting-rooms with sewing-machines in them?"

"I wish you'd come and see."

"Do you?" She had continued to look at him, and now her eyes almost deliberately became dreamy. "I might—if you keep on asking me," she said gravely. "I'm sure I'd hate the West, though."

"Yet, you might come?"

"Ask me again to-morrow."

He was but too glad to be obedient, and asked her again the next day. This was over a table for two at a restaurant on Lafayette Place, where she met him as a surreptitious adventure, suggested by herself and undertaken without notifying her mother. It was a Lochinvar courtship, she said afterward, thus implying that her share in it was passive, though there were indeed days when the young man out of the West found her not merely passive, but dreamily indifferent. And once or twice she was more than that, puzzling and grieving him by an inexplicable coldness almost like anger, so that he consulted George McMillan to find out what could be the matter.

"Moods," George told him. "She's nothing but moods. Just has 'em; that's all. It doesn't matter how you are to her; sometimes she'll treat you like an angel and sometimes like the dickens. It doesn't depend on anything you do."

Dan thought her all the more fascinating, and put off his return home another month, to the increasing mystification of his family, for this month included the Christmas holidays, and Mrs.

18

Oliphant wrote that they all missed him, and that Mrs. Savage really needed him. The McMillans, on the other hand, were not mystified, and Lena appeared to be able to control them. The manner of her parents and her sister toward the suitor was one of endurance—an endurance that intended to be as thoroughbred as it could, but was nevertheless evident. It had no discouraging effect on the ardent young man, who took it as a privilege to be endured by beings so close to her. Besides, George McMillan was helpful with the exalted family, for he showed both tact and sympathy, though the latter sometimes appeared to consist of a compassionate amusement; and once he went so far as to ask Dan, laughingly, if he were quite sure he knew what he was doing.

"Am I sure?" Dan repeated incredulously. "I don't know what you mean."

"I mean about Lena."

"To me," Dan said, with the solemnity he had come to use in speaking of her, "your sister Lena is the finest flower of womanhood ever created!"

Upon that, his friend stared at him and saw that his eyes were bright with a welling moisture, so deep was his worship; and George was himself affected.

"Oh, all right, if you feel that way about it," he said, "I guess it'll be all right. I'm sure it will. You're a mighty right chap, I think."

"I?" Dan exclaimed. "I'm nothin' at all! And when I think that your sister could stoop—could stoop to—to me—why, I—"

He was overcome and could not go on.

The end of it was that when he went home in February it was to acquaint his family with the fact of his engagement; and in spite of his happiness he was a little uneasy. He did not fear the interview with his father and mother; and though he disliked the prospect of talking about Lena with Harlan, who was sure to be critical and superior, he had learned to get along without Harlan's approval. What made him uneasy was his anticipation of the invincible pessimism of that iron old lady, his grandmother.

19

CHAPTER III

THE Oliphants' high white iron fence was a hundred and fifty feet long on National Avenue, a proud frontage, but the next yard to the north had one even prouder: it was of a hundred and eighty feet, and the big house that stood in this yard was almost that far back from the street. Built of brick and painted white, it reached a palatial climax in a facing of smooth white stone under a mansard roof, and the polished black walnut front doors opened upon a stone veranda. From the veranda a broad stone path led through the lawn and passed a stone fountain on its way to the elaborate cast-iron front gate, which was a congenial neighbour to the Oliphants' cast-iron gate to the south. The stone fountain culminated in a bronze swan, usually well supplied with ejectory water in the summertime but somewhat bleak of aspect in winter, when the swan's open beak, perpetually vacant, suggested to an observer the painful strain of unending effort absolutely wasted. It was a relief, after a snowstorm, to see the too-conscientious cavity partially choked.

A little snow remained there, like a cupful of salt that the dutiful bird had firmly refused to swallow, and snow glistened also along its dark green back, one February afternoon, when a lady on her way from the house to the gate paused by the fountain and regarded the swan with apparent thoughtfulness. She was twenty-three or perhaps twenty-four, tall and robust, a large young woman, handsome, and in a state of exuberant good health—her hearty complexion and the brightness of her clear hazel eyes were proof enough of that—and though a powdery new snow, just fallen, lay upon the ground and the air was frosty, she wore her fur coat thrown as far open as possible. And that her thoughtfulness about the bronze swan was only an appearance of thoughtfulness, and not actual, was denoted by the fact that her halt at the fountain coincided with a sound from a short distance to the south of her. This sound was the opening and closing of a heavy door;—it was in fact the Oliphants' front door, one of the ponderous double doors of black walnut, like other front doors of the stately row. The lady looked at the swan only until the young man who had just closed that door behind him emerged from the deep vestibule and came down the steps.

He was a stalwart, dark-haired, blue-eyed young man, comely in feature and of an honest, friendly expression; and although the robust young lady was as familiar with his appearance as one could be who had lived all her life next door, yet when her gaze swept from the swan to him, she looked a little startled, also a little amused. What thus surprised and amused her was the unusual magnificence of his attire. Upon occasion she had seen a high hat upon him and likewise a full-skirted long coat and a puffed scarf, but never spats until now; and never before had she seen him carry a cane. This was of shining ebony, with a gold top, and swung from a hand in a dove-coloured glove. Dove was the exquisite tint, too, of his spats.

"Dan Oliphant!" she cried. "Why, my goodness!"

At the sound of her voice his eye brightened;—he turned at once, left the cement path that led to his own gate and came across the frozen lawn to the partition fence not far from her. Still exclaiming, she went there to meet him.

"My goodness gracious, Dan!" she cried, and shook hands with him between two rods of the iron fence.

"What's the matter, Martha?" he inquired. "I'm mighty glad to see you. I just got home from New York yesterday."

"I know you did," she said. "I mean I see you did. I should say so!"

"What's all the excitement?"

She proved unable to reply otherwise than by continuing her exclamations. "Why, Dan!" she cried. "Dan Oliphant!"

At that he seemed to feel there would be no readier way to solve the puzzle of her behaviour than to adopt her style himself. "Martha!" he exclaimed then, in amiable mockery of her. "Martha Shelby! Well, good gracious me!"

"It's the royal robes," she explained. "I'm overcome. Your mother and father have been worrying about your staying so long in New York, but certainly they understand now what detained you."

"What do you think it was, Martha?" he asked, his colour heightening a little.

"Why, you were learning to wear spats, of course, and how to carry a gold-headed cane. Is the President passing through town this afternoon?"

"No. Why?"

"I thought you might be one of a committee to meet him at the station and give him the keys of the city," said Miss Shelby. "Or are you going to make a speech somewhere?"

"No. I'm going to call on my grandmother."

"I hope dear old Mrs. Savage will be up to it. Would you like to have me walk with you as far as her gate? I'm going that way."

"You bet I'd like it!" Dan said heartily, and without exaggeration; for since this friendly next-door neighbour and he were children there had never been a time when he was not glad to

21

see her or to be with her, walking or otherwise. She had always teased him mildly, now and then, but he bore it equably, not by any means displeased. Nor was he anything but pleased to-day, as they walked down the broad and quiet avenue together, rather slowly, and she resumed her mockery of his metropolitan splendours.

"I suppose your mother had to give up getting you to wear an ulster this afternoon," she said. "It might have hidden that wonderful frock coat."

"You know as well as I do I never wear an overcoat unless it's a lot colder than this," he returned; and he added: "You're a funny girl, Martha Shelby."

"Why?"

"Well, don't you consider you're an old friend of mine? Anyway, I do, and here I haven't seen you since way back last fall, and you haven't said you're glad I'm back, or anything! The truth is, I was kind of lookin' forward to your sayin' something like that."

He spoke lightly, yet there was a hint of genuine grievance in his voice, and she was obviously pleased with it, for she gave him a quick side glance so fond it seemed almost a confession. But she laughed, perhaps to cover the confession, and said cheerfully: "There's one thing neither college nor New York has changed about you, Dan. You'll never learn to sound the final G in a participle; you'll always say 'lookin'' and 'sayin'' and 'goin'' and 'comin'.' Doesn't it worry Harlan?"

"Changin' the subject, aren't you?" he inquired. "Why didn't you tell me you're glad I'm back home again?"

"I am glad," she said obediently. "Are you glad, yourself?"

"To see you? You know it."

"No, I meant: Are you glad to be home?"

He looked thoughtful. "Well, I like New York; there isn't any place else where you can see as much or do as much when you want to; it's always a mighty fine show. And, besides, I like some people that live there." He hesitated, continuing: "I—well, I do like some of the people in New York, but after all I'm glad to get home; I'm mighty glad." Then he added, as a second thought: "In a way, that is."

"In what way particularly, Dan?"

"Well, I do like some New York people," he insisted, a little consciously;—"and I'm sorry to be away from them, but it's pretty nice to get back here where you know 'most everybody you're liable to meet. When you see a dog, for instance, you know who he belongs to and probably even his name—anyhow you probably do, if he belongs in your own part of town—and most likely the dog'll know you, too, and stop and take some interest in you. Of course, I mean

22

here you know everybody that is anybody;—naturally no one knows every soul in a town this big—and growin' bigger every day."

"Hurrah for you!" she cried, laughing at him again. "Why, you already talk like a member of the Chamber of Commerce, Dan."

"How's that?"

"Oh, you know the speeches they make: 'A city of prosperity, a city of homes, a city that produces more wooden butter-dishes than all the rest of the country combined! Yes, ladies and gentlemen, the finest city with the biggest future in the whole extent of these United States!' "

Dan laughed, but there came into his eyes a glint of enthusiasm that was wholly serious. "Well, I believe they're not so far wrong, at that. In some ways I think myself it is about the finest city in the country. It kind of came over me when I got off the train yesterday and drove up home through these broad old streets with the big trees and big houses. It's when you've been away a good while that you find out how you appreciate it when you get back. Harlan's just the other way; he says when he's been away and gets back, the place looks squalid to him. 'Squalid' was what he said. He makes me tired!"

"Does he?"

"Yes; when he talks like that, he does," Dan answered. "Why, the people you see on the streets here, they've all got time enough and interest enough in each other to stop and shake hands and ask about each other's families, and they're mighty nice, intelligent-looking people, too. In New York everybody hurries by; they don't know each other anyway, of course; and if you get off Broadway and Fifth Avenue and Madison Avenue, and one or two other streets, you're liable to see about as many foreigners as you will Americans; but here they're pretty near all Americans. It's kind of a satisfaction to see the good, old-fashioned faces people have in this city."

"I like to hear you praising old-fashioned things," Martha Shelby said slyly. "You must have something dreadfully important to say to your grandmother, Dan."

"Why?"

"Well, don't people put on their robes of state for tremendous occasions? Or did you just get so in the habit of it in New York that you can't give it up?"

"Maybe that's it," he laughed. "But I expect it'll wear off pretty soon if I stay here; and anyhow I am glad to get back. The fact is I'm a lot gladder than I expected to be. The minute I got off the train I had a kind of feeling—a pretty strong feeling—that this is where I honestly belong. It was home, and the people and the streets and the yards and trees and even the air—they all felt homelike to me.

23

And when I went into our good old house—why, I felt as if I hadn't been in a house, not a real house, all the time I was away. But most of all, it's the people."

"Your father and mother?"

"Yes," he said;—"but I mean everybody else, too. I mean you can seem to breathe easier with 'em and let out your voice to a natural tone without gettin' scared you're goin' to break a vase or something. For instance, I mean the way I feel with you, Martha. You see, with some New York people—I don't mean anything against 'em of course; but sometimes, when a person's with 'em, he almost feels as if he ought to be artificial or unnatural or something; but nobody could ever feel anything like that with you, Martha."

"No?" she said, and looked at him with a gravity in which there was a slight apprehension. "Perhaps you might like a little artificiality, though, just for a change. A moment ago you said you thought your New York habits would wear off, and you'd get more natural, if you stay here. What did you mean?"

"Me not natural?" he asked, surprised. "Why, don't I seem natural?"

"Yes, of course. You wouldn't know how not to be. You meant about your clothes. You said you'd probably get over wearing so much finery as a daily habit, if you stay here. Aren't you going to stay here, Dan?"

Her sidelong glance at him took note of a change in his expression, a perplexity that was faintly troubled, whereupon the hint of apprehension in her own look deepened. "Don't tell me you're not!" she exclaimed suddenly, and as he failed to respond at once, she repeated this with emphasis so increased that it seemed a little outcry: "Don't tell me you're not!"

"I certainly hope to stay here," he said seriously. "I didn't realize how much I hoped to until I got back. I certainly would hate to leave this good old place where I grew up."

"But why should you leave it? Your mother told me the other day you expected to go into business here as soon as you get your grandfather's estate settled."

"Yes, I know," he returned, and she observed that his seriousness and his perplexity both increased. "It's always been my idea to do that," he went on, "and I still hope to carry it out. At any rate I'm goin' to try to."

"Then why don't you? What on earth could prevent you?"

Upon this, he seemed to take a sudden resolution. "Martha," he said, "I've got a notion to tell you about something;—it's something beautiful that's happened to me. I haven't told anybody yet. I wanted to tell my father and mother last night; but Harlan

24

kept sittin' around where they were, until they went to bed; and somehow I didn't like to talk about it before him—anyway not at first. And to-day I haven't had a chance to tell 'em; father's been down at his office and mother had two charity board meetings. So you'll be the first person to know it."

"Will I?" Martha said in a low voice.

But he did not notice its altered quality; he was too much preoccupied with what he was saying; and he still looked forward into the perplexing distance. His companion's gaze, on the contrary, was turned steadily upon him; and the sunniness that had been in her eyes had vanished, the colour of her cheeks was not so brave in the cold air. "I'm a little afraid to hear it, Dan," she said. "I'm afraid you're going to say you got engaged to someone in New York. You are?"

"Yes," he answered gravely. "That's what I'm just on the way to tell my grandmother."

"I guessed it," Martha said quietly; and was silent for a moment;—then she laughed. "I might have guessed it from your clothes, Dan. You got all dressed up like this just to talk about her! And to your grandmother!"

A little hurt by her laughter, he turned his head to look at her and saw that there were sudden bright lines along her eyelids. "Why, Martha!" he cried. "Why, what—"

"Isn't it natural?" she asked, smiling at him to contradict the testimony offered by her tears. "I've always had you for a next-door neighbour; you've always been my best friend among the boys I grew up with;—I'm afraid I'll lose you if you get married. Everybody likes you, Dan; I think everybody'll feel the same way. We'll all be afraid we'll lose you."

"Why, Martha!" he exclaimed again, but he had difficulty in misrepresenting a catch in his throat as a cough. "I didn't—I didn't expect you'd think of it like this. I do hope it doesn't mean that I'll have to live in New York. I still hope to get her to come here. I—I'd certainly hate to lose you more than you would to lose me. I've always thought of you as my best friend, too, and I couldn't imagine anything making that different. I'd hoped—I do hope—"

"What, Dan?"

"I hope you—I hope you'll like her, if we come home to live. I hope you'll be her friend, too."

"Indeed I will!" she promised so earnestly that her utterance was but a husky whisper. "I'm glad I'm the first you told, Dan. Thank you."

"No, no," he said awkwardly. "It just happened that way."

"Well, at least I'm glad it did," she returned, and brushing her

25

eyes lightly with the back of a shapely hand, showed him a cheerful countenance. "See! you had just time to tell me."

CHAPTER IV

SHE nodded to where before them a long wooden picket fence outlined the street boundary of Mrs. Savage's lawn. Here was an older quarter than that upper reach of National Avenue whence the two young people had come; the houses here and southward were most of them substantial and ample, but not of the imposing spaciousness prevailing farther up the avenue. Three or four of them had felt the seventies so deeply as to adopt the mansard roof in company with one or two parasite slate turrets; but in the main the houses were without pretentiousness; and among them it was curious and pleasant to see lingering two or three white, low-gabled cottages of a single story.

In the summertime old-fashioned flowers grew in the yards of these, and there might be morning-glories climbing over the front doors; for the cottages were relics of the time when the city was a village and this region was the outlying fringe, beyond the end of the wooden sidewalks. Now, however, it was almost upon the edge of commerce;—there was smoke in the air, and through the haze were seen rising, a few blocks to the south, the blue silhouettes of dozens of office buildings, the court-house tower, and the giant oblong of the first skyscraper, the First National Bank, eleven stories high. Moreover, one of the white cottages had for next-door neighbour the first apartment house to be built in the city;—it was just finished, rose seven stories above its little neighbour, and was significantly narrow. The ground here had already become costly.

Mrs. Savage's gray picket fence joined the white picket fence of the overshadowed white cottage and her house was a good sample of four-square severity, built of brick and painted gray, with two noble old walnut trees in front, one on each side of the brick walk that led from the gate to the small veranda. Here she had lived during little less than half a century;—that is to say, ever since her house had been called "the finest residence in the city," when her husband built it in the decade before the Civil War. Here, too, she "preferred to die," as she said brusquely when her daughter wished her to come and live at the Oliphants', after Mr. Savage's death. She

26

was still "fully able to keep house" for herself, she added, and expected to do so until Smith and Lieven came for her; Smith and Lieven being the undertakers who had conducted all the funerals in her family.

But at ninety-two it is impossible to withhold all concessions; even a lady whose pioneer father whipped her when she was fifteen must bend a little; and although Mrs. Savage still declined to sit in a comfortable chair, she took a daily nap in the afternoon. She had just risen and descended to her parlour, and settled herself by the large front window, when the two young people, coming along the sidewalk, reached the north end of her picket fence.

She did not recognize them at first; for, although her eyes "held out," as she said, they held out not quite well enough for her to see faces except as ivory or pinkish blurs, unless they were close to her. However, the two figures interested her; and because of their slow approach and something intimate in the way they seemed to be communing, she guessed that they might be lovers. To her surprise, they halted at her gate, but, instead of coming in, continued their conversation there for several moments. Then, though they appeared loath to separate, each took both of the other's hands for a moment, in an impulsive gesture distinctly expressive of emotion, and the woman's figure went down the street, walking hurriedly, while the man's came in at the gate and approached the front door. Mrs. Savage recognized her grandson, but no slightest change in her expression or attitude marked the moment of recognition.

Upon the sound of the bell, the old coloured man who had been her servant for thirty years came softly through the hall, but instead of opening the door to the visitor he presented himself before his mistress in the parlour. He was a thin old man of the darkest brown, neat and erect, with a patient expression, a beautifully considerate manner, and a tremulous tenor voice. In addition, his given name was both romantic and religious: Nimbus.

"You like to receive callers, Miz Savage?" he inquired. "Doorbell ring."

"I heard it," the old lady informed him somewhat crisply. "Have you any reason to suppose I can't hear my own doorbell?"

"No'm."

"Then why did you see fit to mention that it rang?"

"I don' know, 'm. You hear good as what I do, Miz Savage," he returned apologetically. "I dess happen say she ring. Mean nothin' 't all. You like me bring 'em in or say ain't home, please?"

"It's my grandson, Dan."

"Yes'm," said Nimbus, turning to the door; "I go git him."

He went out into the broad hall and opened the door to the

27

thoughtful young man waiting there, who shook hands with him and greeted him warmly; whereupon Nimbus glowed visibly, expressing great pleasure and cordiality. "My goo'nuss me!" he said. "Hope I be close on hand when you git ready shed them clo'es, Mist' Dan. You' grammaw cert'n'y be overjoice' to see you ag'in. She settin' in polluh waitin' fer you, if you kinely leave me rest you' silk hat an' gole-head cane. My, look at all the gole on nat cane!"

Receiving this emblem of state with murmurous reverence, he solicitously bore it to the marble-topped table as the young man entered the room where his grandmother awaited him. She sat by the broad window, which had been the first plate-glass window in the town, and in her cap with lace lappets and her full, dark gown, she was not unsuggestive, in spite of her great age, of Whistler's portrait of his mother. Certainly, until her grandson took her hand and sat down beside her, she was as motionless as a portrait.

"Grandma," he said remorsefully, "I'm afraid you feel mighty hurt with me. I know it looked pretty selfish of me not to come home sooner, so we could go ahead and get grandpa's estate settled up. I expect you think I haven't been very thoughtful of you, and you certainly have got a right to feel kind of cross with me, but the truth is—"

"No," she interrupted quietly. "Your father was too busy to attend to the estate himself, and I didn't want Harlan because I know he'd spend all his time criticizing; and besides he didn't offer to do it in the first place, and you did. But your father hired a lawyer for me, and the work's about finished."

"I know what you think of me—" he began but again she interrupted.

"No; you behaved naturally in staying away. Young people always say they like to help old people, but it isn't natural. Mankind are all really just Indians, naturally. In some of the lower Indian tribes they kill off everybody that gets old and useless, and that's really the instinct of the young in what we call civilization. We old people understand how you young people really think of us."

"Oh, my!" the young man groaned. "I was afraid you were a little hurt with me, but I didn't dream you'd feel this way about it."

"No," she said;—"you were having too good a time to dream how anybody'd feel about anything. Your father and mother worried some about you, and once or twice your father talked of going East to see what you were up to. They were afraid you were running wild, but I told 'em they needn't fret about that."

"Did you, grandma?"

"Yes. Your running wild would never amount to much; you

28

come of too steady a stock on both sides not to get over it and settle down. No; what I was afraid of is just what I expect has happened."

"What's that?" Dan asked indulgently. "What do you think's happened, grandma? Think I got too extravagant and threw away a lot of money?"

"No," she replied; and to his uncomfortable amazement continued grimly: "I expect you've fallen in love with some no-account New York girl and want to marry her."

"Grandma!"

"I do!" the old lady asserted. "Isn't that what's been the matter with you?"

She spoke challengingly, with an angry note in the challenge, and Dan's colour, ruddy after his walk, grew ruddier;—the phrase "no-account New York girl" hurt and offended him, even though his grandmother knew nothing whatever of Lena McMillan. "You're very much mistaken," he said gravely.

"I hope so," Mrs. Savage returned. "Who was that you were talking to out at my front gate?"

"Martha Shelby."

"Martha? That's all right," she said, and added abruptly: "If you've got to marry somebody you ought to marry her."

"What?"

"If you've got to marry somebody," this uncomfortable old lady repeated, "why don't you marry Martha?"

"Why, that's just preposterous!" Dan protested. "The last person in the world Martha'd ever think of marrying would be me, and the last person I'd ever think of marrying would be Martha."

"Why?"

"Why?" he repeated incredulously. "Why, because we aren't in love with each other and never could be! Never in the world!"

"It isn't necessary," Mrs. Savage informed him. "You'd get along better if you weren't. Martha comes of good stock, and she's like her stock."

"There are other 'good stocks' in the country," he thought proper to remind her gently. "There are a few people in New York of fairly good 'stock', you know, grandma."

"Maybe a few," she said;—"but not our kind. The surest way to make misery is to mix stocks. You come of the best stock in the country, and you'll be mighty sick some day if you go mixing it with a bad one."

"But good gracious!" he cried, "who's talking of my mixing it with a—"

"Never mind," she interrupted crossly. "I know what those New York girls are like."

29

"But, grandma—"

"I do," she insisted. "They don't know anything in the world except French and soirées, and it's no wonder when you look at their stocks!"

"Grandma—"

"Listen to me," she bade him sharply. "The best stocks in England were the yeoman stocks; you ought to know that much, yourself, after all these years you've spent at school and college. The strongest in mind and body out of the English yeoman stocks came to America; they fought the Indians and the French and the British and got themselves a country of their own. Then, after that, the strongest in mind and body out of those stocks came out here and opened this new country and built it up. All they've got left in the East now are the remnants that didn't have gumption and get-up enough to strike out for the new land. The only thing that keeps the East going is the people that emigrate back there from here in the second and third generations. Don't you mix your stock with any remnants! D'you hear me?"

"Yes, ma'am," he meekly replied, dismayed not only by the extremity of the discouraging old lady's view upon "stocks" and "New York girls," but also by her shrewdness in divining the cause of his long absence. Nevertheless, he ventured to protest again, though feebly. "I think if you could see New York nowadays, grandma, you wouldn't think it's a city built by 'remnants,' exactly."

"I don't have to see it," she retorted. "I know history; and besides, I was there with your grandfather in eighteen fifty-nine. We stayed two weeks at the Astor House, and your grandfather was mighty glad to get back here to home cooking. Even then all the smart men in New York came from somewhere else. Outside of them and the politicians, the only New York people you ever hear anything about are the ones that have had just barely gumption enough to be stingy."

"What? Why, grandma—"

"They never made anything; they've just barely got the gumption to hold on to what's been left to 'em," she insisted. "As soon as anybody gets money, everybody else sets in to try to get it away from him. They try to get him to give it away; they try to trade him out of it, or to swindle him out of it, or to steal it from him. Everybody wants money and the only way to get it is to get it from somebody else; but for all that, the lowest form of owning money is just inheriting it and sitting down on it; and that's just about all they know how to do, these New York folks you seem to think so much of!"

30

"But my goodness, grandma!" the troubled young man exclaimed. "I haven't said—"

She cut him off again, for she was far from the conclusion of her discourse; and he got the impression—a correct one—that during his protracted absence she had been bottling within herself the considerable effervescence she now released upon him. She interrupted him with great spirit. "You wait till I'm through, and then you can have your say! I know these New York girls better than you do. You aren't capable of knowing anything about women anyway, at your age. You're the kind of young man that idealizes anything that'll give you half a chance to idealize it. You are! I've watched you. What do girls mean to a young man like you? If he doesn't think they're good-looking, they don't mean anything at all to him; it's just the same as if they weren't living. But if he thinks some silly little thing is pretty, and she takes special notice of him, that's enough;—he's liable to start right in and act like a crazy man over her! She may be the biggest fool, and the meanest one, too, on earth; he thinks she's got all the goodness and all the wisdom in the universe! You can't help getting into that state about her; but after you've been married awhile the gloss'll wear off and you'll begin to notice what you've tied yourself up to—to live with till you're dead!"

"But I haven't told you—"

Again she disregarded him. "I know these New York highty-tighties!" she said. "Your grandfather and I went to Saratoga the year after the war, and we spent a month there. We saw a plenty of 'em! They aren't fit to do anything but flirt and talk French and go to soirées. They're the most ignorant people I ever met in my life. They're so ignorant if you asked their opinion of Lalla Rookh they wouldn't know what you were talking about; but they think you're funny if you don't know that some fancy milliner of theirs keeps store on Broadway and not on the Bowery. That's about the measure of 'em."

"Well, not nowadays, exactly," her grandson said indulgently. "Some of the ones you saw at Saratoga thirty or forty years ago may have been like that, grandma, but nowadays—"

"Nowadays," she said, taking the word up sharply, "they're just the same. They fooled the young men then just the same as they fool 'em now. They make a young man like you think they know everything, because they're pretty and talk that affected way Harlan does."

"But with them it isn't affected, grandma. It's natural with them. They've always—"

But the obdurate old lady contradicted him instantly. "It's not!

31

It isn't natural for any human being to talk like that! You mustn't bring one of those girls out here to live, Dan."

"Grandma"—he began in an uneasy voice; "Grandma, I came here to tell you—"

"Yes, I was afraid of it," she said. "I was afraid of it."

"Afraid of what?"

A plaintive frown appeared upon her forehead before she answered. She sighed deeply, as if the increased rapidity of her breathing had made her insecure of continuing to breathe at all; and her frail hands, folded in her lap, moved nervously. "Don't do it, Dan," she said. "You ought to wait a few years before you marry, anyway. You're so young, and one of those New York girls wouldn't understand things here; she wouldn't know enough not to feel superior. You'd just make misery for yourself."

But at this he laughed confidently. "You don't know the one I'm thinkin' of," he said. "You've guessed something of what I came to tell you, grandma, but you've certainly missed fire about her! I'll show you." And from his breast pocket he took an exquisite flat case of blue leather and silver; opened it, and handed it to her. "There's her photograph. I'd like to see if you think she's the kind you've been talkin' about!"

Mrs. Savage put on the eye-glasses she wore fastened to a thin chain round her neck, and examined the photograph of Lena McMillan. She looked at it steadily for a long minute, then handed it back to her grandson, removed her glasses, and, without a word, again folding her hands in her lap, looked out of the window.

Under these discomfiting circumstances Dan said, as hopefully as he could, "You've changed your mind now, haven't you, grandma?"

"On account of that picture?" she asked, without altering her attitude.

"Yes. Don't you think she's—don't you think she's—"

"Don't I think she's what?" Mrs. Savage inquired in a dead voice.

"Don't you think she's perfect?"

"Perfect?" Expressionlessly, she turned and looked at him. "What are your plans, Dan?"

"You mean, when do we expect to—"

"No. What business are you going into?"

"Well—" He paused doubtfully; "I still hope—I mean, if I don't have to go to New York to live—"

"So?" she interrupted with seeming placidity. "She declines to come here to live, does she? She hates it here, does she, already?"

"I don't think she would," he said quickly. "Not if she once got

32

used to it. You see she doesn't know anything about it; she's never been west of Rochester, and she only thinks she wouldn't like it. I've been doin' my best to persuade her."

"But you couldn't?"

"Oh, I haven't given up," he said. "I think when the time comes—"

"But if she won't, 'when the time comes'," Mrs. Savage suggested;—"then instead of living here, where you've grown up and want to live, you'll go and spend your life in New York. Is that it?"

"Well, I—"

"So you'd do it," she said, "just to please the face in that photograph!"

"You don't understand, grandma," he returned, and he hurriedly passed a handkerchief across his distressed forehead. "You see, it isn't only Lena herself don't think much of our part of the country. You see, her family—"

"Ah!" the grim lady interrupted. "She's got a family, has she? Indeed?"

"Great goodness!" he groaned, "I mean her father and mother and her sister and her aunts and her married sister, and everybody. They're important people, you see."

"Are they? What do they do that's important?"

"It isn't so much what they do exactly," he explained, "it's what they are. You see, they're descended from General McMillan and—"

"General McMillan? Never heard of him. What was he a general of? New York militia? Knights of Pythias, maybe?"

"I'm not exactly certain," Dan admitted, again applying his handkerchief to his forehead. "I think he had something to do with history before the Revolution. I don't know just what, but anyhow they all feel it was pretty important; and you see to them, why I'm just nobody at all, and of course they must feel I'm pretty crude. It's true, too, because I am crude compared to Lena; and for a good while her family were more or less against any such engagement. Of course, the way they think about my family is even worse than the way you think about them, grandma; and naturally she says herself they're positive it'd be a terrible sacrifice for her to come and live out here. I mean that's the way they look at it."

"Of course they do," said Mrs. Savage. "That's the way those New York people at Saratoga thought about this part of the country. They're just the same nowadays, I told you; they haven't got the kind of brains that can learn anything. Does this photograph girl herself talk about what a 'sacrifice' it would be for her to live here?"

"Lena McMillan is a noble girl," Dan informed her earnestly.

33

"She feels a lot of respect for her family's wishes, and besides she doesn't like the idea of leavin' New York herself; but I don't remember her usin' the word 'sacrifice' exactly. She doesn't put it that way."

"What about you? Do you put it that way? Do you think it would be a sacrifice for her to come and live here?"

"I?" Dan was obviously astonished to be asked such a question. "Why, my goodness!" he exclaimed, "I wouldn't be beggin' her to try it if I thought so, would I? If I can just get her to try it I know she'll like it. How could anybody help likin' it?"

"You're pretty liable to find out how this photograph girl will help it!" his grandmother prophesied, and promptly checked him as he began to protest against her repeated definition of Lena as "this photograph girl." She retorted, "Tut, tut!" as a snub to his protest, then inquired: "What business do you expect to go into, if you live in New York?"

"I don't know," he said gloomily. "I don't see what I could do there."

"What will you do if you stay here?"

At that he brightened instantly. "Why, I think I've got hold of a big idea, grandma. I began to think about it last September, and it's been in my mind all the time I was away;—I've been goin' over it and workin' it out. It's something would make a mighty good profit for me and at the same time I think it'd be a big thing for this city."

"Indeed?" she said. "Yes, you're at the age when everything looks like a 'big thing.' Your grandfather used to talk like that when we were first married."

"Well, he was one of this city's most successful men, wasn't he? He did do big things, didn't he?"

"That was in the early days when he kept us poor," she said, with a short laugh of extreme dryness. "He had ideas about going into things to make this a greater city, and get 'a mighty good profit' for himself, the way you talk now—but what finally made his money was keeping out of big schemes. It was what I kept him from doing that made us well off, not what he did. We saved and went into safe things like the First National Bank stock. When it comes to you and Harlan, after I'm gone, you mustn't ever sell that bank stock, Dan. What is this 'big idea' you spoke of?"

"It's the old Ornaby farm, grandma."

"Oh, I see," she assented with ready satire. "Yes; this photograph girl will make a fine farmer's wife!"

"No, she won't," he returned good-naturedly. "That farm lies right where this city's bound to grow to. I want to take the money

34

grandpa left me and buy it. Then I'll lay it out in lots and make an Addition of it."

"So?" she said. "That's the 'big idea,' is it?"

"That's it, grandma."

She shook her head in pitying skepticism. "You can't carry it out. In the first place, the town'll never grow that far out—"

"Yes, it will," he interrupted eagerly. "Why, in three years at the longest—"

"No," she said; "it won't. Not in three years and not in thirty. Anyhow, your grandfather only left you twenty-five thousand dollars. You'd better keep it and not throw it away, Dan."

"I can get the Ornaby farm for seventeen thousand," he informed her. "That'll leave eight thousand to clear off the lots and put asphalt streets through and—"

"Put asphalt streets through!" she echoed. "How many miles of asphalt streets do you expect to build with eight thousand dollars after you've cleared the lots and advertised enough to boom an Addition?"

"I've been hopin' I'd get help on that," he said, his colour heightening a little. "I thought maybe I could get Harlan to come in with the twenty-five thousand grandpa left him. If he does—"

"He won't. Harlan isn't the kind to risk anything. He won't."

"Well, then," Dan said, "I'll go ahead and get other people. I'm goin' to do it, grandma, if I have to take an ax and a shovel and a wheelbarrow out there and do it all by myself. I've been thinkin' it over a long time, and I know it's a big thing." He laughed a little at his own enthusiasm, but again declared, with earnest determination: "Yes, ma'am! I'm goin' to build 'Ornaby Addition.' "

But his grandmother's compassionate skepticism was not lessened. On the contrary, she asked him quietly: "You're going to build 'Ornaby Addition' at the same time you expect to be living in New York with this photograph girl for a wife? How do you think you'll manage it, Dan?"

"Oh, she'll come here," he said. "I know she will, when I make her see what a big chance this idea of mine gives us. I think I can get her to try it, anyhow; and if she'll just do that it'll come out all right."

"You think she'll be a great help to you, do you, while you're working with a wheelbarrow out on Ornaby's farm?"

"Do I?" he exclaimed, and added radiantly: " 'A help?' Why, grandma, she—she'll be a great deal more than a help; she'll be an inspiration! That's exactly what she'll be, grandma."

Old Mrs. Savage looked at him fixedly, sighed, and spoke as in a reverie. "Ah, me! How many, many young men I've seen believing

35

such things in my long time here! How many, many I've seen that were going to do big things, and how many that thought some no-account girl was going to be their inspiration!"

"Grandma!" he cried indignantly, and rose from his chair. "You haven't any right to speak of her like that."

"No right?" she said quietly. "No, I s'pose not. I wonder how many hundred times in my life I've been told I hadn't any right to speak the truth. It must be so."

"But it isn't the truth," Dan protested, and in a plaintive agitation he moved toward the door. "I showed you a photograph of the sweetest, noblest, most beautiful woman that's ever come into my life, and you speak of her as—as—well, as you just did speak of her, grandma! I wouldn't hurt your feelings for the world, but I—well, you aren't fair. I don't want to say any more than that, so I expect I better go."

"Wait!" she said sharply; and he halted in the doorway. "You wait a minute, young man. I'm going to say my last say to you, and you better listen!"

"Yes, of course I will, if you want me to, grandma," he assented, as he came back into the room and stood before her. "Only I hope you won't say anything against her; and I don't think you ought to call it your 'last say' to me. I'm sure you won't stop speakin' to me."

"Won't I?" she asked; and he was aware of a strange pathos in her glance, and that her head constantly shook a little. "Won't I? I'm going to stop speaking to everybody, Dan, before long."

"But you look so well, grandma; you oughtn't to talk like that."

"Never mind. My talking is about over, but I'm going to tell you something you may remember when I can't talk any more at all. Your father and mother won't even try to have any influence with you; they haven't raised their children the way I did mine. Your father and mother have always been too easy-going with you to really help you by disciplining you when you wanted to do anything wrong, and they'll both act the gentle fool with you now, just as they always have about everything. They won't stop you from going ahead with this photograph girl."

"No," Dan said gently;—"and nothing could stop me, grandma. I told you she's the finest, most beautiful—"

"Be quiet!" the old lady cried. "How much of that same sort of twaddle do you suppose a body's heard in a life of ninety-two years? How many times do you suppose I've had to listen to just such stuff? Good heavens!"

"But, grandma—"

"You listen to me!" she said with sudden ferocity. "You don't

36

know anything about the girl, and you don't know anything about yourself. At your age you don't know anything about anything. You don't even know you don't know. And another thing you don't know is, how much you've told me about this girl and her family without knowing it."

"Grandma, I told you they're fine people and—"

"Fine people!" she said bitterly. "Oh, yes! And how have they treated you?"

"Why, aren't they givin' me their—their dearest treasure? Doesn't that show how they—"

"Yes, doesn't it?" she interrupted. "It shows how much of a treasure they think she is!"

"Grandma—"

"You listen! You're a splendid young man, Dan Oliphant. You're good-looking; you're honourable as the daylight; you're kindhearted, and you'd be just as polite to a nigger or a dog as you would to the President; and anybody can tell all that about you by just looking at you once. But this good-for-nothing girl and her good-for-nothing family have made you feel you weren't anybody at all, and ought to feel flattered to scrub their doormat! Don't tell me! They have! And because you let yourself get as soft as a ninny over a silly little pretty face, you truckle to 'em."

"Grandma!" He laughed despairingly. "I haven't been truckling to anybody."

"You have, and she'll keep you at it all your life!" the old lady said angrily. "I know what that face means. I've seen a thousand just like it! She'll use you and make you truckle to be used! And if you give in to her and live in her town, she'll despise you. If you make her come and live in your town, she'll hate you. But she'll always keep you truckling. Your only chance is to get rid of her."

"Grandma," he said desperately;—"I'm sorry, but I can't hear you talk this way about the sweetest, the most perfect, the loveliest—"

"Get rid of her!" she cried. And as the distressed young man went out into the hall she leaned forward in her chair, shaking at him a piteously bent and emaciated forefinger. "You get rid of her, if you don't want to die in the gutter! Get rid of her!"

37

CHAPTER V

DAN walked home from his grandmother's with the wind blowing a fine snow against his chest, within which something seemed to be displaced and painful. Higher up, under the cold sleek band of his tall hat, there was a stricken puzzlement; and no doubt he was in hard case. For a young lover rebuffed upon speaking of his sweetheart is like a fine artist who has made some fragile, exquisite thing and offers it confidently in tender pride, only to see it buffeted and misprized. To Dan it seemed as though Lena herself had been injuriously mishandled, whereas the injury fell really upon something much more delicate; the lovely image he had made for himself and thought was Lena—an angelic substance most different from the substance of that "little brunette" herself.

He told himself that his grandmother had increased in unreasonableness with increasing age, but in spite of all efforts to reassure himself, and notwithstanding her prediction that he would receive a foolish support from his parents in the matter of his engagement, it was decidedly without jauntiness that he made his announcement to them after dinner that evening.

He found them in the library, a shadowy big room where the fire of soft coal twinkled again upon polished dark woodwork, upon the clear glass doors of the bookcases, and touched with rose the eye-glasses and the shining oval façade of Harlan's shirt as he sat reading Suetonius under a tall lamp in the bay window. Harlan, unlike his father and his brother, always "dressed" for dinner.

He was the thinner and perhaps an inch the shorter of the two brothers; but in spite of their actual likeness of contour, people who knew them most intimately sometimes maintained that there was not even an outward resemblance, so sharp was the contrast in manner and expression. It was Martha Shelby who said that if Harlan had been a year shipwrecked and naked on a savage isle he would still look fastidious and wear "that same old 'How-vulgar-everything-seems-to-be!' expression." Tramps approaching Harlan on the street to beg a dime from him usually decided at the last moment to pass on in philosophic silence.

He was no more like the two handsome, gray-haired people who sat by the library fire, that evening, than he was like his brother. Mr. Oliphant, genial and absent-minded, was the very man of whom any beggar would make sure at first sight; and he was without an important accumulation of fortune now, in fact, because venturous friends of his had too often made sure of him to go on a note or to forestall a bankruptcy that eventually failed to be forestalled. His wife was not the guardian to save him from a disastrous generosity; she was the most ready woman in the world to be recklessly kind, and when kindness brought losses she kept as sunny a heart as her husband did.

Mrs. Savage was right: from this pair no discipline for the good of their son's future need have been expected, although her own effect upon him had been so severe that he began his announcement in the library with a defensive formality that denoted apprehension. His formality, moreover, was elaborate enough to be considered intricate, with the result that his surprised listeners were at first not quite certain of his meaning.

His father withdrew slippered feet from close intimacy with the brass fender enclosing the hearth, stared whimsically at his son, and inquired: "What is it all about, Dan?"

"Sir?"

"It doesn't quite penetrate," Mr. Oliphant informed him. "You seem to be making an address, but I'm not secure as to its drift. I gather that you believe something about there coming a time in a young man's life when his happiness depends upon an important step, and you'd hate to be deprived of something or other. You said something, too, about a union. It didn't seem to connect with labour questions, so I'm puzzled. Could you clarify my mind?"

Harlan, resting his book in his lap, laughed dryly and proffered a suggestion: "It sounds to me, sir, as if he might possibly mean a union with a damsel of marriageable age and propensities."

"Dan!" the mother cried. "Is that what you mean?"

"Yes'm," he said meekly. "I wanted to tell you last night, but— well, anyway it's so. She's the most splendid, noblest, finest girl I ever met, and I know you'll think so, too. Here—well, here's her picture." And he handed the blue case to Mrs. Oliphant.

"Why, Dan!" she said, suddenly tearful, as she took the case and held it open before her.

Her husband, not speaking, got up quickly, came behind her and looked over her shoulder at the photograph of Lena. Then after a moment he looked at Dan, but for a time seemed to be uncertain about what he ought to say. "She's—ah—she's pretty enough, Dan," he said finally, in his kind voice. "She's certainly pretty enough for us to understand your getting this way about her."

"Yes, Dan," his mother agreed. "She—she's quite pretty. I'm sure she's pretty."

"She's beautiful!" Dan declared huskily. "She's beautiful, and she's more than that; she has a character that's perfect. She has an absolutely perfect character, mother."

39

"I hope so," Mrs. Oliphant said gently, bending her head above the blue case. "After all, you can't tell everything from a photograph." She looked up at her husband as if arguing with him. "You can't tell much from a photograph."

"No," he assented readily. "Of course you can't. In fact, you can tell very little; but you can see this is a pretty girl, anyhow. I expect you'd better tell us a little more about her, Dan."

Dan complied. That is to say, he did his best to make them comprehend Lena's perfection; and, touching lightly upon her descent from that somewhat shadowy figure in heroic antiquity, General McMillan—Dan felt sensitive for the general since Mrs. Savage's suggestion about the Knights of Pythias—he kept as much as possible to the subject of Lena herself, and ended by declaring rather oratorically that she had just the qualities he had always admired in the noblest women.

"I do hope so, Dan dear," his mother said, her eyes still shining with tears in the firelight. "I do hope so!"

"Yes," Mr. Oliphant agreed, "I hope so, too, Dan; and anyhow, if you've cared enough about her to ask her to marry you, that's the main thing. You can be sure your mother and father will do their best to be fond of anybody you're fond of."

"But she has those qualities, father," Dan said, not quite sure, himself, why he seemed to be insisting upon this in a tone so plaintively argumentative. "Indeed she has! She has just exactly the qualities I've always admired in the noblest women I've ever known."

"In grandma, for instance?" Harlan inquired.

"What?"

"You said she had just the qualities you've observed in the noblest women. Well, grandma has noble qualities. I was wondering—"

"No," Dan said, swallowing. "Lena—well, she's different."

"If she has the qualities that will help you in building your future," Mrs. Oliphant said, "that will be enough for us."

"She has, mother. Those are just exactly the qualities she's got. Don't you think when—when—" He faltered, obviously in timidity, and glanced nervously at the observant Harlan.

"When what, dear?"

"Well, when—when a wife's an—an inspiration," he said, gulping the word out;—"well, isn't that just everything?"

"Of course, dear," Mrs. Oliphant said comfortingly. Then, when she had touched her eyes with her lace-edged little handkerchief, she spoke more briskly. "This will be quite exciting news for your grandmother, Dan. Poor dear woman! She's been

40

waiting so anxiously for you to come home; and she's grown so frail these last few months; she kept saying she was afraid she wouldn't last till you got here. She's devoted to Harlan, of course, but I think you've always been a little her favourite, Dan."

"A little?" Harlan repeated serenely. "She really doesn't like me at all."

"Oh, yes, she does," his mother protested. "She's devoted to you, too, but she—"

"No," Harlan interrupted quietly; "she's never liked me. I have no doubt when her will is read you'll find it out."

But upon this his father intervened cheerfully. "Let's don't talk about her will just yet," he said. "She's going to be with us a long time, we hope. Dan, you'd better go and tell her your news to-morrow."

"I did, sir. I went this afternoon."

"What did she say?"

Dan passed his hand across his forehead. "Well—she—well, I told her about it and—well, you know how she is, sir. She—isn't apt to get enthusiastic about hardly anything. She seemed to think— well, one thing she seemed to think was that I'm sort of young to be gettin' married."

"Well, maybe," said his father. "Maybe she's right."

"No, sir, I don't believe so. You see grandma is almost ninety-three. Why, to a person of that age almost anybody else looks pretty young. You see, it isn't so much I am young; it's only I look young to grandma."

But upon this argument, delivered in a tone most hopeful of convincing, Mr. Oliphant laughed outright. "So that's the way of it!" he exclaimed, and, returning to his seat by the fire, again extended his feet to the fender. "Well, whether you're really a little too young or only appear so, on account of your grandmother's advanced age, we have to face the fact that you've asked this young lady to marry you, and she's said she will. When that's happened, all the old folks can do is to make the best of it. You know we'll do that, don't you, son?"

"Yes, sir," Dan said a little bleakly. "I knew you would." He took the blue case from his mother's lap, and kissed her as she looked pathetically up at him; then he moved toward the door. "I—I always knew I could count on you and mother, sir."

"Yes, Dan," Mrs. Oliphant murmured, "you know you can."

And her husband, from his chair by the fireside, echoed this with a heartiness that was somewhat husky: "Yes, indeed, Dan. If the young lady is necessary to your happiness—"

"Yes, sir."

"Why, we'll just try to say, 'God bless you both,' my boy."

"Yes, sir," Dan returned, with an inadequacy that he seemed to feel, himself, for he lingered near the doorway some moments more, coughed in a futile and unnecessary manner, then said feebly: "Well—well, thank you," and retired slowly to his own room.

When his steps were no longer heard ascending the broad stairway, the sound of a quick sob, too impulsive to be smothered, was heard in the silent library, and Mr. Oliphant turned to stare at his wife. "Well, what's the matter?" he said. "I told you, you can't tell anything from a photograph, didn't I?"

She pressed her handkerchief to her eyes and shook her head, offering no other response.

Thereupon he struck the poker into the fire, badgered a lump of coal, and said gruffly: "It's all nonsense! She may turn out to be the finest girl in the world. How can you tell anything from a photograph?"

"You can't much," the serene Harlan agreed. He spoke from his easy-chair in the bay window, whither he had returned from an unemotional excursion to the blue leather case when it was exhibited. "You can see, though, that Dan's young person is perfect, as he said, in several ways."

"Think so?"

"Yes; she's perfectly à la mode; she's perfectly pretty—and perfectly what we usually call shallow."

"Oh, I don't know."

"Don't you?" Harlan asked, with a slight amusement, and added reflectively: "Martha Shelby won't like this much, I dare say."

"No," Mrs. Oliphant said faintly. "Poor Martha!"

"Oh, look here!" her husband remonstrated. "What's the use of all this? You're acting as if we were facing a calamity. Dan's got a mighty good head on his shoulders; he wouldn't fall in love with a mere little goose. Besides, didn't I ask you: 'What can you tell from a photograph?'"

"Not everything, sir," Harlan interposed. "But you can usually get an idea of the type of person it's a photograph of."

"Yes, you can," Mrs. Oliphant said. "That's what frightens me. She doesn't seem the type that would want to take care of him when he's sick and be interested in his business and help him. She might even be the type that wouldn't like living here, after New York, and would get to complaining and want to take him away. Of course it is true we can't tell from that photograph, though."

"Can't you?" Harlan asked with a short laugh. "Then why are you so disturbed by it?"

42

"That's sense," his father said approvingly. "If you can't tell anything about her, what's the sense of worrying?"

"It doesn't appear that you got my point, sir," Harlan remarked. "You and mother are both disturbed because you have drawn certain conclusions."

"From that picture?"

"I think so, sir."

"You're talking nonsense," Mr. Oliphant returned testily. "Nobody can tell anything at all from a photograph. Not a thing!"

"No," Mrs. Oliphant agreed, wiping her eyes again. "I hope not. I mean I'm sure not."

"That's right," said her husband heartily. "That's the way to look at it."

"Yes; isn't it!" said the sardonic Harlan, as he resumed his reading; and for a time the library was given over to a reflective silence;—the ceiling, fifteen feet from the floor, was too solid a structure for the pacing that had begun overhead to be heard below.

Up and down his room Dan walked and walked. In the few contemporary novels that he had read the hero's acceptance by a beautiful girl implied general happiness on earth; all the difficulties of mankind seemed to disappear with the happy elimination of those of this favourite twain. Moreover, when friends of his had become engaged there was always joviality; there were congratulations and eager gayeties; there were friendly chaffings from the old stock of jokes on the shelves that afford generation after generation supplies of such humour. Sometimes, as he was growing up, he had thought vaguely of the time when he would be telling people of his own engagement; he had made in his mind momentary sketches of himself, proud, happy, laughing, and a little embarrassed, in a circle of his relatives and friends who would be clamorous with loud felicitations and jocose inquiries. This very vision had come to him on his journey home so vividly that he had chuckled aloud suddenly, in his berth at night, surprising and somewhat abashing himself with the sound.

The picture had not been a successful prophecy he perceived as he walked up and down in his dressing-gown and slippers. Something appeared to have gone wrong somewhere in a mysterious way; and he could not understand what it was, could only pace and grieve, and puzzle himself. Even his talk with Martha Shelby had lacked the stimulating gayety he expected, though she had been "mighty sweet and sympathetic," as he thought; and as for the interview with his grandmother, he must simply try to forget that! So he told himself, and shivered abruptly, recalling the awfulness of her parting instructions. His mother and father had been kind—"just lovely"—but with them, too, something important had been lacking; he could not think why; and so walked and walked without much satisfaction or relief.

An hour after he had left the library there was a knock on his door; and he opened this tall and heavily panelled walnut barrier to admit his father, who looked a little worried.

"Dan," he said, coming in;—"I'm afraid I've got to get you to do something that won't be much fun for you."

"Yes, sir."

"Your aunt Olive's just telephoned me she's in a little trouble to-night."

"Yes, sir," Dan repeated. His aunt Olive, his father's widowed sister-in-law, was often in a little trouble of one kind or another, and the Oliphant family had learned to expect a call for help when she telephoned to them. "Yes, sir. Does she want me?"

"Guess she does," his father said. "Both the children took sick at the same time yesterday morning, she says. Mabel seems to be getting along all right, but Charlie's in a high fever. You see there's an epidemic of la grippe all over town—that's what's the matter with 'em, the doctor thinks; but so many people have got it she can't find a nurse to save her life. Says she's hunted high and low and there simply isn't one to be had, and it seems Charlie's delirious; and he's strong, for fourteen; it's hard to keep him in bed. I offered to go myself, but she said she'd heard you were back in town, so she wondered if you wouldn't come over and sit up with him just a night or so until she—"

"You tell her I'll be right there." Dan had thrown off his dressing-gown and was in a chair, drawing on a shoe. "Tell her—"

"I told her so. You needn't break your neck getting over there, Dan. I don't think there's any particular hurry. She just said—"

"I know, sir. She gets scared about Charlie mighty easy; but still I might as well move along, I guess," Dan said, and continued the hurried resumption of his clothes.

His father stood watching him, and seemed to be a little troubled, showing a tendency toward apologetic embarrassment. "Oh—ah, Dan—" he said, and paused.

"Yes, sir?"

"I—ah—we—don't want you to think—"

"Think what, sir?"

"Why, about your young lady—you took us by surprise, Dan. We weren't looking for what you told us, and so it took your mother and me a little bit off our feet, as it were, Dan."

"I—I suppose so," Dan said. "I expect I didn't go about it with any intelligence in particular, likely. I expect I ought to have—"

44

"No, no. You were all right, Dan. Only as we weren't just looking for it, we've been afraid we didn't seem as hearty about it as we should have."

"Oh, that's all right." Dan was embarrassed in his turn. "You were—you were both just lovely about it, sir. I didn't expect—I mean, it isn't the kind of thing there's any call for you and mother to make a big jollification and fuss over. I wasn't expectin' anything like that."

"No," his father said thoughtfully, "I suppose not. Only we've been afraid you might have been a little disappointed in the quiet way we took it."

"Oh, no, sir!"

"Well, I hope not. And anyway, Dan, we are glad about it, if you're sure you are."

"Yes, sir. Thank you."

"And we want you to know we're with you, Dan. We're with you and for you, and we stand by you," Mr. Oliphant continued; then paused, and concluded with a haste not altogether fortunate— "whatever happens."

"Yes, sir," Dan said, seeming to flinch a little, though meekly; and his father at once added an amendment to the awkward phrase.

"Of course, we think only the pleasantest things will happen, Dan. And we want you to understand that this house must be home for anybody that belongs to you as much as it is for the rest of us. You know we feel that way, don't you, son?"

"Yes, sir. I do hope to bring her here, if you'll let me. I've been thinkin' about it a great deal, and I believe this town is my town"— Dan flushed a little as he spoke—"and I want to prove it, and I want Lena to learn to feel about it the way I do. I believe she'd miss something out of her life if she didn't. And I want you all to learn what a noble girl she is. I know you will, father."

"Why, of course!" Mr. Oliphant took his son's hand and shook it. "We didn't happen to say it downstairs, but we do congratulate you, Dan. As far as anybody can tell from a photograph"—he paused again here, then finished with a great heartiness of voice—"why, as far as you can tell from that, why, she looks like—she looks like a mighty pretty girl."

"Yes, sir." Dan smiled with a little constraint. "There's something else I want to talk over with you when we get time enough. I've got hold of a big idea, father."

"Have you, my boy?"

"It's about our future," Dan said nervously. "I mean Lena's and mine." He hesitated, then went on: "I expect it sounds like big talk from a little man, but I believe it's goin' to be a great thing for the future of our city, too."

Upon this his father's expression of friendly concern became complicated by evidences of a slight inward struggle, but he was able to respond with sufficient gravity: "Do you, Dan? What is it?"

"It's an idea for a big development, sir. I mean a development in the way this city's commenced to grow."

"Indeed?"

"I guess I better tell you another time, sir; it's got lots of details, and I'm afraid I ought to be gettin' on over to Aunt Olive's now, sir."

"I suppose so," Mr. Oliphant said, relinquishing his son's hand. "I only wanted to say—about your engagement—it's all right with us, old fellow, and we just hope we'll be all right with her."

Dan was touched. His father spoke with feeling, and the young man could not trust his eyes to be seen. He hurried out into the spacious upper hall, not looking back, though he said: "Yes, sir; thank you," in a choked voice. Then, when he was halfway down the stairs, he called cheerfully: "I'll let you know to-morrow morning if there's anything much the matter with young Charlie. I'll be home for breakfast, anyway, and I'll tell you about my idea then, too. It's goin' to be a mighty big thing, father!"

"I hope so, my boy," Mr. Oliphant returned; and although there was moisture in his own eyes, he had difficulty in restraining, until the front door closed, a tendency to laughter.

CHAPTER VI

THAT green bronze swan of the fountain in the broad yard next door to the Oliphants' should have been given a new interpretation this season; the open beak, forever addressing itself obliquely to the eastern sky, might well have been thought to complain to heaven of the spiteful hanging on of winter. It was a winter that long outwore its welcome, and then kept returning like a quarrelsome guest forcing his way back to renew argument after repeated ejectments;—the Shelbys' swan was fortunate to be of bronze, for a wet snow filled that exasperated-looking beak of his choke-full one morning a month after the lilacs had shown green

46

buds along their stems. Then, adding mockery to assault, this grotesque weather spent hour after hour patiently constructing a long goatee of ice upon the helpless bird.

Martha Shelby knocked it off late in the afternoon, though by that time the western sun had begun to make all icicles into opals, radiant with frozen fire and beautiful. "Insulting thing!" Martha said, as she brought the ferrule of her umbrella resentfully against the icicle, which broke into pieces that clattered lightly down to the stone basin below. "Of all the Smart Alecks I ever knew I think the worst one's the weather!"

Her companion, a thin young man with an astrakhan collar to his skirted long overcoat, assented negligently. He had happened to overtake her as she walked up National Avenue from downtown, and was evidently disposed to extend the casual encounter at least as far as her door, for he went on with her in that direction as he spoke.

"Yes, I dare say. Nature, in general, has a way of taking liberties with us that we wouldn't tolerate from our most intimate friends. I suspect if we got at the truth of things we'd find that most of our legislation is really an attempt to prevent Nature from getting the better of us."

"Murder!" said Martha. "That's too deep for me, Harlan! Let's go on talking about poor old Dan and things I can understand. Come into the house and I'll give you some tea; you're the only man-citizen I know in town who likes tea. I ought to warn you that papa thinks there's something queer about you since that day after the matinée when you came in and had tea with me. He thought it was bad enough, your being at the matinée—papa says if an old man is seen at a matinée it looks as if he's gone bankrupt and doesn't care, but if it's a young man he must be out of a job and too lazy to look for a new one—and for any man not only to go to a matinée, but to drink tea afterwards, well, papa was terribly mystified about anybody named Oliphant doing such a thing! He can't imagine a man's consenting to drink tea except to help fight off a chill."

"Oh, I know!" Harlan said. "I realize it's a terrible thing for one to do, only three generations away from the pioneers."

As Martha chattered she had opened one of the double front doors, which were unlocked, and now she preceded him into the large central hall, floored with black and white squares of marble. A fine staircase, noble in proportions and inevitably of black walnut, followed a curving upward sweep against curved walls to the third story; while upon both sides of the hall, broad and lofty doorways, with massive double doors standing open, invited the caller to apartments heavily formal in brown velvet and damasks of gold.

In obedience to a casual wave of Martha's hand, as she disappeared through a doorway at the other end of the hall, Harlan left his overcoat and hat upon a baroque gold console-table and entered the drawing-room to his left. Here a fire of soft coal sought to enliven a ponderous black-marble mantelpiece, and Harlan, warming his hands, gazed disapprovingly at the painting hung upon the heavy paper of the wall above. This painting was not without celebrity, but after looking at it seriously for several minutes Harlan shook his head at it, and was caught in the act by Martha, who came in with a light step behind him.

"Don't scold the poor thing, Harlan!" she said; and, as he turned, a little startled, he took note again of a fact he had many times remarked before: she moved with a noiseless rapidity unusual in so large a person. Moreover, her quickness was twice in evidence now; for she had changed her dark cloth dress for a gown of gray silk; and as final testimony to her celerity, when she sat in a chair by the fire and crossed her knees, a silken instep of gray was revealed between the silver buckle of her slipper and the hem of the long skirt she wore in the mode of that time.

"You're like lightning, Martha," Harlan said;—"but not like thunder. I didn't even hear you come into the room. What is it you don't want me to scold?"

"Poor papa's Corot."

"I wasn't scolding it. I was only thinking: What's the use of having a Corot if you hang it so high and so much against the dazzle of the firelight that nobody can see it."

"Oh, that doesn't matter to papa," Martha said cheerfully. "Papa doesn't care to see it; and he doesn't care whether any one else sees it or not. He bought it the summer the doctor made him go abroad, after mamma died. Somebody in Paris convinced him he ought to own an important picture. They took him first to see a Bougereau and he got very indignant. So they apologized and hurried out this Corot and told him who Corot was; so he bought it. All he cares about is that he owns it; he doesn't think about it as a thing to look at any more than the bonds in his safety-deposit boxes. He knows they're there, and they're worth just so much, and they're his; and that's all he cares about. You know papa runs the house to suit himself."

"No," Harlan returned skeptically. "I can't say I quite know that."

"You don't?" She laughed and went on: "Well, he does; especially when he gets set in his head. A few of papa's notions are just molasses, but most of 'em are like plaster of Paris;—if you don't change 'em in a hurry before they set you never can change 'em!

That's the trouble just now; he's turned into plaster of Paris about poor Dan's land operations, confound him!"

She uttered this denunciation with a sharpness of emphasis not ill-natured, but earnest enough to make Harlan look at her seriously across the small table just set between them by a coloured housemaid.

"You've been trying to alter your father's opinion of Dan's commercial ability, have you?" he inquired.

"Yes, I have," she answered crisply. "What's the matter with the business men of this town, anyway? Why won't they help Dan do a big thing?"

At this Harlan allowed his eyes to fall from the troubled and yet spirited inquiry of her direct gaze; he looked at the cup he accepted from her, and frowned slightly as he answered: "Of course they think he's a visionary. The most enthusiastic home boomer in the lot doesn't dream the town'll ever reach out as far as Dan's foolish 'Addition.' "

"How do you know it's foolish?"

"Why, because the population would have to double to reach even the edge of his land, and this town hasn't the kind of impetus that develops suburbs. You know what sort of place it is, yourself, Martha. It's only an overgrown market-town, and an overgrown market-town is what it'll always be."

"Don't you like it?" she asked challengingly. "Don't you even like the town you were born in and grew up in?"

"That sounds like Dan. His latest phase is to become oratorical about the enormous future of our own, our native city—since he bought the Ornaby farm! I suppose I like it as well as I like any city except Florence. I don't think it's as ugly as New York, for instance, because the long stretches of big shade trees palliate our streets half the year, and nothing palliates the unevenness and everlasting tearing down and building up and digging and blasting and steam-riveting of New York. But I do hate the crudeness of things here."

"That's the old, old cheap word for us," she said, " 'Crude!' "

Harlan laughed. "You have been listening to Dan, the civic patriot! Crudeness isn't our specialty; the whole country's crude, Martha."

"Compared to what? China?"

"You'll be telling me all about our literary societies and women's clubs and the factories, if I don't take care," he returned lightly. "How dreadful all that is!" He sighed, and continued: "I suppose you've been trying to convince your father he ought to extend one of his street-car lines out into the wilderness toward

Dan's 'Addition.' Is that what you've been up to with the old gentleman, Martha?"

"Yes, it is," she said quickly. "If he doesn't, how are people to get out there?"

"Quite so! That's one reason why everybody downtown is laughing at Dan. Your father will never do it, Martha. Have you any idea he will?"

"Not much of one," she admitted sadly, and shook her head. "He doesn't understand Dan's theory that the car line would pay for itself by fares from the people who'd build along the line."

"No, I shouldn't think he'd understand that—at least not very sympathetically!"

"Dan isn't discouraged, is he?" she asked.

"No, he isn't the temperament to be discouraged by anything. It's a matter of disposition, not of facts, and Dan was born to be a helpless optimist all his life. For instance, he still believes that when he marries his Miss McMillan and brings her here to live, grandmother will learn to like her! Yet he ought to know by this time that grandmother's a perfect duplicate of your father in the matter of plaster of Paris. I suppose you've seen Miss McMillan's photograph, Martha?"

Harlan glanced at her as if casually, but she answered without any visible embarrassment: "Oh, yes; he brought it over, and talked of her a whole evening. If the photograph's like her—" She paused.

"It's one of those photographs that are like," Harlan observed. "My own judgment is that she's not precisely the girl to put on a pair of overalls and go out and help Dan clear the underbrush off his 'Addition.'"

"Is he doing that himself? I haven't seen him for days and days."

"No," said Harlan. "You wouldn't, because he is doing just about that. I believe he has five or six darkies helping him; but he keeps overalls for himself out there in a shed. He gets up before six, drives out in his runabout, with a nose-bag of oats for his horse under the seat, and he gets home after dark ready to drop, but still talking about what a success he's going to make of the great and only 'Ornaby Addition.' He wears shabby clothes all the time—he seems not to care at all how he looks—and Saturdays he comes home at noon and spends the rest of the day downtown making orations to bankers and business men, especially your father."

"To no effect at all," Martha said gloomily.

"Oh, but I think he's had an extraordinarily distinct effect!"

"What effect is it?"

50

"Well, I'm afraid," Harlan said slowly;—"I'm afraid he's been successful in making himself the laughing stock of the town."

"They—they think he's just a joke?"

"Not 'just' one," the precise Harlan replied. "They think he's the biggest one they've ever seen."

Martha uttered a sound of angry protest, though she did not speak at once, but stared frowningly at the fire; then she turned abruptly to Harlan. "Why don't you help him?"

"I? Well, he hasn't asked me to help him, precisely. Did he tell you I—"

"No; he didn't say anything about you. But why don't you?"

"As a matter of fact," Harlan explained, a little annoyed, "he didn't ask me for help, but he did want me to go in with him on strictly business grounds. He was certain that if I joined him as a partner, it would be a great thing for both of us. He wanted me to do the same thing he did—invest what grandfather left me in making the Ornaby farm blossom with horrible bungalows and corner drug stores."

"And you wouldn't," Martha said affirmatively.

"Why should I, since I don't believe in his scheme?"

"But why couldn't you believe in Dan himself?"

"Good heavens!" Harlan exclaimed, and uttered a sound of impatient laughter. "I've never looked upon Dan as precisely a genius, Martha. Besides, even if by a miracle he could do something of what he dreams he can, what on earth would be the use of it? It would only be an extension of ugliness into a rather inoffensive landscape. I don't believe he can do it in the first place; and in the second, I don't believe in doing it even if it can be done."

"Don't you?" she asked, and looked at him thoughtfully. "What do you believe in, Harlan?"

"A number of things," he said gravely. "For instance, I don't believe in kicking up a lot of dust and confusion to turn a nice old farm into horrible-looking lots with hideous signboards blaring all over 'em."

"How characteristic!"

"What is?"

"I asked you what you believed in," she explained. "You said you believed in 'a number of things,' and went straight on: 'For instance, I don't believe—'"

"Yes," he said, "I was keeping to the argument about Dan."

Martha laughed at his calm sophistry, but was content to seem to accept it and to waive her point. "What do your father and mother think of 'Ornaby Addition'?"

"Oh, you know them! They understand as well as anybody

51

that it's all folly, but they don't say so to Dan. I think poor father would even put something in just to please Dan, if he could spare it after what he's lost in bad loans this year."

"How about Mrs. Savage?"

"Grandmother!" Harlan was amused at this suggestion. "Dan has to keep away from her; she's taken such a magnificently healthy prejudice against his little Miss McMillan she won't talk to him about anything else, and Dan can't stand it. Not much chance for 'Ornaby' there, Martha!"

"No; she is a plaster of Paris old thing!"

"Inordinately. She's always been set about me, Martha," Harlan remarked with a ruefulness in which there was a measure of philosophic amusement. "She's always maintained that I'd never amount to anything—I have the terrible faults of being an egotist and smoking cigarettes—but she's sometimes admitted she thought Dan might. That's why she's furious with him about throwing himself away on this 'spoiled ninny of a photograph girl'—her usual way of referring to Miss McMillan. Grandmother's twice as furious with him as if she hadn't always been like you, Martha."

"Like me? How?"

"I mean about your feeling toward Dan and me." Harlan smiled, but his eyes were expressive of something far from amusement. It was as if here he referred to an old and troubling puzzlement of his, but had long ago resigned himself to the impossibility of finding a solution. "I mean she's like you because she's always thought so much more of Dan than she has of me, Martha."

"Perhaps it's because you've never seemed to think much of anything, yourself," she said gently. "Perhaps we're apt to like people best who do a great deal of liking themselves."

"I might like to have you like me, Martha," Harlan ventured, and there was a quiet wistfulness about him then that touched her. "I might like it better than you know."

She looked at him gravely. "I do like you," she said. "I like you anyhow; but even if I didn't, I'd like you because you're Dan's brother."

Harlan sighed, but contrived a smile to accompany his sigh. "Yes; I've always understood that, Martha; and you're not at all peculiar in your preference. Not only you and grandmother, but everybody else likes Dan much better than me."

"And yet," Martha said, a smouldering glow in her kind eyes, "you tell me that everybody's laughing at him."

"Haven't you heard so yourself?"

52

"Yes, I have," she cried angrily. "But how can they, if they like him?"

"Isn't it plain enough? They like him because he's a democratic, friendly soul, and they laugh at him because he's so absurd about the Ornaby farm."

"And you think he's got to do the whole thing absolutely alone?"

"Why, no," Harlan said, correcting her lightly, "I don't think he's going to be able to do the whole thing at all. He'll get part way and then of course he'll have to quit, because his money'll give out. What he has left may last him a year or even longer, if he keeps on just doing with his little gang of darkies and himself."

"And in the meantime, he'll also keep on being a 'laughing stock?' That's what you said, didn't you?"

"I don't think it was an exaggeration," Harlan returned, defending himself, for her tone was sharply accusing. "After all," he went on, with placative lightness, "isn't it even rather a triumph in its way? You see, Martha, it isn't every young man of his age who'd be well enough known to occupy that position."

"A laughing stock?"

"Why, yes. Don't you see it means a degree of prominence not at all within the reach of every Tom, Dick, and Harry. For instance, I couldn't touch it: I don't know enough people; but Dan's one of those men of whom it's said, 'Oh, everybody in town knows him!' So, you see, since he's run wild over this Ornaby Addition, why, he actually has the whole town laughing at him."

"Since he's run wild!" she echoed scornfully. "And you say you don't exaggerate! How has he 'run wild?'"

"Ask your father," was Harlan's response, delivered quietly, though with some irritation; and Martha said sharply that she would, indeed; but this was mere retort, signifying no genuine intention on her part, for she knew well enough what her father would say. He had been saying it over and over, every evening of late; and her discussions with him of Dan Oliphant and "Ornaby Addition" had reached that point of feeble acrimony at which a participant with any remnant of wisdom falls back upon a despairing silence—a silence despairing of the opponent's sanity. Martha had no mind to release her father from the oppression of this silence of hers, merely to hear him repeat himself.

She knew, moreover, that Harlan had not far overshot the mark when he intimated that Dan had become the laughing stock of the town; nor was it grossly an exaggeration to describe him as "making orations to bankers and business men, especially your father." The enthusiast for "Ornaby Addition" had indeed become

53

somewhat oratorical upon his great subject; and the bankers and business men to whom he made speeches not only laughed about him, as did their secretaries and clerks and stenographers, distributing this humour widely, but often they laughed at him and rallied him, interrupting him as he prophesied coming splendours.

"You'll see!" he would answer, laughing himself, albeit rather plaintively. "You can sit there and make all the fun o' me you want to, but the day'll come when you'll wish you'd had a hand in makin' this city what it is goin' to be made! It isn't only the money you'd get out of it, but the pride you'd take in it, and what you'd be able to tell your grandchildren about it. Why, gentlemen, ten years from now—" Then he would go on painting his air castles for them while they chuckled or sometimes grew noisily hilarious.

But the toughest and most powerful of them all declined to chuckle; there was little good-nature and no hilarity left in dry old Mr. Shelby. He was seventy, and, as he crisply expressed himself, at his age he hated to have his time wasted for him; he didn't see any pleasure in listening to the goings-on of a fool-boy about two minutes out of school! This viewpoint he went so far as to communicate to Dan directly, as the latter stood before him in the old gentleman's office. For that matter, Mr. Shelby seldom cared to be anything except direct; it was his declared belief that directness was the only thing that paid, in the long run. "Usin' a lot of tact and all that stuff to spare touchy people's vanity, it's all a waste of energy and they only hate you worse in the long run," he said. "So I'm not goin' to trouble to use any tact on you, young Mr. Dan Oliphant!"

He was a formidable old figure as he sat in his mahogany swivel-chair, which every instant threatened to swing him about to face his big, clean desk again with his back to the visitor. Neat with an extremity of precision, this old man had not altered perceptibly in appearance for many years, not even in his clothes; he was now exactly as he was in Dan's childhood. The gray chin-beard was the same precisely trimmed short oblong, and no whiter; the same incessant slight frown was set between the thin gray eyebrows; the same small black necktie showed a reticent bow beneath the flat white collar that was too large for the emaciated neck; and the same clean white waistcoat was worn under the same black "cutaway" coat; the same gray-and-black-striped trousers descended to the same patent-leather "congress gaiters." Twice a year Mr. Shelby gave an order—always the same order—to his tailor; he never left his house in the evening; had not taken any exercise whatever since his youth; went to bed always at nine o'clock; always ate exactly the same breakfast of oatmeal, an egg, and one cup of coffee; was never even slightly indisposed; and appeared to be everlasting. Compared to such a man, granite or basalt might be imagined as of an amiable plasticity; yet the ardent Dan hopefully persisted in seeking to remodel him.

"Why, of course, Mr. Shelby," he assented;—"that's just the way I want you to feel; I don't want you to use any tact on me. I don't need it. When I'm layin' out a proposition like this before a real business man, all I want is his attention to the facts."

"What facts?"

"The facts of the future," the enthusiast replied instantly. "The future—"

"What d'you mean talkin' about the facts of the future? There ain't any facts in the future. How you goin' to have any facts that haven't happened yet? A fact is something that's either happened or is happening right now."

"No, sir!" Dan exclaimed. "The present is only a fraction of a second, if it's even that much; the past isn't any time at all—it's gone; everything that amounts to anything is in the future. The future is all that's worth anybody's thinkin' about. That's why I want you to think about the future of your car lines, Mr. Shelby."

"Oh, you do, do you?" the old gentleman said sardonically. "You think I ain't thinkin' about it, so you called around for the fourth time to draw my attention to it?"

"Yes, sir," the undaunted young man replied. "I don't mean exactly you don't think about it; I just mean you don't seem to me to consider all the possibilities."

"Such as old Ranse Ornaby's ex-hog-wallow and corn-patch, for instance?"

"That ex-hog-wallow and corn-patch, Mr. Shelby," Dan said proudly, "consists of five hundred and thirty-one and two-thirds acres. If you'd only drive out there in your carriage as I've asked you to—"

"Good heavens!" Mr. Shelby interrupted. "I chopped wood there thirty years before you were born! D'you think I got to hitch up and go buggy-ridin' to know where Ranse Ornaby's farm is?"

"It isn't his, sir," Dan reminded him. "It belongs to me. I only meant, if you'd come out there I think you'd see some changes since I've been layin' it out in city lots."

"City lots? What city you talkin' about? Where's any city in that part o' the county? I never knew there was any city up that way."

"But there is, sir!"

"What's the name of it?"

"The city of the future!" Dan proclaimed, his eyes brightening

55

as he heard his own phrase. "This city when it begins to reach its growth! Why, in ten years from now—"

"Ten years from now!" the old man echoed, with angry mockery. "What in Constantinople you talkin' about? D'you know you're gettin' to be a regular by-word in this town? Old George Rowe told me yesterday at his bank, he says you got a nickname like some Indian. It's 'Young Ten-Years-From-Now.' That's what they call you: 'Young Ten-Years-From-Now'! George Rowe asked me: he says, 'Has Young Ten-Years-From-Now been around your way makin' any more speeches?' he says. He says that's the nickname everybody's got for you. It's all over town, he says."

Dan's colour heightened, but he laughed and said: "Well, I expect I can stand it. It isn't a mean nickname, particularly, and I don't guess they intend any harm by it. I shouldn't be surprised if it turned out to be good advertisin' for the Addition, Mr. Shelby."

"I should," the old man remarked promptly. "I'd be surprised if anything turned out good for the Addition!"

"No," said Dan. "That nickname might do a lot o' good; though the truth is I'm not talkin' about ten years from now nearly as much as I am about only two or three years from now. Ten years from now this city'll be way out beyond Ornaby Addition!"

"Oh, lord! Hear him holler!"

"It will," Dan insisted, his colour glowing the more. "It will! Why, you go down to the East Side in New York and look at the way people are crowded, with millions and millions more every year tryin' to find footroom. They can't do it! They've got to go somewhere. They've got to spread all over the country. Thousands and hundreds of thousands of 'em have got to come here. That's not all; we've got the finest climate in the world, and the babies that get born here practically all of 'em live, and there's tens of thousands of 'em born every year. Besides that, this city's not only the natural market of a tremendous agricultural area, but the railroads make it an absolutely ideal manufacturing centre. Why, it's just naturally impossible to stop the growth that's comin', even if anybody wanted to, and the funny thing to me is that so few of you business men see it!"

"You listen to me," the old man said;—"that is, unless you got the habit of talkin' so much you can't listen! You been tellin' the men that run this town quite a few things about our own business lately; it's time somebody told you something about your own. You're a good deal like your grandfather Savage used to be before your grandmother sat on him and never let him up. He was always wantin' to put his money into any fool thing and lose it, until she did that, and I hear she tried to stop you, but you didn't have the

56

gumption to see she's right. Now, look here: I've been here since there was a population of seven hundred people chillin' every other day, eatin' quinine by the handful, and draggin' one foot after the other out of two-foot mud if they had to get off a horse and walk anywhere. Last census we had a hundred and eighty thousand. I've seen it all! D'you expect you can tell me anything about this town?"

"No, sir; not about the history of it or anything that's past. But about the future—"

"You listen!" Shelby commanded irascibly. "You come around here blowin' out your chest and tellin' us old settlers that this town has grown some—"

"No, sir; I know you know all about that a thousand times better'n I do. I only use it to prove the town's goin' to keep on growin'. Why, Mr. Shelby, ten years from now—"

"Great Gee-mun-nently!" the old man shouted. "Can't you listen at all? Of course it's goin' to keep on growin', but not the way you think it is. It's already reached its land size, or mighty near it, because there's plenty vacant lots inside the city limits—hunderds and hunderds of 'em—and people want to live near their business; they don't want to go way out in the country where there ain't any sewers nor any gas nor city water."

"But they'll get all that, Mr. Shelby. They will as soon as there's enough of 'em to make it pay the water company and the gas company to run their pipes out; and there'd be enough of 'em, if you'd lay even a single track out to—"

"Out to Ranse Ornaby's frog pond!" the old man interrupted angrily. "You think if I'd throw away a hundred thousand dollars like so much dirt, that'd bring the millennium to the old hog-wallow, do you, young man? Look out that window behind you. What's the biggest thing you see?"

"The First National Bank Building."

"Yes, sir. Eleven stories high, and the Sheridan Trust Company's got plans to put up a block higher'n that. People'll build up in the air, not only for business, but to live in flats, but they won't go 'way out to a hog-wallow in the country when there ain't a reason on earth for 'em to. You seem to think people ride on street-cars for pleasure! Well, I've had some experience in the business, and I can tell you they don't, except in mighty hot weather; they ride on street-cars to get somewhere they want to go; and goodness knows nobody wants to go to Ranse Ornaby's farm."

"But, Mr. Shelby, if you'd listen just a minute—"

"I've listened all I'm a-goin' to," the old man said decisively. "This is the fourth time you been here tellin' me all about this town that wouldn't be here if it wasn't for me and some the other men you

57

been lecturin' to about it. You go at me as if I'd just put up at the hotel and never saw the place before, and what's worse you've gone and got Martha so she keeps ding-dongin' at me till I can't eat my supper in peace! It's about time for you to understand it's no use."

"But, Mr. Shelby, if you'd just let me put the facts before you-"

"Facts about what's goin' to happen ten years from now? No, sir!" The swivel-chair began to turn, making it clear that this interview had drawn to a close. "I thank you, but I can make up my own facts, if I so desire!" And the back of the chair and its occupant were offered to the view of the caller.

Dan made a final effort. "Mr. Shelby, I hope you don't mean this for your last word on the subject, because just as sure as you're born the day will come when—"

"Will it?" the old man interrupted; and turned his head angrily, so that his neat beard was thrust upward by his shoulder and seemed to bristle. "You go teach your grandma Savage to suck eggs," he said with fierce mockery, "but don't come around here any more tellin' me where I better lay my car tracks!"

"Well, sir, I—"

"That's all!"

"Yes, sir," Dan said, a little depressed for the moment.

But in the hall, outside the office, he recovered his cheerfulness, and, after consulting a memorandum book, decided to call on Mr. George Howe, the president of the First National Bank. Since yesterday Dan had thought of several new things that were certain to happen within the next ten years.

CHAPTER VII

NO FIGURE was more familiar to the downtown streets of those days than that of the young promoter of Ornaby Addition. Always in a hurry and usually with eyes fixed on what appeared to be something important in the distance, he had the air of a man hastening to complete a profitable transaction before traintime. Now and then, as he strode along, his coat blowing out behind him in the spring breeze, his gaze would be not upon the distance, but eagerly engaged in computations, with the aid of a shabby memorandum book and an obviously dangerous fountain pen.

58

Moreover, the shabbiness of the memorandum book was not out of keeping with the rest of him; for here again Harlan's sketch of his brother failed to exaggerate. Dan's metropolitan gloss had disappeared almost in a day, and though it might make a brief reappearance upon Sundays, when he walked to church with his mother and swung the gold-topped cane as he talked earnestly to her of Ornaby Addition, yet for the rest of the week he did seem to be almost unconscious, as Harlan said, of what he wore; so much so that his mother gently scolded him about it.

"What will people think of me," she asked, "if you insist on going about with two buttons off your vest, and looking as if you haven't had anything pressed since the flood? Whenever I do get one of your suits to look respectable, you wear it out to the farm and forget to put your overalls on, and then you climb trees, I suppose, or something else as destructive; and after that you rush off downtown where everybody sees you looking like the Old Scratch—that's what your father said, and it troubles him, too, dear. You were so particular all through college, always just the very pink of fashion, and now, all of a sudden, you've changed the way some young men do when they've married and get careworn over having two or three babies at home. Won't you try to reform, dear?"

He laughed and petted her, and went on as before, unreformed. Clerks, glancing out of the great plate-glass windows of a trust company, would giggle as they saw him hurrying by on his way from one office to another, rehearsing to himself as he went and disfiguring his memorandum book with hasty new mathematics. "There it goes again!" they would say, perhaps. "Big Chief Ten-Years-From-Now, rushin' the season in year-before-last's straw hat and a Seymour coat! Look at him talkin' to his old notebook, though! Guess that's about all he's got left he can talk to without gettin' laughed to death!"

Dan found one listener, however, who did not laugh, but listened to him without interruption, until the oration was concluded, although it was unduly protracted under the encouragement of such benevolent circumstance. This was Mr. Joseph Kohn, the father of Dan's former partner in the ornamental bracket business. Kohn & Sons was an establishment formerly mentioned by National Avenue as a "cheap Jew dry-goods store"; and prosperous housewives usually laughed apologetically about anything they happened to have bought there. But, as the years went by, the façade of Kohn & Sons widened; small shops on each side were annexed, and the "cheap dry-goods store" was spoken of as a "cheap department store," until in time it became customary to omit the word "cheap." Old Joe Kohn was one of the directors of the

59

First National Bank; he enjoyed the friendship of the president of that institution, and was mentioned in a tone of respect by even the acrid Shelby.

In the presence of this power in the land, then, Dan was profuse of his utmost possible eloquence. Unchecked, he became even grandiose, while the quiet figure at the desk smoked a cigar thoughtfully; and young Sam Kohn, not yet admitted to partnership with his father and older brother, but a floor-walker in the salesrooms below, sat with his elbows on his knees and his chin on his fists, listening with admiration.

"My gracious, Dan," he said, when the conclusion at last appeared to have been reached;—"you are certainly a natural-born goods seller! I wish we had you on the road for us."

"Yes, Sam," his father agreed pleasantly. "He talks pretty good. I don't know as I seldom heard no better."

"But what do you think of it?" the eager Dan urged. "What I want to know: Don't you think I've made my case? Don't you believe that Ornaby Addition—"

"Let's wait a minute," Mr. Kohn interrupted quietly. "Let's listen here a minute. First, there's the distance. You say yourself Shelby says he ain't goin' to put no car line out there; and it's true he ain't."

"But I told you I haven't given that up, Mr. Kohn. I expect to have another talk with Mr. Shelby next week."

"He don't," Mr. Kohn remarked. "He spoke to me yesterday a good deal about it at bank directors' meeting. No, Mr. Oliphant; don't you expect it. You ain't goin' to git no car line until you got people out there, and how can you git people out there till you git a car line? Now wait!" With a placative gesture he checked Dan, who had instantly begun to explain that with enough capital the Addition could build its own tracks. "Wait a minute," Mr. Kohn went on. "If you can't git enough capital for your Addition how could you git it for a car line, too? No, Mr. Oliphant; but I want to tell you I got some idea maybe you're right about how this city's goin' to grow. I've watched it for thirty years, and also I know something myself how the people been comin' from Europe, and how they're still comin'. It ain't only them;—people come to the cities from the country like they didn't used to. The more they git a little bit education, the more they want to live in a city; that's where you're goin' to git a big puportion the people you claim's goin' to crowd in here.

"But listen a minute, Mr. Oliphant; that there Ornaby's farm is awful far out in the country. Now wait! I'm tellin' you now, Mr. Oliphant, please. Times are changin' because all the time we git so

60

much new invented machinery. Workin' people are willin' to live some ways from where they work, even if they ain't on a car line. Why is that? It's because they can't afford a horse and buggy, but now they got bicycles. But you can't git 'em to live as far out as that there Ornaby's farm, even with bicycles, because except in summer the roads ain't nothing but mud or frozen ruts and snow, and you can't git no asphalt street put out there. The city council wouldn't ever—"

"Not to-day," Dan admitted. "I don't expect to do this all in a week or so, Mr. Kohn. But ten years from now—"

"Yes; that's it!" Mr. Kohn interrupted. "You come around and talk to me ten years from now about it, and I might put some money into it then. To-day I can't see it. All at the same time if I was you I wouldn't be discouraged. I won't put a cent in it, Mr. Oliphant, because the way it stands now, it don't look to me like no good proposition. But you already got your own money in; you should go ahead and not git discouraged because who can swear you won't git it out again? Many's the time I seen a man git his money out and clean up nice when everybody believed against him, the way they all believe against this here Ornaby's farm right to-day." He rose from his chair and offered his hand. "I got a business date, Mr. Oliphant, so I must excuse. I'm glad to talk with you because you're old friends with Sam here, and he always speaks so much about you at our family meals at the home. Good-bye, Mr. Oliphant;—I only got to say I'm wishin' you good luck, and hope you keep on at it till you win. You got as good a chance as many a man, so don't give it up."

Dan repeated the last four words a little ruefully as he went down in the elevator with Sam, who was his escort. "'Don't give it up.' Well, not very likely!" He laughed at the idea of giving it up; then sighed reflectively. "Well, anyhow, he's the first one I've talked to that said it. Most of the others just had a grand time laughin' at me and told me to give it up! I appreciate your father's friendliness, Sam."

Sam shook his head. "It ain't that exactly," he said, with a cautious glance at the young man who operated the elevator. "Wait a minute and I'll tell you." And when they had emerged upon the ground floor, he followed his friend through the busy aisles and out to the sidewalk. "It's this way, Dan," he said. "You ain't got any bigger ideas of how we're goin' to have a great city here than what papa has; he don't talk so much in public, as it were, the way you been doin', but home I wonder how many thousand times we got to listen to him! That's why you had him so interested he sat still like that. But he ain't goin' to put money in it now. I know papa awful well; it ain't his way. I wouldn't say it to anybody but you, Dan, but I

61

expect right now he'll own a good many shares stock in that Ornaby farm some day."

"What?" Dan cried, surprised. "Why, you just said—"

"I said he won't put money in now," Sam explained, with a look of some compassion. "Papa won't ever take a gamble, Dan; he ain't the kind. He'll wait till you go broke on this Ornaby farm; then, if it looks good by that time, he'll get a couple his business friends in with him, maybe, and they'll send some feller after dark to buy it for thirty-five cents. He wouldn't never mean you no ill will by it, though, Dan."

"Oh, I know that," Dan said, and laughed. "But you're mistaken about one thing, Sam, and so's he, if he counts on it."

"What's that?"

"I'm not goin' broke on it. Why, Sam, ten years from now—"

"You told papa all about that," Sam interrupted hurriedly. "You talked fine about it, and I wish I could run off an argument half as good. It's a shame when a man's got a line o' talk like that he ain't got a good proposition behind it."

"But it is good. Why, even two years from now—"

"Yes; by then it might be," Sam said. "But now you got an awful hard gang to get any backin' out of in the business men of our city, Dan. They didn't make their money so easy they're willin' to take a chance once in a while, you see."

"I expect so," Dan sighed; and then, consulting his memorandum book, shook hands with this sympathetic friend and hurried away to see if he could obtain another interview with John W. Johns, the president of the Chamber of Commerce. He was successful to just that extent; he was readily granted the hearing, but failed to arouse a more serious interest in Ornaby Addition than had hitherto been shown by this too-humorous official.

Mr. Johns was cordial, told Dan that he did "just actually love to listen about Ornaby Addition"; that he was always delighted to listen when he had the time, and went on to mention that he had said openly to the whole Chamber at the Chamber's Friday lunch, "Why, to hear young Dan Oliphant take on about Ornaby Addition, it's as good as a variety show any day!" Mr. Johns was by no means unfriendly; on the contrary, he ended by becoming complimentary on the subject of Dan's good nature. "Of course, you aren't goin' to get any business man to sink a dollar in that old farm, my boy; but I do like the way you stand up to the roastin' you get about it. 'Tisn't every young fellow your age could take everybody's whoopin' and hollerin' about him without gettin' pretty hot under the collar."

"Oh, no," Dan said. "If I can get some of you to put in a little money, I don't care how you laugh."

62

"But you can't," Mr. Johns pointed out. "That's why I kind o' like the way you take it. We don't put in a cent, and we get hunderds of dollars' worth o' fun out of it!"

"I guess that's so," Dan admitted, and he went away somewhat crestfallen in spite of Mr. Johns's compliment.

As Sam Kohn said, these men of business had not made their money easily; they had made it by persistent caution and shrewdness, by patient saving, and by self-denial in the days of their youth; they were not the men to "take a chance once in a while." Orations delighted them but would never convince them; and as the weeks and months went by, Dan began to understand that if Ornaby Addition was to be saved, he alone would have to save it.

He worked himself thin at the task; for he was far from losing heart and never admitted even to himself that he was attempting an impossibility. His letters to Lena were filled with Ornaby Addition, of which her own ideas appeared to be so indefinite that sometimes he wondered if she didn't "skip" in her perusal of his missives. She wrote him:

It seems to me you must spend a great deal of time over that Ornaby thing. Is it really so beautifully interesting as you say it is? Of course I do understand you're immensely keen on it though, and I'm glad it will be such a great success and all that. I certainly hope it will because as I warned you I'm an extravagant little wretch and always in a row with papa about it. But I do hope you don't feel you'll have to spend lots of time out there after we're married. Of course we must be as practical—disgusting word!—as we can, but I do hope you'll arrange so that you won't need to do more out West than just oversee this Ornaby affair for a week or so every year, because I adore you and I'll want you to be with me all the time.

Cousin Oliver has some works—I don't know what it is they make but I think it's metal things for plumbers or something equally heinous!—and his works are out in the West somewhere, too. He only has to go there once or twice a year and gets home again the next night. I do hope you'll be sure to make arrangements like that about yours. At any rate, be sure not to have to go out there next year, not unless you just hate your poor Me! I couldn't bear for anything to interfere with our having a full year abroad. I won't let you leave me in Nice or Mentone and run back to your old Ornaby thing for weeks and weeks! If you dare to try anything like that, sir, I'll flirt my little head off with some dashing maître d'hôtel! Write instantly and tell me nothing shall spoil our full year abroad together. Instantly! Or I'll think you hate me!

This letter gave Dan a bad hour as he sat in his room at home trying to construct a reply to it. The full year abroad now considered so definite by Lena had been rather sketchily mentioned between them in New York; he had agreed, with a faint and concealed uneasiness, that a wedding journey to southern France, if he could "manage" it, would be lovely; but afterwards he had forgotten all about it; and, being in his twenties, he was yet to learn how often the casual implications of men in their tender moments are construed by women to be attested bonds, sworn to, signed and sealed. So now, as he answered Lena, he found himself on the defensive, as if the impossibility of the full year abroad were a wrong to her, an unintended one, but nevertheless a wrong for him to explain and for her to forgive. He added to his opening explanations:

We might go to Europe two or three years from now. Of course I don't expect to make the Addition my life work. I hope to be going into other things as soon as I've put this on its own feet. You show you've got a wonderful business head in your letter, dear, because a man's business ought to be just the way you say—it ought to be so he only needs to oversee it. The broad principles of business aren't often understood by a woman, and it makes me proud that you are one of the few who can. You do understand them so well I see it must be my own fault I haven't given you the right idea about Ornaby Addition. For one thing, you see, an addition isn't a works exactly, though not as unlike as it might seem, because both need a great deal of attention and energy to get them started. What I am trying to do is to lay out an Addition to the city, making streets and building lots that afterwhile will become part of the city, and my land won't be really an addition until that is accomplished. It is a wonderful piece of land, with superb trees and good clean air, though I have to cut down many of the trees, which I hate to do, in order to lay out the building lots.

What troubles me so much since reading your last letter is that I don't see any way to leave here at all, except for a few days for our wedding and a stop at Niagara Falls if you would like that—it is a sight you ought to see, dear, and well worth the time—on our way here. I'm afraid I didn't think enough about the trip abroad when we spoke of it and didn't fully understand it was a settled thing, as you do. That is all my fault and I'm going to be mighty sorry if this is a big disappointment to you. I would sooner cut off my right hand than let anything be a disappointment to you, Lena, and I don't know just how it happened that I didn't know before how much you were counting on spending the year in Europe.

Another thing that hurts me and I hardly know how to speak of it is this: I ought to have consulted you before I plunged into this work—I see that now—but I got so enthusiastic over it I just went ahead, and now it's impossible for me not to keep on going ahead with it, and that means we have to live here, Lena. I did hope to persuade you to be willing for us to live here, but I only hoped to persuade you to it, and now I'm afraid this may look to you as if I forced it on you. That would just break my heart, to have you believe it, and I never thought of such an aspect when I bought the Ornaby farm. I just thought it would be a big thing and make us a fortune and help build up my city. But now it's done and all my money's tied up in it, we'll have to settle down till the job's put through—don't ever doubt it's going to be a big thing; but I see how you might look at it. If you do look at it as forcing you, please just try to forgive me and believe I did mean for the best for both of us, Lena, dear.

My mother and father want us to live with them, and I think it would be the best and most sensible thing for us to do. There's a great deal of room and if we rented a house we couldn't get a very comfortable or good-looking one, I'm afraid, because all we can possibly spare of what I have left will just have to go into the Addition.

I'm so afraid this letter will worry you. I don't know what to do or what else to say except please write as soon as you can to tell me how it strikes you, and if you can say so please say you don't think I meant to force our living here, and you still care something about me.

The trouble is you don't know what a great place to live this is, because you haven't ever been anywhere except a few places East and Europe. You would soon get used to the difference between living here and New York and after that you'd never want to live anywhere else. Of course it's mighty pleasant to go to New York or Europe for a visit now and then, and most of the people you'd meet here do that, just as you and I would hope to when we could afford it, but for a place to settle down and live in, I know you'd get to feeling we've got the most satisfactory one on the face of the globe right here. Won't you write me right away as soon as you read this and tell me you don't think I've tried to force anything, and anyhow no matter what you think you forgive me and haven't changed toward me, dear?

65

CHAPTER VIII

BUT Lena did not respond right away. Instead, she allowed a fortnight to elapse, during which her state of mind was one of indecision and her continuous emotion a sharp irritation; both of these symptoms being manifest in an interview she had with her brother George, one day, when she finally decided to consult him. "It's so indecently unfair!" she complained. "It is forcing me; and his letter was a perfectly abject confession of it. He admits himself he's compelling me to go out to that awful place and live with him."

"How do you know it's awful?" George inquired mildly. "He's the most likable chap I ever knew, and he comes from there. Doesn't that look as if—"

"No, it doesn't. Just think of being compelled to listen to everybody speaking with that awful Western accent! I can stand it in him because I like his voice, and he's only one; but imagine hearing nothing else!" Lena shivered, flinging out her beautiful little hands in a despairing gesture, illuminated by tiny stars of fire from her rings. "Just imagine having hundreds of 'em talking about 'waturr' and 'butturr' all day long!"

"Oh, I dare say they speak of other matters at intervals," George said. "If that's the supremest agony you have to face, Lena, I don't see why you're kicking up such a row with yourself. I'd rather like to go out there, myself."

"What in the world for?"

"Well, for one reason," he answered seriously, "because I like Dan, but principally because I'd do well to get away from New York."

"To live?" she cried incredulously. "I could understand that, if you meant you'd like to get away in order to live in Paris, but to want to go out and bury yourself in one of those awful Western—"

"Paris!" George exclaimed. "For me? I suppose your idea is a short life but a merry one!"

"Why not? It might be better than living to a hundred on 'watturr' and 'butturr!' What's the matter with you and New York?"

"Nothing's the matter with New York except that it's got so many sides it can be whatever one chooses to make it, so that a weak character like me gets too many chances to increase his weaknesses here. There's no question about it, Lena; I'm a weak character. I've proved it to myself too many times to doubt it. A smaller city is pretty much one thing, but New York is anything because it's everything. The trouble is with me I've slid into making

66

a New York for myself that I can't break away from unless I emigrate. My New York is Uncle Nick's offices for as few hours a day as I can fool 'em with; and after that it's three clubs and the Waldorf, the Holland House, Martin's, Jack's, two or three roulette holes, incidental bars, and sometimes the stage door of the Casino. The rest of the time I live in a hansom cab. A pretty thing, isn't it!"

"Then why don't you change it?"

"Because I can't. I can't get myself away from the crowd I've picked up, and that's the life they lead. Funny, too, I don't really like one of 'em, yet I can't keep away from 'em because I'm in the same ruts and talk the same lingo and drink the same drinks. That's the real trouble, I suppose, and there's a certain future ahead of me—a pleasant one to look forward to!"

"What is?"

"Drunken stockbroker," George replied with laconic despondency. "That's me, if I live to forty."

"I'd rather be one than buried in a mudhole on the prairie," said Lena. "I'd rather be anything than that; yet it's precisely what my thoughtful fiancé informs me I have no choice about. I think perhaps he'll learn whether I have or not, though!"

"Better think it over," George advised, with a thoughtful glance at his sister's flushed and petulant face. "It might be the best thing for you."

"What!"

"It might," he insisted. "You've made a pretty quick-stepping New York of your own, Lena. Tea at Sherry's means mighty little tea for you, my dear. A man told me the other day he'd never met a human being who could survive as many Benedictines in the afternoon as you can. Besides that, you get too much music."

"You're crazy!" Lena cried. "I live on music!"

"No, you don't," he said. "You keep yourself woozy with it. You go on music debauches, Lena. You don't take it as an art; you take it as an excitement. You keep your emotions frothing with it, and that's why you can't get along without it. If you hadn't been in the habit of getting yourself woozy with music, that Venable affair would never have happened."

"George!" she said sharply, and her eyes, already angry, grew more brilliant with increased emotion. "Shame on you!"

"Oh, well—" he said placatively.

"It's a thing you have no right to make me remember."

"Other people remember it," he said, with a brother's grimness. "You needn't think because nobody outside the family ever speaks of it to you it isn't thought of and referred to when you're spoken of."

She looked pathetic at this, and reproached him in a broken voice. "Unmanly! One would think my own—my own brother—"

"Your own brother is about the only person that could speak of it to you in a friendly way, Lena. You know how the rest of the family speak of it to you—when they do."

"It's so unfair!" she moaned. "Nobody ever understood—"

"We needn't to go into that," George said gently. "I think myself it was your musical emotions on top of a constitutional lack of discretion. Oh, I don't blame you! I've spent too much time trying to cover my own indiscretions from the family. I'm really more the family black sheep than you are, only you had worse luck; that's all. I only mention it to get you to think a little before you talk of throwing Dan Oliphant over rather than to go and live in the town he's so proud of."

She wiped her eyes, choked a little, and protested feebly: "But the two things haven't any connection. What—what's Venable got to do with—"

"Well, you make me say it," George remarked as she paused. "I think you understand as well as I do; but if you want me to be definite, I will."

"Not too definite, please, George!"

"How can I be anything else? There isn't any tactful way to say some things, Lena. You may get proposals from some of these men you meet at parties and father don't know about—"

"Never mind, please, George. Do you have to be quite so—"

"Yes," he said decisively. "Quite. The family have made it clear what they'll do, if you ever try again to marry one of the wrong sort, like Venable."

"'The wrong sort!'" she echoed pathetically, though with some bitterness toward her brother. "He was the most interesting man I ever knew, and a great artist. He was—"

"Unfortunate in his domestic experiences," George interrupted, concluding the sentence for her dryly. "And you were unfortunate in overlooking—well, to put it tactlessly, in seeming to have no objection to what I'm afraid I must call his somewhat bigamous tendencies, Lena."

"George!"

"My dear, I'm trying to say something helpful. Eligibles of our own walk in life enjoy dancing with you or buying Benedictines for you, but after Venable, none of 'em would be likely to—"

"That's enough, please, George!"

"No," he said, "I'm explaining that Dan's the best thing in sight. The family weren't too pleased about him, I admit; but they couldn't help seeing that. For my part, I think it might be the making of you."

"I don't care to be made, thanks."

"I mean you might have a chance to improve, living somewhere else," he explained calmly. "But more than that, Dan Oliphant looks up to you so worshipfully—he pictures you as such spotless perfection—it seems to me you'd just have to live up to his idea of you. If you want to know the truth, I took such a fancy to him I wasn't too delighted on his account when I saw he was getting serious about you; but when he seemed to be so much so, I thought maybe it might turn out pretty well for both of you. It's good sometimes for a man to have such ideals, and it's always good for a woman to live up to 'em. Besides, you do care about him, don't you?"

"Yes," she said. "I wouldn't have said I'd marry him if I didn't. I really did fall a lot in love with him, but that's not being in love with spending my life in some terrible place, is it? And besides I'm not going to live up to his ideals; nothing bores me more than pretending to be somebody I'm not. I get enough of that with the family, thanks!"

"You think you won't try to be the girl he believes you are?" George asked gravely.

"Don't be silly! Why on earth should I pretend to be anybody but myself?"

"In that case," George said, "I hope you'll write poor Dan that you refuse to be compelled and have decided to break your engagement. He'll be pretty sick over it, I'm afraid, but I think you'd both live happier—and longer!"

With this brotherly tribute, spoken in a rueful humour, he departed, leaving her at her small French desk, where the sheet of blue-tinted note paper before her remained blank, except for a few teardrops. In spite of his parting advice, George had relieved neither her indecision nor her conviction that she was being ill-treated by her lover. Nevertheless, except for one thing, she was inclined to accept that advice.

The one deterrent was the group of people defined by George and herself, in tones never enthusiastic, as "the family." Aunts, uncles, and cousins were included, all of them persons of weight, and some of them of such prodigious substance in wealth as to figure as personages in the metropolis; though all McMillans were personages to themselves, on the score of what they believed to be clan greatness due to historical descent and hereditary merit. To their view, New York was a conglomerate background for the McMillans and a not extensive additional gentry, principally English

69

and Dutch in origin. Beyond the conglomerate background, the McMillans permitted themselves to be aware of certain foreigners as gentry, and also of some flavourings of gentry, similar to their own, in Philadelphia, Boston, and one or two smaller cities, but there perfected civilization ended. All else they believed to be a kind of climbing barbarism, able to show forth talent or power, perhaps, in a spasmodic way, or even isolated greatness, as in Abraham Lincoln, but never gentry, except in imitations laughably pinchbeck.

To the McMillan view, Lena's adventure with that dashing sculpture, half genius and half Grecian-shaped meat, Perry Venable, had placed her gentryship in jeopardy, damaged her as a McMillan;—in fact, her infatuation for so conspicuous a baritone could not avoid being itself conspicuous; it "made talk," and in answer to the talk she had announced her engagement to him. Then, in the face of the family's formidable opposition, she made preparations for a clandestine wedding, which Mr. Venable was unable to attend on account of his wife's arrival from Poland. Thereupon, standing alone against the shock of heavy McMillan explosives, Lena's impulsive loyalty in defending the godlike baritone led her to make an unfortunate statement: great artists were not to be bound by the ordinary fetters upon conduct, she said;—and this prelude not being accepted as of any great force and originality, she followed it hotly with the declaration that she had long been aware of the Polish lady's existence.

It was in great part to this admission of hers that the unwitting Dan Oliphant owed the family's consent to his suit for the hand of a McMillan. A McMillan who got herself talked about, and then confessed, not in the manner of confession but with anger, that she had not been deceived—such a McMillan would conceivably do such a thing again, and a respectable barbarian bridegroom might be the best substitute for those unfortunately obsolete family resources in times of youthful revolt, lettres de cachet and the enforced taking of veils. But, in good truth, Dan may have owed to Lena's celebrated admission more than the family's consent, for the family's austerity of manner toward Lena became so protracted an oppression that she was the readier to be pleased with anything as cheerfully different from that family as Dan was.

Without doubt, too, he owed it to this McMillan austerity that she did not write to him now and break her engagement with him. The Venable affair was two years past, but the austerity went on, unabated. Dan was at least an avenue of escape, and, as Lena had said to her brother, she was "a lot in love" with him. Yet she hesitated, angry with him because he could not offer what she wanted, and half convinced that escape from what she hated might be an escape into what she would hate more. So she wrote to him finally:

You said you loved me! That isn't quite easy to believe just now. Why did you let me go on counting upon our having a year abroad? I'm afraid I'll never be able to understand it. I don't know what to say or what to do. I think the best thing you could do would be to come East at once. Maybe I could understand better if we talked it over together. It seems to me that you couldn't have cared for me with any depth or you wouldn't have allowed things to be as you say they are. A man can always do anything he really wants to, and if you had really wanted—oh, I know it's futile to be writing of that! You simply didn't care enough, and I thought you did! The only thing for you to do is to come at once. We must settle what's to be done, because I can't go on in the state of unhappiness I've suffered since your last letter. Maybe you can convince me that you do care a little in spite of having forced me to give up what I counted on. If you do convince me, I suppose there's no use putting off things—I don't want a large, fussy wedding. If we are going ahead with it, we might as well get it over. I don't know what to do, I admit that; but I'm still

Your half-heartbroken
Lena.

CHAPTER IX

NOT long ago there was found everywhere in the Midland country a kind of wood then most characteristic of it but now almost disappeared, a vanishment not inexpressive of nature's way of striking chords; for the wood is no longer so like the Midlands as it was. But in the days when Ornaby Addition struggled in embryo, hickory still grew in profusion, and that tough and seasoned old sample of it, Mr. Shelby, withstood at his office desk the hottest summer in several years. He permitted himself the alleviation of a palm-leaf fan, and when his open carriage came for him at a little before six o'clock, every afternoon, he had the elderly negro coachman drive him out to the end of the cedar-block pavement of Amberson Boulevard before going home; but on the day that began the hottest hot spell of the summer he forebore to indulge himself with this excursion, albeit he forebore somewhat peevishly.

71

"We got to go straight home this evening, Jim," he said, and added, "Plague take it!"

"Yes, suh," the coachman assented. "She lay it down she want me ca'y you home quick as I kin git you. I tell 'er bettuh not be too quick or I'm goin' have me two nice dead trottin' hosses. Hoss die same as a man, day like this, an' it ain't cool off airy bit sense noon. Look to me like gittin' hottuh, 'stid o' simmerin' down some, way ought to!" He widened one fat brown cheek in a slight distortion, producing a sound not vocal, but correctly interpreted by the horses as the call for an advance. Then, as they obediently set off at a trot, he chuckled; for although he complained of the heat he really liked it; and was not ill-equipped for it in shapeless linen, a straw hat, and slippers. "Tell me be'n five six whi' men drop down dade right out in a middle the sidewalk to-day," he said. "Way it keepin' up, they be mo' of 'em befo' mawnin'. Look at them hosses bustin' out an' lathun theyse'f a'ready, an' I ain't trot 'em a full square yit!"

"You needn't push 'em on my account," Mr. Shelby said, "I'm not in any hurry."

"No, suh," the coloured man agreed, smiling over some private thought of his own. "I guess you ain't! But she said, hot or no hot, git you home early's I could fix it." And then he laughed outright.

"Plague take it!" Mr. Shelby said again; for what amused the coachman made the master all the more peevish. Unquestionably, he was a deeply annoyed old gentleman, in spite of the fact that he was the coolest looking human being up and down the full length of National Avenue, into which thoroughfare the carriage had turned.

The long avenue might well have been mistaken for a colony of invalids and listless convalescents. Damp and languid citizens, their coats over bared forearms, made their painful way homeward from downtown, mopping fiery brows and throats; other coatless citizens, arrived at home, reclined melting in wicker rocking-chairs upon their verandas or lawns, likewise mopping as they melted; while beside them their wives and daughters, in flimsiest white, sat fanning plaintively. Here and there the stout father of a family stood near his front fence and played a weak and tepid stream from the garden hose over his lawn, or sprinkled the street, while his children, too hot to be importunate, begged lifelessly to relieve him of the task. The leaves of the massed foliage that made the street a green tunnel hung flaccidly gilding in the sun; and the sun abated not at all as it approached its setting. The air drooped upon the people with a weight too heavy to let them move readily, yet for breathing there seemed to be no air; and it had no motion, so that the transparent bits of paper, where the popcorn man or the hokey-pokey man had passed, lay in the street and on the sidewalks as still as so much lead.

"Seem like ev'thing wilted down flat," Mr. Shelby's fat coachman remarked as they turned into the driveway at home. "Me, I reckon if you's to take little slim string o' cobweb up on the roof an' push 'er off, she'd fall ri' down on the groun' same as a flatiron. Look fountain, Mist' Shelby!" He laughed happily, and waved his whip toward the bronze swan. "That duck, let alone he ain't got stren'f 'nough to spout, he ain't but jes' hodly able to goggle his th'oat little bit."

The swan was indeed put to it to eject a faint spray, for all over the town the people were making such demands on the water, already low with the dry season, that the depleted river whence it came threatened to disappear unless the drought were broken. However, neither drought nor heat had to do with Mr. Shelby's peevishness, which visibly increased when the carriage turned into his driveway;—what made him frown so bitterly was the sight of his daughter, charmingly dressed in fabrics of gossamer weight, her shapely hands gloved in spite of the weather, and her hazel eyes bright under a hat of ivory lace. She was sitting upon a wicker bench on the big veranda, but when the lathered bay horses trotted through the driveway gate, she jumped up and hurried to meet her father as he stepped out upon a stone horseblock near the veranda steps.

"Papa!" she cried, "you must hurry; we're terribly late! I wouldn't have waited for you, but I was afraid you wouldn't go unless I took you."

"I wouldn't," he said grimly. "You bet your sweet life I wouldn't!"

"Won't you hurry?" she urged.

"What for? Ain't I dressed up enough? All I'm goin' to do is wash my hands."

"Then do," she cried, as he moved to go indoors. "Please hurry!"

"Never you mind," he returned crossly. "I don't usually take more'n half a jiffy to just wash my hands, thank you!" And as he disappeared he was heard to mutter, not without vehemence: "Plague take it!"

A few moments later he reappeared, not visibly altered except that his irritated expression had become one of revolt. "Look a-here!" he said. "I don't see as I'm called upon to promenade over there and join in with all this high jinks and goin's-on!"

"Papa—"

"I don't mind an old-fashioned party," he went on. "I used to

73

go to plenty of 'em in my time, but when all they got for you to do is listen to half the women in town tryin' to out-holler each other, why, you bet your bottom dollar I'm through!"

"But, papa—"

"No, sir-ree!" he protested loudly. "You can well as not go on over there without me. Why, just look at the crowd they got in there already."

He waved his hand to the neighbouring domain on the south, where the crowd he bitterly mentioned was not in sight, but was indicated by external manifestations. Open family carriages, surreys, runabouts, phaetons, and "station wagons" filled the Oliphants' driveway, and, for a hundred yards or more, were drawn up to the curb on each side of the avenue. Coloured drivers sat at leisure, gossiping from one vehicle to another, or shouting over jokes about the hot weather. The horses drooped, or, with heads tossing at intervals, protested against their check-reins—and one of them, detained in position by a strap fastened to a portable iron weight, alternately backed and advanced with such persistence that he now and then produced enough commotion to bring profane bellows of reproof from the drivers, after which he would subside momentarily, then misbehave again.

One of the coachmen decided to settle the matter, and, sliding to the ground from the hot leather front cushion of a "two-horse surrey", went to chide the nervous animal. "Look a-me, hoss!" the man shouted fiercely. "You gone spoil ev'ybody's pleasure. Whyn't you behave youse'f an' listen to music?" He pointed eloquently to the Oliphants' open windows, whence came the sound of violins, a harp and a flute. "You git a chance listen nice music when you stan' all day in you' stall, hoss? An' look at all them dressed-up white folks goin' junketin'. What they goin' think about you, you keep on ackin' a fool?" Here, to clarify his meaning to the disturber, he gestured toward some young people—girls in pretty summer flimsies and young men in white flannels—who were going in through the iron gateway. "You think anybody goin' respect you, cuttin' up that fool way? You look out, hoss, you look out! You back into my surrey ag'in I'm goin' take an' smack you so's you won't fergit it long's you live!"

Mr. Shelby, becoming more obdurate on his veranda, found this altercation helpful to his argument. "Why, just listen! That crowd's makin' so much noise I'd lose my hearin' if I went in there. I won't do it!"

"But, papa," his daughter pleaded, "it isn't the people in the house who are making the noise; it's that darkey yelling at a horse. You've got to come."

74

"Why have I?"

"Because you're their next-door neighbour. Because it's a time when all their friends should go."

"Why is it?" he asked stubbornly. "What they want to make all this fuss over her for, anyway? I guess, from what I hear, her folks didn't make any fuss over them in New York. Just barely let 'em come to the weddin' and never even asked 'em to a single meal! I should think the Oliphant family'd have too much pride to go and get up a big doin's like this over a girl when her family treated them like that!"

"Please come," Martha begged. "All that matters to Dan's father and mother is that he is married and they want their old friends to meet the bride and say a word of welcome to her."

"Well, I don't want to say any welcome to her. Dan Oliphant hadn't got any more business to get married right now than a muskrat; he's as poor as one! I don't want to go over there and take on like I approve of any such a foolishness."

"You're only making excuses," Martha said, frowning, and she took his arm firmly, propelling him toward the veranda steps. "You know how they'd all feel if their oldest neighbour didn't go. You are going, papa."

"I won't!" he protested fiercely; then unexpectedly giving way to what at least appeared to be superior physical force, he descended the steps. "Plague take it!" he said, and walked on beside his daughter without further resistance.

At the Oliphants' open front doors they seemed to step into the breath of a furnace stoked with flowers. Moreover, this hot and fragrant breath was laden with clamour, the conglomerate voices of two hundred people exhausting themselves to be heard in spite of one another and in spite of the music.

"Gee-mun-nently!" Mr. Shelby groaned, as this turmoil buffeted his ears. "Why, this is worse'n a chicken farm when they're killin' for market! I'm goin' straight home!" And he made a serious attempt to depart through the portal they had just entered, but Martha had taken his arm too firmly for him to succeed without creating scandal.

A head taller than her father, she was both powerful and determined; and his resistance could be but momentary. She said "Papa!" indignantly under her breath; he succumbed, indistinctly muttering obsolete profanity; and they went into a drawing-room that was the very pit of the clamour and the flowery heat, in spite of generous floor space and high ceilings. The big room was so crowded with hot, well-dressed people that Martha had difficulty in passing between the vociferous groups, especially as many sought to

75

detain her with greetings, and women clutched her, demanding in confidential shouts: "What do you think of her?"

But she pressed on, keeping a sure hold upon her outraged father, until they reached the other end of the room; for there, in a trellised floral bower, with all the flowers wilted in the heat, Dan Oliphant stood with his bride and his father and mother.

The reception party appeared to be little less wilted than the flowers; Mr. Oliphant and Dan, in their thick frock coats, suffering more than the two ladies; but all four smiled with a brave fixity, as they had been smiling for more than an hour; and the three Oliphants were still able to speak with a cordiality that even this ordeal had been unable to exhaust.

The bride might have been taken for a somewhat bewildered automaton, greatly needing a rewinding of its mechanism. In white satin, with pearls in her black hair, she was waxy pale under the rouge it was her habit to use, and she only murmured indistinguishably as Mr. Oliphant presented his guests to her. The faint smile she wore upon her lips she did indeed appear to wear, and to have worn so long that it was almost worn-out;—no one could doubt that she longed for the time when she could permit herself to get rid of it. As a matter of fact, she granted herself that privilege when Mr. Oliphant presented Miss Shelby to her; for the smile faded to an indiscernible tracing as Lena found the statuesque amplitude of Martha towering over her. The small bride looked almost apprehensive.

"I hope—I do hope you'll be able to like me," Martha said, a little nervously. "I live next door, and I hope—I do hope you'll be able to." Then, as Lena said nothing, Martha gave Mr. Shelby's arm a tug, unseen, and brought him unwillingly to face the bride. "This is my father. He's a new neighbour for you, too."

The old gentleman made a slight, hostile duck with his head. "Pleased to meet ye, ma'am," he said severely.

At that the bride seemed to be astonished. "What?" she said.

"I bid you good afternoon, ma'am," he returned, ducked his head again, and passed on as rapidly as he could.

Martha whispered hurriedly to Dan: "She is beautiful!" and would have followed her father, but Dan detained her.

"Martha, will you help us to get her to like it here?" he said. "You see she's such an utter stranger and everything's bound to seem sort of different at first. I've been hoping you'd let her be your best friend, because you—you'd—"

"If she'll let me, Dan," Martha said, her voice faltering as she continued, "You know that I'd always—I'd always want to—" She stopped, glancing back at Lena, whose own glances seemed to be noting with some interest the heartiness with which Dan still grasped the hand of this next-door Juno. "I know she's lovely!" Martha said; and she moved away to overtake her father, who had every intention of leaving the house at once, but found himself again balked by his daughter's taking his arm.

"What you so upset over?" he asked crossly. "What's the matter your face?"

"Nothing, papa. Why?"

"Looks as though you're takin' cold. It's the heat, maybe. Let's go."

"Not yet, papa."

"Look a-here!" he said, "I'm not goin' to promenade out in that dining-room and ruin my stomach on lemonade and doodaddle refreshments. It's suppertime right now, and I want to go home!"

"Hush!" she bade him. "It wouldn't be polite to rush right out. Just stay a minute or two longer; then you can go."

"But what's the use? I don't want to hang around here with all the fat women in town perspiring against my clo'es. I hate the whole possytucky of 'em!"

"Sh, papa!"

"I don't care," he went on with husky vehemence. "Nothin' to do here except stare at the bride, and she's so little it don't take much time to see her; she's just about half your size—you made her seem like a wax doll beside you, and the way she looked at you, I guess she thought so, too. Anyway, she does look like a wax doll. Looks worse'n that, too!"

"No, no!"

"Yes, she does," he insisted. "She's got paint on her. Her face is all over paint."

"It isn't paint. It's only rouge."

"What's the difference? It ain't decent. She paints. She's got red paint on her cheeks and black paint on her eye-winkers. Looks to me like Dan Oliphant's gone and married a New York fast woman."

"Hush!" Martha commanded him sharply. "People will hear you!"

"I can't hardly hear myself!" he retorted. "Never got in such a gibblety-gabble in my born days. I tell you she paints! Her mother-in-law ought to take her out to a washstand and clean her up like a respectable woman. The Oliphant family ought to know what people'll take her for, if they let her go around all painted up like that. If she was my daughter-in-law—"

But here Martha's protest was so vehement as to check him. "Everybody will hear you! Be quiet! Look there!"

77

She caught her breath, staring wide-eyed; and, turning to see what had so decisively fixed her attention, he realized that the clamorous place had become almost silent. Old Mrs. Savage, leaning upon her grandson Harlan's arm, had entered the room and was on her way to the bride.

The guests made a passage for her, crowding back upon themselves until there was an aisle through which she and Harlan slowly passed. She was in fine gray silk and lace; and her hair, covered only in part by the lace cap, was still browner than it was white. But she could no longer hold herself upright as of yore; a cruel stoop had got into the indomitable back at last, and she was visibly tremulous all over. The emaciation, too, of such great age had come upon her; the last few months had begun the final shrivelling of everything except the self, but in her eyes that ageless self almost flamed;—it had a kind of majesty, for its will alone and no other force could have made the spent body walk. Thus, among these people who had known her all their lives, there was an awe of her, so that they had hushed themselves, silently making room for her to pass; and she was so frail, so nearly gone from life, that to many of them it seemed almost as if a woman already dead walked among them. They perceived that she could never again do what she was doing to-day, nor could any fail to comprehend in her look her own gaunt recognition that this was the last time she would thus be seen.

Slowly, with Harlan helping her, she went through the room, came to Lena, and stood before her, looking at her and making little sighing murmurs that told of the effort it cost her still to live and move. Then, in a voice not cracked or quavering, though broken a little, she said: "I thought so! But you're welcome."

Lena looked frightened, but Dan laughed and kissed his grandmother's cheek, talking cheerfully. "Well, this is an honour, grandma! We hardly hoped you'd come out in all this heat. We certainly appreciate it, grandma, and we'll never forget you thought enough of us to do it. It's just the best thing could happen to us in the world!"

His free and easy full voice released the guests from the sympathetic hush put upon them by the apparition; they turned to one another again and the interrupted chatter was loudly resumed; but Mrs. Savage extended her right arm and with her gloved hand abruptly touched the bride's cheek.

Startled, Lena uttered a faint outcry, protesting. "What—why, what do you mean?"

Mrs. Savage was looking fiercely at the tremulous fingertips of the white glove that had touched the rouged cheek.

"She's painted!"

Dan laughed and patted the old lady's shoulder. "You'd better go and get some iced coffee, grandma," he said, and turned to his mother. "Couldn't we all go and get something cold now with grandma? I don't believe there are any more people coming and Lena's pretty tired, I'm afraid."

"I am," Lena said. "I really am." She came close to him, pleading in a faint voice: "For heaven's sake let me go up to my room and lie down. I can't stand any more!"

"Why, Lena—"

"Please let me go, Dan."

"Why—but—" he began. "Couldn't you stick out just a little longer? If we go to the dining-room with grandma I think it might please her. Besides, if the bride disappeared at her own reception I'm afraid they might think—"

"Please, Dan!"

"Well—but, dear—"

But Lena waited for no more argument; she made a gesture of most poignant appeal, slipped by him and went quickly out through a door that led into a rear hallway. Dan's impulse was to follow her, but he decided that his first duty led him in another direction, and joined his grandmother who was on her way to the dining-room. When he had helped Harlan to bring the old lady iced coffee and such accompaniments as she would consent to nibble, it was time to return to the drawing-room to say farewell to the guests; for, according to a prevalent custom, they could not depart without assuring him that they had enjoyed themselves.

He explained to them that the heat had been too much for Lena, received their messages of sympathy for her and their renewed congratulations for himself, and finally, when they were all gone, ran anxiously upstairs to her. He found her lying face downward upon her bed in her bridal gown, an attitude less of exhaustion than of agitation, though it spoke of both. Both were manifest, too, in the disorder of her curled black hair and in the way one of her delicate arms was stretched upward across the pillow with a damp handkerchief half clenched in the childlike fingers.

"Why, Lena—"

"You'd better let me alone!"

"But what is the matter?"

"Nothing!"

He touched the small hand on the pillow solicitously. "I'm afraid I let you get tired, dear."

"'Tired!'" she echoed, withdrawing her hand instantly. "'Tired!'" And with that she abruptly sat upright upon the bed,

79

showing him a face misshapen with emotion. What added to the disastrous effect upon her young husband was that her movement completed the disorder of her hair so that some heavy strands of it hung down, with the string of pearls, still enmeshed, dangling unheeded against her cheek. The picture she thus presented was almost unnerving to Dan, who had never seen a woman so greatly discomposed. His mother had wept heartbrokenly when her father died; but she had kept her face covered; and he had no recollection of ever seeing her with her hair in disorder.

"Why, Lena!" he cried. "What on earth—"

"Nothing!" she said, and laughed painfully, satirizing the word. "Nothing! Nothing at all!"

"But, dear—"

"Never mind!" She shivered, then sighed profoundly, and stared at him with curiosity, as if she were examining something unfamiliar. "So this is what it's going to be like, is it?" she asked.

"What?"

"I mean this place! These people! This—this climate!"

But here Dan was touched upon his native pride. "Climate? Why, this is the best climate in the world, Lena! There isn't any climate to compare with it! And as for this little warm spell just now, why, you see we do need some hot weather."

"Like this?"

"Why, certainly! You see this is the greatest corn belt in the country, dear. If it wasn't for a stretch or two of good corn-growin' weather like this every summer, the farmers wouldn't get half a crop, and there'd be a big drop in prosperity."

"And you'd rather have it hot like this, then?" Lena asked, seeming to find him increasingly strange. "You want the farmers to grow their corn, no matter what happens to your wife?"

"But, my goodness!" he cried, in his perplexity. "I don't run the weather, Lena! It don't make any difference how I might want it, the weather just is the way it is. Besides, we don't mind it so much."

"Don't you?" She laughed briefly, and shook her head as though marvelling at the plight in which she found herself, wondering how she had come to it. "No, I suppose you were born and brought up to such weather. I suppose that's why you didn't tell me about it before I came here. You probably didn't realize what this deathly suffocating air might do to the nerves of a human being who's always lived near the sea. And for your mother to make me stand hours in that oven, trying to talk to all those awful people—"

"Lena!" Dan was as profoundly astonished as he was distressed. "Why, those are the best people in town; they're our old family friends, and I don't know where in the world you'd expect to

80

find better. What fault could you find with 'em, dear? They were all so cordial and pleasant, and so anxious to be friends with you, I thought you'd enjoy—"

"Oh, yes!" she cried. " 'Enjoy!' Oh, yes!"

"What's the matter with 'em? Weren't their clothes—"

"Their clothes!" she echoed desperately. "What do I care about their clothes!"

"Then what—"

"Oh, don't!" she moaned. "Don't ask me what's wrong with such people!"

"But I do ask you, Lena."

"Don't! My life wouldn't be long enough to tell you."

"Well, I declare!" the dismayed young husband exclaimed, and sat down beside her on the bed.

But she leaned away from him as he would have put his arm about her. "Please don't try petting me," she said. "You'll never be able to make me stand such people. I couldn't! It isn't in me to!"

"This is just a little spell you've got, Lena; it won't last. In a few days you'll begin to feel mighty different, and then when you get to knowing mother a little better, and some of the younger people, like Martha Shelby—"

"Who's Martha Shelby?"

"You met her and her father this afternoon," Dan explained. "Harlan and I grew up with her, and she's one of the finest girls in the world. She's always just the same—cheerful, you know, and dependable, no matter what happens. You'll get mighty fond of her, Lena. Everybody always does."

"Was she that great hulking thing with the dried-up little old father that said, 'Pleased to meet ye, ma'am?' "

Dan laughed uneasily. "Why, Martha isn't 'hulking.' She's a mighty fine-lookin' girl! She's tall, but she isn't as tall as I am, and she's—"

"She is that big girl, then," Lena said with conviction. "I hope you don't intend to ask me to see anything of her!"

"But, Lena—"

"She's an awful person!"

"But you've just barely met her," he cried, his distress and perplexity increasing. "You don't know—"

"She was perfectly awful," Lena insisted sharply. "Do you have to let her call you 'Dan?' "

"Why, good gracious, everybody in town calls me 'Dan,' and Martha lives next door."

"I don't see why you need to be intimate with people merely because they live next door," Lena said coldly. "I suppose, though, in this heavenly climate you feel because a girl lives next door to you it's necessary to let her hold your hand quite a little!"

"But she didn't hold my hand."

"Didn't she? It seemed to me I noticed—"

"No, no, no!" he exclaimed. "I only wanted to stop her a minute to say I hoped she'd help make you like it here and be as good a friend to you as she's always been to me."

"I see. That's why you held her hand."

"But I didn't—"

"Of course not!" Lena interrupted. "Not more than five minutes or so! And she's the one you especially want me to be friends with! I never saw a more awful person."

"But what's 'awful' about her?"

Lena shook her head, as if in despair of him for not comprehending Martha's awfulness. "She's just awful," she said, implying that if he didn't perceive for himself why Martha was awful he hadn't a mind capable of being enlightened. "I suppose you expect me to be intimate with her father, too?"

Dan laughed desperately. "I wouldn't be apt to ask you to be particularly intimate with anybody his age, Lena."

"I hope not," she said, and became rigid, looking at him with a cold hostility that was new to his experience and almost appalled him. "I was afraid you might intend to ask me to be intimate with your grandmother."

Dan seemed to crumple; he groaned, grew red, apologized unhappily: "Oh, Lord! I was afraid that'd upset you, but I kind of hoped you'd forget it."

" 'Forget it?' When she did it before everybody! Pawing me—croaking at me—"

"Oh, Lord!" he groaned. "I was afraid it bothered you."

" 'Bothered' me! Is that your word for it?"

"Nobody else noticed it, Lena," he went on. "Nobody except just our family—"

"Oh, yes!" she said. "The next-door person you admire so much was one of those that took it all in. She was in at the death—my death, thank you!"

"Lena, you don't understand at all. Nobody thinks anything about anything grandma does. You see she's a good deal what people call a 'privileged character.' "

" 'Privileged?' Yes! I should say she takes privileges perhaps!"

"Oh, dear me!" he sighed. "Lena, you just mustn't mind it. You see, she belongs to two generations back, and besides I suppose most people here wouldn't know just what to make of your puttin' artificial colour on your face. For that matter, your own mother and sister used to be against it, even in New York, and probably people would take notice of it here a little more than they would there. I kind of hoped myself, when you got here—"

"How kind of you!" she said. "Possibly some day you'll understand a little of what I've had to go through since you brought me to this place. Yesterday, when we got here, I thought I just couldn't live in such heat. You're used to it; you don't know what it is to a person who'd never even imagined it. And in spite of the fact that I was absolutely prostrate with it, your mother informs me that she's invited people to come and shake my hand and arm off for two hours in an oven. Then, because I'm so deathly pale that I look ghastly, I use a little rouge and am publicly insulted for it; after which my husband reproves me for trying to look a little less like a dead person."

Dan was miserable with remorse. "No, no, no! I don't mind your puttin' it on, Lena. I didn't mean to reprove you; I only—"

"You only meant to say your grandmother's insult was justified."

"But it wasn't an insult, Lena. After you get to know grandma better—"

"After I what?" Lena interrupted.

"You'll understand her better after you get to know her."

"After I what?" Lena said again.

"I said—"

"Listen!" she interrupted fiercely. "You must understand this. On absolutely no account must you expect me ever to go into that frightful old woman's house, or to see her, or to speak to her, or to allow her to speak to me. Never!"

"Oh, Lord!" Dan groaned; then rose, rubbed his damp forehead, crossed the room with a troubled and lagging step, and, upon the sound of a bell-toned gong below, turned again to his bride. "There's supper. Mother said we'd just have a light supper this evening instead of dinner. Could you—"

"Could I what?"

"Could you wash your face and fix your hair up a little?" he said hopefully, yet with a warranted nervousness. "It'll do you good to freshen up and eat a little. Except the family there'll be nobody there except—except—"

"Except whom?" she demanded.

"Well—except Martha," he faltered. "Mother asked her yesterday because she thought you'd—well, I mean except Martha and—and grandma."

Lena again threw herself face downward upon the bed; and

83

when he tried to comfort her she struck at him feebly without lifting her head.

CHAPTER X

HALF an hour later he brought her a tray, a dainty one prepared by his mother, and set it upon a table close beside the bed.

"Here you are, dearie," he said gayly. "Jellied chicken, cold as ice, and iced tea and ice-cold salad. Not a thing hot except some nice crisp toast. You'll feel like running a foot-race after you eat it, Lena!"

She spoke without moving, keeping her face away from him. "Are those women still downstairs?"

"Who?"

"Your grandmother and that big girl—the awful one."

"You don't mean—"

"I asked you if they're still in the house."

"They're just goin' home, Lena. Martha told me to tell you how sorry she is you feel the heat so badly. Won't you eat something now, please, dear?"

"No, thank you."

"Please! You'll feel all right again if you'll eat something, and to-morrow morning we'll drive out to Ornaby Addition. Then you'll feel like a queen, Lena; because it's all yours and you'll see what it's goin' to do for us."

"Do you think it will get us away from here?" she asked in a dead voice.

"Well, by that time," Dan answered cheerfully, "I expect maybe you won't want to get away."

" 'By that time,' " she said, quoting him dismally. "You mean it's going to be a long time?"

"Lena, I wish you'd just look at this tray. I know if you'd only look at it, you couldn't help eating. You'd—"

"Oh, hush!" she moaned, and struck her pillow a futile blow. "Someone told me once that you people out here always were trying to get everybody to eat, that you thought just eating would cure everything. I suppose you and all your family have been eating away, downstairs there, just the same as ever. It makes me die to think of it! I've had delirium in fevers, but I never was delirious

84

enough to imagine a place where there wasn't some mercy in the heat! There isn't any here; it's almost dusk and hotter than ever. I couldn't any more eat than if I were some poor thing cooking alive on a grill. What on earth do you want me to eat for?"

"Well, dearie," he said placatively. "I think it would strengthen you and make you feel so much better, maybe you'd be willing to—to—" He hesitated, faltering.

"To what?"

"Well, you see grandma's so terribly old—and just these last few months she's broken so—we know we can't hope to see much more of her, dear; and so we make quite a little fuss over her when she's able to come here. I did hope maybe you'd feel able to go down with me to tell her good-night."

At that, Lena struck the pillow again, and then again and again; she beat it with a listless desperation. "Didn't you understand what I said to you about her?"

"Oh, yes; but I know that was just a little nervousness, Lena; you didn't really mean it. I know you feel differently about it already."

"No!" she cried, interrupting him sharply. "No! No!" And then, in her pain, her voice became so passionately vehement that Dan was alarmed. "No! No! No!"

"Lena! I'm afraid they'll hear you downstairs."

"What do I care!" she cried so loudly that Martha Shelby, in the twilight of the yard below, on her way to the gate, paused and half turned; and Dan saw her through the open window. "What do I care!" Lena screamed. "What do I care!"

"Oh, dear me!" he groaned, and though Martha hurried on he was sure that she had heard.

"I don't care!"

"Oh, dear me!" he groaned again, and went to close the door which he had thoughtlessly left open when he came into the room. But, to his dismay, before he closed it he heard Mrs. Savage's still sonorous voice in the hall downstairs: "No, don't bother him. Harlan's enough to get me home. But if I had a daughter-in-law with tantrums I'd mighty soon cure her."

At that point Dan shut the door hurriedly, and went back to the bedside. "Lena," he said, in great distress, "if you won't eat anything, I just don't see what I can do!"

"You don't?" she asked, and turned to look at him. "It seems to me nothing could be simpler. You know perfectly well what you can do."

"What?"

85

"Take me out of this. Keep your promise to me and take me abroad."

"But I can't, dearie," he explained. "You see I didn't realize it was a promise exactly, and now it's just out of the question. You see everything we've got is in Ornaby Addition and so—"

"Then sell it."

"What? Why, I wouldn't have anything left at all if I did that at this stage of the work. You see—"

"Then put a mortgage on it. People can always get money by mortgages."

Dan rubbed his forehead. "I've already got a mortgage on it," he said. "That's where the money came from I'm workin' with now." He sighed, then went on more cheerfully. "But just wait till you see it, Lena. We'll drive out there first thing to-morrow morning and you'll understand right away what a big thing you and I own together. You just wait! Why, two or three weeks from now—maybe only two or three days from now—you'll be as enthusiastic over Ornaby as I am!" He leaned over her, smiling, and took her hand. "Honestly, Lena, I don't want to brag—I wouldn't want to brag to you, the last person in the world—but honestly, I believe it's goin' to be the biggest thing that's ever been done in this town. You see if we can only get the city limits extended and run a boulevard out there-"

But here she startled him; she snatched her hand away and burst into a convulsive sobbing that shook every inch of her. "Oh, dear!" she wailed. "I'm trapped! I'm trapped!"

This was all he could get from her during the next half hour; that she was "trapped," repeated over and over in a heartbroken voice at intervals in the sobbing; and Dan, agonized at the sight and sound of such poignantly genuine suffering, found nothing to offer in the way of effective solace. He tried to pet her, to stroke her forehead, but at every such impulse of his she tossed away from his extended hand. Then, in desperation, he fell back upon renewed entreaties that she would eat, tempting her with appetizing descriptions of the food he had brought and, when these were so unsuccessful that she made him carry the untouched tray out into the hall and leave it there, he returned to make further prophecies of the restorative powers of Ornaby Addition.

Once she saw Ornaby, he said, she would be fairly in love with it; and he was so unfortunate as to add that he knew she would soon get used to his grandmother and like her.

Lena was growing somewhat more composed until he spoke of his grandmother; but instantly, as if the relation between this cause and its effect had already established itself as permanently automatic, she uttered a loud cry of pain, the sobbing again became convulsive; and Dan perceived that for a considerable time to come it would be better to omit even the mention of Mrs. Savage in his wife's presence.

Darkness came upon the room where Lena tossed and lamented, and the young husband walked up and down until she begged him to stop. He sat by an open window, helplessly distressed to find that whatever he did seemed to hurt her; for, when he had been silent awhile she wailed piteously, "Oh, heavens! Why can't you say something?" And when he began to speak reassuringly of the climate, telling her that the oppressive weather was only "a little hot spell," she tossed and moaned the more.

So the long evening passed in slow, hot hours laden with emotions that also burned. From the window Dan saw the family carriage return from Mrs. Savage's; the horses shaking themselves in their lathered harness when they halted on the driveway to let Harlan out. He went indoors, to the library as usual, Dan guessed vaguely; and after a while Mr. and Mrs. Oliphant came from the house and walked slowly up and down the path that led through the lawn to the gate. They were "taking the air"—or as much of it as there was to be taken—and, walking, thus together, the two figures seemed to express a congeniality Dan had never before noticed with attention, although he had been aware of it all his life. Both of them had retained their slenderness, and in the night were so youthful looking that they might have been taken for a pair of young lovers, except for the peacefulness seeming to be theirs. This emanation of a serenity between them suddenly became perceptible to their son as a surprising thing; and he looked down upon them wonderingly.

There came a querulous inquiry from the bed. "What on earth are you staring at?"

"Only father and mother. They're outdoors coolin' off."

"Good heavens!" Lena said. "Cooling off!"

"You're feelin' better now, aren't you, Lena?" he asked hopefully.

" 'Better!' " she wailed. "Oh, heavens!"

Dan rested his elbows on the window-sill, and his chin on his hands. "They're comin' in, now," he said after a while. "They've had their little evening walk in the yard together. They nearly always do that when the weather isn't too cold."

" 'Cold?' I suppose this place gets just as cold in winter as it does hot in summer!"

"It does get pretty cold here in winter sometimes," the thoughtless Dan said, with a touch of pride. "Why, last February—"

"Oh, heavens!" Lena wailed; and she began to weep again.

About midnight she was quiet, and Dan, going near her,

87

discovered that she drowsed. His foot touched something upon the carpet, and he picked up the string of artificial pearls, put it upon the table beside the bed, then tiptoed out of the room, closing the door with great care to make no noise. The house was silent and solidly dark as he went down the broad stairway and opened the front door to let himself out into the faint illumination of the summer night. It was a night profoundly hushed and motionless; and within it, enclosed in heat, the town lay prostrate.

Sighing heavily, the young husband walked to and fro upon the short grass of the lawn, wondering what had "happened" to Lena—as he thought of it—to upset her so; wondering, too, what had happened to himself, that since he had married her she had most of the time seemed to him to be, not the Lena he thought he knew, but an inexplicable stranger. This was a mystery beyond his experience, and he could only sigh and shake his inadequate head; meanwhile pacing beneath the midnight stars. But they were neither puzzled nor surprised, those experienced stars, so delicately bright in the warm sky, for they had looked down upon uncounted other young husbands in his plight and pacing as he did.

By and by he stood still, aware of another presence in the dimness of the neighbouring yard. The only sound in all the world seemed to be a minute tinkling and plashing of water where the stoic swan maintained himself at his duty while other birds slept; but upon the stone rim of the fountain Dan thought he discerned a white figure sitting. He went to the fence between the two lawns to make sure, and found that he was right; a large and graceful woman sat there, leaning over and drawing one hand meditatively to and fro through the water.

"Martha?" he said in a low voice.

She looked up, said "Dan!" under her breath, and came to the fence. "Why, you poor thing! You're still in that heavy long coat!"

"Am I?" he asked vaguely. "I hadn't noticed."

" 'Hadn't noticed?' In this weather!"

"It is fairly hot," he said, as though this circumstance had just been called to his attention.

"Then why don't you take it off?"

"My coat?" he returned absently. "I don't mind it."

"I do," Martha said. "You don't need to bother about talking to me with your coat off, do you? It's only a dozen years or so since we hid our shoes and stockings in the harness closet in your stable and ran off barefoot to go wading in the street after a thunderstorm. Take it off."

"Well—" He complied, explaining, "I just came out to get cool."

"So did I; but I don't believe it can be done, Dan. I believe this is the worst night for sheer hotness we've had in two or three years. I haven't felt it so much since the day I landed in New York from Cherbourg, summer before last. I'll never forget that day!"

"In New York?" he asked, astonished.

"I should say so! I suppose I felt it more because I was just from abroad, but I think people from our part of the country suffer fearfully from the heat in New York, anyhow."

"I believe they do," he said thoughtfully. "And New York people suffer from the heat when they come out here. That must be it."

"Do you think so?" She appeared to be surprised. "I don't see how New York people could mind the heat anywhere else very much after what they get at home."

"Oh, but they do, Martha! They suffer terribly from heat if they come out here, for instance. You see they don't spend the summers in New York. They either go abroad in summer or else to the country."

"Does she?" Martha asked quickly; but corrected herself. "Do they?"

"Yes," he said, seeming to be unaware of the correction. "That's why it upsets her so. You see—"

"Yes?"

"Well—" he said, hesitating. "It—it does kind of upset her. It—" He paused, then added lamely, "It's just the heat, though. That's all seems to be really the matter; she can't stand the weather."

"She'll get used to it," Martha said gently. "You mustn't worry, Dan."

"Oh, I don't. In a few days she'll probably see how lovely it really is here, and she'll begin to enjoy it and be more like herself. Everything'll be all right in a day or so; I'm sure of that."

"Yes, Dan."

"Of course just now, what with the heat and all and everybody strangers to her, why, it's no wonder it makes her feel a little upset. Anybody would be, but in a few days from now"—he hesitated, and concluded, with a somewhat lame insistence, "Well, it'll all be entirely different."

"Yes, Dan," she said again, but there was an almost imperceptible tremble in her voice, and his attention was oddly caught by it.

All his mind had been upon the suffering little bride, but there was something in the quality of this tremulousness in Martha's voice that made him think about Martha, instead. And suddenly he looked at her with the same wonder he had felt earlier this queer

89

evening, when he noticed for the first time that emanation of serenity between his father and mother. For there seemed to be something about Martha, too, that he had known familiarly all his life, but had never thought of before.

There is indeed a light that is light in darkness, and these strange moments of revelation, when they come, are brought most often by the night. Daylight, showing too many things, may afterwards doubt them, but they are real and not to be forgotten. They are only moments; and yet, while this one had its mystic little life, Dan was possessed in part by the feeling, altogether vague, that somewhere a peculiar but indefinable mistake had been made by somebody not identified to him.

Moreover, here was matter more curious still: this thing he had all his life known about Martha, but had never realized until now, made her in a moment a woman new to him, so that she seemed to stand there, facing him across the iron fence, a new Martha. He had no definition in words for what he felt, nor sought one; but it was as if he found himself in possession of an ineffable gift, inexpressibly valuable and shining vaguely in the darkness. This shining, wan and touching, seemed to come from Martha herself; and this newness of hers, that was yet so old, put a glamour about her. The dim, kind face and shimmering familiar figure were beautiful, he saw, never before having had consciousness of her as beautiful; but what most seemed to glow upon him out of the glamour about her was the steadfastness within her; for that was the jewel worn by the very self of her and shining upon him in the night.

"Martha—" he said in a low voice.

"Yes, Dan?"

"You've always been such a friend of mine, I—I—I've never said much about how I feel about it. I haven't got anything I wouldn't sooner part with, Martha."

"I hope so," she said gently, and bowed her head in a kind of meekness. "I hope so, Dan, but—" She stopped.

"But what, Martha?"

"I'm afraid," she said slowly, "your wife isn't going to like me."

"Oh, but she will," he returned, trying to put heartiness into this assurance. "She's bound to! Why, everybody in the world likes you, Martha."

"No; I had the feeling as soon as I spoke to her that she never would, Dan. It was just a feeling, but I'm afraid it'll turn out so. That doesn't mean I won't try my best to make her."

"You won't need to try. Of course just now she's suffering so terribly, poor little thing—"

"Poor Dan!" Martha said, as he stopped speaking and sighed instead. "You never could bear to see anybody suffer. The trouble is it always makes you suffer more than the person that's doing the original suffering."

"Oh, no. But I don't know what on earth to do for her. Of course, in a few days, when she begins to see what it's really like here, and I get her to understand a little more about the Addition—"

He stopped, startled to hear his name called in a querulous little voice from an upstairs window.

"She's awake," he said in a whisper.

"Who on earth are you talking with out there?" called the querulous voice.

"Good-night," he whispered, moving away hurriedly; but, looking back, he saw that Martha remained at the separating iron fence, leaning upon it now; and he could feel, rather than see, that she was not looking at him, but that her head was again bowed in the same meekness with which she had said she hoped he prized her feeling for him.

CHAPTER XI

THE doleful bride remained in bed all the next day, prostrate under the continuing heat;—in fact, it was not until a week had passed that she felt herself able to make the excursion projected by the hopeful bridegroom; and when they finally did set forth, in Dan's light runabout, she began to suffer before they reached the gates of the carriage driveway.

"Oh, dear!" she said. "Is it going to be bumpy like this all the way? It hurts my back."

Dan apologized. "I'm sorry I didn't have those holes in the drive filled up; I'll do it myself this evening. But here on the avenue," he said, as they turned north from the gates, "we'll have this fine cedar-block pavement for quite a good way."

"Oh, dear!" she complained. "It's worse on the cedar-block pavement than it was in your driveway."

"It is a little teeny bit jolty," Dan admitted. "You see this pavement's been down over five years now, but it's held out mighty well when you consider the traffic that's been over it—mighty well! It's been one of the finest pavements I ever saw in any town."

91

She gave a little moan. "You talk as if what it has been were a great help to us now. It does hurt my back, Dan."

"Oh, it isn't goin' to keep on like this," he assured her comfortingly. "The contracts are already signed for a new pavement. Six months from now this'll all be as smooth as a billiard table."

"But we have to go over it to-day!"

"That's why I thought the runabout would be pleasanter for you," he said. "Our old family carriage is more comfortable in some ways, but it hasn't got rubber tires. I hardly notice the bumps myself with these tires."

"I do!"

"Think what a great invention it is, though," he said cheerfully. "Why, before long I shouldn't wonder if you'd see almost everything that rolls usin' rubber tires, and a good many such light traps as this with inflated ones like bicycles. If horseless carriages ever amount to anything, they'll get to usin' inflated rubber tires, too, most likely."

"Oh, dear me!" Lena sighed. "Doesn't this heat ever relent a little?"

He assured her that it did; that the hot spell would soon be over, and that she wouldn't mind it when they reached the Addition, which was on higher ground. "It's always cool out at Ornaby," he said proudly. "The mean level's twenty-eight feet higher than it is in this part of the city; and I never saw the day when you couldn't find a breeze out there."

"Then hurry and get there! It must be a terribly long way. I don't see any higher ground ahead of us—nothing but this eternal flatness and flatness and flatness! I don't see how you people stand it. I should think somebody would build a hill!"

He laughed and told her that Ornaby was almost a hill. "Practically, it is," he said. "Anyhow it's a sort of plateau—practically. You see the mean level—"

"Oh, dear!" she sighed; and for a time they jogged on in silence.

He drove with one hand, holding over her with the other a green silk parasol, a performance not lacking in gallantry, nor altogether without difficulty, for his young horse was lively, in spite of the weather; yet it is doubtful if strangers, seeing the runabout pass, would have guessed the occupants a bride and groom.

Beneath the broad white rim of Lena's straw hat the pretty little face was contorted with discontent; while her companion's expression showed a puzzled discouragement not customarily associated with the expressions of bridegrooms. True, the discouragement passed before long, but it came back again after a

92

little more conversation. Then it disappeared again, but returned when signs of capricious weather were seen in the sky. For it is new knowledge to nobody that the weather has an uneducated humour and will as soon play the baboon with a bride and groom, or with a kind cripple on an errand of mercy, as it will with the hardiest ruffian. But at first Dan welcomed the hints of change in the southwest.

"By George!" he said, nodding across the vast flat cornfields upon their left, for the runabout had now come into the open country. "There's good news, Lena."

"What is?"

"Look over yonder. We're goin' to get rain, and Heaven knows we need it! Look."

Along the southwest horizon of cornfields and distant groves they saw a thickening nucleus of dark haze. Out of it, clouds of robust sculpture were slowly rising, muttering faintly as they rose, as if another planet approached and its giants grumbled, being roused from sleep to begin the assault.

"By George, that's great!" Dan exclaimed in high delight. "That's worth millions of dollars to the farmers, Lena."

But Lena was as far as possible from sharing his enthusiasm. "I believe it's going to be a thunderstorm. Turn back. I hate thunderstorms. I'm afraid of them."

"Why, they won't hurt you, Lena."

"They frighten me and they do kill people. Please turn back."

"But we're almost there, dear. I think the rain'll hold off, probably, but if it doesn't we'd be more likely to get wet goin' all the way back home than if we went ahead. I've got a tool shed out there we could wait under."

"A tool shed? With all the tools in it? That's just where the lightning would strike first!"

Dan laughed and tried to reassure her, but although they drove on in the bright sunshine for a time, she became more and more nervous. "It almost seems to me you don't want to do things I want you to. We should have turned back when I first spoke of it."

"Look, dear," he said. "Just ahead of us there's something you're goin' to be mighty proud of some day. It's Ornaby Addition, Lena!"

Before them the dirt road, grown with long grass between the ruts, had been widened to the dimensions of a city street as it passed between old forest groves of beech and elm, through which other wide rough roads had recently been cut. Beyond the woods were some open fields, where lines of stakes were driven in the ground to outline—apparently in a mood of over-optimistic prophecy—some

93

scores of building lots and various broad avenues. But so far as could be seen from the runabout, felled trees and wooden stakes were all that proved Ornaby to be an Addition and not a farm, though a few negroes were burning the remnants of a rail fence in a field not far from the road. And what made the whole prospect rather desolate was the malicious caprice of the weather;—the very moment when Dan stopped the runabout and waved his hand in a proud semicircle of display, the first of the robust clouds passed over the sun and Ornaby lay threatened in a monstrous shadow.

"Look, Lena!" the exultant proprietor cried. "This is Ornaby!"

"Is it?" she said desolately. "I do wish you'd turned round when I said. It's going to thunder and lighten horribly, and I know I'm going to be frightened to death."

Then, as a louder rumble sounded in the sky, she shivered, clutching Dan's arm. "I know that struck somewhere!"

"It might have struck somewhere in the next county," he laughed.

"What! Why, look at the sky right over us. I never saw anything so awful."

Dan laughed again and patted her small, clutching hand soothingly. "It's just a pleasant little summer thundershower, Lena."

"Little!" she cried. "Do you call storms like this 'little' out here?"

For, in truth, Dan's reassuring word was not well supported by the aspect of the sky. Above them hung what appeared to be a field of inverted gray haystacks, while from westward ragged, vast draperies advanced through a saffron light that suddenly lay upon all the land. A snort of wind tore at the road, carrying dust high aloft; then there was a curious silence throughout all the great space of the saffron light, and some large raindrops fell in a casual way, then stopped.

"You see?" said the cheery Dan. "That's all we'll get, likely enough. I shouldn't be surprised it'd clear up now."

"'Clear up!'" Lena cried incredulously. "I do believe you're crazy! Oh, heavens!"

And the heavens she thus adjured appeared heartily inclined to warrant her outcry. Satan fell from the sky in a demoniac swoop of lightning, carrying darkness with him; wind and water struck the runabout together; and Dan was fain to drive into the woods beside the road, while Lena clung to him and wailed. He tied the trembling horse to a tree, and got the bride and her wrecked parasol under the inadequate shelter of the tool house he had mentioned, but found little happiness there. A hinge had broken; the negroes had carried the door away to repair it; the roof leaked everywhere and was sonorous with the hail that fell presently with the heavy rain. At every bedazzlement of the lightning Lena gasped, then shrieked throughout the ensuing uproar, and before long whimpered that she was freezing. In fact, her wet clothes, little more than gauze, appeared to be dissolving upon her, while the air grew cold with the hail.

Dan put his soggy coat about her, petted her, and piled wet sticks together, saying that he would make a fire for her if he could. Whereupon she wept and uttered a pathetic laughter. "Burn up with the heat one minute," she said, through chattering teeth, "and the next freeze to death if you can't make a fire! What a place!"

Of course Dan defended his climate, but his argument was of as little avail as were his attempts to build a fire with sodden wood and drenched matches. Lena suffered from the cold as expressively as she had from the heat, and forgetting that these changes in temperature had not been unknown to her in her own native habitat and elsewhere, she convinced herself perfectly that all of her troubles were put upon her by "the West." Yet in this she was not so unreasonable as might appear;—our sufferings from interior disturbances are adept in disguising themselves as inflictions from outside.

These troubles of hers were not alleviated by two unfortunate remarks made by her young husband in the course of his efforts to hearten her. After one of the numerous electrical outrages, appalling in brilliancy and uproar, he said he was sorry he couldn't have taken her to the old Ornaby farmhouse for shelter; and when Lena reproached him for not having thought of this sooner, he explained too hastily that the house had been struck by lightning and burned to the ground during a thunderstorm earlier in the summer. After that, as she became almost hysterical, he straightway went on to his second blunder. "But nobody was hurt," he said. "Nobody at all, Lena. There wasn't anybody in the house; and anyhow I don't believe the lightning's really struck right near us during this whole shower. Why, it's nothin' at all; I've seen storms a thousand times worse than this. Only last summer I got caught out on a little lake, north of here, in a canoe, and pretty near a real tornado came up, with thunder and lightning that would make this little racket to-day look like something you'd get from a baby's toy. We didn't mind it; we just—"

" 'We?' Who?"

"Martha Shelby was with me," the incautious Dan replied. "Why, you ought to've seen how she behaved, Lena! She didn't mind it; she just laughed and kept on paddlin' like a soldier. I honestly think she enjoyed it. Now, why can't you—"

95

"You hush!" Lena cried.

"But I only—"

"Haven't I enough to bear? Be quiet!"

He obeyed, gazing out upon the tumultuous landscape, and wondering sadly what made her so angry with him. Then, all at once, beyond and through the mazes of tossing rain he seemed to see, however vaguely, the new Martha he had recognized in that queer night after his homecoming; and the recollection of their strange moment together brought him another not unlike it now. Something mystic operated here; he felt again that same enrichment, charged with an indefinite regret; and though the moment was no more than a moment, passing quickly, it comforted him a little. "There! Don't worry!" Martha seemed to say to him gently. So he said it to himself and felt in better spirits.

"Oh! Oh! Oh!" Lena wept, huddling in a corner of the shed. "How this horrible old world does make us pay for not knowing what to do!" And when he turned to try again to soothe her, she shrank but farther away from him and bade him let her alone.

"But it'll be all cleared up, half an hour from now," he said. "You'll be warm as toast as soon as the sun comes out again, and then we'll go over the whole Addition and see what's what, Lena!"

The first half of this prediction was amply fulfilled; Lena was indeed warm soon after the sun reappeared; but they did not inspect the Addition further. They went home, and a few days later Lena wrote an account of the expedition in a letter to her brother George. Not altogether happy when she wrote, she was unable to refrain from a little natural exaggeration.

You said to me once you'd like to come here to live. Read Martin Chuzzlewit again before you do. "Eden!" That's what the famous Ornaby Addition looks like! It isn't swampy, but that's all the difference I could see. We drove miles in the heat and choking dust and there wasn't anything to see when we got there! Just absolutely nothing! People had been digging around in spots and cutting a lot of trees down and after a cyclone and cloudburst that came up while we were there he pointed out a post sticking out of the ground and showed the greatest pride because it had "47th St." painted on it! This was when we were driving out of the woods. He wanted to poke all over the dreary place, looking at other posts and stumps of trees, but I couldn't stand any more of it.

We had the most horrible storm I was ever out in, and it hailed so that after being ill in bed for a week with the ghastly heat, it got so cold I almost died, and then as soon as the cyclone was over it got hot again—it isn't like ordinary heat; it gets hot with a sticky heaviness I can't express and the thermometer must stay up over

100 even at night—and as soon as we got home I had to go to bed where I've been ever since—hence this pencil—and I've just escaped pneumonia! And during the cyclone when I was really ill with the nervous anguish lightning always causes me, he began telling me how wonderfully a former sweetheart of his behaved in a storm on a lake! It was his idea of how to make me not mind it. Of course he only meant to cheer me up—but really!

His father and mother aren't bad, I must say. They're quite like him, good-looking and full of kindness; his mother is really sweet and I like them both, though I'll never get used to hearing people talk with this terrible Western accent. To a sensitive ear, it's actual pain. The brother looks rather like Dan, too; but he's pompous in a dry way and affected. Reads heavy things and seems to me a cold-hearted sort of prig, though he's always polite. The father and mother read, too. Their idea is Carlyle and Emerson and Thoreau—you know the type of mind—and Harlan (the brother) talks about that Englishman, Shaw, who writes the queer plays. They say they have two theatres open in winter, but of course there's no music here except something they brag about called the "April Festival," when there's a week of imported orchestra and some singing. Pleasant for me!—one week in the year!—though I suppose you'll think it's all I should have.

They meant to be kind, but they gave me the most fearful "reception." I never endured such a ghastly ordeal. The weather was over 100 in the shade—and in crowded rooms, well, imagine it! The people were dressed well enough—some of them were rather queer, but so are some at home—but I wish you could have seen the vehicles they drive in and their coachmen! Slouchy darkies in old straw hats with long-tailed horses that get the reins under their tails—and fringed surreys and family carryalls, something like what you'd see out in the country towns in Connecticut. They have phaetons and runabouts and a few respectable traps, but I've seen just one good-looking victoria since I came here. They don't like smartness really. I believe they think it's effeminate!

The real head of the Oliphant family is an outrageous old hag, Dan's grandmother, who behaved terribly to me at my only meeting with her—it will remain our only meeting! They're all afraid of her, and she has a lot of money. Queer—I understand he's tried to raise money for his Eden all over the town, but never asked the terrible grandmother. She doesn't believe in it, and I must say she's right about that! Rather!

How strange that any girl should do what I've done—and with my eyes wide open! I did it, and yet I knew he didn't understand me. I ought to have known that he can never understand me, that we don't speak the same language and never will. I ought to have realized what it means to know that I must live days, weeks, months, years with a person who will never understand anything whatever of my real self!

Yet I still care for him, and he is good. He does a thousand little kind things for me that do not help me at all, and the truth is most of them only irritate me. How odd it is that I write to you about not being understood—you who are seldom kind to me and often most unjust! Yet in a way I have always felt that you do understand me a little—perhaps unsympathetically—but at least you give me the luxury of being partly understood.

Yes, I still care for him, but when I think of his awful Ornaby thing I sometimes believe I have married a madman. It is nothing as I said—hopeless—a devastated farm—and yet when he speaks of it his eye lights up and he begins to walk about and gesture and talk as if he actually saw houses and streets—and shops—and thousands of people living there! If this isn't hallucination, I don't know what hallucination means.

But since our excursion to the place I've almost cured him of talking about it to me! I just can't stand it! And what is pleasant, I think he probably goes to talk about it to another woman. Already! A perfectly enormous girl seven or eight feet tall that he'd picked out to be my most intimate friend! Because she's been his most intimate friend, of course. But I suppose all men are like that.

The heat did relax for a day or two—but it's back again. Sometimes I can't believe I am actually in this place—apparently for life—and I begin to hope that I'll wake up. I think even you would pity me sometimes, George.

CHAPTER XII

IN THE minds of Mrs. Savage's neighbours across the street and of the habitual passers-by, that broad plate-glass window where it was her custom to sit for the last hour of every afternoon had come to bear the significance of a glass over a portrait. All long thoroughfares and many of even the shortest have such windows; and the people who repeatedly pass that way will often find the portrait window becoming a part, however slight, of their own lives;

98

but it will seldom be an enduring part, except as a fugitive, pathetic memory. For a time the silent old face is seen framed there every day, or it may be a pale and wistful child looking out gravely upon the noisy world. Then abruptly one day the window is only a window and no more a portrait; the passer-by has a moment of wonder whenever he goes by, but presently may have his faintly troubled question answered by a wreath on the door; and afterwards the window that was once a portrait will seem to him a little haunted.

Mrs. Savage's window had been a portrait so long that even the school children who went homeward that way in the autumn afternoons noticed a vacancy behind the glass and missed her from the frame; but new seasons came and passed, and no wreath appeared upon her door. She had been so thoroughly alive for so many years that the separation of herself from life could not be abrupt, even if she wished it. She did not wish it she told Harlan, one rainy night, as he sat beside her bed after bringing her the news that she was a great-grandmother.

"I suppose it seems funny to you," she said. "You must wonder why an old woman with nothing to live for would still want to live. I suppose you think it's because I just want to eat a little more and to lie here listening to that!" With a hand now become the very ghost of a hand, she gestured toward a window where the parted curtains revealed black panes slushed with noisy water by the strong west wind. "How you must wonder!"

"Oh, no," Harlan said, though she spoke the truth. "I don't wonder at all, grandma."

"Yes, you do! How could a young person help wondering about such a thing? Year before last I could still go out for a little walk; last year I could only go for a drive in the afternoons. After that I could still get downstairs and sit by the window; then I couldn't even do that, and could only hobble around upstairs;—then I couldn't even get into another room without being helped. And now for a month I've not been able to get out of bed—and I'll never be able to. No wonder you wonder I want to hang on!"

"But I don't," he insisted. "I don't, indeed."

"You do. What do you think I have to live for?"

"Why, partly for your family, grandma. We're all devoted to you; and besides you have your memories—I know you have many happy memories."

She laughed feebly, but nevertheless with audible asperity, interrupting his rather stumbling reassurances. " 'Happy memories!' Young people are always talking about 'happy memories'; and they think old people 'live in their happy memories.' I advise you not to

99

look forward to spending your old age in that way! There's no such thing, young man."

"No such thing as a happy memory?"

"Not when you're as old as I am," she said. "You can only have a happy memory of something when you can look forward to something of the same kind happening again; but I can't look forward to anything. Yet I still want to hang on!"

Harlan laughed gently. "Then doesn't that prove you do look forward to something, grandma?"

"No," she said. "It only proves I still have a little curiosity. I'd like to live twenty years just to prove I'm right about how this baby's going to turn out."

The implication of her tone was grim with conviction—clearly she spoke of a baby who could not turn out well—and Harlan was amused by his own perception of a little drama: his grandmother, clinging with difficulty to one extreme edge of life and prophesying only black doom for this new person who had just crawled up into life over the opposite extreme edge. "I'm sorry you feel so gloomy about that baby, grandma. I'm rather pleased, myself, to be an uncle, and so far I haven't been worrying about his future. Don't you think there's a chance for him?"

"Not with such a mother and father," the old lady promptly replied. "Dan oughtn't to have mixed with such a stock as that painted-up little photograph girl."

Harlan protested a little; coming to Lena's defense at least in this detail. "But I understand that the particular foible of the McMillan family is the magnificence of their stock, as you call it, grandma. It seems they're so proud of it they don't think of much else."

"Yes; that's always a sign a stock's petered out. When people put a lot on what their folks used to do, it always means they haven't got gimp enough left to do anything themselves. The minute I laid eyes on her picture I knew she came from a no-account stock; and when your mother gave her that reception everybody in town could tell right off what she was. Painted! That tells the story!"

Again Harlan protested on behalf of his sister-in-law. "Oh, I shouldn't make too much of that, grandma. A little rouge now and then—"

"'A little rouge!'" the old lady echoed satirically. "She was plastered with it! That doesn't make any difference though, because a woman that uses it at all is a bad woman and wants the men to know it."

"Oh, no, no!"

"It's so," the old lady cried as fiercely as her enfeebled voice

100

permitted. "It's the truth, and you'll live to see I'm right. I don't want you to forget then that I told you so. You remember it, Harlan."

"Yes, grandma," he said placatively. "I will if—"

"I don't want any 'if' about it. You remember what I'm telling you! She's bad!" Mrs. Savage spoke so vehemently that she had to pause and let her quickened breathing become more regular;—then she went on: "Look how she's treated me. If she'd had the right stuff in her, she'd have been grateful to me for giving her a lesson. If she'd been just a foolish girl who'd made a mistake and painted herself because she wanted to look healthier when she met her new husband's friends, why, she might have got a little pettish with me for showing her it was a mistake the way I did, but long before now she'd have forgiven me and thanked me for doing it. Not she! That was the last time I set foot out of doors; and has she ever come to see me? She's never been near me! What's more, she's done her best to keep Dan from ever coming here. When he has come I know he hasn't dared to tell her. Do you deny it?"

Harlan shook his head. "No, I'm afraid I can't, grandma."

"Do you know why she hates me so?" the old lady demanded. "It's because she's bad, and she knows I know it. People never forgive you for knowing they're bad. And now she's brought this baby into the world to inherit her badness, and you sit there and wonder I say the child's bound to turn out wrong."

"Grandma!" the young man exclaimed, laughing. "I only wonder you don't take into account the fact that the baby is Dan's, too. Dan may be a rather foolish sort of person—in fact, I think he is—but surely you've never thought him bad."

The old lady looked at her grandson querulously. "Don't be so superior, young man. That's always been your trouble—you think you're the only perfect person in the world." And when he would have protested, defending himself, she checked him sharply and went on: "Never mind! I'm talking about other things now. The trouble with Dan is that he's never seen anything as it really is and never will—not in all the days of his life! He was that way even when he was a boy. I remember once you hurt his feelings about some poor little brackets he was making with a little Jew boy. He thought the brackets were perfect, and he thought the little Jew boy was perfect, too. When you criticized them both he got into such a spasm of crying he had to go home to bed."

"Yes," Harlan said, smiling faintly; "I remember. He was always like that."

"Yes, and always will be. So he'll think this child of his is perfect, and it'll never get any discipline. I'd like to live twenty years just to see the wrack and ruin that's going to be made by these children born nowadays. Their parents got hardly any discipline at all, and they won't get any, so they'll never know how to respect anything at all. It only takes a little common sense to see from the start how this child'll turn out. With no discipline or respect for anything, and with such a mother from a petered-out stock, and a father that hasn't got a practical thought in his head, you can just as well as not expect the child to be in the penitentiary by the time he's twenty years old!" Then, as Harlan laughed, the old lady uttered a faint sound of laughter herself, not as if admitting that she exaggerated anything, however, but grimly. "You'll see!"

"You're right about it this far," Harlan said. "Dan already thinks the baby's perfect."

"Happy, is he?"

"The usual triumphant young father. More triumphant than the usual one, I should say. He went whooping over the house till mother had to stop him and send him outdoors to keep him from disturbing Lena."

"Yes; that's like him," the old lady said. "How queer it is; there are people who can always find something to whoop about, no matter what happens. Your grandfather was like that when he was a young man. Even when we were poor as Job's turkey he'd burst out cackling and laughing over anything at all. I used to just look at him and wonder. Dan's desperate for money, isn't he?"

Harlan coughed, frowned, and then looked faintly amused. "Yes, I should just about use the word 'desperate.' I think he is."

"He'll not get any of mine!" Mrs. Savage said. "I'd not be very apt to help him anyhow, after the way his wife's treated me. He wouldn't listen to me; he would marry her, and he would throw all he had away on that miserable old farm! Now I guess he's got nothing more to throw away."

"He's got rather less than nothing now, grandma. The place wouldn't sell for enough to pay the mortgages, and he hasn't been able to meet the interest. Father managed to let him have a thousand dollars two months ago, but it didn't go very far. The truth is, I think Dan's begun to be a little out of his head over the thing;— he had twenty teams hauling dirt while poor father's thousand lasted. Now he's going to lose the place, and I'd think it a fortunate misfortune if I believed he'd learn anything by it; but he won't."

"No," Mrs. Savage agreed gloomily. "He's like his grandfather, but he hasn't got a wife to watch over him as his grandfather had. He'll just be up to some new wastefulness."

"He already is," Harlan laughed. "You're extraordinary, the

102

way you put your finger on things, grandma. He's already up to a new wastefulness."

"What is it?"

"Horseless carriages," Harlan informed her. "Automobiles;— 'les autos,' I believe the French call them now. Since old Shelby wouldn't run a car line out to the farm, and the city council wouldn't build a street to the city boundary, and the county wouldn't improve the road, Dan's got the really magnificent idea that his Ornaby place could be reached by automobiles. He believes if the things could be made cheap enough everybody that's going to live in Ornaby Addition could own one and go back and forth in it. And besides, he expects to build some horseless omnibuses to run out there from town."

"He expects to?" Mrs. Savage cried, aghast. "He's just about to lose everything, yet he expects to manufacture horseless carriages and omnibuses?"

"Oh, yes," Harlan said easily. "He doesn't know he's bankrupt! To hear him you'd think he's just beginning to make his fortune and create great public works."

"Jehoshaphat!" In a few extremities during her long life Mrs. Savage had sought an outlet for her emotions in this expression; and after using it now she lay silent for some moments; then gave utterance to a dry little gasp of laughter. "I guess it's a good thing I've made a new will! Maybe this girl might have sense enough to clear out."

"Lena?" Harlan asked, for his grandmother's voice was little more than a whisper, as if she spoke to herself; and he was not sure of her words. "Do you mean you think Lena might leave Dan?"

"If he didn't have any money she might. What did she marry him for? She's hated being married to him, hasn't she? She must have believed he had money."

Harlan shook his head. "No," he said thoughtfully;—"I don't believe she's mercenary. I don't think that's why she married him."

"Can't you use your reason?" the old lady complained petulantly. "Hasn't she whined and scolded every minute since he brought her here?"

"Oh, it's not so bad as that, grandma."

"Your mother says she stays in her room for days at a time."

"Yes, she gets spells when she's moody—or at least just quiet," Harlan admitted. "But she's not always in them by any means. She's rather amusing sometimes, and she seems to try to be kind to Dan."

"Oh, she 'seems to try?'" Mrs. Savage echoed. "You seem to try to stand up for her! Do you like her?"

Faced with this abrupt question, Harlan was somewhat

103

disturbed. "Well, possibly not," he replied honestly, after a moment. "No, I can't say I do."

"I thought not. And does she like any of you?"

"Well, she's evidently rather fond of mother—and of father, too."

"Who on earth could help liking them?" Mrs. Savage cried, and, in her vehemence, seemed about to rise from her bed. "Do you think that's to her credit? She hates everybody and everything else here, and she nags Dan. That means she thought he had money, and she married him for it, and now she's disappointed. Well, she'll keep on being disappointed a good while, so far as my property is concerned! Then maybe she'll have sense enough to leave him and give him a chance to get the woman he ought to've married in the first place."

Harlan looked a little startled as his grandmother sank back, panting with exhaustion; the spirit within her was too high and still too passionate for the frail material left to it. The self of her was indeed without age, unaltered, and as dominant as it had ever been, though the instrument through which it communicated, her strengthless body, was almost perished out of any serviceableness. To her grandson there came an odd comparison: it seemed to him that she was like a vigorous person shouting through an almost useless telephone that could make only the tiniest, just perceptible sounds; and he had an odder thought than this: When the telephone was entirely broken and silent would she still be trying to shout through it? She would be shouting somewhere, he felt sure. But what he said, rather sadly, was, "Martha? I suppose you mean Martha Shelby?"

"Of course! Martha could make something out of Dan, and she's never looked at anybody but him, and she never will. You needn't expect her to, either, young man."

Harlan's colour heightened at this, and some shadows of sensitiveness about his mouth became quickly more visible. "Oh, no; of course I don't," he said quietly.

"She'll never marry you," the terrible old lady went on. "I know what you've been up to—I've had my eyes about me—but you'll never get her to quit thinking of Dan. And if this painted-up photograph girl takes her baby and goes away some day, things might have a chance to come out right. But you, young man—" She stopped, beset by a little cough as feeble as a baby's, yet enough to check her; and upon this the professional nurse who now took care of her appeared in the doorway and gave Harlan the smiling glance that let him know his call had lasted long enough.

He rose from his chair by the bedside, murmuring the

104

appropriate cheering phrases;—he was sure his grandmother would be stronger the next time he came, and she would soon "get downstairs again," he said; while she looked up at him with a strange contemplation that he sometimes remembered afterwards; she had so many times in her life said to others what he was saying to her now. But she let him thus ease his departure, and responded with only a faintly gasped, "We'll hope so," and "Good-night."

Though he bent over her, her voice was almost inaudible against the sound of the rain spitefully hammering the windows; and in the light of the single green-shaded bulb that hung above the table of tonics and medicines at the foot of the bed, the whiteness of her face was almost indistinguishable from the whiteness of the pillow. She was so nearly a ghost, indeed, that as he touched the cold hand in farewell, it seemed to him that if there were ghosts about—his grandfather, for instance—she might almost as easily be communing with them as with the living. She was of their world more than of this wherein she still wished to linger.

Downstairs, the elderly negro who had served her so long waited to open the door for the parting guest.

"You ought to brung you' papa's an' mamma's carri'ge, Mist' Hollun," he said. "You goin' git mighty wet, umbrella or no umbrella."

"No doubt, Nimbus."

"Yes, suh," said Nimbus reflectively. "You goin' swim. How you think you' grammaw feel to-night?"

"I'm afraid she's not any stronger. I'm afraid she won't be here much longer."

"No, suh?" The thin old man chuckled a little, as if to himself. "She awready did be here some few days! She stay li'l' while yet, Mist' Hollun."

"You think so?"

"Yes, suh," said Nimbus, chuckling again. "Same way as 'tis 'bout anything else. Some people come call on you; stay li'l' while; git up to go, they walk right out. Some people, they set an' set an' set; then when they git up to go, they don't go; they keep on talk, talk, talk. You grammaw she aw-ways do like that. She goin' take her time before she walk out the big door."

"I hope so," Harlan said, as Nimbus unfastened the old-fashioned brass door-chain for him. "I hope so, indeed."

"Yes, suh; she take her own time," the coloured man insisted;—then, opening the door, he stood aside and inclined himself in a bow that obviously gave him a satisfaction more than worth the effort. "I expeck she do you well, Mist' Hollun."

105

"What?" Harlan asked, pausing to unfurl the umbrella he had left just outside. "What did you say, Nimbus?"

"I mean: What she goin' do with all that propaty?" Nimbus explained. "Door she goin' out of when she git ready, it's a mighty big door, but 'tain't big enough to tote all that propaty with her—no, suh! I expeck you goin' git mighty big slice all that propaty, Mist' Hollun. Goo' ni', suh."

Harlan laughed, bade him good-night, and strode forward into the gusty water that drove through the darkness. Outside the gate, as he turned toward home, he laughed again, amused by the old negro's view of things, but not amused by the things themselves. Harlan knew that he had never won his grandmother's affection; her thought had always been of his brother and was still of Dan now, as she lay upon the bed from which she would never rise. Whatever the terms of her new will might be, and whatever their actual consequences, she had made it clear that they were at least designed for Dan's ultimate benefit.

Harlan had little expectation of any immediate benefit to himself, notwithstanding the lively hints of Nimbus; nor were his hopes greater than his expectations. He had no wish to supplant his brother.

CHAPTER XIII

HE HAD no wish to supplant his brother in Mrs. Savage's will or in anything;—last of all did he wish to supplant him in the heart of Martha Shelby. Mrs. Savage had been far from understanding her grandson's deep pride, and, as he strode homeward in the slashing rain, her acrid warnings that he must not hope for anything from Martha repeated themselves over and over in his mind, as such things will, and upon each repetition stung the more.

He thought ruefully of the ancient popular notion that such stingings come from only the unpleasant truth. "It hurts him because it's true," people say, sometimes, as if mere insult must ever fail to rankle, and all accusation not well-founded fall but painlessly upon the righteous. What Harlan recognized as possibly nearest the truth among his grandmother's unfavourable implications was what hurt him the least. He did not wholly lack the power of self-criticism; and he was able to perceive that the old lady had at least a foundation when she said, "Don't be so superior, young man. That's always been your trouble." Harlan was ready to admit that superiority had always been his trouble.

Not definitely, or in so many words, but nevertheless in fact, he believed himself superior to other people—even to all other people. Thus, when he and his brother were children, and their father took them to Mr. Forepaugh's circus, Dan was enthusiastic about a giant seven and a half feet high; but Harlan remained cold in the lofty presence. True giants were never less than nine feet tall and this one was "a pretty poor specimen," he declared, becoming so superior in the matter that Dan fell back upon personalities. "Well, anyhow, he's taller than you are, Harlan."

"I'm not in the business of being a giant, thank you," Harlan said; and Dan, helplessly baffled by the retort, because he was unable to analyze it, missed the chance to understand a fundamental part of his brother's character.

Harlan did not go into the giant business, yet he grew up looking down on all giants, since they all failed to reach the somewhat arbitrary nine feet he had set for them. He could not give credit to a struggling giant of seven feet and a half, and admire him for the difficulties overcome in getting to be at least that tall; Harlan really looked down upon such a giant from a height of nine feet.

Yet he was able, at times, to perceive his superiority as an unendearing characteristic and even to look upon it with some philosophic detachment; he did not resent his grandmother's remarks upon that subject. What he minded was her assumption that he was trying to take Dan's place in Martha Shelby's heart; Harlan wanted his own place there, or none.

He had wanted it ever since Martha was a handsome romping girl of fourteen and he a fastidious observer a little older. She was a romp, yet her boyish romping never lacked a laughing charm; for, although she was one of those big young girls who seem to grow almost overwhelmingly, she had the fortunate gift of gracefulness; she was somehow able to be large without ever being heavy. And one evening at a "German" for young people of the age that begins to be fretful about a correct definition of the word "children," she danced lightly to Harlan and unexpectedly "favoured" him; whereupon something profound straightway happened to the boy's emotions.

No visible manifestations betrayed the change within so self-contained a youth; for here his pride, deep-set even then, was touched;—the lively Martha's too obvious preference was always for the brother so much more of her own sort. Dan was her fellow-romp, and she would come shouting under the Oliphants' windows

107

for him as if she were a boy. They were an effervescent pair, and often rough in their horseplay with each other; while Harlan, aloof and cold of eye, would watch them with an inward protest so sharp that it made him ache.

He wanted to make Martha over from a model of his own devising; he wished her to be more dignified, and could not understand her childish love of what to him seemed mere senseless caperings with the boisterous Dan. Yet neither her caperings nor her devotion to Dan was able to disperse Harlan's feeling for her, which gradually became a kind of customary faint pain. In a little time—a year or two—the caperings ceased; Martha went eastward, as did the brothers, for the acquisition of a polish believed to be richer in that direction; and when she returned she had become dignified, as Harlan wished, but otherwise did not appear to be greatly altered. Certainly her devotion to Dan was the same; and her merely becoming dignified failed to alleviate that customary faint pain of Harlan's. He still had it, and with it his long mystification;—he had never been able to understand why she cared for Dan.

Harlan's view of his brother as a rather foolish person might have meant no more than superiority's tolerant amusement, had that pain and mystification of his not been involved; but, as matters were, Harlan would have been superior indeed if all bitterness had passed him by. He could have submitted, though with a sorrowing perplexity, to Martha's inability to be in love with him; but what sometimes drove him to utter a burst of stung laughter was the thought that she had given her heart to a man who did not even perceive the gift. To Harlan that seemed to be the supreme foolishness of his foolish brother.

Through the rain, as he opened his own gate, he saw in the direction of the house next door a line of faintly glowing oblongs, swept across by wet black silhouettes of tossing foliage; and since these lighted windows at Martha's were all downstairs, he concluded that she must have callers; for when she was alone she went up to her own room to read, and just before nine o'clock Mr. Shelby put out all the lights of the lower floor. The old gentleman was sensitive about uselessly high gas bills, in spite of the fact that he was, himself, to an almost exclusive extent, the company that produced the gas.

In the vestibule at his own door Harlan furled his umbrella, shook the spray from his waterproof overcoat, and was groping in his waistcoat pocket for the latchkey, when his mother unexpectedly opened the door for him from the inside. "I was standing at a window looking out, and saw you come up the walk," she explained. "Your mackintosh looks soaking wet; you must be drowned! The

108

doctor was here again awhile ago and says Lena's doing splendidly, and the nurse just told me she and the baby are both asleep. Come into the library and dry off. Your father's gone to bed, but he lit the fire for you before he went up. We were afraid you'd be chilled. How did you find mother?"

"About the same, I should say." Harlan hung his dripping overcoat upon the ponderous walnut hatrack, the base of which was equipped for such emergencies with a pair of iron soup plates in a high state of ornamentation. Then he followed his mother into the library and went to sit by the fire, extending his long legs to its warmth, so that presently the drenched light shoes he wore began to emit a perceptible vapour.

"You ought to have worn your rubbers," Mrs. Oliphant said reproachfully; and then as he only murmured "Oh, no," in response, she said in a tone of inquiry: "I suppose you didn't happen to see anything of Dan?"

"Not very likely! Not much to be seen between here and grandma's just now except night and water."

"I suppose so," she assented. "I thought possibly you might have gone somewhere else after you left mother's."

"No." But there had been something a little perturbed in her voice and he turned to look at her. "Were you at the window on Dan's account, mother? Are you anxious about him?"

"Not exactly anxious," she answered. "But—well, I just thought—" She paused.

Harlan laughed. "Don't be worried about it. I'll sit up for him, if you like. I dare say your surmise is correct."

"My surmise?" she repeated, a little embarrassed. "What surmise?"

"About how your wandering boy has spent his evening," Harlan returned lightly. "I haven't a doubt you're right, and he's followed the good old custom."

Mrs. Oliphant coloured a little. "I don't know what you mean."

"Oh, yes, you do!"

"I don't," she protested, with a consciousness of manner that betrayed how well she understood him in spite of her denial. "I don't, indeed!"

"No?" the amused Harlan said mockingly. "You don't know that upon the birth of an heir—especially when it's the first and a boy—it's always understood by every good citizen of these parts that it's the proud father's business to go out and celebrate? Don't worry, mother: Dan won't go so far with it that he'll be unable to get home. Even in his liveliest times at college he always kept his head."

"I'm not exactly worried," she explained, with a troubled air.

"I know young fathers usually do cut up a little like that;—the only time in his life when your father didn't seem to be quite himself was the night after Dan was born. I'm afraid he was really almost a little tight, and I gave him such a talking to when I was well enough, that he didn't repeat it when you came along. But I haven't been worrying so much about Dan's going downtown and celebrating a little, as you call it—he's so steady nowadays, and works so hard I don't think it would be much harm—but I thought—I was a little afraid—I—"

"Afraid of what, mother?"

"Well, he was so exhilarated, so excited about his having a son—he was so much that way before he went out, I was a little afraid that when he added stimulants to the tremendous spirits he was already in, he might do something foolish."

"Why, of course he will," Harlan assured her cheerfully. "But it will only amount to some uproariousness and singing at the club, probably."

"I know," she said. "But I've been afraid he'd do something that would put him in a foolish position."

"I shouldn't have that on my mind if I were you, mother. There's hardly ever anybody at the club in the evening, and the one or two who'd be there on a night like this certainly wouldn't be critical! Besides, they'd expect a little boisterousness from him, under the circumstances."

"I know—I know," she said, but neither her tone nor her expression denoted that his reassurances completely soothed her. On the contrary, her anxiety seemed to increase;—she had remained near the open door leading into the hall, and her attitude was that of one who uneasily awaits an event.

"Mother, why don't you go to bed? I'll see that he gets in all right and I won't let him go near Lena's room, if that's what's bothering you."

"It isn't," she returned; was silent a moment; then she said abruptly: "Harlan, would you mind going over to Martha's?"

"What?"

"Would you mind going over there? You could make up some excuse; you could say you wanted to borrow a book or something."

"Why, it's after half-past ten," Harlan said, astonished. "What on earth do you want me to go over there for, as late as this?"

"Well, it's why I am a little worried," she explained. "I'd been standing at the window a long while before you came, Harlan; and about half an hour ago I thought I saw Dan and someone else come along the sidewalk and stop at our gate. At any rate two men did stop at the gate."

110

"You recognized Dan?"

"No; it was too dark and raining too hard. I thought at first perhaps it was you with someone you knew and had happened to walk along with. I went to the front door and opened it, but I could only make out that they seemed to be talking and gesturing a good deal, and I thought I recognized your cousin Fred Oliphant's voice. I waited, with the door open, but they didn't come in, and pretty soon they went on. I called, 'Dan! Oh, Dan!' but the wind was blowing so I don't suppose they heard me. Then I thought I saw the same two going up the Shelbys' walk to the front veranda. They must have gone in, because a minute or so afterwards the downstairs windows over there were lighted up. Couldn't you make some excuse to go over and see if it's Dan?"

Harlan jumped up from his chair by the fire. "It just might be Dan," he said, frowning. "I don't think so, but—"

"I'm so afraid it is!" Mrs. Oliphant exclaimed. "I don't like to bother you, and it may be a little awkward for you, going in so late, but you can surely think of some reasonable excuse, if it isn't Dan. If it is, do get him away as quickly as you can; I'd be terribly upset to have him make an exhibition of himself before Martha—she's always had such a high opinion of him."

"Yes, she has!" Harlan interrupted dryly, as he strode out into the hall; and he added: "I don't suppose Lena'd be too pleased!"

"She'd be furious," his mother lamented in a whisper. She helped him to put on his wet waterproof coat, and continued her whisper. "She's never been able to like poor Martha, and if she heard he went there to-night when she's still so sick, she—she—"

"Yes, she would!" Harlan said grimly, finishing the thought for her. "You might as well go to bed now, mother."

"No, no," she said. "If it is Dan, I won't let him see me when you get back, but I just want to know he's safely in. And try to—try to—"

"Try to what, mother?" he asked, pausing with the door open.

"Try to explain it a little to Martha. She's always been such a good friend of his, and he needs friends. Try to keep her from losing her high opinion of him. She's always—"

"She has indeed!" Harlan returned with a wry smile. "I'll do what I can." And he closed the door behind him as gently as he could, against the turbulent wind.

111

CHAPTER XIV

ADMITTED by a coloured housemaid who drowsily said, "Yes'm, she still up," in response to his inquiry, Harlan had only to step into the Shelbys' marble-floored "front hall" to dispel his slight doubts concerning the identity of Martha's callers; his brother was unquestionably one of them.

The heavy doors leading from the hall into the drawing-room sheltering Mr. Shelby's Corot were closed, but Dan's voice was audible and although his words were indistinguishable he was evidently in high spirits and holding forth upon some subject that required a great deal of emphatic expounding. Harlan stepped forward to open the doors and go in but halted abruptly, for at this moment Martha made her appearance at the other end of the hall. She came from the rear of the house and carried an oval silver tray whereon gleamed, among delicate napery and china, a silver coffee pot of unusually ample dimensions.

Her serious but untroubled look was upon the tray; then she glanced up, saw Harlan, and in surprise uttered a vague sound of exclamation. He went quickly toward her, but before he reached her she nodded to the housemaid in dismissal. "You can go to bed now, Emma."

"Yes'm, thank you," said Emma. "I'm full ready," she added, as she disappeared.

"I came over because I was afraid you—" Harlan began.

But Martha interrupted him at once. "You needn't be," she said. "There's nothing the matter."

"I only thought their coming here—disturbing you at this hour—"

"It doesn't disturb me," she said. "It isn't very late."

"But wouldn't your father—"

At that Martha laughed. "The chandelier in there fell down one night last winter, and it didn't wake him up! At least I do run the house when he's asleep. Don't look so tragic!"

"But I'm afraid they—"

"It's nothing at all, Harlan. I'd gone upstairs, but not to bed, when the bell rang; and when Emma told me Dan and Fred Oliphant were here, I came down and brought them in and lit the fire for them. They were rather damp!"

"But why didn't you—"

"Send them home? Because Dan wanted to tell me all about the baby."

112

"Good heavens!"

"Not at all!" she said; and as his expression still remained gloomy, she laughed. "Won't you open the door for me? I made coffee for them because I thought it might do them good—especially your cousin Fred."

Harlan uttered an exclamation of reproach addressed to himself: "Idiot! To let you stand there holding that heavy tray!" He would have taken it from her, but she objected.

"No; you might spill something. Just open the door for me."

He obeyed, then followed her into the drawing-room and closed the door. Before him, in a damask-covered armchair, was seated his second cousin, Mr. Frederic Oliphant, a young gentleman of considerable pretensions to elegance, especially when he had spent an evening at the club. In fact, since the installation of this club, which the well-to-do of the town had not recognized as a necessary bit of comfort until recently, Fred had formed the habit of arriving home every evening with such a complete set of eighteenth-century manners that there was no little uneasiness about him in his branch of the Oliphant family.

At present he was leaning forward in his chair, a hand politely cupped about his ear to give an appearance of more profound attention to what Dan was saying. The latter stood at the other end of the room, before the fire, and with great earnestness addressed this ardent listener; but Harlan was relieved to see that although his brother's eyes were extraordinarily bright and his cheeks ruddier than usual, there appeared no other symptoms, except his eloquence, of his dalliance at the club. "No, and always no!" he was protesting as the door opened. "If we lose that, we lose everything! This country—"

But here Fred sprang up to take the tray from Martha. "Permit me! Indeed permit me!" he begged. "It must not be said of an Oliphant that he allowed a lady to perform menial—"

"No, no!" She laughed, and evading his assistance, set the tray upon a table. "Do sit down, Fred."

"Since it is you who command it!" he said gallantly and returned to his chair; but on the way perceived the gloomy Harlan and bowed to him. "My dear sir!" he said. "This is an honour as unexpected as it is gracious; an honour not only to our hostess but to—"

"Sit down!" Harlan said brusquely.

"Since it is you who command it!" the other returned with the happy air of a man who delivers an entirely novel bit of repartee; then bowed again and complied.

Dan came forward from his place before the fire. "Why,

Harlan!" he exclaimed. "I thought you went to spend the evening with grandma."

"I did," Harlan returned, and added pointedly: "Several hours ago!"

"But it isn't late, is it?"

"No," Martha said quickly;—"it isn't. Won't you both please sit down and let me give you some coffee?"

"Really—" Harlan began, but she checked him and had her way; though Dan did not sit down. Instead, he returned to the fireplace with the coffee she gave him. "What I was tryin' to explain to Fred when you came in," he said;—"it was something I don't think he understood at all, but I believe you would, Martha."

"I beg you; I beg you," the courtly Frederic interposed. "I was never gifted, yet I understood you perfectly. You said, 'If we lose that, we lose everything.' I think you must have been speaking of champagne."

"No, no," Dan said, and for a moment appeared to be slightly annoyed; then he brightened. "I told you several times I meant our work for the new generation. The minute a man gets to be a father he belongs to the old generation, and the only use he is, it's to plan for the new one. From then on, that's what his whole life ought to be—just buildin' up the world for his son. Now you take this boy o' mine—"

"Excuse me," his cousin interrupted earnestly. "You're referring now to the one who was born late this afternoon?"

"I mean my boy!" Dan replied; and his face glowed with the triumphant word. "I have a son! Didn't you know it?"

"It's been mentioned, I believe, during the evening," Frederic answered. "Excuse me, pray."

"When he grows up," Dan went on radiantly, "he's got to find everything better because of the work the old generation's got to do to make it that way. That's what we're put in the world for! I never knew what I was for until to-day. I knew I was meant for something; I knew I ought to be makin' plans and tryin' to build up; but I didn't see just what for. I thought I did, but I didn't. That's what I wanted to explain to Martha, because she's the only one that could understand. It's the reason for the universe."

"You surprise me," Frederic remarked; and he replaced his cup with careful accuracy upon its saucer on the arm of his chair. "Correct me if I fail to follow you, but are you fair to your son? If he's the reason for the universe he ought to be able to grasp a few simple truths. You say Martha is the only person who could understand, but have you even tried to make him understand?"

Dan laughed happily, in high good humour. "That boy'll

114

understand soon enough!" he cried. "You wait till he's old enough for me to drive him out to Ornaby and let him look it over and see where his father fought, bled, and died to build it for him! You wait till he learns to drive an automobile from his father's and his uncle's own factory!"

"His uncle's?" Frederic repeated, turning to Harlan. "Forgive me if I trespass upon private ground, but I haven't heard—"

"I have nothing to do with it," Harlan said, frowning with an annoyance that had been increasing since his entrance into the room. "He means his wife's brother." He leaned toward Martha, who sat looking quietly at the radiant Dan. "Did you ever hear wilder nonsense?" he said in a low voice. "I really suspect he's a little mad. Do tell us to go home."

"No, no," she whispered, and returned her attention instantly to Dan, who was explaining to his cousin.

"My brother-in-law in New York, George McMillan, wrote me he'd got hold of an engineer who'd made designs for a wonderful improvement in automobile engines. McMillan wants to come out here, and he and I think of goin' into it together. We want to build a factory over on the west edge of Ornaby, where it won't interfere with the residential section."

"The residential section?" his cousin repeated in a tone of gentle inquiry. "Do I comprehend you? It's over where you've got that tool shed?"

"No, sir!" Dan exclaimed triumphantly. "We moved the tool shed this very morning because yesterday the lot it stood on was sold. Yes, sir; Ornaby Addition has begun to exist!"

At this Martha's quiet attitude altered; she leaned forward and clapped her hands. "Dan! Is it true? Have you sold some lots?"

"The first one," he answered proudly. "The very first lot was sold the day before my son was born!"

"How splendid!" she cried. "And they'll build on it right away?"

"No; not right away," he admitted. "That is, not much of a house, so to speak. It was bought by a man that wants to own a small picnic ground of his own, because he's got a large family; and at first he's only goin' to have a sort of shack there. But he will build when he sees the other houses goin' up all around him."

"Pardon me," said Frederic Oliphant. "Which other houses are you mentioning now?"

"The houses that will go up there," Dan returned promptly. "The houses that'll be there for my young son to see."

"Your 'young son?'" Fred repeated. "Your son is still young yet, then? It's remarkable when you consider he's the meaning of

115

the universe. You feel that when he grows up he'll have houses to look at?"

Dan's chest expanded with the great breath he took; his high colour grew higher, his bright eyes brighter. "Just think what he'll have to look at when he grows up! Why, the nurse let me hold him a few minutes, and I got to thinkin' about how I'm goin' to work for him, and then about how this country's moved ahead every minute since it was begun, goin' ahead faster and faster till now it just jumps out from under your feet if you stand still a second—and it grows so big and it grows so magnificent that when I thought of what sort of a world it's goin to be for my son, I declare I was almost afraid to look at him; it was like lookin' at somebody that's born to be a god!"

He spoke with such honest fervour, and with such belief in what he said, that, for the moment, even his bibulous cousin said nothing, but sat in an emotional silence, staring at him. As for Martha, an edge of tears suddenly showed along her eyelids; but Harlan was not so susceptible. "Dear me!" he said dryly. "After that burst of eloquence don't you think we'd better be starting for home? At least it would avoid an anti-climax."

Dan had been so rapt in his moment of vision, his exultant glimpse of a transcendent world for his son's heritage, that his brother's dry voice confused him;—he was like a balloonist who unexpectedly finds the earth rising swiftly to meet him. "What?" he said blankly; and then, as secondary perceptions clarified Harlan's suggestion to him, he laughed. "Why, yes; of course we ought to be goin'; we mustn't keep Martha up," he said. "Harlan, you always do find a way to make me look mighty ridiculous. I guess I am, too!"

With that, shaking his head and laughing, he brought his cup and saucer to the tray upon the table beside Martha, and turned to her. "Good-night, Martha. I guess I talk like a fool, but you know it doesn't happen every day, my gettin' to be a father! I want to bring him over to see you the first time they'll let him outdoors. I want you to be his godmother, Martha. I want you to help bring him up." She rose, and he took her hand as he said good-night again; and then, going toward the door, he added cheerfully, with a complete unconsciousness that there might be thought something a little odd about such a speech: "What I hope most is, I hope he'll grow up to be like you!"

Martha's colour deepened as she met Harlan's gaze for an instant; and she turned quickly to say good-night to the solemn Frederic, who was bowing profoundly before her. "Permit me, indeed," he murmured, and followed Dan out into the hall.

Thus, for a moment, Martha and Harlan were alone together;

116

and he stepped nearer to her. "Mother wanted me to apologize for him," he said. "I do hope you'll—"

"Apologize for him?" she echoed incredulously. "Why? Don't you suppose I'm glad he wanted to come here?"

"But under the circumstances—"

"No," she said proudly. "I'd always be glad—under any circumstances."

He looked at her, smiled with a melancholy humour not devoid of some compassion for her, as well as for himself, and assented in a rueful voice, "I suppose so!" But, having turned to go, he paused and asked wistfully: "Are there any circumstances under which anything I could do would make you glad?"

"In some ways, why, of course," she answered with a cordiality that did not hearten him; for he sighed, understanding in what ways he had no power to make her glad.

"All right," he said, and, straightening his drooped shoulders, strode out to join his brother and cousin in the hall.

Young Mr. Frederic Oliphant was lost in a thoughtful silence while the three went down the path to the gate, but as they passed this portal, his attention was caught by external circumstances. "Excuse me if I appear to seek assistance upon a point of natural history," he said;—"but wasn't it raining or something when we came in here?" And, being assured that rain had fallen at the time he mentioned, he went on: "That makes it all the more remarkable, my not noticing it's cleared up until we got all the way out here to the sidewalk. I was thinking about Dan's speech."

"Never you mind about my 'speech.'" Dan returned jovially. "You'll make speeches yourself if you ever have a son. I could make speeches all night long! Want to hear me?"

"Don't begin till we reach your gate," Fred said. "I'm going to leave you and Harlan there and go back to the club. But when I spoke of your speech I didn't mean the one you made over by the fireplace, the one all about your son's being the meaning of the universe and gods and everything. I meant your last speech—not a speech exactly, but what you said to Martha."

"I didn't say anything to her except 'good-night.'"

"It seemed to me you did," Fred said apologetically. "I may be wrong, but it seemed to me you said something more. Didn't it seem so to you, Harlan?"

"Yes, it did," Harlan answered briefly. The group had paused at the Oliphants' gate, and he opened it, about to pass within.

But his cousin detained him. "Wait a moment, I mean about Dan's hoping the baby would grow up to look like Martha. Didn't it strike you—"

117

Dan laughed. "Oh, that? No; I said something about hoping he'd grow up to be like her: I meant I hoped he'd have her qualities."

"I see," young Mr. Oliphant said pensively. "The only reason it struck me as peculiar was I thought that was what the father usually said to the mother."

Thereupon he lifted his hat politely, bowed and walked away, leaving both of the brothers staring after him.

CHAPTER XV

HIS humour was misplaced, and both of them would have been nothing less than dismayed could they have foreseen in what manner he was destined to misplace it again, and to what damage; for not gossip, nor scandal, nor slander's very self can leave a trail more ruinous than may a merry bit of drollery misplaced. The occasion of the catastrophe was not immediate, however; it befell a month later, when the Oliphants made a celebration to mark the arrival of the baby and the completed recovery of the baby's mother. Mrs. Oliphant gave a "family dinner."

She felt that something in the nature of a mild banquet was called for, and her interpretation of "the family" was a liberal one. Except those within her household, and except her mother, who was still somehow "hanging on," she had no relatives of her own; but the kinsfolk of her husband were numerous, and she invited them all to meet their new little kinsman.

They were presented to this personage; and then the jubilant father, carrying him high in his arms and shouting, led a lively procession into the dining-room. The baby behaved well, in spite of the noise his father made, and showed no alarm to be held so far aloft in the air, even when he was lifted as high as his bearer's arms could reach.

"Ladies and gentlemen," Dan shouted, thus interpreting his offspring's thoughts in the matter, "grandparents, great-uncles, great-aunts, uncle Harlan, second-cousins and third-cousins, kindly sit down and eat as much as you can. And please remember I invite you to my christening, one week from next Sunday; and if you want to know what's goin' to be my name, why, it's Henry for my grandpa, and Daniel for my papa, and Oliphant for all of us. Take a

118

good look at me, because I'm Henry Daniel Oliphant, ladies and gentlemen, the son and heir to Ornaby Addition!"

There was cheering and applause; then the company sat down; the nurse took the little lacy white bundle from the protesting father's arms; and Henry Daniel Oliphant was borne away amid the customary demonstrations, and carried upstairs to his cradle.

Dan, at the head of the table, held forth in the immemorial manner of young fathers: the baby had laughed his first laugh that very morning;—Dan was sure it was neither an illusion of his own nor a chance configuration of the baby's features. It was absolutely an actual human laugh, although at first the astounded parent hadn't been able to believe it, because he'd never heard of any baby's laughing when it was only a month old. But when Henry Daniel laughed not once, but twice, and moreover went on laughing for certainly as long as thirty-five seconds, the fact was proven and no longer to be doubted. "No, sir, I just had to believe my own eyes when he kept right on laughin' up at me that way, as if he thought I was a mighty funny lookin' old thing to be his daddy. My, but it does seem like a miracle to have your son look up at you that way and laugh! I hope he'll keep doin' it his whole life long, too. I'm certainly goin' to do all I can to keep him from ever havin' anything happen he can't laugh at!"

He continued, becoming jovially oratorical upon his theme, while down at the other end of the long table, sitting between the baby's grandfather and grandmother, Lena now and then gave him a half-veiled, quick glance that a chance observer might have defined as inscrutable.

Her pretty black-and-white dress of fluffy chiffon was designed with a more revealing coquetry than the times sanctioned; so that her amiable father-in-law, though not himself conscious of any disapproval, withheld from expression his thought that it was just as well that Mrs. Savage could not be of the company. The ruthless old lady might have supplemented her "lesson" to Lena, although it had produced somewhat pointedly the reverse of its intended effect. The young mother was "painted" more dashingly than the bride had been, and her lips as well as her cheeks were made so vivid that probably her friends in New York would have found her more than ever the French doll—a discontented French doll, they might have said.

Yet, to her credit, if she was discontented, she made an effort not to seem so; she chattered gayly to her mother-in-law and Mr. Oliphant, laughed with them about Dan's bragging of his offspring, and coquetted demurely with one or two elderly cousins-in-law. A young one, Mr. Frederic Oliphant, seemed genuinely to amuse her, which was what led to misfortune. He found her laughter a sweet fluting in his ears, and, wishing to hear more of it, elaborated the solemn-mannered waggeries that produced it.

"It's a great thing to be the only father in the world," he said. "I suppose it's even greater than being an earl."

"Why than an earl particularly?" she asked.

"Didn't you know? At the club and downtown nowadays they speak of your husband as the 'Earl of Ornaby.' You may not have noticed it, but he sometimes mentions a place called Ornaby Addition. Now that he's got another subject though, I suspect his title ought to be changed to 'Father of the Heir to Ornaby.' Doesn't that seem more intriguing, if I may employ the expression?"

"Most intriguing!" she agreed. "But since my husband's the 'Earl,' am I called the 'Countess of Ornaby'?"

"No; they leave you out of it, and I'm afraid you'll be left out of it again if the new title's conferred on him. No one would get an idea from his orations that the Heir to Ornaby has a mother. A father would seem to be Henry Daniel's sole and total ancestry." Then, as she laughed again, Fred added his unfortunate afterthought. "No; I forgot. I believe he does include a godmother as a sort of secondary necessity."

"Does he? We haven't talked about who's to be the godmother yet. We haven't selected one."

" 'We?' " Fred repeated, affecting surprise. "You seem to think you have something to do with it! Perhaps when the father of the Heir to Ornaby gets around to it, he may condescend to inform you that the godmother was selected the very night after the heir was born."

"Was she?" Lena laughed. "Where? At the club?"

"Goodness, no! Don't you know where Dan went that night?"

"Just to the club, didn't he?" Lena said cheerfully, a little surprised. "That's all I heard mentioned about it afterwards, at least."

"Ah, they cover up these things from you, I see. It's time somebody warned you of what's going on." And Fred was inspired to add: "Haven't you realized yet there's an enchantress living right next door to you?"

From the young man's own point of view, this was foolery altogether harmless: Martha Shelby was almost "one of the family"—so near to being one of them, in fact, that he would not have been at all surprised to find her included in this family party— and the episode of his call upon her, with his cousin, upon the night after the baby's birth, seemed to him of no other than a jocose significance. Like Dan's "speech" to Martha, it merely illustrated the

120

hare-brained condition of a new-made father, and in that light was handy material for a family dinner-table humorist.

In this capacity, therefore, he blundered on. "Yes, indeed—right next door! Old Dan may look like the steady, plodding homebody sort of husband, but when that type really breaks out it's the wildest of all."

Lena gave the farceur a sidelong glance the sobriety of which he failed to perceive; but at once she seemed to fall in with the spirit of his burlesquing, and, assuming a mock solemnity herself, "This is terrible news!" she said. "I suspected him of being rather wild, but I didn't suppose he'd go so far as to appoint an enchantress to be the godmother."

"And not only appointed her, but called on her in the middle of the night to notify her of the appointment," Fred added. "Not only that, but dragged me along to be a chaperon!"

"No! Did he? How funny!"

"The way he behaved when we got there, I think he needed one!" the youth continued, expanding in the warmth of her eagerly responsive laughter. "We did get oratory! He explained to the enchantress that she was the only person who could understand his son's being a god and the meaning of the universe; but that wasn't all. Oh, not by any means!"

"But he couldn't have done worse than that!" she laughed. "Are you sure?"

Fred was so overcome by mirthful recollection that he was unable to retain his affectation of solemnity;—a sputtering chuckle escaped him. "I wish you'd been there to hear him telling Martha he wanted Henry Daniel to grow up to be like her!"

"No! Did he?"

The jovial Frederic failed to catch the overtone in her voice, but happening to glance at Harlan, who sat opposite him, he was surprised, too late, by a brief pantomime of warning. Harlan frowned and pointedly shook his head; and at the same time Mrs. Oliphant, across whom the merry colloquy had taken place, began hastily to talk to Fred about his health. His mother had told her that he was ruining it at the club, she said amiably, and, to his mystification, became voluble upon the subject; but she also was too late. Lena continued to laugh, and, turning to Mr. Oliphant, prattled cheerily about nothing;—but Harlan saw her covert glance at the other end of the table where her husband was still bragging of Henry Daniel; and, although her eyelids quickly descended upon it, this glance was an evanescent spark glowing brightly for an instant through the fringe of blackened lashes.

When the party left the table to prepare for the charades—the customary entertainment offered to one another by the Oliphants on such occasions—Frederic sought an opportunity to speak privately with Harlan.

"What on earth were you shaking your head at me like that for? I wasn't saying anything."

"Weren't you?"

"Certainly not! And your mother kept talking to me as fast as she could all the rest of the time we were at the table. Looked as if she was afraid for me to open my mouth again! What was it all about?"

"Nothing."

"Then what made you act as if it was something?" Fred inquired. "You certainly don't think your sister-in-law would ever be jealous of dear old Martha, do you?"

"Oh, no," Harlan said. "Not jealous. They don't get on very well, though, I believe."

"What? Why, I passed by here only the other day and saw Martha coming out of the front door. She was laughing and waving her hand back to some one in the doorway and—"

"Oh, yes. She still comes to see mother sometimes, as she always did; but I believe she doesn't ask for Lena any more when she comes. I understand Lena has never returned her call. You may have noticed that ladies regard those things as important?"

"What of it? Lena would certainly understand. I'd never have mentioned our going in there that night, if there'd been any reason for her to mind it," Fred protested. "What's more, she doesn't mind it. Look at her now."

He nodded toward where, across the broad drawing-room, Lena was helping to set the stage for the first of the charades. She moved with a dancing step, laughing and chattering to the group about her; and as she dropped a green velvet table cover over the back of an armchair, announcing that this drapery made the chair into a throne, she flung out her graceful little arms and whirled herself round and round in an airy pirouette. Fred laughed aloud, finding himself well-warranted in thinking his cousin's uneasiness superfluous; for Lena seemed to be, indeed, the life of the party. Moreover, she remained in these high spirits all evening; and Harlan began to feel reassured, for this was what he and his mother and father had learned to think of as "Lena's other mood"; and sometimes it lasted for several days.

The present example of it was not to cover so extensive a period, however; although when the guests had gone she kissed her mother-in-law good-night affectionately, patted Mr. Oliphant's shoulder, and then waved a sparkling little hand over the banisters

122

to Harlan as she skipped upstairs and he stood below, locking the front doors. Humming "Tell me, pretty maiden," from "Floradora," she disappeared from his sight in the direction of her own room, but it was not there she went.

Instead, she opened the door beyond hers, stepped within and closed it;—and during this slight and simple series of commonplace movements she underwent a sharp alteration. She had carried her liveliness all the way to the very doorknob, and, until she touched it, was still the pirouetting Lena who had been the life of the party; then suddenly she stood in the room, haggard; so that what happened to her was like the necromantic withering of a bright flower during the mere opening and closing of a door.

It was Dan's room, and he had just taken off his coat, preparing for bed. "Got to be out at Ornaby by six to-morrow morning," he explained. "A contractor's goin' to meet me there to pick out a site for our automobile works. I won't get much sleep, I guess—up at five this morning, too." He yawned, and then, laughing, apologized. "I beg your pardon, Lena; I don't mean I'm sleepy, if you want to talk the party over. You were just lovely this evening, and the whole family thought so, too. You made it a great success, and you can be certain we all appreciate it. I certainly do."

Facing him blankly, leaning back against the door with her hands behind her, she said nothing; and he stepped toward her solicitously. "I'm afraid you tired yourself out at it—only a week out of bed, poor child! You look—"

"Never mind how I look," she said in a low voice, and as his hand was extended placatively, to pet her, she struck at it. "Just you keep away from me!"

"Why, Lena!" he cried. "What in the world's the matter?"

She continued to stare at him, not replying, and he saw that she was trembling slightly from head to foot. "Lena! You're lettin' yourself get all upset over something or other again. You've gone ever since Henry was born without gettin' this way. I was almost in hopes—in hopes—"

"Yes?" she said, as he faltered. "What were your hopes?"

"Why, I was almost in hopes it—it wouldn' happen again."

"What wouldn't happen again?"

"Your gettin' upset like this," he answered apologetically. "I honestly did pretty near hope it, Lena. It seemed to me we'd maybe kind of reached a turning point and could get along all right together, now Henry's come to us."

"Maybe we have reached a turning point," she said. "I suppose it's generally considered quite a turning point when a wife leaves her husband for just cause, isn't it?"

123

"Oh, dear me!" Dan sighed, and sat down heavily on the side of his bed, taking his head between his hands. "I guess we've got to go through another of 'em."

"Another of what?"

"Another of these troubles," he sighed. "Well, what's this one all about, Lena?"

She came toward him angrily. "I'd like to know what you'd think of any other man that treated his wife as you do me! What would you say of any other man who went out the very night his child was born and did what you did?"

"Why, I didn't do anything," he said, and looked up at her, surprised.

"You didn't? Don't you call it anything to go to see that woman at midnight?"

"You mean our goin' in to Martha's?" Dan asked, his surprise increasing. "It wasn't midnight; it was about ten o'clock, and we only stayed a few minutes—half an hour maybe. I just wanted to tell her about the baby."

"Yes, so I hear," Lena returned bitterly. "You took particularly good care not to mention that little call to me afterwards!"

"No; I didn't," he protested. "I never thought of it; I've been too busy thinkin' about the baby and Ornaby. I don't say though"— he paused, and then went on with painful honesty: "I don't say I would have mentioned it to you, if I had thought of it. I know you've never liked Martha. We could all see that, and it's been sort of a trouble to us—"

"To 'us'?" she interrupted sharply. "To whom?"

"Well, to me, of course; but I mean mother, too, though she's never said anything about it. We've all been as fond of Martha all her life as if she was one of our own family, and, for instance, I think mother was probably a little worried because she thought she'd better not invite her to-night, on your account. What I mean, though, is that I probably mightn't have told you about our goin' in to see her that night, even if I had thought of it afterwards, because as I knew how you felt about her I'd have been afraid of it's gettin' you into one of these upsetnesses. I guess I'd have been right, too," he added, with a rueful laugh. "Somebody's told you about it, and you have got into one."

"How kind of you! So you admit you went running to her the minute the baby was born, and yet you knew perfectly well how I felt about her."

"Well—I knew how unreasonably you felt about her."

" 'Unreasonably?' " Lena cried shrilly. "What a wise little

124

word! When you told her she was the only woman in the world who understands you!"

"No, no! I don't care who understands me," Dan protested unhappily. "I meant she was the only one that would understand what I was sayin' about the baby. I just had to talk about him, and she always understands anything at a time like that—or any time, for that matter. She—"

"Go on!" Lena said. "Go on making it worse!"

"But I'm only tryin' to explain how—"

"Explain this, then! You told her you wanted my child to grow up to be like her."

"Why, yes," Dan said reasonably. "I didn't mean to look like her; I only meant I hoped he'd have her qualities. Anybody that knows Martha would feel that way, Lena. Why, except my own father and mother, she's the most even-tempered, understanding, helpful kind of person I ever knew in my life. Why, everybody in town looks up to her just the same as I do, and anybody'd have said that to her, Lena. You would yourself, if you had only not let yourself get prejudiced against her about nothin' at all and just been sensible enough to really get acquainted with her."

Lena stood before him rigidly, except for the trembling, which had increased a little. "Tell me another thing," she said. "When a young wife becomes a mother, does her husband ever consult her before inviting a woman she doesn't like to act as godmother for the child?"

Dan got up and began to pace the room, his face reddening with a prophetic distress. "Oh, golly!" he groaned. "You're goin' to object to it. I see that now!"

"You do see it, do you? How remarkable!"

He turned to her appealingly. "Look here, Lena; I did speak about it to her too soon. Of course I ought to've consulted you first;—I was just so enthusiastic about bein' the boy's father, and she's such a dear, good, old friend—well, I guess I was excited. I know I ought to've waited and asked you who you wanted—but I didn't. I did just blurt out and ask her, so it's done and can't be helped. Well, I can't go back on it; I can't go over there and just plain tell her you don't want her!"

"Can't you?" Lena said. "It doesn't matter to me what you tell her."

"You're not goin' to make me, are you?" he asked piteously.

"No. Tell her anything you like."

Mistaking this icy permission, he uttered an almost vociferous sigh of relief. "Well, I do truly thank you, Lena. If you're noble enough to overlook my selfishness in not thinkin' about who you'd want to have for Henry's godmother—well, my goodness, I am grateful to you, and I know it's more'n I deserve. It's a noble action on your part, and I'm sure it's goin' to lead to splendid results, because now you can't help but get better acquainted with Martha, and you'll do what I've hoped for so long: you'll get to likin' her and thinkin' as much of her as everybody else does. With her in that relation—"

"In what relation?"

"In the relation of the baby's godmother. From the very day of the christening you'll—"

"There may not be any such day," Lena interrupted. "You seem to have mistaken me. There may not be any christening—at least not here. If she's to be the godmother, the baby and I will be with my own family in New York."

"Oh, golly!" Dan said, and sank down on the side of the bed again. "Oh, golly!"

Lena became vehement. "I should think you would say 'golly'! If you had a spark of remorse in you, I think you'd say more than that!"

"Remorse? I don't see—"

"You don't?" she cried. "You don't see what you have to be remorseful for? You bring me out here to the life you've given me, and you see nothing to regret? You bring me to this flat town and its flat people, where not once in months can I hear a note of real music and where there's no art and no beauty and no life—after you'd given me your word I should have a full year in Europe!—and you watch me struggling to bear it, to bear it with the best bravery I have in me, and the most kindness to you—and to be cheerful—and I dare you to say I haven't made the best of it! I have—and how hard I've had to try most of the time to accomplish it! And what have you been? Who was the man I found I'd married? Even in this hole of a town he's called a failure—the town failure! That's who you got me to marry! Even these people out here—your own people—even they take you as a joke—the town joke! And when I make the best of it I can and bear it the best I can, and go on, month after month, not complaining, and suffer what I suffered when the baby came, you go gayly over to the woman whose hand you held the very first day I came here—yes, you did!—and the woman you've compared me to unfavourably every time you've ever dared to speak of me to her— yes, you have; every single time!—and you ask her to come and be the godmother to my child! You can go over there and tell her anything you like—tell her again you want my baby to be like her— but there's one thing you'd better tell her besides, and that is, there won't be any christening if she comes to it!"

126

She ran out, the closing of the door reverberating eloquently through the house; and Dan remained seated upon the side of the bed, his head between his hands. It was by no means the first time he had remained in that position when Lena slammed the door.

CHAPTER XVI

HIS attitude had not changed, fifteen minutes later, when there came a light tapping upon that mishandled door of his; and at the sound he rose quickly, said, "Yes, mother," and tried to regain his usual cheerfulness of aspect as Mrs. Oliphant came in noiselessly. She was smiling, and he was able to construct a smile in return, telling her she looked "mighty pretty" in her rose-coloured negligee—a compliment not exaggerated. Serenity, a good faith, and a cheerful disposition bring beauty in time even where it has not been; and, where beauty has always been, as it had with Mrs. Oliphant, white hair is only that crowning prettiness so knowingly sought by the ladies of the eighteenth-century when they powdered their blonde or brunette ringlets.

"I just thought I'd slip in for a minute," she said apologetically. "I was afraid you might forget you had to be up so early to-morrow morning, and get to thinking about something and not go to bed at all."

"Oh, no; don't worry. I'll not do that again," he said. "It doesn't do any good, I know. I suppose you heard her?"

She patted his cheek, smiling up at him and resolutely withholding from expression the compassion that had brought her to him. "I just wanted to tell you not to be troubled. You'll have to give her a little more time to get adjusted, Dan. A great many young couples don't manage all these little adjustments until after the first few years of marriage; and I think my own father and mother didn't manage it even that soon;—I'm afraid I remember their having some rather troubled times when I was a pretty old little girl. You mustn't let yourself be discouraged, dear. Lena really tries to get the best of herself, and though she fails sometimes—"

"It isn't that," he interrupted. "At least it seemed to be something more definite than usual this time. You see, I didn't stop to think about consulting her, and asked Martha to be Henry Daniel's godmother."

"I heard Fred Oliphant say so, but I thought perhaps he was only trying to tease Lena." For a moment Mrs. Oliphant looked disturbed, but brightened with a quickly reassuring second thought. "Well, that would be lovely, and I'm glad you did it; but Martha'll decline."

"She didn't, though, when I asked her."

"What did she say?"

Dan rubbed his forehead. "Well, I don't remember that she said anything."

"No?" His mother laughed. "You won't have to withdraw your invitation, if that's what's troubling you, Dan."

"It is troubling me," he admitted despondently. "I just couldn't go over there and tell her—"

"No," Mrs. Oliphant said. "And Martha'd never let you."

"You mean you'd tell her—"

"No. Nobody'll say a word to her about it. Don't you know Martha well enough yet to understand that she won't expect to be Henry's godmother?"

"But she must."

"No. If she did, she'd have spoken of it to me."

"That does look like it a little," he said with some relief; then frowned again. "But I want her to be the godmother; and she ought to be. Lena hasn't any great friend of her own that she wants for it; and Martha's the best friend I ever—"

"No, no," his mother interrupted hurriedly. "It wouldn't do, Dan."

"But why?"

"Well—" she hesitated, sighed, and went on: "We all love Martha—except Lena. I'm afraid that's reason enough. You must give it up."

"I'm afraid so," he agreed gloomily. "Oh, lordy!"

"Now, now! Martha knows you wanted her, and that's all she'll care about. She—" Mrs. Oliphant paused with the bothered air of one who fears to elaborate an indiscretion already committed. Then she continued nervously: "There was something else I wanted to speak to you about. Your father and I—we've been a little afraid—" She hesitated again.

"Afraid of what, mother?"

"Well, we were talking over this long struggle of yours to make a success of the Addition, Dan; and of course we've seen how hard you've been pressed from the very first, and yet you've always kept the thing a little alive and held on to it when time after time everybody said you'd just have to let go."

"Yes, mother?"

128

"Well, it seems your father heard downtown to-day that this time you'd—you'd—"

"This time I'd what, mother?"

She put her arms about him and, in spite of her resolution, the compassion she felt for him was evident in her voice and in her eyes. "Oh, Dan, if this time you can't hold on to it any longer, you mustn't feel too badly, please!"

He had bent over her as she embraced him; but now he threw back his shoulders and laughed. "So that's what father heard to-day," he said. "You tell him he was listening to the wrong crowd, mother!" He moved her gently toward the door, his arm about her. "You go to bed, and so will I." He laughed again, not grimly or bitterly, but with deep and hearty mirth. "Why, there isn't any more chance of my not keepin' hold of Ornaby than there is of this house fallin' off the earth onto the moon! They can't foreclose on me for anyhow two weeks more, and by that time I'll show 'em what's what! I sold a lot only last month, and there've been three more men out there already to look at locations. Two weeks is plenty of time for things to happen, mother. Don't you worry."

He kissed her good-night, and as she smiled back at him from the hall and told him she wouldn't worry if he'd get some sleep, he went on: "Why, they haven't any more chance to get Ornaby away from me than they have to—than they have to"—he paused, searching for a sufficient comparison, and, finding it, finished with cheery explosiveness—"than they have to get Henry Daniel Oliphant himself away from me!"

Upon this she went to her own door down the hall, where she nodded and whispered back to him a smiling good-night, and disappeared, glad to see him so abundantly recovered from his brief depression. "Somehow I believe he will manage to keep on going, even this time," she told her husband. "He's so sure failure's an absolute impossibility that I do think maybe—"

"No, I don't see even a 'maybe' in it for him," Mr. Oliphant said, and shook his head. "Not this time, I'm afraid."

But the Earl of Ornaby was in the field by sunrise the next morning, and armoured in convictions so strong that he began the day with plans, not for the retention of the threatened domain, but for an extension of it; he went to see a farmer who owned sixty acres north of Ornaby and got an option on them before keeping his appointment with a contractor to select a site for the airily projected automobile factory.

Not until the afternoon did he go downtown to see about raising a little money on a note to fend off the impending foreclosure; and he was still undiscouraged when he came home that evening without having succeeded. There were thirteen long days left, he told his mother, in the hall near the front door, where she met him when he came in; and she responded sunnily that thirteen was a lucky number, then gave him a note of a kind different from the one he had spent the afternoon trying to negotiate.

"You see I was right," she said. "Didn't I tell you she'd understand? Their housemaid brought it in this morning after breakfast."

Martha had written to Mrs. Oliphant:

We're in such a rush of packing I won't have time to come in and say good-bye, as I'd like to. Papa has to go to New York, and I've decided I ought to go with him, because there are so many automobiles there now, and he hasn't learned that they're getting even worse than the bicycle "speeders" about running over people.

We'll be there two or three weeks and I've almost persuaded him to let me show him Quebec and the Saguenay—and he says he might be willing to take the boat from Montreal for a little run to England after that!

Please give my love to Mr. Oliphant and Harlan for me, and of course to Dan, whom I haven't seen since his great evening after the baby was born. He was so funny and delightful, and he talked with such really true wisdom, too! I wanted to remember everything he said, but the trouble was that he talked so fast and said so much that the next day I couldn't remember any of it at all!

Please say good-bye for us to Mrs. Savage. Tell her when we get home we expect to find her downstairs again and enjoying the view from that big window of hers where she's always loved to sit. Tell her papa wants to come with me to see her. He wants to talk with her about the old days when this was a little town. There aren't so many left now he can do that with, though I know Mrs. Savage regards him as a mere youth, comparatively! He asks me to say good-bye to Mr. Oliphant and all of you for him—and for myself I close with good-bye to you and send you my best love, always.

"Lordy!" Dan said, staring at this missive when he had finished reading it. "She is goin' to be gone a long while! I don't get to see her often, but it's always mighty satisfactory to know she's there—just next door. That house'll look pretty empty for a while, won't it?" He sighed. "Well, I suppose I'd better go and let Lena know there's nothin' to disturb her now about the christening."

Mrs. Oliphant told him lightly that she had already informed her daughter-in-law of Martha's departure, and that it would be better for him not to mention the subject again;—Lena had selected his aunt Olive as a proper godmother. Dan looked rueful, but

130

muttered an unenthusiastic consent and went into the library to consult his father upon the best way to raise money in thirteen days.

Mr. Oliphant was unable to offer him either the money itself or practical advice how to get it. "I'm afraid it looks like pretty hard luck this time, Dan, old fellow," he said. "It's funny a man with as good a practice as mine can't ever seem to be able to lay his hands on a little cash that doesn't have to go right out on some old debt. If I just didn't have to meet that confounded note I went on for poor old Tom Vertrees I—"

"No, no," his son protested;—"I wouldn't let you, if you could. My conscience'd trouble me about what I did let you do for me if I wasn't so sure you'll get paid back with seven per cent. interest as soon as I begin to get these lots to sellin' off a little faster."

"What about the three men your mother tells me have been out there looking at lots since you sold the first one? Couldn't you offer them a reduction in the price for a little cash in hand?"

"I did," Dan replied. "I did that the first thing with each of 'em. But one of 'em told a darkey I've got workin' out there he thought he could get what he wanted still cheaper after the mortgage is foreclosed; and I guess maybe the other two thought the same way about it. I guess that's the way those seven people felt that came when I tried to auction off some lots awhile back."

"I'm afraid so. I hope you aren't going to take it too hard, Dan."

"Take what too hard, sir?"

"There are other things you can go into, my boy. You've shown you've got immense energy and perseverance. They may laugh at you, but you can be sure they like the grit you've shown, and if you do have to give up the idea—"

"What idea, sir?"

"I mean the idea of this Addition," his father explained. "If the time's come when you have to let it go—"

"Ornaby?" Dan interrupted with an incredulity wholly untouched by the facts confronting him. "Why, you just put any such notion out of your mind, sir." And he repeated the extreme comparison he had made the night before. "Why, I'm not goin' to let Ornaby go any more than I am our little namesake upstairs in his cradle! I'm goin' to keep it this time and every time! I've got thirteen days left and I'll find some way!"

He kept Ornaby "this time," but in spite of his determined prophecy and all he did to fulfil it, six of his thirteen days passed and he had not found the way. Indeed, he did not find the way at all; for it was found through none of his seeking. On the seventh of the thirteen days his grandmother sent for him to come to talk to her in

131

the evening; and when he sat down beside her and for a moment covered the ghostly hand on the coverlet with his own, he told her truthfully that she was looking better.

"Why, a great deal better!" he said. "I guess you're goin' to do what Martha said in her message, grandma, and get downstairs again before she comes home."

"Do you think so?" she said in a voice a little stronger than it was when he had last talked with her. "You think I might fool that doctor after all?"

"But doesn't he say you're better, grandma?"

"Yes," she said, and smiled faintly. "But he doesn't think so. Told me this morning I was better and then came three times during the day! He doesn't fool anybody."

"But you're goin' to get well," her grandson assured her. "What I want to know is: When are you goin' to let me bring that baby to see you? Mother says you don't—"

"No, no," she interrupted peevishly. "I don't want to see any babies."

"But, grandma, you've never seen any baby like—"

"No, no!"

"But you don't understand what a baby can be like," he persisted. "I don't know I ever thought much of babies generally, either; but I've found out there's just as much difference between 'em as there is between people. Think of this, for instance: one day I was bendin' down over him, just lookin' at him—and this was before he was even four weeks old, remember—and all at once he took the notion I must be kind of funny. He broke right out in a laugh! He did! It was a real laugh, too, though a good many people might think I imagined it; because I've asked everybody I know, pretty near, and not one of 'em said they ever heard of a baby only four weeks old that could—"

"Stop!" she protested. "I didn't send for you to talk about your baby."

"But, grandma, if you'd just let me bring him to see you—"

"I don't want to hear anything about him, and I've only got one thing to say about him myself. You better not let him listen to his mother when he learns to talk, or to Harlan either—not if you want to save him from that affected Eastern way of talking. You've had enough to do with Eastern people, young man! You take care of yourself and have as little to do with 'em after this as you can manage. They may seem mighty fine and highty-tighty, and let you think it's a great thing to be in with 'em, but all they're after is to get something out of you; and after they've got it, they'll give you the go-by quick enough! Now I haven't got strength enough to talk very long, and I don't want to talk any more about your baby."

"All right," he said submissively. "What do you want to talk about, grandma?"

She turned her head on the pillow to look at him; and it seemed to him that her eyes were vague, as if they found him indistinct;—she frowned plaintively in an effort to see him more clearly, and was silent for a time.

"It's Dan, is it?" she said finally.

"Why, yes, grandma," he answered in surprise. "We've just been talkin' about the baby, grandma; and how much better you are and everything."

"I know," she returned with a feeble petulance. "I know what we're talking about. I wanted you to come to-night because I want to tell you something."

"Yes, grandma?"

"It's this," she said; then closed her eyes, and when she opened them, asked again: "Is it Dan?"

"Why, yes, of course, grandma! You just said—"

"I know what I said! I wanted to tell you—to tell you—"

"Yes, grandma," he said, and added indulgently, "Tell me anything you like to."

"I wanted to tell you not to mind," she went on. "You mustn't mind anything that happens. I mean anything I have to do with."

"No; of course," he returned without any idea of what she might mean. "Of course I won't. I won't mind it."

"You must be sure not to," she insisted. "You won't understand, but you mustn't let it make you feel hurt with me. You mustn't—"

"Of course I won't. Why, I'd never dream of feelin' hurt with you about anything in the world, grandma."

"Listen, Dan. I've always liked you best since you were a little boy. If you don't understand something that happens, you remember I said this, will you? What may happen is for your own good and to help you, though it may seem just the other way to you. Will you promise to remember?"

"Of course," he returned promptly; but she was not satisfied.

"No; I want you to think what you're saying. You speak too quickly to make me sure you'll remember. Say it slower, Dan. Say, 'I promise to remember.'"

"I promise to remember," he repeated slowly, to indulge this whim of hers; and then asked, "To remember what, grandma?"

"What I've just told you. That's all I have to say, Dan."

"All right, grandma;—I hope I haven't stayed long enough to

tire you," he said, and patted her hand as he rose. "I expect you want to drowse a little now. Good-night, grandma."

"Good-bye," she said. And her cold and bent fingers feebly clasped his hand, giving it an impulse which he allowed it to follow until he found it resting against her cheek. "Dear boy!" she said faintly; and he was touched by this, the first caress she had given him since he was a child. She retained his hand, keeping it against her cheek a moment longer; then relinquished it gently and said "Good-bye" again.

"Not 'good-bye,' grandma," he protested heartily. " 'Good-night,' not 'good-bye.' You are better, and the doctor himself says so. Why, by next week—"

"Next week?" she said in the faintest voice in the world and with the remotest shadow of an elfin smile to herself. "Next week? Yes. You can—you can bring the baby to see me—next week."

She just reached the end of that permission, her voice was so infinitely small and so drowsy; and her eyes closed before the last word;—she seemed to fall asleep even while she spoke. Dan tiptoed out, nodding to the nurse, who had been close at hand in the hall and came into the room as he left it.

Downstairs he found the courteous Nimbus waiting, as always, to unlatch the front door. But to-night the elderly servitor was solemn and unloquacious beyond his custom. "Goo'-ni', suh," he said. "I reckon you' grammaw 'bout ready to let that big door swing. Yes, suh. Goo'-ni', suh."

Dan walked home, wondering what door Nimbus conceived himself to be talking about, and wondering more what his grandmother had meant him to remember. But at his own door he was abruptly enlightened upon Nimbus's meaning about a "big" one. Harlan met him there and told him that the nurse had just telephoned.

Mrs. Savage would never explain what she had asked him to remember; she would never explain anything—never, forever.

134

CHAPTER XVII

THE day after her funeral Mr. Oliphant brought home a copy of her will and read it to his wife and their sons and daughter-in-law in the library. He read slowly, while his four auditors sat in a silence broken only once, though the document was a long one. The single interruption was a vocal sound from Dan when the bequest to himself was mentioned, an exclamation the import of which was not determinable by the others.

But before the reading Mr. Oliphant made some introductory remarks as he wiped his glasses: The estate appeared to be "somewhat larger than anticipated," he said, as Mrs. Savage's boxes in the bank's deposit vaults contained securities she had never mentioned;—she had always been "very reticent in such matters." The value of her possessions might be "estimated roughly at probably upward of eight hundred thousand dollars, in addition to her house and a small amount of other real estate." Then he took up the typewritten sheets of the will.

Mrs. Savage had always been known in the town as "pretty close"; for her early youth was of the "old-settler" days when people who failed to be thrifty might also fail to keep themselves alive; and something of this quality had the air of striving to survive her in the posthumous expression of her wishes. She had left one hundred and thirty-five dollars to each of her three elderly servants; and seven hundred and fifty dollars to every "established charitable institution of worth and merit" in the city, the "worth and merit" to be determined by her executors, those two discreet men of substance, Mr. George Rowe and Mr. John P. Johns.

Mr. Oliphant's throat seemed to trouble him when he came to the next clause, for he read it huskily, the papers trembling slightly in his hand. The paragraph concerned Mrs. Savage's "dearly and well-beloved grandson, Daniel Oliphant" and carefully explained her reasons for making what might seem an unfair division of her property.

Inasmuch as my said grandson, Daniel, has not seen fit to avail himself of the sound advice of those more experienced, and in particular has acted directly contrary to my own counsel for his well-being, both in the conduct of his business and in other affairs, wherein I have endeavoured to assist him and offer him guidance, and although I intend this clause in no manner to reflect upon or in any way impugn his probity and honour, which have always been above reproach, I am compelled to draw the conclusion that he has

135

not shown that discretion in the management of his affairs which would convince me that in his hands any large sum or parcel of my estate might not soon be dispersed and disappear without profit to himself. Therefore, out of regard to his welfare, as well as to my own peace of mind, and as a token only of the sincere affection I bear him, I devise and bequeath to my said grandson, Daniel Oliphant, to be paid to him in cash by my executors out of the sum remaining on deposit to my credit at the First National Bank of this city after my funeral expenses and other just debts and the above mentioned bequests shall have been paid, the sum of thirty-five hundred dollars.

It was then that the indeterminable vocal sound came from the corner where Dan sat—a sound not unlike a slight, irrepressible gasp, though not distinctly that; nor was the nature of the emotion producing it indicated by the sound itself. No one looked at Dan, and his father hastily went on with the reading.

To Mrs. Oliphant her mother had left the income to be derived from "securities to the value of two hundred and twenty-five thousand dollars, these securities to be held in trust for her." Mrs. Oliphant was to have the income from them during her life, but she could not sell them or give them away, though she was left at liberty to bequeath them to whom she pleased. And the rest of the estate, much the greater part of it, was left without condition—and also without defining him as "dearly and well-beloved"—to her grandson, Harlan, the residuary legatee.

"Good Lord!" Harlan said loudly, and, without further explanation of his feelings, sat staring blankly at the wall opposite him.

Wiping her eyes, Mrs. Oliphant looked at Dan; and her husband also turned in that direction.

"Dan, old fellow," he began, in a distressed voice, "you mustn't think—"

But Lena interrupted him. She jumped up from her chair, and her cheeks and temples were alive with a colour that outdid all the extraneous tinting her grandmother-in-law had so hated. "This is aimed at me!" she cried. "I understand perfectly the real meaning of that precious document! Heaven knows why, but she must have disliked me before Dan ever brought me here! She showed spite at her first sight of me, and tried to hurt me, and did hurt me. And now she cuts us off with nothing and gives it all to Harlan just to show she thought that all I care about is money—yes, and to prove she can still injure me and insult me even after she's dead!"

But here the hot little voice was choked with anger and tears;—she ran to the door. "What are such people?" she sobbed,

136

stopping there for a moment, and addressing to the upper air of the room this inquiry of passionate wonderment. "Oh, my heavens! What are these people I've got to spend my life among?"

Then she ran through the hall and up the stairs, sobbing more and more uncontrollably, and audible below until the vigorous action of her splendidly constructed bedroom door produced a sonorous climax, followed by instantaneous silence. Dan had risen, apparently intending to follow her, but he paused as his father spoke to him.

"I believe I wouldn't, if I were you, Dan."

"Wouldn't what, sir?"

"I think I'd just let her alone to have it out with herself. I've noticed it seems to work better, she gets herself in hand sooner that way."

"Yes, sir," Dan said, and moved to depart.

"Wait just a minute. I think your mother has something she wants to say to you." Mrs. Oliphant, who was holding her handkerchief to her eyes, had made a slight gesture, which her husband thus interpreted, and Dan turned back quickly and stood before her.

"What is it, mother?"

She caught his hand and held it, speaking brokenly:

"You—you mustn't think—Mother loved you—she did! She—she left it so that I could always—always take care of you, if you—if you needed it. She didn't mean anything unkind to you."

Mr. Oliphant supplemented this. "I believe your mother's entirely right, Dan. The division may seem unfair, but I'm strongly of the opinion there was no intention to be unkind or to—or to hurt you!"

" 'Hurt me!' " Dan exclaimed loudly. His face was aglow and his eyes were shining. "Hurt me? Why, she didn't leave you anything, sir, and you're not hurt. And just look what she's done for me! Why, even you and mother had begun to think I couldn't hold on to Ornaby this time, but grandma's left me not only enough to tide me over, but to go ahead with! I'm goin' to set out the stakes for that automobile factory to-morrow!"

He turned again toward the door as he spoke; and his father again mistook his intention. "Dan, I—I really wouldn't go up to talk to Lena just now. If we all just let her alone when she's in one of these—ah—that is, I've noticed if we keep away—"

"Yes, so have I," Dan agreed heartily. "That's not where I'm headed for, sir."

His mother had retained his hand in spite of his movement to go, and now she tried to draw him nearer her. "Stay with us, dear,"

137

she pleaded. "You're so plucky, you poor boy, but I know it has hurt you. I know you want to get outdoors and walk and walk and grieve to yourself, but if you'd stay with your father and me—"

"I can't," he said, and detached his hand from hers though she still sought to keep it. "I got to go, mother."

"But where?" she begged. "Where do you want to go at such a time as this, dear?"

"Where?" he cried triumphantly. "Why, to see those executors and get that money! I'm goin' to make George Rowe and old John P. Johns agree to advance it to me the first thing to-morrow morning. Grandma's saved Ornaby for me, God bless her!"

He waved an exultant hand over his head and departed at a long and rapid stride, leaving his father and mother to stare at one another with pathetic inquiry; but after a moment or two of this Mr. Oliphant laughed vaguely, sighed, shook his head, and said: "Why, he means it!"

"You don't think he's just covering up what he feels? Pretending—"

"Pretending? No!" her husband returned. "All your mother's will means to him is that he can go on with his Addition!"

"But he can't. Thirty-five hundred dollars won't—"

"No, not long," Mr. Oliphant admitted. "But it looks like a million to him to-day, because it pulls him around this particular corner. Of course in a little while there'll be another corner that he can't get pulled around, but he doesn't see that one now. All he's thinking about—"

"But he expects to begin a factory!" she exclaimed. "I haven't a doubt he'll try to."

"Neither have I; and that'll bring the corner he can't turn just so much nearer."

"It seems so pitiful," the mother lamented. "I'll help him all I can. There's the income of what she's given me—"

"It won't go very far," Oliphant informed her, ruefully amused. "Not with the kind of plans Dan'll be making now that he's got hold of thirty-five hundred dollars!"

"Well, but then," she said brightly, yet with a little timidity, "you see, there's Harlan. Harlan could—" She hesitated; and both of them turned, though not confidently, toward their younger son who still continued to sit motionless in his chair, in the bay window, staring at the opposite wall. He seemed unaware that they were looking at him, until his mother addressed him directly. "Harlan, you would, wouldn't you?"

He merged from his deep interior of thought like a man blinking in the sun after exploring a cavern. "What?"

138

"I said, wouldn't you—"

"Oh, yes," he interrupted. "Yes, I heard what you said, though I was thinking of something else. I wonder if either of you understand just what grandma was up to."

"It seems to be plain enough," his father said. "She'd always been a pretty sharp business woman; she was convinced that your grandfather's success was mainly due to her advice, and I expect it was, myself—anyhow a good deal of it—so she thought Dan ought to've listened to her when she opposed his putting what your grandfather left him and all he could borrow besides into this real-estate venture. I'm afraid she felt rather bitter when he went ahead with it in spite of all she said against it. So it seems pretty clear that she thought if she left him anything substantial it would all be thrown away on a scheme she thinks is bound to fail—she couldn't imagine the city's ever growing out that far—and she didn't want her money wasted. So she left it to you. I don't see anything particularly enigmatic about it, Harlan."

"No," Harlan agreed, though his dry smile was evidence that he withheld his true thought on the matter; "I suppose not. At least, there's nothing enigmatic about it to me." He was obviously not elated over his good fortune; and his mother saw fit to commend him for this.

"I think—I think it's so sweet of you, dear," she said timidly;— "I mean especially while Dan was here—your not showing any pleasure in having so much come to you. I think it's noble, Harlan."

"You do?" he asked, and he laughed briefly without any merriment. "Perhaps I'd better explain what I believe grandma really meant. She never liked me, and she always adored Dan. It's curious, too, because Dan's disposition is like grandfather's, and she certainly never seemed to think much of grandfather! Well, she did hate Dan's throwing his money away on a wild scheme that can't possibly do anything in the end but leave him bankrupt; and she certainly understood him—she knew no matter how much he could lay his hands on, he'd pour it all in after the rest—and it's true she didn't want her money wasted that way, and knew I wouldn't let it be wasted at all, if she left it to me; but that wasn't what she really had in mind. Lord, no!"

"Wasn't it?" his father inquired gravely. "I don't see anything else."

Harlan laughed again with the same dry brevity. "She always hoped Dan would marry Martha Shelby—and she kept on hoping it, even after he married Lena."

"Harlan!" his mother protested. "You oughtn't to speak like

that! Why, mother couldn't any more have thought of such a thing, when Dan was already married—"

"She died hoping it," Harlan insisted. "I tell you—"

Mr. Oliphant interrupted. "That seems to me about as far-fetched an idea as I've often heard, Harlan."

"Does it, sir? Didn't you ever hear grandmother express her opinion of Lena?"

"Somewhat frequently."

"Did you ever hear her mention her conviction that Lena was entirely mercenary and married Dan because she thought he was rich?"

"She talked that way sometimes—yes."

"And didn't Lena just show us she thinks that's what the will means, herself?"

"Possibly," Mr. Oliphant admitted. "But that doesn't prove—"

"You might just read over that document of grandma's again," Harlan suggested. "She appears to leave me everything and Dan nothing, but gives mother a very comfortable living income, and she knew mother will take care of him when he needs it. What's most significant, she provides that mother can leave the principal to any one she pleases. Don't you suppose grandma knew it will naturally come to Dan eventually? She's really taken care of him, and at the same time made it appear that he's cut off with this thirty-five hundred dollars that'll last him about a minute. She did it because she hoped Lena would leave him and get a divorce."

"No, no!" Mrs. Oliphant cried out. "Mother wouldn't have had such a wicked thought. She had the strictest ideas about morality I ever—"

"Yes, she did," Harlan agreed. "Yet that's just what she planned. You may not see it, but it's as plain to me as if she had written it in her will. And there's something more than that in it, too."

"What is it?" Mr. Oliphant inquired skeptically. "What is the something more that's hidden from every eye but yours?"

Harlan reddened and failed to reply at once;—then he said with a reluctant humour: "I'm afraid she's played it rather low down on me, sir."

"What!" Mr. Oliphant stared at him. "You call leaving you five or six hundred thousand dollars playing it rather low down?"

"You'd say it's a fantastic view, would you, sir?"

"Yes, I believe I should—considerably!"

"Maybe so," Harlan said. "Yet there seems some ground for it. Grandma knew—that is, I mean she thought—she thought that I had certain hopes about Martha myself, and she told me pretty plainly

I'd better keep out of the way. Well, she's put me in a fine light before Martha, hasn't she? Here's Dan, all his life supposed to be the favourite, with great expectations, and now he's cut off with a shilling, and I get it all! In the eyes of a sympathetic woman who's always liked him best anyhow, isn't he the suffering hero, and don't I play the rôle of the brother that undermined him and supplanted him?"

"That's nonsense," his father said a little irritably. "You don't suppose your grandmother deliberately—"

"I don't suppose she meant unkindly by me," Harlan interrupted. "Naturally I don't suppose my grandmother made me her residuary legatee for the purpose of injuring me. Probably she thought I'd be consoled by what she was leaving me."

"Oh, Harlan!" his mother cried reproachfully.

But Harlan only smiled at her faintly and did not defend himself.

"So Lena will leave Dan now, will she?" Mr. Oliphant inquired, with satire. "And then Dan will proceed in freedom to carry out the rest of this programme?"

"No, sir; not at all."

"But haven't you just been saying—"

"I've been saying what I see in the will," Harlan explained. "I've been saying what grandma hoped, and I think she was pretty shrewd, but I believe that her dislike of Lena led her into an error. I haven't the remotest idea that Lena will leave her husband."

"I see!" Mr. Oliphant returned sharply. "You mean you haven't any fantastic ideas yourself, Harlan; it's only your grandmother who had them, though she's just left you a fortune!"

His tone was hard; and Harlan, looking at him gravely, pointed out a significance in the hardness. "There it is, sir. Already I'm a little more unpopular with you than usual, because you can't help sympathizing with Dan and feeling that I've got his share as well as my own. Don't you think other people may feel the same way?"

For a moment Mr. Oliphant looked slightly disconcerted by this bit of analysis, but, recovering himself, "Not necessarily," he replied. "I'm not criticizing you because of your inheritance, but because it doesn't seem fair in you to impute all this surreptitious planning to a person who's shown such generosity to you. You don't seem to realize—"

"Oh, but I do," Harlan interrupted. "Mother spoke of my not seeming elated and praised me for it. I don't deserve her praise. You see, if I don't feel much elated just at first it's because to my mind the whole thing is another example of how much better grandma

141

liked Dan and how much better other people are going to go on liking him. Naturally, I'm glad to have the money; I know she meant well by me, and I appreciate it. I appreciate another thing, too. One of the reasons she left it to me was that she knew I put what I had from grandfather into the safest type of municipal bonds. She knew that I'd understand the value of whatever she left me. She knew I'd take care of it."

He put a slight but sharp and dry emphasis upon the final words, "She knew I'd take care of it," so that there was a hint of warning in them; and he added, making this note more definite: "She was right about that, because I will take care of it."

Upon that, he struck both arms of his chair decisively with the palms of his hands, and, as a continuation of this action, rose and turned to the window, his back to his parents. They glanced nervously at each other, each knowing that the other had the same hope and the same doubt; the glance they exchanged meaning, "You speak to him about it!" Mr. Oliphant yielded and coughed uncomfortably as a prelude, but his wife impulsively decided to begin the task for him.

"Harlan, dear," she said, "your father and I both know you've always acted conscientiously in everything you've ever done; and of course what mother's given you ought to be regarded as a sacred trust. You're right to say you'll take care if it, but we feel—I mean your father and I feel—" She faltered, and appealed to her husband: "You do feel that perhaps—perhaps under the circumstances—perhaps—"

"Yes," Mr. Oliphant said as she came to a helpless stop;—"I think under the circumstances Harlan might—might properly see fit to—" But here he, too, hesitated and seemed unable to continue.

Their son, however, understood them perfectly, and turned sharply to face them. "Of course I knew you'd ask it," he said, and an old bitterness, long held down within him, came to the surface. "I knew you wanted me to let Dan have even that twenty-five thousand dollars grandfather left me. You really wanted me to let him throw it away along with his own, though you never spoke out and asked me to do it. Martha Shelby did, though. She spoke out plainly enough! The fact that grandfather gave it to me never entered her head. She only thought I was miserly for not putting it into Dan's hands to be squandered. That's what she thought, and I've understood all along that my mother and my father had a great deal the same feeling."

"No, no," his mother protested, for the bitterness in his voice had increased as he spoke. "We never reproached you, dear."

"No, not in words maybe."

"No, not in any way," she said. "It was right of you to take care

142

of it, and you'd be right now to take care of what you'll have. Your father and I only mean that now you have so much—"

"Now that I have so much," Harlan echoed, "I ought to throw away part of it, even though grandma's trusted me to save it from just this very wastage and to take care of every bit of it?"

"No, no; it isn't that," Mrs. Oliphant said; and with pathetically naïve artfulness she changed the basis of her appeal. "But you know, dear, you were just telling us how much Martha had wanted you to help Dan—she's always been such a devoted friend of his—and you said that after she hears about mother's bequest to you, she may take it as a kind of supplanting your brother, and it would be harder than ever for you to make her fond of you; so don't you see—don't you see what a splendid effect it would have on her now, when you've got so much, dear, and could spare it—don't you see, if you'd—if you'd—"

"Yes, I see," Harlan said grimly. "You think Martha might even admire me enough to marry me, if I'd say to Dan: 'Here! I won't accept all this that should have been yours. Here's half of it.'"

"Oh, no," she cried, "I didn't mean half of it; I only meant you might—"

"No," Harlan said; "not any, mother—not a dime! I won't impress Martha with a pose. I don't want her or anybody else to like me because of a pose."

"Would it be a pose," Mr. Oliphant asked gravely, "to help your brother?"

"Wouldn't it?" Harlan returned as gravely. "Isn't it a pose to do something that isn't natural to you, simply to make a woman admire you? I'd call that a pose, myself, though you may have another definition of the word. I'm not caring to get admiration that way, sir."

"All right," his father said, nodding, as the fragile edifice of Mrs. Oliphant's gentle cunning was thus dispersed upon the air. "I should say you had the right spirit there. But why need it be an attitude? Wouldn't you really like to help Dan out a little, Harlan?"

Harlan sighed. "Not in a failure, sir. First and last he's had a pretty long chance to prove what he could do with his Addition, and he's no nearer succeeding to-day than he was when he began. Instead, he's lost all his money and all his time. All he's done was to spoil a farm."

"But if he had some really substantial assistance, it's not absolutely impossible he might—"

"No, sir," Harlan said definitely; "I don't believe in it, and I'll never do it. I didn't want to supplant him. I didn't ask for what grandma's done for me; I never did one thing to get it, or for the

143

purpose of making her like me; and, as a matter of fact, she didn't do it because she liked me. But she did know I'd take care of it, and I'm going to prove she was right about that, anyhow. I won't throw any of it away on an attitude to make Martha Shelby think well of me. Of course she'll be all the surer she's right about me, now that I don't do anything for him, though I have so much!" He picked up the copy of Mrs. Savage's will from the table where his father had left it, and, sitting down again, prepared to look over it; but, as he placed in position the eye-glasses already necessary to him when he read, he sent a sidelong glance toward his parents, a glance in which there was the bitterness of an ancient pain. "I wouldn't even throw any of it away to make my father and mother like me a little better, either," he said.

Mrs. Oliphant cried out reproachfully: "Oh, Harlan!" and she would have said more; but her husband shook his head at her, and she was silent. Harlan finished his reading, set the manuscript down upon the table, and went away without speaking again, so that his parents were left to themselves and a thoughtful, somewhat melancholy silence.

Mrs. Oliphant broke it diffidently. "You don't think mother ever dreamed that—"

"That he might help Dan? No; not with the Addition. Harlan's right when he says that's just what she trusted him not to do."

"I didn't mean that," Mrs. Oliphant explained. "I mean—you know what he said about mother's hoping—I mean his saying he thought mother had those wild ideas about Lena's going away and—and Martha Shelby—"

"No," her husband said. "No; I don't think so. It seems unlikely. I don't think your mother would have—"

"No," Mrs. Oliphant assented thoughtfully. "I can't believe she would. Of course there isn't any way of being sure—now."

"No; but it's probably just Harlan's imagination. He's sensitive, and that always means imaginative, too. I don't think we need to dwell on it."

"I suppose not. Especially as she couldn't have meant anything like that. You don't think she could, do you, dear?"

"No, no; I don't think so," he answered. "We'd better be worrying over other matters, I suspect."

"You mean about getting Harlan to help Dan out?"

"Yes."

"Of course I can do something," she said. "I'll help all I can with the income mother's given me; we've always managed to live very comfortably without it. But Harlan—why, I almost believe Dan could make a success of the Addition, if Harlan would do something substantial about it. Yes; we ought to be able to think of some way to get him to do it."

CHAPTER XVIII

THEY thought of many ways to get him to do it, but none of such ingenuity as to inspire them with confidence. Mrs. Oliphant made more suggestions than her husband did, and she put most of them into the form of little dramatic dialogues imagined as taking place between Mr. Oliphant and Harlan. Mr. Oliphant was to say such-and-such things to Harlan, who would necessarily reply in certain terms, which she sketched;—whereupon his father could triumphantly turn the words just uttered into proof that Harlan would not only be doing his duty by helping Dan, but at the same time would make great headway with Martha Shelby in a straightforward manner involving not the slightest pose.

Unfortunately, after each of these small dramas in turn, becoming eager in her opinion that "this time" she had "got it," she was forced into pessimism by Mr. Oliphant's pointing out that Harlan wouldn't say what she had sketched for him; but, on the contrary, was certain to express himself to an effect precisely the opposite.

Many times that afternoon the poor lady murmured, "No, I suppose perhaps it wouldn't do after all," and pondered again. "But why don't you think of a way that would do?" she asked, with more spirit, after one of her failures. "You're a lawyer; you ought to be able to think of something."

He laughed and made the gesture of a man helpless between opposing viewpoints of his own. "What provokes me is that I can't help seeing Harlan's side of it, too. There's a good deal to be said on his side, you know."

"Yes, indeed," she readily assented. "He thinks he's perfectly right; but of course he isn't."

"Well, why isn't he? After all, your mother trusted him to do just what we're planning to get him not to do."

"But her will doesn't say he can't help Dan. So why shouldn't he?"

"No," Mr. Oliphant interrupted; "it doesn't say he mustn't; but

145

that's what she counted on. In our hearts we're blaming him for not betraying a trust, and for being unwilling to put money into the fire;—he honestly believes it would be putting it into the fire. And he won't do it, even though he knows his refusing makes him look mean in the eyes of pretty much everybody he cares about, even in the eyes of the person he seems to care most about. Well, there's something rather fine in a stand like that, after all."

"Martha'd never forgive him!" Mrs. Oliphant said emphatically. "Never! If he doesn't help Dan, now that he's got so much, she'd always believe him terribly stingy. So you see we ought to persuade him for his own good, too—if we could only think of a way."

But they continued to find that elusive way beset by baffling afterthoughts; and when Dan came home from his excursion, successful and in high fettle, they spoke to him of the subject that had been engrossing them—and were straightway baffled again. Dan even declined the proffer of future assistance from his mother.

"Not a penny!" he said. "She didn't have any faith in me, and she despised the whole idea of Ornaby. She gave me thirty-five hundred dollars of my own—bless her for it! She gave me that to do with as I please, and it's plenty. Why, to-morrow I'm goin' to fix up the interest on what's owed on the land, and then I've got to settle another little matter, and after that I—"

"Wait, Dan," his father interposed. "What other little matter is it you have to settle? I didn't know anything had been worrying you except the probable foreclosure."

"It didn't, sir. I didn't worry about this at all. I knew I could fix it all right, if I could just hold off the foreclosure. It seems I've never paid any of the taxes on the Addition—I've had so many other things on my mind, it seems I just kind of neglected that—and so somebody's got a tax title to it; but now I can settle with him to-morrow morning and clear it off—and then I'm goin' to turn up some sod out there! I'm goin' to get ready to lay the foundation for my first factory!"

"But the money, dear!" his mother cried. "How in the world do you expect even to lay the foundations unless we can get Harlan—"

"No, ma'am! I wouldn't take a nickel of it if he begged me to! I've been pretty near where I was ready to steal to get money to pull me out of a hole; but I'll never take one single cent of what grandma left Harlan, or of what she left you either. If she'd meant me to have it she'd have given it to me herself; but she didn't have any faith in me, and she says so in plain words in her will. You don't expect me

146

to take help from her that she wanted to prevent, do you? Never in this world!"

"There! You see?" Mrs. Oliphant lamented, appealing to her husband. "I knew it hurt him, in spite of what he said. I knew it!"

"You're all wrong," Dan stoutly maintained. "She kind of explained to me what she was goin' to do, though I didn't see what she meant. It was just a few minutes before she died. She told me to remember not to be hurt, but she needn't have worried about it, and I told her so. So don't you worry about it. I didn't begin to build Ornaby on my expectations from her; I've carried it along this far by myself, and I expect to carry it the rest of the way. And I'm goin' to build that factory! George McMillan thinks maybe he can float some of the stock for it in New York, and I don't know but he's got a little money of his own he may want to put in. The way I feel, why, it looks to me as if I was about ready to climb out on the top o' the heap right now; and I'm certainly not baby enough to be hurt because my grandmother didn't have any faith in me."

He continued to protest and perhaps protested too much; for although it was clear enough to his parents that he was so heartened by his thirty-five hundred dollars as to anticipate miracles, yet it was not to be believed that his pride had suffered no injury at all. What appeared in his grandmother's will as a severe criticism of his ability and judgment was more than a mere neutral lack of faith; and Mrs. Oliphant's intuition had touched the truth; he was indeed hurt—but he never admitted it.

Moreover, he remained steadfast in refusal; he would neither allow his mother to help him with money nor countenance any appeal of hers, or his father's, to Harlan. Both of them, uncountenanced, did with faint hope reopen the subject to Harlan, though they did it indirectly;—they made allusions to the pathos of the brave and independent position his brother had taken. But Harlan only looked slightly badgered, and replied that this extolled position of Dan's was the only possible correct one under the circumstances.

From time to time the troubled parents tried other diplomacies of increasing feebleness, until finally it seemed best to mention the subject, even indirectly, no more. In the evenings the silences in the library were charged with feeling withheld from expression; though Dan enlivened the room when he came in, and made it boisterous if he brought the baby with him. Certainly no depression could be recorded against either of this pair; Henry Daniel glowed with health and became livelier with every month of increasing age and weight. As for Lena, after her outburst upon the reading of Mrs. Savage's will, she was another of this household who

147

was surcharged with repressed feeling; but her repression became a habit;—weeks went by when she did not slam a door. She appeared to become more tolerant of her husband at this period than she had ever been; and when she spoke to him at all, it was in a tone suggesting that her tolerance had in it something of compassion.

She devoted herself to her baby, perhaps finding a refuge in her devotion; but she declined to accompany Dan on Sunday afternoons when he went for a sidewalk excursion with the perambulator. This was an established custom in the town, she observed: every Sunday, early in the afternoon, the young fathers and mothers began to appear upon the sidewalks, the fathers pushing the baby-carriages and the mothers strolling a little way behind with the toddlers, if there were any of these, or perhaps lingering for a moment of gossip with friends encountered by the way, then scurrying on to overtake the perambulator.

High and low followed the custom; it was as well observed by the South Side, where lived most of the followers of handicrafts, as it was upon National Avenue and Amberson Boulevard. The perambulators of these two thoroughfares were the more luxurious; fine lace was to be seen upon the occupants, and the accompanying parents were well dressed; though Lena, looking from her window, sometimes shivered to see one of the passing young husbands wearing a Derby hat as a complement to the long frock coat that appeared to be a regalia garment necessary to this occasion.

By four o'clock, which was Dan's favourite hour for his weekly perambulator stroll, most of the pedestrian families were on their way homeward from "Sunday dinner at grandpa's and grandma's," the grandma and grandpa being almost invariably the parents of the young mother. Lena objected to the parade as "publicly provincial," and pointed out that Dan lacked any plausible reason for joining it;—if the baby needed air he could be taken for a drive in the family carriage; and if Dan insisted on pushing him in the perambulator, the Oliphants' back yard was "twice the size of Madison Square," she said with elaborate exaggeration; but Henry Daniel's father only laughed and continued to follow the custom of his fellow-townsmen.

The Sunday-afternoon excursion with the perambulator gave him his greatest happiness, and all through his bustling week days of work he looked forward to it, chuckling as he thought of it. And when the rewarding hour arrived, he went forth wheeling his son before him and cheerily unconscious that he was the only father in sight not accompanied (even at a distance) by a second parent for the occupant of the perambulator. He was proud to exhibit Henry Daniel and loved nothing better than to lift him out of the little carriage and talk uproarious baby-talk to him, and tickle him to make him laugh, and in every other possible manner show him off to other young parents—or to anybody who had time to listen to these hilarious paternal banalities. If other parents bragged of their own young, showing them off in turn, Dan's manifestations with Henry Daniel would become but the louder; and if the other parents, being two to one, succeeded in drowning him out, he would restore his child to the perambulator tenderly and move on, sorry for people who had so little to make such a fuss about.

Sunday, he said, was the only day when he had a chance to get really acquainted with the baby; for all the rest of the week Dan was out hustling so early and so late that opportunities for making the acquaintance more intimate were few. A great part of his activity at this time was in the chase of possible buyers of Ornaby ground; and a driven life was led by those three men who had thought they might buy lots after the foreclosure. The Earl of Ornaby gave them little rest; and although he sometimes remained away from one or another of them for days at a time—perhaps upon the ardent request, "Well, for heaven's sakes can't you even give me a chance to think it over?"—he would write frequent letters to the pursued creature in the interval. Incessantly he persuaded, argued, and prophesied; seldom has a half-accepted, half-rejected lover shown such hot persistence in convincing his lady; and probably never have three dismal men in moderate circumstances been so urgently courted into the buying of lots.

They were not friends, these men; they had gone separately to Ornaby and had no knowledge of one another when the pursuit of them began; but they knew one another well before it was over. The vehement salesman had so quoted them to one another, making such glorifying use of their every admission not actually condemning Ornaby, that a conference of the quoted seemed to be a necessity. They thought to meet in secret; but within ten minutes found the hunter upon them.

"Gentlemen," he began, "you wish to be alone, and I will not interrupt you"—and talked until two of them went home.

He went with them, and then returned to talk some more to the man at whose house the conference had been called.

Such deadly persistence finally prevailed upon a majority of the three and two more lots were sold in the Addition upon the liberal terms of nothing down and little more than nothing to be paid in periodical installments. Nevertheless, here were three actual sales, and if there ever lived a salesman who knew how to make three appear to be a hundred, because he himself believed three to be a hundred, that multi-visioned salesman was Daniel Oliphant.

In a day of quieter art certain academicians now gone from

149

their academies had frequently the desire to paint pretty young women blue-robed and poised as if alighting from the air. Sometimes, upon the lower part of his canvas, beneath the poising lady's alighting toe, such a painter would twirl a golden circle, then swathe her eyes with a blue kerchief and name the picture, "Dame Fortune on her Wheel." The effect was of the dame blind, but dancing; and sometimes the course of events in the life of a human creature will warrant the conception, yet it has usually been observed that Fortune seldom dances to one who has not diligently begged the favour. It would seem the blinded lady has a little bit of her kerchief up.

The man who had built a picnic shack at Ornaby for his large family found his wife and children so reluctant to come home from the picnics that he enlarged the shack, put a cooking-stove and cots in it, and began to stay there from Saturday afternoon until Monday morning. His house was far down in the city where the smoke had begun to discourage his wife, and, in the unavailing struggle to keep things clean, she grew querulous. "If we could only live out here!" she wailed one day when they were at the shack; and this outcry produced the first house in Ornaby Addition. It was a cottage of the "New Colonial" kind; and Dan drove all of his other Ornaby boosters to see every new phase of its construction, from the digging of the cellar to the polishing of the floors; for when the cottage was begun the purchasers of land in the Addition were increased in number to eight. By the time the cottage was finished there were fourteen, and several of these intended to build "right the first minute next spring," Dan said.

He called them his "Ornaby boosters"; for he readily adopted the new vocabulary of commercial argot then being developed by "promoters," by writers of advertisements, and by New York hustlers for trade. "Every Ornaby buyer is an Ornaby booster," he said one day, when the new cottages in the Addition had brought him new buyers of lots; and, falling instantly in love with the cadence of this alliteration, went straight to the billboard men. Thereafter no one could go northward of the city for an afternoon drive and fail to find the gentle landscape wrecked. On every road the earl blazoned his great defacements: "Every Ornaby Buyer is an Ornaby Booster!"

At home he had two subjects, both subdivided. One was Henry Daniel, his growth, his wit, and his precocity; and the other was Ornaby Addition, its present magnificence and prospective splendour.

"And the queer thing is," Harlan told Martha Shelby, "he

150

believes every word of it. He actually still believes he's making a success of that dreadful place. Isn't it strange?"

But Martha said that she knew something stranger, and when he asked her what it was, she answered: "Why, it's your still believing he isn't making a success of the 'dreadful place.'"

CHAPTER XIX

HARLAN laughed ruefully and told her that time, tide, and travel failed to alter her. "You don't change as much as—as much as"—he looked about him for a comparison, and found one ready to hand in the material of which the Shelbys' veranda was made. "You don't change as much as this Western limestone does. It's made of stone, too, but years and weather take its edges off and give it the look of being not so hard as it used to be."

Not defending herself from the criticism, she gazed thoughtfully at Harlan as he sat fanning himself with his straw hat—he was warm and flushed after their walk on this hot June morning—then she turned her eyes again to the wide lawn stretching before her down to the National Avenue sidewalk. Looking out from the shade of the veranda, her eyes needed the shelter of the curved fingers of her hand, a protection she gave them, resting her elbow on the stone railing beside her. The trimmed grass of the lawn was a blazing green, seen waveringly through visible pulsations of the heated air; the fountain swan, still diligent under every discouragement, sprayed forth no skyward rainbow mists, but ejected a limpid rod of water of so brief an uplift that the bird seemed to carry in his throat the curved tip of a shepherd's crook made of glass. The asphalt street, beyond the shade of its bordering maples, lay steaming and smelled of tar;— drooping bicyclists rode there, tinkling their little bells for a right of way. Surreys and phaetons gave them courteous passage, and frequently a swifter, noisier vehicle went by, grinding, squawking, and leaving blue oil-smoke on the air.

There were many more automobiles than when she had last gone away, Martha noticed; yet the outlook from the veranda was the old familiar one. To her eyes, however, it bore the familiar unfamiliar appearance that well-known things bear to the traveller

151

at home again, but not yet quite adjusted after a long absence. For this was not her return from the little run she had made to England at the time of the baby's christening next door, though that excursion was itself a longer one—much to her taste—than she had planned. The bit of old hickory serving her as a father resisted stiffly, but finally proved flexible under great pressure, and she took him even to Russia before she got through bending him. When his protestive squeakings at last became unbearable, she brought him home, but did not remain herself. In the Italian Alps there was a valley town with which she had fallen in love;—she returned to her native land merely as an escort for Mr. Shelby, and, having deposited him safely, hurried back to the terraced vineyards, the whitewashed walls with strings of red peppers dangling against them, and the frescoed old villa she had rented in the foreground of this picture.

It was a commonplace, she said, that the new Twentieth Century was the age of the annihilation of distances; people talked from New York to Chicago over a wire; the Atlantic was crossed in six days, the American continent in four; and her father could remember when it took him three weeks to get to Philadelphia; he "wouldn't mind being taken care of by correspondence."

Old Hickory, well-warranted in his outburst, replied that he didn't "need any takin' care of, thank you"—he was tired of being bossed to death, and he wanted her to understand she was mighty welcome to go and stay as long as she had a mind to! If she remained at home, he wouldn't know when she might be draggin' him off again without his exactly knowin' how it happened. It was "curious," he continued; he had sense enough never to let her interfere with him in his business; but in other matters he never knew when he mightn't find himself in some dog-gone place he didn't want to be in—at a plague-taken pink tea maybe, or even right spang in the middle of Europe in some heaven-forsaken garlic heap, with nothin' to think about but old dead monks and nothin' to do but hate the smell. If Martha liked hangin' around those old worn-out nations that never showed a sign o' life except advertisin' chocolate and keepin' their fertilizer right under their front parlour window for fear somebody'd steal it, why, she was certainly good and welcome to all she wanted of 'em! For himself, he had his business to 'tend to; and he didn't want any aunt Ella to pester him, either; "aunt Ella" being his widowed sister, whom Martha had proposed as a housekeeper in substitute for herself. He was full and able—thank you again!—to get up in the morning and eat his ham and eggs without somebody's pinning a bib around his neck, and he believed he knew how to wash and go to bed at night without any fussy woman fixin' up his bureau every other day, so as to hide his nightshirts from him! Altogether, he was lookin' forward to a little rest and liberty, thank you!

So Martha had gone with his earnest consent; for his complaint of her did not lack reason—she was headstrong and a compelling daughter—and she stayed until she had her fill of Italy for that while. Meantime, the abandoned father contentedly lived alone, except for his negro servants, and declared that at last he was his own man and began to feel as if he owned his own house; he felt that way for the first time since his daughter was born, he said. But a different view of his condition was maintained by a member of the household next door.

"A fine exhibition of filial duty!" Lena cried, in one of the irritated moods that returned upon her as the growing Henry Daniel began to be a little boy instead of a little baby. When he was a noisy little boy during the day his mother often became reminiscent, not happily, by the time his father came home in the evening. "You told me once she had a heart as big as she was," Lena went on. "It looks like it, doesn't it? Leaving that poor old man alone over there, month after month and year after year!"

Dan listened absently, his mind on a new customer for a lot. "Who you talkin' about now?"

"You know! That big girl of yours."

"Martha?" he said, his tone a weary one instantly. "How often have I told you she never was any girl of mine, big or little? What's started you on that again?"

"I shouldn't think you'd expect it would take much to start me," Lena exclaimed, "when you remember you gave me your sacred promise I should have a year in Europe—"

"Oh, Lordy! Have we got to go all over that again?"

"—And when you remember you deliberately broke your word to me," Lena went on, "and haven't ever even made the slightest effort to keep it! You hold me here, suffocating in this place, year after year—"

"Now, see here," he interrupted; "just think a minute, please! Is that fair? Haven't you been back to New York every year for at least two or three—"

But Lena almost shouted her interruption. "Yes! Two or three weeks! To visit my family! Do you think it means happiness for me to be with them?—and all of 'em watching to see how I take care of my baby! Is that keeping your word to take me abroad? Oh," she cried, with bitter laughter, "doesn't it seem ironical even to you? That big creature next door was so jealous of me because I had what

153

she wanted she couldn't bear to stay where she had to look at it, so she goes away and gets what I wanted! Isn't it ironical, Dan? Don't you see it at all?"

"I see you've got your imagination all stirred up again, that's all."

"Imagination!" she cried. "Yes; I should think my imagination would get 'all stirred up!' Why, it's funny! She can go and take what I want, but it can't be any good to her; she hasn't culture enough to see it or to feel it or to hear it. I can see her carrying that accent around Europe, and asking waiters for 'ice wat-urr' and 'please to pass the but-urr!' Yet she can go and I can't!"

"But I didn't send her," Dan explained, since his wife clearly implied his responsibility. "You talk as if I—"

"No; but you had no right not to send me after giving me your sacred—"

Dan interrupted her genially; he smiled and patted her pretty little shoulder, though it twitched away from his touch. "Lena, look here: I've got some big deals on, and I'm just about certain they're goin' to work out the right way. You see up to now the trouble's been that all the money comin' in had to be put right out again almost before I'd get hold of it. If it hadn't been for that, I'd had that factory up and running long ago. But as I look ahead now, everything is mighty good—mighty good! If I can just put these deals through—"

"Yes; it's always 'if,'" she reminded him. "When have I ever talked to you that you weren't just about to put through some 'mighty big deals'? You said exactly the same last year."

"Well, but this is a better year than last year. Why, I've done twice the business—yes, better'n that; it's more like four times what I did last year. If Ornaby keeps on like this, why, a few years from now—"

She stopped him; informing him that she'd long since heard more than enough about "a few years from now"; whereupon, being full of the subject, he went down to the library to tell his father and mother what was inevitable within a few years. No skepticism dampened his library prophecies now; Harlan was no longer there to listen, staring with dry incredulity through his glasses.

Harlan had not sold Mrs. Savage's old house, but had moved into it, and kept as precise a routine there as she had kept, and with the same servants. He had two bedrooms upstairs made into a library, but changed nothing on the lower floor; and often the old lady seemed still to be there in authority. At twilight, before Nimbus lit the electric table lamp in the "south front parlour," the room to which she had always descended from her afternoon nap, it was not difficult to imagine that she was sitting in the stiff chair beside the plate-glass window. Of course Nimbus believed that he saw her there when he came in to light the lamp; and he often mumbled to her—always upon the same theme. He was grateful for the one hundred and thirty-five dollars she had left him, but considered the sum inadequate.

"No'm, indeed," he said to the figure he saw in the stiff chair. "I thank you kindly, but didn' I used you right all my days? How much it cost you slip down ten hunderd thirty-five on that paper, 'stead of one hunderd thirty-five? You ain't got it, are you? Ain't doin' you no good, do it? No'm, indeedy! 'Tain't no use you bein' sorry, neither. Make all the fuss you want to; you too late; nobody ain't goin' pay no 'tention to you!"

And in the kitchen he would discuss the apparition with his fourth wife, the fat cook, Myrtle. "Look to me like she can't keep away," he would say. "Set there same as ever. Set up straight in that stiff chair. See her plain as I see you, till I git that lamp lit."

"Landy me, Nimbus, I wouldn' go in that room unlessen the light bright as day if you give me trottin' horse an' gole harniss! How you keep from hollerin'?"

At this the tall, thin old fellow would laugh without making a sound; deep wrinkles in the design of half of a symmetrical cobweb appearing on each side of his face. Some profoundly interior secret of his might have been betrayed, it seemed, if he had allowed his merriment to become vocal; and this noiseless laugh of his awed his wife in much the same way, no doubt, that the laugh of a jungle witch-doctor ancestor of his had awed wives not unlike Myrtle. "She ain't goin' bother me ner you," he explained. "She ain't settin' there 'count o' me ner you. She settin' there 'cause she so mad."

"Who? Who she mad at?"

"Mad at somep'm!" Nimbus would say, and, becoming less uncomfortably mystic might allow a human chuckle to escape him. "Set there mad long as she want to; 'tain't goin' do her no good. She ain't fixed to make no changes now!"

The new owner lived in the old house almost as quietly as Mrs. Savage, in the visions of Nimbus, went on living there. Harlan had several times thought of going to Italy, but the idea never culminated in action.

"I wanted to come, though," he told Martha, as they sat on her veranda that hot morning, the day after her return. "I wanted to more than I ever wanted to do anything else. You see I've almost stopped going to the office; I just dangle about there sometimes to please father, but I don't care to practise law. It's a silly way of spending one's life after all, fighting the sordid disputes of squabbling people. There was really nothing to keep me here."

She did not alter her attitude, but still looked out upon the old familiar unfamiliar scene from beneath her sheltering curved fingers. "If you wanted to come, why didn't you?"

"Because I'd only have done it to see you, and I suppose I have a remnant of pride. If you'd like a better answer, think of what I told you about yourself. I didn't come because I know you're stony. I knew you hadn't changed."

"About what?"

"About me," he said, and added: "About anything!"

At this she turned her head and looked at him, for he spoke with a sour significance. "Well, have you changed, Harlan?" she asked gravely.

"About you," he answered. "I haven't—unfortunately."

"But I meant: Have you changed about anything? Aren't you just what you were five or six years ago, only a little intensified—and richer?"

"Ah, I knew I'd get that," he said. "I knew it would come before I could be with you long. I told my father and mother the very day my grandmother's will was read that you'd hate me for it, and mother agreed quickly enough."

"Why, no," Martha said, and her surprise was genuine. "Why should I hate you because Mrs. Savage—"

"Because she left it to me and not to Dan, and because I didn't think it was right or sensible to help him with any of it."

"But he hasn't needed any help," Martha said. "It's much better for him to be doing it without any help, and so splendidly."

"So splendidly?" Harlan repeated, and he stared at her. "But you don't take what Dan says seriously, do you? You don't think that just because he says—"

"I haven't seen him, Harlan."

"But you speak as if you believe he's actually succeeding in making that old fantasia of his into a reality."

"Well," she said, "isn't he?"

"What? Why, he's still just barely keeping his head above water. He sells vacant lots out there, yes—but to keep on selling them he has to put all they sell for into developing the land he hasn't sold. It amounts precisely to the same thing as giving the property away. His mortgages used to worry him to death, but he's got most of the place mortgaged now for three times what it was five years ago. You see—"

"I see that the land must be worth three times as much as it was five years ago, since he can borrow three times as much on it."

"But, my dear Martha—"

"But, my dear Harlan!" she echoed mockingly, and thus

156

disposed of his argument before he could deliver it. "The truth is, you've had the habit of undervaluing Dan so long that you can't get over it. You can't see that at last he's begun to make a success of his 'fantasia.' Given time enough, critics who aren't careful to keep themselves humble-minded always lose the power to see things as they are."

Harlan winced a little under this sententious assault, and laughed at himself for wincing; then explained his rather painful laughter. "It's almost amusing to me to find myself still cowering away from your humble-minded criticisms of me—just as I used to, Martha!"

"Yes, I know it," she admitted. "I hate myself for the way I talk to you, Harlan;—somehow you always make me smug and superior. I'm the foolish kind of person who's always made critical by superior criticism—critical of the critic, I mean."

"But I'm not more critical of Dan than other people are. Have you asked your father what he thinks of Ornaby now, for instance?"

"Yes, I asked him last night."

"What does he think of it?"

"He thinks the same as I do," she said. "He's been compelled to recognize that it's going to be a tremendous success."

"Then he's changed his mind since last week," Harlan returned, somewhat discomfited. "He told me—"

"Oh, yes, I know," she said. "He didn't say he thought it would be a success. He said he thought the Addition idea was just as crazy as he ever did, and Dan Oliphant was the biggest fool in seven states, and the noisiest! Those were his words precisely, Harlan."

"But you just told me—"

"No," she explained;—"you asked me what he thought. Do you suppose he'd admit to me that he ever made a business mistake? He knows perfectly well that he did make one when he refused to follow my advice and buy some of Dan's stock when the poor boy was trying to finance his plan at the beginning. Papa confessed it absolutely."

"He did?"

"Certainly," she replied. "If he'd meant what he said he'd just have grunted it. Instead, he yelled it at me. With papa, that's exactly the same as a perfectly open confession."

Harlan shook his head, remaining more than doubtful of this interpretation. "So you believe if Dan tried now to organize a stock company for Ornaby—"

"They'd gobble it!" she said. "Papa especially! But he and others like him wouldn't buy a single share when poor Dan went

157

begging and peddling all over town; and now I'm glad they didn't. It's so much better for him to have done it alone."

"But, my dear," Harlan insisted, not altogether without exasperation, "he hasn't done it."

"My dear," she returned promptly; "he's going to!"

"But, Martha—"

"Listen," she said. "I'll tell you something that you don't understand, because you've been living here all along. When I went off to college, I spent the Christmas holidays visiting some Eastern girls, and papa didn't see me for a whole year. Then he nearly fainted—I'd grown so! Yet I'd grown just as much the year before, but he never noticed it because I was living at home where he saw me every day. It's the same way with a city like this, Harlan. I haven't been here for so long that I can see the change. Everything is going to happen that Dan prophesied."

She had spoken with gravity, but Harlan laughed, not impressed. "Yes, the boosters brag of the increase in population shown by the last census," he said. "We've got a few thousand more Italians and Polish Jews and negroes, I suppose; and some new ugly factories and dwelling-houses of objectionable architecture. They're beginning to build awful little shacks they call 'bungalows,' hurrying them up by the dozen. Is that the glorious cosmopolis of your hero's prophecies, Martha? To my mind it's only an extension of hideousness, and down where I live, in my grandmother's old house, it's getting so smoky in winter that the air is noxious—the whole town's dirty, for that matter."

"Yes," she said. "Yesterday, as soon as I got here, I noticed that even in summer the air's smokier than it used to be. I think the city was a cleaner place and a better-looking place when I went away. There's the smoke, of course, and I've already seen how they're beginning to tear old buildings down and put up bigger ones, and no building has any thought of having the slightest relation to the ones on each side of it. In a way, as you say, it's getting hideous, though some of these long, wide streets are pleasant, even to a person who's stayed in Europe too long perhaps—and National Avenue is really beautiful. I don't know where except in towns like this you'll find a long street of such big, solid, comfortable houses with green trees and clean lawns about them. This part of the town, at least, hasn't changed; but a change has begun, and I believe it's the growth—I think it's the incredible growth that Dan predicted, Harlan. I think it's begun."

Again she had spoken gravely, though with a glinting look at him which had in it some hint of triumph, and piqued him.

"Well, if this fabulous growth has begun," he said

incautiously, "you're surely not hero-worshipper enough to think it's going to extend as far as Ornaby Addition, are you?"

She had hoped for this, had led him into it. "Papa's going to begin building an extension of the Tennessee Avenue car line next month," she said. "I forced him to admit how far out it would run."

"Not so far as the Addition?"

"Within an eighth of a mile of it," said Martha. "That's what made him so noisy!"

CHAPTER XX

HARLAN was astonished, but he took his little defeat well; and Martha in turn encountered a surprise, for he showed a discomfited kind of pleasure. "So Ornaby Addition's going to get its rapid transit at last," he said. "That's not so bad, you know. Why, Dan might come out pretty well on the thing after all!"

"But doesn't that annoy you, Harlan?" she asked.

"You mean that I want to see my brother beaten? That I really haven't good will toward him?"

"No, indeed I don't. I mean: Wouldn't it annoy you to find you'd always been mistaken about him?"

"But I'm not. I grew up in the same house with him, and I ought to know him. If he does happen to do anything with his wild old idea after all, it'll be by the grace of a series of miracles no one could possibly have foreseen."

"That is to say," Martha observed, "you'd call him 'a fool for luck.'"

"Let's put it, I hope he is."

"And you were just telling me I didn't change!" she cried.

"Yes," he returned placidly;—"it seems we're neither of us wiser than we used to be. We sit here talking of Dan and his Addition just as we'd have been talking about them if you'd never been away. You really ought to be speaking with a slight foreign accent and unable to put your mind on anything later than the seventeenth century."

She nodded, agreeing. "Yes, it's queer; and it makes me feel a little queer. You go away and stay for ever and ever; then you come back home and by the time your trunk's unpacked you're ready to

159

wonder if you've been away at all;—maybe you've just had a long dream. Of course, too, I knew what was going on at home—not through papa!—but some of the girls of our old set here have been faithful about writing, in spite of their every single one of 'em getting married. That makes me feel I belong to the seventeenth century—almost 'cinquecento!' "

"I'd prefer the 'cinquecento,'" Harlan said, and immediately added: "Not that I care for it myself."

"What!" she cried, her eyes widening. "You'd even criticize the Renaissance?"

It appeared that he would, and willingly. Offhand he called the Renaissance "a naïve movement amusingly overrated and with the single merit that it was better than what had gone before." Martha was indignant, and they had an argument in which she proved to be no match for him. He had not been abroad since his junior vacation as an undergraduate, but he knew a great deal more about Italy than she did, though she had just come from long residence there. She continued to disagree with him, and presently was surprised by the suspicion that she enjoyed hearing him talk, and in a way, found him congenial in spite of their differences.

"You're the only person I ever heard of that criticized the Renaissance," she said, when he got up to go. "You're all wrong, of course, even if I can't prove it. You're too much for me, but that's only because you're such an admirable bookworm."

Then, as he went down the long path to the gate, she observed that his shoulders had acquired a little more habitual stoop in them than she remembered. Otherwise the tall figure might have been that of a thin athlete; and Harlan had a well-shaped head;—she was readily able to comprehend what one of her friends had written her of him: "And Harlan Oliphant seems to be just as sarcastic as he used to be, but he is awfully distinguished-looking as he grows older." Nevertheless, even in this view of his back, Martha found something irritating, something consciously aristocratic, over-fastidious, skeptical, and precise. "That's just what you are!" she said half-aloud, before she turned to go into the house. "You can be rather fascinating, but you're really only an admirable bookworm in a nice, clean white collar!"

The admirable bookworm, unconscious that the definition of him had been enlarged, walked down National Avenue, keeping within the continuous shade of the big maple trees and perplexing himself with introspections as he went. He was dry and cold, as he knew, yet far from incapable of ardour, and he had never entirely lost the ardour he felt for Martha; but what surprised him was the renewed liveliness of that ancient pain she evoked within him. He had thought it dead, but evidently it had only fallen into a doze in her absence.

Of course he asked himself why he should ache because she had at once resumed with him her old critical attitude, and why, moreover, he should care about her at all. She had almost no coquetry and little more of the quality called "sheer feminine charm"; she was too downright and plain-minded to possess much of either. She was not masculine yet, as her father said with the plaintive irascibility of a man who knows because he has suffered, she was imperious. "A man might as well be dead as bossed to death," he often complained. And although she was a handsome creature and graceful, Harlan saw a dozen prettier girls at the new Country Club every day that he played golf there. Notwithstanding all this, she had only to let him see her again after years of absence, and at once his heart leaped, then ached, and he could think of nothing but this Martha who thought so little of himself.

He was not the only member of his family who found Martha's return disturbing; his sister-in-law also had long thoughts connected with the arrival from Italy. That evening before dinner, Dan was whistling in his bathroom, shampooing himself lavishly, when Lena came into his bedroom and addressed him through the open door.

"I suppose you've seen her," she said, and gave utterance to an emotional little titter that quickly stopped his whistling.

He had heard such semblances of amusement from her often enough to understand their prophetic meaning. "In for it again!" was instantly his thought. "Seen her?" he said. "Who do you mean?"

"Your fair mountain range," Lena replied, affecting a light mockery. "Of course you didn't know she's home again! Innocent old Dannie!"

"I heard she was to get here to-day, so I suppose she's here; but I haven't seen her. What about it?"

"Oh, nothing!" Lena returned, continuing her archness. "Do you suppose she can stand it?"

"Stand what?"

"Why, the sight of us—of her old sweetheart married to me," Lena explained. "She's stayed away till she thought she could bear it, but do you suppose she will be able to?"

"Yes, I think she'll bear it," he said gruffly and went on with his lathering.

"How about you? Do you think you'll be able to contain yourself when you—"

"I expect so."

"Why don't you ask me how she looks?" Lena inquired, still

161

affecting to rally him gaily. "I know you're dying to. I've seen her; I was looking from my window and saw her go out and walk up the street this afternoon. I laughed so!"

"What about?"

"She was such a perfect picture of a big Western woman! Absolutely typical!"

"You mean like mother, for instance?"

"No; your mother's a dear thing who'd be lovely anywhere; I never think of her as Western at all," Lena said. "She isn't."

"She is as much as Martha is—or anybody else. She was born here and—"

"Not at all!" Lena interrupted airily. "The real Western woman is like your mountain girl. They love to be huge; that's why they live in the prairie country—so they'll look even bigger. One reason I laughed was because your friend was just exactly as much the typical Western woman after all this time abroad as she was before she went. She was wearing all kinds of expensive clothes, and I haven't a doubt she'd got them in Paris, but on her they looked perfectly as Western as if she'd just bought 'em and put 'em on downtown at Kohn & Sons! Do you suppose you'll be able to control your raptures at all when you meet her again, old innocent Dannie?"

"See here," he said, "I wish you'd let me get fixed for dinner. I had a pretty hot day's work and I'd like to—"

"Of course you would!" Lena said. "You'd like to make yourself beautiful because you're going to hurry over there to her just as soon as you've finished your dinner, aren't you? That's what you have been planning, isn't it?"

"Why, yes; certainly," he answered. "I'd like to have you go with me. She's an old friend of mine and all our family; she's been away a long time, and it wouldn't look very cordial not to—"

"Why, no; so it wouldn't!" Lena mocked, but now her mockery was openly acrid. "It wouldn't look cordial and naturally you'd hate to have her think you lacked cordiality—a woman you were so cordial with you wanted your child to grow up to be like her instead of like its mother!—a woman you were so cordial with you had to hold her hand the very day you brought your bride home! It would be terrible to have her think—"

But here Dan closed the door, though not so sharply as Lena closed the outer door of his bedroom when she went out of it an instant later.

The subject of Martha's return was not again mentioned directly during the evening; and after dinner, when Lena with arch significance inquired of her silent husband why he had settled down at the library table to write business letters when there was "so

162

much to do in the neighbourhood," Dan replied, without looking up, that his letters were important—he'd have to beg to be excused from talking. Lena picked up a book, and retired to the easy-chair and the lamp in the bay window, which had once been Harlan's favourite reading place; but she did not read. She sat looking steadily at her husband—as he thoroughly and uncomfortably understood, though he kept doggedly at his writing.

After a time his mother and father were heard in the hall, going out; and he knew that they were "going over next door" to bid Martha welcome home. They had not mentioned where they were going, and he understood the significance of their not mentioning it—and so did Lena, as she sat watching him. He wondered why he did not rise and say to her: "There's an old friend of mine next door; I haven't seen her for years; I ought to go over and tell her I'm glad she's home, and I want to! There's no reason I shouldn't, and you can make the most of it—I'm going!"

Lena had her own wonderings. She wondered why she was keeping her husband from going. Her thought was that she ought to say: "I don't think I care for you enough any more to have a right to be jealous. Go to your old friend and tell her you're glad she's home again, since you wish to. I'm not so small about it as I'm making you think, and I really don't care."

Lena wondered why she did not say this to her husband;—in a manner she wanted to say it, and at the same time she knew that she would say nothing of the kind, but on the contrary, intended to keep him in fear of what she might do if he made any effort to appear "cordial," as he had said, to Martha. Thus the husband and wife sat—the husband bent over his writing and the wife looking at him, her book in her lap. When she looked away from him it was not to the book that her gaze went, but to the wall across the room, where she saw nothing to please her; and when she had looked at the wall for a time she always looked again at Dan. His own eyes were kept to the writing upon the table, yet he must have been conscious of hers when they were upon him, for a deeper frown came upon his forehead whenever she looked away from the wall and again at him.

After a while Mr. and Mrs. Oliphant were heard returning, and in the library it somehow seemed strange, and like an event out of nature's order, to hear such brisk and cheerful sounds, when the front door opened, letting in the two voices and their owners simultaneously.

"Indeed she is!" Mrs. Oliphant was heard to say, while her husband continued a narrative evidently begun outside.

"And I told her so. I said, 'By George, if an old maid's a person

163

who just gets lovelier and lovelier, Martha, why, then, maybe you're—'"

But here his voice so abruptly dropped to a mumble no one could have doubted that the suppression was in obedience to a tactful gesture of his wife's; nor was it difficult to picture this gesture as a movement of Mrs. Oliphant's hand toward the open door of the library. Immediately afterward the two were heard ascending the stairs; the house again became as quiet as before; Dan went on with his writing, and Lena with her looking and wondering.

Often such a vigil between husband and wife does not end by leaving things as they were before it began. Between the two silent people appear to have taken place communications so imperceptible that neither is definitely aware of them, yet each may be affected by them as if by words spoken. It would seem that there is a danger here; for with couples not well wedded the unspoken words may be too true, or may carry altogether too much revelation. Lena stopped wondering; and then rather slowly it became clear to her that she and her husband no longer cared for each other at all. Long, long she had clung to her belief that she was still in love with him; and now all she had left to her of this was that she could still be jealous of him. "A fine reason for not leaving a man!" she said to herself;— especially a man who really cared about nothing but his business and his boy!

Suddenly she rose from her chair, the book in her lap falling to the floor, where she let it remain; and then she stood still, while Dan glanced up inquiringly from his work and met the strange, examining, hostile look she gave him.

There was a final moment of silence between them before Lena hurried across the room and left him. A minute later Dan rubbed his forehead, wondering again. Upstairs, Lena had not slammed her door.

He had an absent-minded impression that something had happened, but as its nature seemed indefinite, and he had now become more interested in his letters than in Martha's return or Lena's temper, he bent again to his work and kept at it with zest until after midnight.

164

CHAPTER XXI

DAN did not go next day to bid the returned neighbour welcome home—he thought it better to postpone the call of greeting he should have made at once. He knew he should have made it, if even out of no more than mere neighbourliness; but gradually it became postponed into the indefiniteness that means never, a postponement not without parallel when old friends of husbands return. Meanwhile, Martha was not again mentioned by either Lena or her husband; though this is only to say that she was not orally mentioned between them, but continued to be the subject of their silences. Dan did not dare to go to see her; and his own silence, when he was with his wife, was doggedly protestive, while Lena's was inscrutable, though she sometimes gave him evidences of a faintly amused contempt. She permitted him to perceive that she despised him, but not to understand whether she despised him because he wanted to see Martha or because he was afraid to do what he wanted.

Once or twice, when he came from his long day's work, he caught a glimpse of a white figure in the twilight of the Shelbys' veranda, and waved his hat, and thought a hand waved to him in return; but weeks passed and limp midsummer was almost upon the town before he had speech again with the slighted lady, though the slight was always upon his conscience.

Upon a hot Sunday noon, when his father and mother returned from church, he took them to see the "carpenter shop" he had spent the morning making in the old summer-house for young Henry—Henry Daniel no longer, at the boy's own vehement request. The grandparents praised the "carpenter shop" but chided their son for staying away from church to construct it, and their grandson for missing Sunday-school. Dan laughed; he had not been to church in a year; and Henry distorted the cherubic rotundities of his small face into as much ferocity as he could accomplish. "I hate Sunday-school," he declared; and, as his mother joined them just then, he seized her hand. "I don't haf to go 'lessen I want to. You'll never get me in that ole hole again!"

"My gracious!" Dan laughed. "It isn't as bad as all that. You and I might decide to begin goin' again sometime, Henry."

"I won't," Henry said stoutly, and as the group moved across the lawn, returning toward the house, he clung to his mother's hand and repeated that he didn't "haf to." He appealed to Lena piercingly: "I don't haf to if I don't want to, do I, mamma?"

165

"Why, no," his father assured him. "Of course you don't. It wouldn't do you much good, I expect, if you don't like it. You needn't fret, Henry. I guess you'll be a good enough boy without Sunday-school."

"I expect so, maybe," Mr. Oliphant agreed, chuckling at his grandson's vehemence. "It's a good thing your grandmother Savage can't hear you, though, Dan. I never did know what she really believed; in fact, I rather suspect she was an agnostic in her heart—but she'd have been shocked to hear you letting your offspring out of Sunday-school—or anything else—merely because he doesn't like it."

"I expect she would, sir," Dan said. "But all that's changed since her day. People don't believe in—" He stopped speaking and moving simultaneously, and stood staring out at the sidewalk where his brother and Martha Shelby, walking slowly, were returning from church.

"People don't believe in what?" Mr. Oliphant inquired, stopping also.

"I—I don't know, sir," Dan said vaguely, and he began to grow red. Harlan and Martha had turned in at the gate and were coming across the lawn to them.

Martha went first to Lena. "I haven't had a chance to say 'Howdy-do' to you since I came back," she said easily. "I'm ever so glad to see you again." Then she turned to Dan, and gave him her hand with a cordial emphasis of gesture. "It's fine to see you again, too, Dan. I want to congratulate you about Ornaby Addition. You'll have to look out, though."

"I will?" Dan said and added awkwardly, "Well—well, the—the truth is, I'm mighty glad to see you. I mean we're all glad you're back home again, Martha." He was visibly in a state of that almost certain contagion, embarrassment, and so flounderingly that he was embarrassing. He dropped Martha's cordial hand almost as soon as he touched it, and at the same instant turned upon his wife a look of helpless apprehension that would have revealed everything, if revelation were needed. But Lena showed herself as little disconcerted as the steady Martha was; and the look she sent back to her husband held in it something of the hostile examination that had come into her eyes on the evening after Martha's return, though now it was accompanied by a bright glint almost hilariously jeering. It was strikingly successful in effect. Dan gulped, then he stammered: "How—how do you—how do you mean I must look out, Martha?"

She laughed cheerfully. "I mean you must look out for some of those wicked old men downtown. You tried to get them to come in

166

with you at the start, but they wouldn't, and pretty soon they're going to be furious that they let the chance slip. They'll try to get Ornaby away from you, Dan." She turned to the little boy, who had been silenced for a moment by the arrival of this stranger. "I ought to know you," she said. "That's why I stopped on my way home: I wanted to meet you. I live next door. Will you shake hands?"

"No," Henry replied, because his momentary shyness had passed and he felt that this refusal would help to restore the conspicuousness he had been enjoying as the owner of a new "carpenter shop" and a rebel against Sunday-school. "I don't want to. I don't want to shake hands."

"Why, Henry dear!" Mrs. Oliphant intervened, touching her grandson lightly upon the shoulder. "You don't mean that! This is our dear friend that lives next door and likes little boys. You must—"

"I won't!" Henry shouted. "I don't care who she likes, I don't want to shake hands." He intended no discourtesy; he merely wished to be distinguished, and in continuance of that desire immediately doubled himself, placing the top of his head upon the ground. "I can turn a summerset," he said. "Want to see me do it? Watch me! Look!"

He failed to accomplish the proposed feat, but at once attempted it again. "Watch me!" he shouted. "Look at me! Why don't you watch me?"

He went on with his attempts, more and more shrilly demanding the public attention that had wandered from him. Martha had begun to talk to Mrs. Oliphant; and Lena came close to Harlan for a moment. "Didn't leave her accent in Italy!" she murmured in her little voice; and passed on toward the house, displaying daintily upon the short grass pretty white slippers that a girl of twelve might have worn.

Harlan shrugged his shoulders, and his thought was, "Parisian doll!" as it usually was when his sister-in-law irritated him. Certainly, if there were a Parisienne present it was Lena and not the unchanging Martha in her Paris clothes.

The little boy shouted louder and louder, since attention was still denied him;—he tugged at his father's coat, wailing shrilly, "Look at me, papa! Oh, my goodness, can't you watch me?"

Meanwhile Martha, beaming down upon Mrs. Oliphant, nevertheless sent an impersonal glance over that amiable lady's head to where the child thus besieged his father, who seemed to be in a temporary stupor. Dan looked much older, Martha thought, than when she had gone away; and, though she had not expected him to retain for ever an unlined face and his fine figure, she felt a little dismay at finding him settling into what was strikingly like middle-age. He was older and heavier than he need have been, she thought, and a stranger might well have guessed Harlan to be ten years the younger of the two.

Nowhere in Dan, with his broadened, preoccupied, and lined face, his heavy, careless figure and his middle-aged careless clothes, could she discover the jolly boy she had known, or the youth she had danced with in college holidays, or the jaunty young man so dashingly clad who had come home from New York engaged to be married, and told her so on a February walk she would always remember. What was more to her, nowhere in this almost middle-aged man of business, now beginning to be successful, could she discover signs of the spirit that once would have brought him instantly to welcome home an old friend, even if a wife did threaten. Yet he was a man who would have swept Lena aside if she had attempted to interfere with his business, Martha thought—and it was not a thought that made her happier. She moved to depart.

But at this, the insistent Henry, irritated beyond measure by the general indifference to his acrobatics, flung himself upon her, pulling fiercely at her dress. "My goodnuss! Can't you watch me? What's the matter with you? You got to watch me!"

There was a sound of tearing as he pulled at her;—Mr. Oliphant sprang to him and removed him, but Martha picked up the lace flounce partly torn from her skirt, and laughed at the mutilation of her finery. "No harm at all," she said, as both Mr. and Mrs. Oliphant began to apologize for Henry; but their apologies and her reassurances were not distinctly audible; nor were her words of departure as she turned toward the gate with Harlan. Henry had instantly squirmed from his grandfather's grasp and was shriller and louder than ever.

"Now I guess you'll watch me!" he shrieked. "Look at me, gran'pa! Look at me, everybody!" He appealed also to his mother, who had paused near the front steps and stood there, laughing. "Look at me, mamma! Watch me, now! I'm goin' to turn a summerset!" He charged into his father's legs, yelling, "You're not lookin' at me, papa! My goodnuss! Can't you watch me?" And he continued to be overwhelmingly vociferous, but Dan, for the moment, paid no attention.

He was wondering how it had happened that Martha had been so long at home and he had not taken the few steps—just to next door—to tell her he was glad she had come back. What if Lena had made a fuss? It would have been right to go. And there came to him faintly, faintly, the ghost of a recollection of a starry night when he and Martha stood not far from where they were now in this glaring noon. It had strangely seemed to him then that he had had a gift

168

from her, something made of no earthly stuff, something enriching and ineffable. He had forgotten it; but now he remembered, and at the very moment of remembering, it seemed to him that the gift was gone.

He stared blankly at her as she passed through the open gateway, holding her torn dress and chatting with Harlan; while against Dan's legs the vehement Henry was battering himself and shrieking, "Look at me, papa! My goodnuss! Can't you look at me!"

Dan consented, and when Martha and Harlan entered the Shelbys' gate, beyond, they saw that the acrobat, still piercingly vociferous, had collected the attention of all of his audience but one. His mother still stood near the stone front steps, laughing, not looking at him; but his grandparents and his father were applauding him. He was insatiable, however; keeping them in the hot sun while he performed other athletic feats. "You shan't go in the house, gran'ma!" he screamed. "I'm goin' to hop on one leg all across the yard. You got to watch me. You watch me, gran'ma!"

Mrs. Oliphant obediently returned, and the new entertainment began.

"Isn't it awful?" Harlan groaned. "Isn't it dismaying to think what children are coming to nowadays? I'd hoped you'd let me sit on the veranda a little while with you, Martha; but I can't ask you to stay out in an air made hideous by all this squawking and squealing."

"Then you might come in with me," she laughed. "Our walls are pretty thick."

The walls of the big old house were as she said, but open windows brought the shrill, incessant "Watch me!" indoors, and the annoyed Harlan complained further of his nephew. "It makes one respect the Chinese," he said. "They at least pay some attention to ancestors. Only certain tribes biologically very low worship children, I understand; but that seems to be our most prevalent American habit to-day. We're deliberately making this the age of the abject worship of children—and I wish my grandmother could have lived to give her opinion of it!"

"What do you think she'd say, Harlan?"

"Isn't hard to guess! She'd have said we're heading the children straight for perdition. In fact, she thought that about our own generation; she thought father and mother were heading Dan and me that way; yet we were under heavy discipline compared to the way this terrible little Henry's being brought up. Lena's family were severe with her, I understand, and she doesn't believe in discipline. As for Dan, he's always been just the child's slave."

169

Martha looked compassionate. "Yes," she said slowly. "I suppose he had to have something he could worship."

"Well, he's got Ornaby Addition," Harlan suggested dryly.

"No. He had to have something besides. I think he'd have worshipped his wife, if she had ever let him, but I suppose she—"

"No," Harlan said, breaking the indefinite pause into which Martha had absently strayed. "But she's always capable of being jealous." And he looked at Martha from the side of his eye.

"Jealous of me?"

"You've certainly been made well enough aware of it from the very day he brought her home, Martha."

"Oh, yes," she assented cheerfully. "She's never doubted that I've always cared for Dan, but she knows that he wasn't in love with me. She must have always been sure of that, because—well, here I was—he had only to step over next door and ask me, but he asked her, instead. And yet, as you say, she disliked me from the start. She certainly saw I wasn't the sort to take him away from her, even if I'd thought I could—and I knew I couldn't. Yet it's true she was jealous. Do you know what I think really made her so, Harlan? I think almost the principal reason was because I'm so tall."

"What?"

"Yes, I do believe it," Martha insisted. "Someone told me she used to be called 'French doll' in New York, and was very sensitive about it. She wanted to be thought a temperamental and romantic opera heroine, and would never stand near a tall woman because she was afraid of being made to look more like a French doll. I think she couldn't endure the thought of her husband's having a woman friend as big as I am."

"No doubt she's never wanted to be near you herself," Harlan said. "But I think her feeling isn't quite so much on the physical plane as that."

"Oh, yes, it was. A man mightn't understand it, but—"

"A man might, though," he interrupted. "Lena's always been afraid that you're just what she'd call the type of big Western woman Dan ought to have married in order to be happy."

"What?" Martha cried, but her colour deepened, and there was agitation in her voice, though she laughed. "Why, what nonsense!"

"Is it?" Harlan said, and now agitation became evident in his own voice, though he controlled it manfully. "It's what I've always been afraid of, myself."

"No, no!" she cried, her colour still deepening. "That's just nonsense!"

"Is it?" he repeated grimly. "My grandmother Savage didn't

170

think so. She cut Dan off with a shilling because she hoped Lena would leave him and give him a chance to marry you—eventually!"

"Harlan Oliphant! What on earth are you talking about?"

"I think you understand me," he said. "Grandmother was a shrewd old lady, and as good a judge of character as one often sees; but sometimes she overshot the mark, as most of us do, no doubt, when we think we understand other people so thoroughly that we can manipulate their destinies. She thought a good deal that was true about Lena; but she despised her too much, and made the mistake of thinking her purely mercenary. That's why I was the residuary legatee, Martha."

"Of all the nonsense!" she protested, and continued to protest. She'd never heard anything so far-fetched in all her life, she declared—people didn't put such Machiavellian subtleties into their wills; and Harlan was a creative romanticist instead of the critic she'd always believed him to be. But his romancing wasn't successful; it was too incredible.

He listened, skeptically marking the difference between the vehemence of the words she used and the lack of conviction in the voice that uttered them. "Never mind, Martha," he said at last. "I see you believe it and agree with me."

"I don't," she still protested; but her tone was now so feeble that it only proved her determined never to make the open admission of what she denied. "It would be too tragic."

"Why?"

"To think of that poor old woman—"

"Yes," he agreed. "I'm afraid it must irritate her now if she knows."

"To think of her—" Martha said. "Poor thing! I mean it would be too tragic to think of her hoping and planning such—such preposterousness!"

At this Harlan looked at her so sharply, so gravely, that he seemed to ask much more than appeared upon the surface of his question: "But would it be preposterous? Suppose Lena and Dan should—"

"Separate?" she said, as he stopped at the word. "They never will."

"But I asked you, if they should?"

Martha shook her head, smiling faintly; and she looked away from him—far away, it seemed—as she spoke. "People don't stay ardently in love forever, Harlan. I don't suppose anybody stays in love with anybody—forever. I think I used to believe I'd always be in love with Dan, and in a way that was true—whatever is left in me of the girl I used to be will always be in love with the boy he used to be. But I don't know where that boy is any more. Do you understand?"

Harlan looked melancholy, as he nodded. "I suppose so."

"I mean I'm true to my memory of him, perhaps. I'm afraid I don't know just what I do mean."

"I'm afraid I do, though," he said. "I'm afraid it's only that you're hurt with him because Lena frightened him into keeping from even stepping over here for a minute to say, 'Welcome home.'"

"No; it didn't hurt—not exactly," she returned. "But he does seem changed." She frowned. "Do you think he's lost something, Harlan? Is it something—something fine about him—that's lost? It seems to me—it seems to me there must be. How could anybody expect a man to go through such a struggle for success as the one he's been through and not bear the marks of it? Or maybe is it only his youthfulness he's lost?"

"I don't see anything missing," Harlan replied. "He's certainly not lost his optimistic oratory; he can still out-talk any man in town on the subject of Our Glorious Future. In fact, I think he's even more that way than he used to be. Years ago he may have shown a few very faint traces of having been through a university, but you could sandpaper him to powder now and not find them: I don't believe he could translate the first sentence of Cæsar, or 'Arma, virumque cano!' The only things he ever talks about are his business and his boy and local politics. I think that's all he can talk about."

"Whereas," Martha said, with a flash of the old championing, "the learned Mr. Harlan Oliphant has only to open his mouth in order to destroy a lonely woman's whole joy in the Italian Renaissance."

He lifted his hands, protesting, then dropped them in despair. "So I've lost it already!" he said. "And lost it in the old, old way!"

"Lost what?"

"Hope," he explained. "You see I'm years and years older than Freddie Oliphant, and he was complaining to me the other day;— he's now considered so much 'one of the older men' that some of the pretty young things one sees at the Country Club were leaving him out of their festivities. You see where that puts me. So I hoped that when you came home—"

"Yes?"

"Well, I hoped that maybe you and I shouldn't quarrel any more, and—"

"Quarrel? No; we mustn't, indeed!" she said. "What else is there left for left-overs to do but to make the best of each other?"

"Nothing else, I'm afraid."

"And I'd hoped," he went on a little nervously;—"I'd hoped

maybe you'd let me see you a good deal—that you'd let me take you places and—"

"Good gracious!" Martha cried; and she laughed and blushed. "Haven't you just taken me to church? Aren't you already taking me places, Harlan?"

CHAPTER XXII

MARTHA had said that Dan's remaining away "didn't hurt—not exactly"; and by this she meant to give Harlan the impression that she was less than hurt; but such a denial, thus qualified, means in truth more than hurt. She was a "big Western woman," but she could be sensitive, and had her resentments and her smallnesses. Perhaps she was not quite genuinely sorry to believe that the old friend who neglected to bid her welcome home had begun to look almost middle-aged and seemed to have lost something fine that he had possessed in his youth. There were characteristic possessions of his that he had not lost, however; he had even acquired more of them, as she discovered one evening a few weeks after the Sunday noon when little Henry tore her dress.

Mr. Shelby had come home from his office in a state of irritability, which he made audible even before he entered the house; and from her windows upstairs she heard him denouncing his old negro driver. There had been a thunderstorm earlier in the afternoon, but that was no excuse—"not a dog-gone bit of excuse!" Mr. Shelby declared—for a carriage to be "all so sploshed-over with mud that a decent man'd be ashamed to get caught dead in it!" And he seemed to resent the fat old servitor's wheezy explanation that the mud was the work of a malevolent motor-car. "Cain't go nowhur them automob'les ain' goin' to git you these days! I had my carri'ge all spick-an'-span. Automob'le come zimmin' by jes' as we turn onto the avenoo. 'Splickety-splick-splash!' she say, an' zoosh! jes' look at my nice clean carri'ge solid mud! No, suh, Mist' Shelby; I had my carri'ge all wash up fresh. Nasty ole automob'le spoil ev'ything! No, suh, I—"

"Gee-mun-nent-ly!" Martha heard her father exclaim. "What you tryin' to do? Talk me to death? I already heard enough talk in my office for one day, thank you! By Cripey, you stop that eternal

173

gab o' yours and get those horses into the barn and sponge their mouths out! Hear me?"

He came into the house and could be heard muttering snappishly to himself on the stairway, as he ascended to his room to "wash his face and hands for dinner." But at the table he proved that soap and water were ineffective, at least to remove bitterness from a face; and he found fault with everything. The most unbearable of his troubles finally appeared to be put upon him by the salt, which the humidity of the weather had affected. "I s'pose this is the way you keep house in Italy!" he said. "Nothin' but smell and deggeredation over there anyway—they prob'ly don't care whether they can get salt out o' their saltcellars or not. But in this country, in a decent man's house, he'd like to see at least one saltcellar on his table that'd work!"

"It's apt to be like that in hot weather after a rain," Martha returned placidly. "What went wrong at the office this afternoon, papa?"

"Nothin'!" he said fiercely. "What's my office got to do with wet salt? Why can't you ever learn to keep some connection between your thoughts? Geemunently!"

"So you had a good day, did you, papa?"

"It would 'a' been," he replied angrily, "if it hadn't been for a fool friend o' yours!"

"Somebody I'm responsible for?" she inquired with a genial sarcasm that exasperated him into attempted mockery—for when he was angriest with her he would repeat something she said, and, to point the burlesque, would speak in a tinny and whining falsetto which he seemed to believe was a crushing imitation of his daughter's voice. " 'Somebody I'm responsible for?' " he squeaked, using this form of reprisal now. "No; it ain't somebody you're responsible for!" Here he fell back upon downright ferocity. "Doggone him! Somebody better be responsible for him!"

At this Martha made a good guess. "Dan Oliphant!"

"Yes, ma'am! And I came within just one o' throwin' him out o' my office! Stood up there and grinned at me in front o' my own desk and told me what I had to do! What I had to do!"

"And do you have to, papa?" she asked.

"What!"

"I only wondered—"

"Why, plague take him, I never saw the beat of it!" he went on, disregarding her. "Walked right into my office and told me I had to run my car line all the way across his Addition. Told me I had to! I told him we were goin' almost to the edge of it and that'd be every last speck o' the way we'd move until he does the right thing."

174

"Until he does what 'right thing,' papa?"

"Until he quits bein' a hog!" the old man returned violently. "He seems to think the best men in this town got nothin' on earth to do but spend their time buildin' up his property for him and makin' it more valuable, all for his benefit. I told him when he was ready to act like a decent man and reorganize his holdings with a good trust company's advice, and issue stock, and let somebody else in, we might talk to him and not before."

"What did Dan say?"

"Said he tried to get us in at the start, and now we could go plum to! Said I'd put that car line through there whether I wanted to or not. Threatened me with a petition of his lot owners, and said they were liable to go before the legislature and get my charter annulled, if I didn't do it."

"Was he angry, papa?"

"Angry? No!" Mr. Shelby vociferated. "What in continental did he have to be angry about? I was the one that was angry. He stood up there and laughed and bragged about what he was goin' to do till you'd thought he'd bust with the gas of it! Why, Great Geemunently!—you'd thought this whole city's got nothin' to do but turn in and run around doin' what Ornaby Addition says it's got to! I says, 'Yes!' I says. 'So from now on the tail's goin' to wag the dog, is it?' 'I don't know but it might,' he says. 'This town's done considerable laughin' at me,' he says. 'I expect it's about time I did some laughin' myself,' he says. 'You'll have to look out for your charter, Mr. Shelby,' he says."

Martha ventured to continue her naïveté, and unfortunately carried it too far. "And will you have to look out for it, papa?" she asked gently.

With his thin but hard old fist he struck the table a blow that jarred the china and jingled the silver. "Haven't you got any sense?" he shouted. "I'll show him who he's talkin' to! There's a few men left in this town that'll teach him a little before he gets through with 'em! I'm not the only one he thinks he can lay down the law to." He glared at her, his small gray face flushing with his increased anger. "Are you still standin' up for him after the way he's treated you?"

This took Martha's breath, and for an instant she was at a loss. Never before had her father seemed to notice how she was "treated"—by anybody. "I don't know what you—I don't know what you mean," she said.

"Don't you?" he returned sharply, and, before the bright stare of his angry eyes, her own troubled gaze fell. "You say you don't know what I mean?"

"Why—no. Not—not at all," she murmured.

175

"Well, I do!" And with a brief shot of breath between his almost closed lips, he further expressed an emotion that remained enigmatic to her. He rose. "Seems to me it's about time you quit standin' up for him," he said; and stalked out of the room, leaving her still at the table.

She sat there in an attitude of some rigidity after she had heard him go upstairs, and she continued to sit there, though she had finished her dinner before he departed. The conclusion she reached in her thoughts was that there was a question she would never ask him;—she would never ask him what he had meant by that final remark of his. She hoped he meant only that her pride ought to resent a neighbour's failure to come to say he was glad to see her at home again—but she feared her father meant more than this. She feared he meant much more, and she so feared it that she would never dare to ask him.

Yet she wondered why she wouldn't dare. How could it ever be "about time" for her to stop standing up for an old friend? And when Harlan was announced to her, as she sat alone at the table, she rose with a little sigh. She did not sigh because she was sorry he had come; it was because she had just realized how much more his brother was still the heart of her thoughts than was this faithful and constant escort.

For she and Harlan had already fallen into a relation not uncommon among those she had spoken of as "left-overs": a relation that becomes a habit—a habit that in turn becomes a relation. She "went everywhere" with him; and continued to go everywhere with him; and so, after a while, their contemporaries, all married, never sent an invitation to one without including the other. Then, as time went on, and the habit continued and continued, it became common stock in the prattle of more dashing and precipitous younger people. When talk languished and even weather stencils failed to cover a blank, those who felt such covering a necessity could always fall back on this, and wonder why the two didn't "get married and be done with it."

In that manner a worn woman-of-the-world, aged twenty, complained to Frederic Oliphant one evening at the Country Club, as he sat with her after unsuccessfully attempting an imported dance he found himself too old to learn. "You aren't too old to learn it, if you wouldn't insist on being too polite to hold a girl as tight as these boys do," the woman-of-the-world informed him with the new frankness then becoming fashionable. "You aren't as old as your cousin Harlan. Why on earth don't he and Miss Shelby get married and be done with it? They've certainly been just the same as engaged for almost as long as I can remember. Everybody says they

176

must be engaged—by this time! They say she used to be in love with his brother. I don't see how anybody could be in love with him!"

She glanced through an archway, near by, to where Dan and his wife and Martha and Harlan and a dozen other people were gravely straggling out of the dining-room; all of this party having the air of concluding a festival that had not proved too hilarious. Dan, in particular, appeared to have thought the occasion a solemn one. He had been placed next to Martha; and she remarked cheerfully that it was the first time he had been so near her "in ages." After that, however, she found little more to say to him, since he seemed to encounter certain definite difficulties in saying anything to her in return.

"I am coming in to—to call, some evening," he stammered, laughing uncomfortably to express his cordiality. "I'd have been to see you—I'd have been over oftener, except—" He paused, then concluded his ill-fated excuses hurriedly—"except I'm so busy these days." And he glanced uneasily across the table to where Lena sat smiling mysteriously at him.

Martha thought it tactful, and the part of a true friend, to talk to Harlan, who sat next to her on the other side.

CHAPTER XXIII

"HOW in the world did that cunning little wife of his ever fall in love with him?" Frederic's companion inquired, watching the emerging procession of the dining party. "He always looks as if he had something else on his mind when he's with women—as if he didn't think they're worth talkin' to. She looks about half his age. Of course you can't tell, though; everybody uses so much makeup nowadays. They say she belongs to awf'ly important people in New York and never liked it here because she couldn't get enough music. You didn't answer my question: Aren't they ever goin' to get married? I mean your cousin Harlan and that big Miss Shelby. How in the world do they find anything to say to each other? Gosh, if I kept a man hangin' on that long I'd certainly be talked out! How in the world can two people stand seein' each other all the time like that?"

"I can comprehend the gentleman's half of it," said the gallant

177

Frederic. "I believe Miss Shelby goes abroad for a few months now and then to make her own share of the association more endurable."

Martha had been at home only a week, in fact, after one of these excursions; though she did not make them for the reason set forth by Frederic Oliphant, who was now much given to the reading of eighteenth-century French memoirs and the polishing of his diction. She went, she airily explained to Harlan, to gather materials that would enable her to defend the Renaissance; but as he drove home with her from the dinner at the Country Club, this evening, he observed that the materials she had gathered impressed him as "about as deep into the twentieth century as mechanics and upholsterers were able to go." His allusion was to the expensive closed car she had brought from Paris;—her old bit of hickory, impossible to be bent an atom's width in business, yielded with no more than a faint squeak when his daughter was lavish with herself. "Spend what you plague-taken want to," he said, "so long as you don't ask me to ride in the devilish contrapshun!"

"He says he'll stick to his horses and our old carriage until they're 'chased off the road,'" Martha told Harlan, on this homeward drive. "It doesn't seem to me that's so far ahead. Why hasn't Dan ever done anything about the motor-car factory he was going to build?"

"He has," Harlan said, and laughed. "In talk he has, that is! He's been talking about it for years, almost as much as he has about Ornaby."

"Then why doesn't he—"

"Still dancing on the tight-rope!" Harlan laughed. "He's got his car line through the Addition—I understand your father explodes completely whenever it's mentioned to him—but Dan's spending fortunes on new streets and sewers and what not. He's actually trying to open a big tract still farther out, north of Ornaby; and I don't believe he's able to keep money in his hands long enough to go into building cars. You'd think he's building them though, if you'd listen to him! He talks about the 'Ornaby Car' to everybody; I suppose he believes it's a lucky name. He has got his Addition booming though—no question. He's making the countryside more and more horrible every day. It's much worse than it was last year."

"How is it horrible?"

"I could tell you, but it's ten to one that if I merely told you, you'd become Ornaby's defender—you're so everlastingly its defender! I'd rather show you, if you'd take me as a passenger in this jewelled palanquin of yours to-morrow."

Martha assented, and the next afternoon her neat young

178

mechanic drove them northward over the road once travelled on a hot and threatening morning by a "rubber-tired runabout" in which sat a disappointed little bride and a perplexed bridegroom. On that dusty morning, already of the long ago, the way had soon become rustic; the cedar-block paving, itself worn and jolty, had stopped short not much more than a mile from its beginning; then came macadam, but not for long; and then the rough country road, leading north between the great flat fields of corn and wheat to where it became a slough in winter, and tall grass and even ironweed grew between the ruts in summer—for there it reached the soggy and tangled groves of Ornaby.

But on this brisk autumn afternoon, the crystal and enamel of the silent French car went glistening serenely along a level white way of asphalt. The fields, above which the troubled bride and groom had seen rising the clouds of the summer storm, were fields no longer; for here was bungalow-land, acres and acres of bungalows, with brick groceries and drug stores at some of the street corners, and two or three wooden church spires slenderly asserting their right to look down on all the rest. Cross streets gave glimpses of trolley cars on other north-and-south thoroughfares; great brick schoolhouses, unbearably plain, were to be seen, and a few apartment buildings, not made more beautiful by pinchbeck torturing of their façades.

"Of course Dan has no responsibility for this particular awfulness," Harlan explained. "Without rime or reason the town just decided to grow, and luckily for him it's grown faster out this northern way than it has in any other direction. Some people seem to think he performed an enchantment to make it do it, but it just happened."

"It seems to happen faster and faster," Martha observed. "The last time I drove out this far was in our old carriage with papa, not quite a year ago, I think; and there were dozens of vacant lots; but now there are hardly any. The asphalt wasn't finished clear into Ornaby then, though Dan had built a fine road through. I suppose now—"

"Oh, yes; now he's got asphalt on his cross streets, too; and the southern part of Ornaby is so like this you couldn't tell when you get into it, if it weren't for the disasters he calls his signboards. Look at that!"

As they spoke the swift car had brought them into a region where there was more vacant ground; and the little houses, nearly all of wood, were not so closely crowded. On a stretch of weedy land, rising slightly above new cement sidewalks, there smote the eye a painted wooden wall two hundred feet long. With enormous yellow

179

words on a black background the thing not only staggered the vision of a passer-by, but seemed to bellow in his ear: "You Are Now Entering Ornaby Addition! Build a Home in Ornaby the Beautiful! Every Ornaby Buyer is an Ornaby Booster."

Beyond came a region of more bungalows: "Homes Beautiful of Ornaby the Beautiful" another bellowing signboard declared them to be; and, not blushing in the very presence of the dwellings and dwellers it thus made proclamation for, went on to insist once more upon the enthusiasm necessarily a consequence in the bosom of any one who became an "Ornaby Buyer." There was a briskness about the place: children went busily roller-skating over the new sidewalks; clotheslines were flying their Monday white pennants on the breeze; other bungalows were noisily getting themselves built, and farther on were some white cottages;—"quite pretty," Martha said they were. Beyond them the open spaces were broader, and the little houses more infrequent; but the asphalt street went on, with numbered white posts marking the building lots, paved cross streets running to right and left into thicket-bordered distances, and Dan's great signboards shouting along the front of untouched acres of old forest.

"You see for yourself," Harlan said. "This was beautiful before 'Ornaby the Beautiful' insulted the landscape. But now, with all these flimsy and dreadful bungalows and the signboards screeching at the trees—"

"Yes," she interrupted, "but he's spared all the trees he could, even back there where the bungalows and little houses were so thick. And I noticed the people were planting shrubberies and trying to make little gardens grow. It might be really very pretty some day. And just here—"

"Oh, here," Harlan said, "where he hasn't touched it yet, it's well enough, of course. But you'll find it's only a question of time till he spoils it, though I understand he intends this to be what he calls a 'restricted residence district.'"

The paved street ran between tall woods now; the numbered lots were broad, and the car passed a few proudly marked "Sold." Then Martha noticed one that was several hundred feet wide, and in depth extended indefinitely into a grove of magnificent beech trees. Stone pillars gave entrance upon a partly completed driveway that disappeared round an evergreen thicket, not long planted. "What a pleasant place to live! It's getting so smoky in town it seems to me people will have to be moving out even this far some day. Whose place is that?"

"Dan's," Harlan said, with his dry laugh. "At least he says he plans to build there sometime. I don't think Lena cares about it

180

much! I heard her speaking of it as 'out at the end of Nowhere.' One of the interesting things about my sister-in-law, to me, is the fact that she's really never wanted a house of her own. She's never once proposed such a thing in all this time, I believe, but goes on living with father and mother; and year after year passes without altering that air of hers of being only temporarily marooned in what she still calls 'the West.'"

Martha looked serious, but said nothing, and he spoke to the chauffeur, who turned westward at the next cross street. At the end of a block it ceased to be a street and became a newly gravelled road, a transformation that interested Harlan. "Funny!" he said. "I was out this way a couple of months ago and this was a dirt road with a good deal of grass on it. Now he's had it gravelled. It leads over to the west side of his land, where he laid out the site for his factory, years ago. I thought you might like to see that."

But before they approached the site of Dan's factory, they passed a long line of trucks and wagons bound their way; wagon after wagon laden with bricks, and truck loads of lumber, of drainage tile, of steel girders and of cement, and there were great-wheeled carriers of stone. As they came closer they saw that many two-story double houses for workmen and their families were being built on both sides of the road; and, beyond these, long lines of brick walls were rising, broken into regular open oblongs where the ample glass of a modern factory building was to be set.

"By George!" Harlan exclaimed, surprised almost to the point of dismay. "He is going it! Why, he's got the thing half up!" And he said, "By George!" again, seeing the figure of his brother on a section of roof and outlined against the sky. "There he is—and in his element!"

"You mean in the sky?" Martha asked, her eyes brightening.

"No; I mean hustling. Keeping everybody on the jump while he defaces the landscape some more! That's his element, isn't it?"

Dan was indeed in that element and it was truly his. He could be seen waving his arms at the workmen; shouting to foremen; running along the roof and calling to teamsters, instructing them where to dump their loads. His voice was audible to the occupants of the French car that stopped for a few moments in the road; and they became aware that he addressed the workmen, both white and coloured, by their first names or their nicknames exclusively; his shoutings were all to "Jim" or "Mike" or "Shorty" or "Tony" or "Gumbo."

A moment after the car stopped, a smaller figure climbed up the slope of the low roof and joined the towering and bulky one on the ridge. "He's got my charming-mannered nephew with him,"

181

Harlan said. "What time he can spare from spoiling the landscape he puts into spoiling Henry!"

"Is that Henry?" Martha asked incredulously; then, as she saw Dan put his right arm about the boy's shoulder, guarding him carefully from a misstep, she replied to herself. "Yes, it really is. Gracious, how time runs away from us!"

Turning to shout at some one in their direction, Dan saw them, and waved his free arm cordially in greeting; but he made no motion as if to descend, and went on immediately with his shouting to the men. Martha said, "We'll go now," to the chauffeur; and the car instantly moved forward.

She leaned back, smiling. "He's in his glory," she said. "It all goes on arriving, Harlan. His great days have come!"

CHAPTER XXIV

SHE was right; the growth was now visibly upon the pleasant and substantial town, where all had once appeared to be so settled and so finished; for, just as with some of man's disorders that develop slowly, at first merely hinting in mild prophetic symptoms, then becoming more sinister, and attacking one member after another until the whole body writhes and alters, so it is with this disorder that comes racking the midland towns through distortions and turmoil into the vaster likenesses of cities: haphazard and insignificant destructions begin casually, but gradually grow more sweeping and more violent until the victim town becomes aware of great crashings;—and then lies choking in a cloud of dust and smoke wherein huge new excrescences appear.

Cameras of the new age sometimes record upon strips of moving film the slow life of a plant from the seed to the blossoming of its flower; and then there is thrown upon the screen a picture in which time is so quickened that the plant is seen in the very motions of its growth, twisting itself out of the ground and stretching and swelling to its maturity, all within a few minutes. So might a film record be made of the new growth bringing to full life a quiet and elderly midland town; but the picture would be dumfounding. Cyclone, earthquake, and miracle would seem to stalk hand-in-hand upon the screen; thunder and avalanche should play in the orchestra pit.

182

In such a picture, block after block of heavy old mansions would be seen to topple; row on row of stout buildings would vanish almost simultaneously; families would be shown in flight, carrying away their goods with them from houses about to crumble; miles of tall trees would be uprooted; the earth would gape, opening in great holes and long chasms;—the very streets would unskin themselves and twist in agony; every landmark would fly dispersed in powder upon the wind, and all old-established things disappear.

Such a picture would be but the truth with time condensed;— that is to say, the truth made like a man's recollection of events— and yet it would not be like the truth as the truth appeared to Daniel Oliphant and the other men who made the growth, nor like their subsequent memories. For these men saw, not the destruction, but only the city they were building; and they shouted their worship of that vision and were exultant in the uproar. They shouted as each new skyscraper rose swimming through the vast drifts of smoke, and shouted again as the plain, clean, old business streets collapsed and the magnificent and dirty new ones climbed above the ruins. They shouted when business went sweeping outward from its centre, tearing away the houses where people had lived contentedly for so long; and they shouted again as the new factory suburbs marched upon the countryside, far and wide, and the colossal black plumes of new chimneys went undulating off into a perpetual smoke-mist, so that the distant level plain seemed to be a plain surrounding not a city, but an ever-fuming volcano.

Once again, in the interminably cycling repetition of the new displacing the old, then becoming the old and being displaced in turn, an old order was perishing. The "New Materialism" that had begun to grow with the renewed growing of the country after the Civil War, and staggered under the Panic of '73, but recovered and went on growing egregiously, had become an old materialism now. It had done great things and little things. Amongst the latter, it had furnished Europe with a caricature type of the American—the "successful American business man." On the shelf, beside the figure of the loud-tweeded Boxing Briton with his "side whiskers," Europe set the lank-and-drawling, chin-bearded, palace-buying Boaster of the Almighty Dollar, the Yankee of the great boom period.

That had been a great railroad-making and railroad-breaking period; the great steel period; the great oil period; the great electric-invention period; the great Barnum-and-Bunkum period; the period of "corrupt senators"; of reform; and of skyscrapers thirty stories high. All this was old now, routed by a newer and more gorgeous materialism. The old had still its disciplines for the young and its general appearance of piety; bad children were still whipped

183

sometimes, and the people of best reputation played no games on Sunday, but went to church and seemed to believe in God and the Bible with almost the faith of their fathers. But many of these people went down with their falling houses; a new society, swarming upward above the old surfaces, became dominant. It began to breed, among other things, a new critic who attacked every faith, and offered, instead of mysteries, full knowledge of all creation as merely a bit of easily comprehended mechanics. And in addition to discovering the secret of the universe, the new society discovered golf, communism, the movies, and the turkey trot; it spread the great American cocktail over the whole world, abolished horses, and produced buildings fifty stories high.

. . . The slow beginnings of the new growth in the town had been imperceptible except to a few exuberant dreamers—the most persistent somnambulist of whom was Dan Oliphant—but now that the motion was daily more visible to all men, there was no stopping it. Hard times and prosperity were all one to it;—it marched, and so did its chief herald and those who went shouting before it with him, while the "old conservative business men," the Shelbys and Rowes and John P. Johnses, sat shaking their heads and muttering "Gamblers!"

Gamblers, or destroying angels, or prophets, whatever they were, they went trampling forward in thunder and dust. The great Sheridan, of the Trust Company and the Pump Works, had joined them. Unscrupulous and noisiest of the noisy, he was like a war band drumming and brassily trumpeting with the vanguard. There was Eugene Morgan who had begun building the "Morgan Car" when automobiles were a joke, and now puffed forth from his long lanes of shops black smoke that trailed off unendingly to the horizon that it dimmed. Pendleton, of the new "Pendleton Tractor," marched with these, and old Sam Kohn and Sol Kohn and Sam Kohn, Junior—the Kohns were tearing down the Amberson Block, the very centre and business temple of the old town, the corner of National Avenue and First Street—and there were the Rosenberg Brothers, apartment builders who would buy and obliterate half a dozen solid old houses at a time. There were the Schmidts, the Reillys, the younger Johnsons, third generation of the old firm of Abner Johnson's Sons, and there were the Caldinis, the Comiskeys, and the Hensels, as well as all the never-resting optimists who had come to the town from farms and villages to blast it into nothingness and build their own city and build themselves into it.

In the din of all the tearing down and building up, most of the old family names were not heard, or were heard but obscurely, or perhaps in connection with misfortunes; for many of the old families were vanishing. They and their fathers and grandfathers had slowly made the town; they had always thought of it as their own, and they had expected to sit looking out upon it complacently forever from the plate glass of their big houses on National Avenue and the two other streets parallel to the avenue and nearest it. They had built thick walls round themselves, these "old families," not only when they built the walls of their houses, but when they built the walls encircling their close association with one another. The growth razed all these walls; the "sets" had resisted the "climbers," but the defences fell now; and those who had sheltered behind them were dispersed, groping for one another in the smoke.

It was Dan Oliphant who began the destruction of National Avenue. Among the crumbling families were the Vertreeses;—they retired to what was left of their country estate, which had already been overtaken by the expanding town and compressed to half an acre. Dan bought the old Vertrees Mansion on National Avenue, tore it down and built upon its site a tremendous square box of concrete fronted with glass—the "sales building" of the "Ornaby Four, the Car of Excellent Service." This was just across the street from where his grandmother had lived, and Harlan protested long and loudly; but Dan was too busy to give his brother a complete attention. He said mildly that his new building seemed at least an improvement upon the shabby boarding-house, which the Vertrees Mansion had become when he bought it; and, when Harlan hotly denied the improvement, Dan sat listening with an expression of indulgence, the while occupying his mind with computations concerning other matters.

For, as Martha had felt, these were his great days, and he was "in on" everything. The Earl of Ornaby was earl of more than Ornaby now; Ornaby and the "Ornaby Four" were but two of the adventurous fleets he had at sea. He was "in on" a dozen "promotions" at once; "in on" the stock of new "industrials"; inventors and exploiters lived at his office doors. And although all of his fellow-hustlers used the phrase, none could say "my city" with a greater right than he. When he began one of his boostings with, "I believe first of all in my own city," the voice of a religion was heard. He was his city; he was its spirit, and more than any other he was its guide, and yet its slave and worshipper. He could not speak of it except with reverence, nor go on speaking of it long unless he made the eagle scream.

He had become a juggler of money, which poured streaming into one hand as fast as he hurled it aloft with the other. He was one of those men of whom it is said, "Nobody knows what he's worth. He couldn't tell you, himself, to save his life!" He was called "rich," and sometimes he was said to be the richest man in town. He juggled with money, with land, with houses, with skyscrapers, and with factories, keeping them all in the air at once; and his brother said that even so, Dan still "danced the tight-rope," maintaining his balance dangerously during the juggling. Meanwhile, as he balanced and tossed the glittering and ponderous things through the air, the rest of the deafening show went on; the hustling and booming and boosting moving round and round him in clouds of dust to the sound of brass bands, while crowds gazed marvelling up at the juggler, and admired and envied him.

Of all the admirers who now looked up to him, cheering, probably the most enthusiastic was his brother-in-law, George McMillan, whom Dan had made "General Manager of the Ornaby Four." George had not quite fulfilled his own prediction that at forty he was to be a "drunken broker"; but he had come, as he said, "near enough to it"; and he was glad when Dan finally sent for him and his designer of a new gasoline engine, the prospective "Ornaby Four."

"It's the greatest idea in the world," George told his sister. "It's cheap, but not the cheapest; it doesn't compete with the commonest little cars, nor, on the other hand, with even the moderately expensive ones. It's got a place of its own in between, where there are millions of people that can afford a little better car than the cheapest, but wouldn't dream of a luxurious one like the 'Morgan.' It was an inspiration of Dan's to set the price of the 'Ornaby' at eight hundred and eighty-five dollars. I like the sense of adventure you get in a game like this. I like getting out of my New York, and I like the way things move in a place so friendly as this. It's immensely alive, but somehow it does manage to be friendly, too. I don't understand why you've always hated it so."

She explained that she had hated it less when she was in Europe, where she had at last got her year, having taken young Henry with her in spite of her husband's strong protest. The mother and son had just returned. "I think I could stand the place perfectly well, George," she said, "if I were quite sure I'd never have to see it again!"

"But don't you begin to understand yet what a husband you've got?" George cried. "Why, he's a great man, Lena!"

Lena laughed and looked at him pityingly; but contented herself with that for argument. To her mind Dan was not made great by becoming the great figure of a city that was merely growing larger, noisier, and dirtier. She had never cared for anything but Beauty, she said; and, to her mind, as to that of the fastidious Harlan, Dan was only helping to increase hideousness; so she joined her brother-in-law in habitually referring to "Ornaby the Beautiful"

186

as "Ornaby the Horrible." Moreover, although she had never manifested any interest in National Avenue before its destruction began, she became almost vehement upon the subject of its merit as the razing of its old houses continued; and Harlan was again in agreement with her here.

"You and Eugene Morgan and that rascally old Sheridan and your Jew friends are doing an awful thing," he said to Dan at a family dinner. "You're ruining the one decent thing the city possessed—a splendid, dignified old street. It's happening all over the country—one doesn't need half an hour in New York to see that Fifth Avenue is ruined; but I did think we might have escaped here. I doubt if it would ever have occurred to Morgan to put up his awful sales building—with a repair shop in it!—on National Avenue, if you hadn't done it first. Then the others thought they had to follow; and if something isn't done to stop you fellows, the whole avenue will be nothing but a mile row of motor-car sales buildings and pneumatic tire warehouses and garages—a market!—and with hundred-foot smoke-stacks! It may reach even here to our old house and the Shelbys'; and already you've made the peaceful neighbourhood around my house horrible. I'd like to know what grandma Savage would have said about the things you people have done to this town! Why, you've made National Avenue begin to look like an old pipe-smoking hag's mouth with every other tooth missing and the rest sticking up all black in the smoke."

Dan laughed absent-mindedly, but remained impervious. Like the ardent Sheridan, he loved the smoke, called it "Prosperity," and drew his lungs full of it, breathing in it the glory of his city. More and more, the city became his city, and with all his juggling and tight-rope dancing he found time to be mayor of it for a year, and to begin the "Park System" that was afterwards to bring so much beauty to it. One day he drove his father over the ground he had planned to include in this chain of groves and meadows; and he was glad afterwards that they had made the excursion together.

"It'll be a great thing for the city," his father said, as Dan's car turned homeward with them. "It's a great thing for you to do and to be remembered by. You were a good boy, Dan; and you're a good man and a good citizen. You serve your fellow-men well, I think."

Dan laughed, a little embarrassed by this praise; but although Mr. Oliphant perceived his son's embarrassment, he had more to say, and went on with something like timidity, yet with a gentle persistence: "I'd like to tell you another thing, Dan. It's something your mother and I never felt we ought to talk about to you, but I believe I'll mention it to you to-day. We—you see your mother and I have always thought there's a danger sometimes in letting a person see that you sympathize with him, because it might make him feel that he's unhappy, or in trouble, whereas, if you just leave him to himself he may go on cheerfully enough and never think about it. But I would like to tell you—I'd like to say—"

He paused, and Dan asked: "You'd like to say what, sir?"

"Well—I'd like just to tell you that your mother and I think you've always been as kind as you could to Lena."

Surprised, Dan stared at him; and Mr. Oliphant gravely and affectionately returned his look. "Yes, sir," the son said awkwardly. "I hope so. Thank you, sir." And he thought that the handsome, kind old face seemed whiter and more fragile than usual.

That was natural, Dan told himself; people couldn't help growing old, and they grew whiter and thinner as age came upon them; but age didn't necessarily mean ill-health. For that matter, his father hadn't nearly reached a really venerable old age; he was more than a decade younger than old-hickory Shelby, who still never missed a day's work. Nevertheless, there had been something a little disquieting in Mr. Oliphant's manner; it was as if he had thought that perhaps he might never have another chance to say what he had said;—and that night, on the train to which he had hurried after their drive, Dan thought about his father often.

He thought about him often, too, the next day, in New York; and during the conferences there with the landscape architects who were designing the new parks, his thoughts went uneasily westward;—not to the green stretches of grove and sward that were to be, but to the quiet old man who had walked so slowly between the tall white gateposts after bidding his son good-bye. Recalling this, it seemed to Dan that he had never before seen him walk so slowly; and he went over in his mind, for the fiftieth time, his father's manner in speaking of Lena—the slight, timid insistence, as if there might never be another opportunity to say something he had always wished to say. It had given what he said the air of a blessing bestowed—and of a valedictory.

Thus Dan's vague uneasiness grew, and although he scolded himself for it, and told himself he was imaginative beyond reason, he could not be rid of it. That was well for him; since such uneasiness may be of help when life is like a path whereon tigers leap from nowhere, as it is, sometimes;—the wayfarer will not avoid wounds, but may better survive them for having been in some expectance of them.

For a year Mr. Oliphant's heart had been "not just what it ought to be"; but he told no one that this was his physician's report to him. Harlan's telegram reached New York just as Dan was starting home. Mr. Oliphant had indeed taken his last opportunity

188

to say what he had so long wished to say, for now the kind heart beat no longer;—but he had died proud of his son.

CHAPTER XXV

NEITHER Mr. Oliphant's daughter-in-law nor his grandson was at home at the time of his death. Lena had gone abroad again, for a "three-months' furlough," as she called it; and again in spite of Dan's vehement protest that the boy "ought to see his own country first," she had taken Henry with her.

"I wouldn't mind it so much," Dan said to her before they went;—"but you never even stop off and show him Niagara Falls when you take him to New York to visit your family; and when I want to take him with me, you always say he's got a cold or something and has to stay at home. It seems to me pretty near a disgrace for parents to carry their children all over Europe and pay no attention to the greatest natural wonders in the world, right here at home. My father and mother went to Europe with Harlan and me, but not before they'd taken us to see Mammoth Cave and Niagara Falls. Why, it'd take five Europes to give me the thrill I got the first time I ever looked at the Falls! It's not fair to Henry, and besides, look what it does to his school work! He picked up some French, yes, the other time you had him over there; but he dropped a whole year in his classes. And how much French is he goin' to need when I take him into business with me? Not a thimbleful in a lifetime! He's the best boy I ever knew and got the finest nature; and he ought to be given the opportunity to learn something about his own country instead of too much Paris!"

This patriotic vehemence went for nothing, since Henry intended to accompany his mother and announced his intentions with a firmness that left his father nothing to do but grumble helplessly, while Lena laughed. At fifteen, Henry had his precocities, and among them a desire (not mentioned) to revisit the Bal Tabarin, as he retained a pleasant memory of a quiet excursion to this entertainment, during his previous travels, when he was twelve and already influential with Parisian hotel guides. Lena had her way, and, having placed the ocean between herself and further argument on the part of her husband, remained twice as long as the "furlough"

189

she had proposed. She did not return until Dan's term as mayor was concluded, four months after Mr. Oliphant's death.

When she finally did arrive, her appearance was mollifying;— she had always looked far less than her age, and now, fresh from amazing cosmetic artists, and brilliantly studied by superb milliners, she was prettier than she had ever been. Strangers would have believed a firm declaration that she was twenty-four; she knew this, and her homecoming mood was lively—but when Dan within the hour of her arrival wished to drive her out to Ornaby to see the new house, which he had at last begun to build, after years of planting and landscaping, she declined. Her look of gayety vanished into the faraway expression that had always come upon her face when the new house was mentioned.

"Not to-day," she said. "I'm not so sure we ought to go ahead with it at all. I don't think we ought to leave your mother; she'd be too lonely in the old house now—living here all alone."

"But I never dreamed of such a thing," Dan protested. "She'll come with us, of course. This old place is going to be sold before long; I've just about talked her into it, and she can get real money for it now. Land along here is worth something mighty pretty these days. Why, Fred Oliphant's family got seven hundred a front foot for their place three months ago, and an absolutely magnificent office-building for doctors is goin' to be put up there. They've got the foundations all in and the first story's almost up already. That's only two blocks below here; and I can get mother almost any price she wants. I'd buy it myself and sell it again, only I wouldn't like to feel I'd taken advantage of her. Why don't you come on out now with Henry and me and take a look at our own doin's? It'll surprise you!"

"Oh, some day," she said, the absent look not disappearing from her eyes. "I'd rather lie down now, I believe. You run along with Henry."

Henry showed no great enthusiasm about accompanying his father, and when they arrived at the new house seemed indifferent to the busy work going on there. Dan was loud and jocose with him, slapping him on the back at intervals, and inquiring in a shout how it felt to "be back in God's country again." Upon each of these manifestations, Henry smiled with a politeness somewhat constrained, replying indistinctly; and, as they went over the building, now in a skeleton stage of structure, Dan would stop frequently and address a workman with hearty familiarity: "Look what I got with me, Shorty! Just got him back all the way from Europe! How'd you like to have a boy as near a man as this? Pretty fine! Yes, sir; pretty fine, Shorty!" And he would throw his ponderous arm about his son's thin shoulders, and Henry would bear the embrace with a bored patience, but move away as soon as he could find an excuse to do so.

He was a dark, slender, rather sallow boy, short for the sixteen years he verged upon, though his face, with its small and shapely features, like his mother's, looked older and profoundly reticent. It was one of those oldish young faces that seem too experienced not to understand the wisdom of withholding everything; and Henry appeared to be most of all withholding when he was with his boisterous, adoring father. Obviously this was not because the boy had any awe of Dan. On the contrary, as one of the friendly and admiring carpenters observed, "The Big Fellow, he's so glad to have that son of his back he just can't keep his hands off him; wants to jest hug him all the time, and it makes the kid tired. Well, I can remember when I was like that—thought I knew it all, and my old man didn't know nothin'! I expect this kid does know a few things the Big Fellow doesn't know he knows, mebbe! Looks like that kind of a kid to me."

The estimate was not ill-founded, as Henry presently demonstrated. Escaping from his father's fond and heavy arm, he seated himself upon a slab of carved stone, produced a beautiful flat gold case, the size and shape of a letter envelope, and drew from it a tiny cigarette of a type made in France for women.

Dan stared at him, frowned, and inquired uncomfortably, but with some severity: "Don't you think you're too young for that, Henry?"

"Young?" Henry seemed to be mildly surprised as he lighted the cigarette. "No, I shouldn't think so. I've smoked for quite some time now, you know."

"No; I certainly didn't know."

"Oh, yes," Henry returned placidly. "It's years since I first began it."

"Well, but see here—" Dan began; then paused, reddening. "I don't believe it'll be very good for your health," he concluded feebly.

"My health's all right," the youth said, with an air that began to be slightly annoyed. "Mother's known I smoked a long while."

"Well, but—" Dan stopped again, his embarrassment increasing and his perplexity increasing with it as he remembered that he himself had smoked at fifteen, surreptitiously. "Well—" he began again, after a pause, during which Henry blew a beautifully formed little smoke ring. "Well—"

"Yes, sir?"

"Well—" Dan said. "Well, I'm glad if you do smoke, you do it openly, anyhow."

"Yes, sir?" Henry returned, with a slight accent of surprise

191

that suggested his inability to perceive any reason for not smoking openly. Then, regarding the incident as closed, he asked: "I suppose you'll put up a garage in proportion to the house, won't you? It's about time I had a car of my own, don't you think, sir?"

"I expect so," Dan said, still uncomfortable. "I expect we'll have to see about it before long. Anyhow, I would rather you did it openly, Henry. I—I don't—I—" He stopped, in difficulties with a depth of feeling that affected his voice. "I—I don't ever expect to be half as good a father to you, Henry, as my—as my own father was to me, but I—well, your uncle Harlan and I were afraid to smoke before him until we were almost grown up. We used to sneak out to the stable to smoke—or in alleys—and though my father was so much better a man than I am, and so much better a father to me than I can ever hope to be to you, I guess—I guess this is better, Henry. I mean I guess it's better to have you open with me, like this. It's an advance, I expect. I don't know why we were afraid to smoke before father; he never whipped us and he was the kindest man—the best—the best father that ever—" He was unable to continue; and Henry glanced up to see him, red-faced and swallowing, struggling with an emotion that made the boy wonder what in the world was the matter with him.

"I suppose he was, probably," Henry said. "How about that car? Don't you think I might as well have it pretty soon? How about this week's being as good as any other time?"

Dan recovered himself, smiled, and patted his son's shoulder. "I expect so, maybe. We'll drive down to our agents on the avenue before we go home."

And at this Henry proved that he could still show some animation. He sprang up, shouting. "Ya-ay!" he cried. "Vive le sport!" And he leaped into the big Morgan limousine that stood waiting for them in the cluttered driveway. "Come on!" he shouted. "I'll show you how to shoot a little life into this old town!"

Rising from her nap, an hour later, Lena looked from her window and saw them returning. Henry was still animated, talking busily, and, as they came into the house, seemed willing to bear the weight of his father's arm across his shoulders. The mother, looking down upon the pair, smiled thoughtfully to herself;—she was not more indulgent with the boy than his father was; but she knew that Henry was more hers than he was his father's. He had always been so, because of some chord of subtle understanding struck by her nature and Henry's. She had sometimes been in a temper with him when he was a noisy little boy, but as he grew older she had begun to feel only amusement over his naughtinesses, because she understood them so well;—she laughed at him sometimes, but had long since ceased to chide him. She had no blame for him, and she knew that he would never find fault with her, no matter what she did. They had a mysterious comprehension of each other—a comprehension so complete that they had never needed to speak of it.

She heard him chattering to his grandmother in the hall downstairs, and knew by his tone that his father had bought him something, of which the boy would presently tell her;—she remained standing beside the closed window, waiting for him to come in with his news. Then, as she stood there, a gust drove down a multitude of soot flakes from the smokestack of an apartment house that had been built near by, on the cross street just south of the Oliphants', while she was away. After the soot, which flecked the window, the smoke itself descended, enveloping the house so thickly that the window became opaque. Sounds were not shut out, however, and she could still hear all too well the chattering of a steam drill at work across the street, where a public garage was being built. She frowned at the noise, for the drill had disturbed her sleep; and so had the almost unceasing rumble of trucks passing the house; and so had the constant yelp of automobile signals rasping at one another for right of way.

The smoke thinned out, revealing the busy street that had been so different when she had first looked forth upon it from this same window, a bride. She remembered how quiet it had been then—and suddenly she spoke aloud.

"Well, I'm still here!"

Then she laughed softly, as her eyes wandered to the north, crossed the iron picket fence that divided the Oliphants' yard from the Shelbys', and beheld the fountain swan. He was green no longer; his colour was that of the smoke; and though he still shot a crystal spray, the flying water was the only clean thing about him, or in sight.

"Ridiculous old beast!" Lena said; but there was no bitterness in her tone. It was a long time since she had felt jealous of Martha; and, although she often told Harlan that Martha would never marry him, "because she still hopes Dan'll be a widower some day," the warning had come to be merely jocular, without intended sting. Moreover, she practised the same raillery with her brother after he had taken up his residence in the town; for George offered himself as a rival to Harlan in the half-serious manner of a portly bachelor of forty mildly courting a contemporary.

Lena repeated her opinion of the swan. "Ridiculous old beast!" This time she did not murmur the words as before; but spoke them in her mind, and she immediately followed them with others, the connection being made without any more feeling than she had about the swan. Her thought was merely speculative, even a little compassionate: "I suppose she does still hope it, poor old thing! She thinks maybe, if I leave him—"

But Henry came in with the news of his father's munificence, and interrupted this thought that had been in her mind ever since the night of Martha's return from the long absence in Italy. Throughout all the long time since then, there had always been in Lena's mind a conviction, however obscured or half-forgotten, that some day she would leave her husband.

CHAPTER XXVI

SHE was mistaken about Martha, who never had the definite hope Lena's imagination attributed to her. Martha was steadfast because she could not help it, having been born with this endowment evidently; and her tenderness for the boy she had loved so heartily was imperishable; but the Dan Oliphant of the middle years did not seem to her to be that boy. What she felt for the big middle-aged man, she felt only because he had long ago been the beloved youth; she was not in love with him, nor with anybody. This was the explanation she still found it necessary to make to his brother about once a year—usually on New Year's Day; for it was Harlan's habit to select that hopeful anniversary as a good time to dwell a little upon his patience.

"You call it your patience, but it became only your habit long ago," she told him. "It would really unsettle you badly if I ever said I'd marry you, Harlan; and it would unsettle you even more if I not only said I would, but went ahead and did it. You'd find you'd never forgive me for upsetting your routine. If we were married, where in the world would you ever go? You haven't been anywhere for so long, except to see me, that you'd be left without the destination you've been accustomed to. It's gallant of you to still mention your willingness, every now and then, and I own up that I rather expect it and should miss it if you didn't; but if you want to marry, you ought to look about for—well, say a pretty widow of twenty-nine, Harlan. She'd be better for you than one of the 'buds,' though you could have whichever you chose;—they'd jump at the chance! The trouble with me is that I'm too old—and I'm horribly afraid I look my age."

194

The fear was warranted, though it need not have been a fear. She had escaped the portliness that seemed to threaten her at thirty, and had escaped too far, perhaps; but her thinness was not angular; and if she looked her age, then that age was no more than a pleasantly responsible age, as Harlan told her, and neither a careworn nor a gray-haired age. In fact, it must be the perfect age, he said—and he wondered if it mightn't be as kind as it looked, and be the perfect age for him.

At that, she became more serious. "I'm surprised at myself every year I grow older," she said. "I'm so much more romantic than I was at twenty, and it seems I keep growing more so. At twenty how I'd have laughed if I'd heard of a woman of forty who said she couldn't marry because she was in love with no one! I suppose what would have struck me as funniest would have been the idea of a woman of forty talking about marrying at all."

She was "in love with no one," but she could still be Harlan's brother's champion, if need arose; and after George McMillan took up his residence in the town, and began his mild rivalry, she had this amiable bachelor to second her. Moreover, it is to be admitted for her that she, who in the bloom of youth had never known how to display the faintest symptoms of coquetry, now sometimes enjoyed tokens of disturbance unwillingly exhibited by Harlan when the rival appeared to win an advantage. McMillan, dark and growing a little bald, counterbalanced what was lacking above by a decoration below already rare in the land, but not yet a curiosity, a Van Dyke beard, well suited to his face. In manner, too, he was equal to the flavour of a fine old portrait, and he had spoken from his childhood in the accent Harlan had carefully acquired. Thus the latter was sometimes but too well encountered on his own ground.

He met one of these defeats in an early April twilight when he had expected to find Martha alone, as he knew a meeting of the board of directors of the "Ornaby Four" had been called for that evening, and George McMillan was a member of the board. The air was warm with one of the misplacements of this season, when sometimes a midsummer day wanders from its proper moorings and irrationally ascends almost to the chilly headwaters of spring. Martha was upon the veranda, occupied with a fan and the conversation of Mr. McMillan when Harlan arrived; and the newcomer was so maladroit as to make his disappointed expectations plain.

"I thought you had a directors' meeting," he said, almost with his greeting and before he had seated himself in one of the wicker chairs brought out upon the veranda by the unseasonable warmth. "I thought there was—"

George assented placidly. "There was, but it couldn't be held. Our president had to go to another one that he's president of—the Broadwood Interurban. It's in difficulties, I'm afraid, because of too high wages and too much competition by motorcycles and small cars. I hope Dan can straighten it out."

"I hope so," Harlan said. "That is, strictly as his brother I hope so. As a human being still trying to exist in what was once a comfortable house, I might take another attitude. I live deep in the downtown district now, for my worst sins, and those long Broadwood cars screech every hour, night and day, on a curve not a hundred yards from my library." He sighed. "But why should I waste my breath, still complaining? It all grows steadily worse and worse, year after year, and if one happens to like living in a city in his own native land, there's nowhere to escape to. I suppose National Avenue—poor thing, look at the wreck of it!—I say I suppose it couldn't have hoped to escape the fate of Fifth Avenue; for the same miserable ruction is going on all over the country. My illustrious brother and his kind have ruined everything that was peaceful and everything that was clean—they began by murdering the English language, and now they've murdered all whiteness. Beauty is dead."

"Isn't that only a question of your definition?" McMillan inquired.

"Why is it?"

"For one reason, because everything's a question of definitions."

"No, it isn't," Harlan returned somewhat brusquely; and Martha sat in silence, amused to perceive that her two callers had straightway resumed a tilting not infrequent when they met. A lady's part was only to preside at the joust. "There's only one definition of beauty," Harlan added to his contradiction.

"What is it?"

"The one Athens believed in."

"It won't do for that brother of yours," his antagonist returned. "The Greeks are dead, and you can't tie Dan and his sort down to a dead definition. The growth isn't beautiful to you, but it is to them, or else they wouldn't make it. Of course you're sure you're right about your own definition, but they're so busy making what they're sure is beautiful they don't even know that anybody disagrees with them. It won't do you the slightest good to disagree with them, either."

"Why not?"

"Because they've got everything in their hands," George

196

McMillan replied cheerfully;—"and they're too busy to listen to any one who isn't making something besides criticisms."

"And for that reason," Harlan began, "all of us who care for what's quiet and cool and charming in life are to hold our peace and let—"

He was interrupted, unable to make himself heard because of a shattering uproar that came from beyond the iron fence to the south. A long and narrow motor car, enamelled Chinese red, stood in the Oliphants' driveway, and an undersized boy of sixteen had just run out of the house and jumped into the driver's seat. Dusk had not fallen darkly; he saw the group upon the neighbouring veranda well enough, but either thought it too much effort to salute Martha and his uncles, or was preoccupied with the starting of his car;—he gave no sign of being aware of them. Evidently the unmuffled machine-gun firing of his exhaust was delightful to his young ears, for he increased its violence to the utmost, although the noise was unlawful, and continued it as he shot the car down the drive, out of the gates and down the street at a speed also unlawful.

"There, at least," Harlan said, "is something of which criticism might possibly be listened to with good effect—even by my busy brother."

But George laughed and shook his head. "No. That's the very last thing he'd allow you to criticize. He'd only tell you that Henry is 'the finest young man God ever made!' In fact, that's what he told me yesterday evening when I dined there; and I had more than a suspicion I'd caught a whiff of something suggesting a cocktail from our mutual nephew, as he came in for a hurried dinner between speedings. But that isn't Dan's fault."

"Yes, it is," Harlan said. "Giving a sixteen-year-old boy a car like that!"

"No, the fault is my sister's. What's a boy to do when his mother keeps him hanging around Paris so long in the autumn that it's too late for him to make up his class-work, and he has only a tutor to cajole? I don't blame Henry much. In fact, the older I grow the less I blame anything."

"No?" Harlan said. "I'm afraid the world won't get anywhere very fast unless there are some people to point out its mistakes."

But the other bachelor jouster was not at all disconcerted by this reproof, nor by the tone of it, which was incautiously superior. "By George, Oliphant, I always have believed you were really a true Westerner under that surface of yours! The way you said 'the world won't get anywhere very fast' was precisely in the right tone. You're reverting to type, and if the reversion doesn't stop I shan't be surprised to hear of your breathing deep of the smoke and calling it 'Prosperity' with the best of them!"

Harlan was displeased. "I suppose the smoke comes under your definition of beauty, too, doesn't it?"

"It isn't my definition," George explained. "I was groping for Dan's. Yes, I think the smoke's beautiful to him because he believes it means growth and power, and he thinks they're beautiful."

"I dare say. Would you consider it a rational view for any even half-educated man to hold—that soft-coal smoke is beautiful? Do you think so, Martha, when it makes pneumonia epidemic, ruins everything white that you have in your house and everything white that you wear? Do you?"

"It's pretty trying," she answered, as a conscientious housewife, but added hopefully: "We'll get rid of it some day, though. So many people are complaining of it I'm sure they'll do something about it before long."

Harlan laughed dryly, for he had hoped she would say that. "I've been re-reading John Evelyn's diary," he said. "Evelyn declared the London smoke was getting so dreadful that a stop would have to be put to it somehow. The king told him to devise a plan for getting rid of it, and Evelyn set about it quite hopefully. That was in the latter part of the seventeenth century. Evelyn is dead, but the smoke's still there."

"And yet," George McMillan said coolly, "I'm told they've made quite a place of London, in spite of that!"

Martha laughed aloud, and Harlan was so unfortunate as to be annoyed. "It seems rather a childish argument in view of the fact that we sit here in the atmosphere of what might well be a freight yard," he said; and, turning to Martha he spoke in a lowered voice, audible to his opponent, yet carrying the implication that McMillan was excluded from the conference. "My committee have at last got the symphony organization completed," he said. "The orchestra knows it can depend on a reliable support now, and the first concert will be two weeks from to-night. I hope you won't mind going with me."

"No; I won't mind," she said, and hospitably explained to McMillan: "We've been trying for years to expand our week of the 'April Festival' into something more permanent. Mr. Oliphant has done most of the work, and it's really a public service. It will be good news for your sister;—I understand she's always felt we were a lost people, in music particularly."

"We'll have a start at any rate," Harlan said, as he rose to go. "That is, if the smoke doesn't throttle our singers. Venable is back

198

from South America and there ought to be some interest to hear him."

"Venable?" George repeated. "Did you say Venable?"

"Yes; the baritone. He's still just in his prime; at least so his agent says. Have you ever heard him?"

"Long ago," the other returned. "I—" He stopped abruptly.

"Did you know him?" Martha asked.

"No. That is, I had a short interview with him once, but—no, I shouldn't say I know him." He rose, in courtesy to the departing Harlan, and extended his hand. "You mustn't wait behind the next corner and leap out on me with a bowie-knife, Oliphant," he said. "I didn't mean to be such a disagreeable arguer."

"Not at all," Harlan returned, somewhat coldly, though he added an effect of geniality to his departure by a murmur of laughter, and got away without any further emphasis upon his disappointment at finding his rival in possession. The latter gentleman, however, made little use of the field left open to him. Not long after Harlan had gone Martha noticed that her remaining guest seemed to be rather absent-minded, and she rallied him upon it.

"I'm afraid you thrive upon conflict, Mr. McMillan."

"Why?"

"Peace doesn't seem to stimulate you—or else I don't! You've hardly spoken since Mr. Oliphant left. I'm afraid you're—"

"You're afraid I'm what?" he said, as she paused; and although the dusk had fallen now, it was not too dark for her to see that his preoccupation was serious.

"Are you troubled about anything?" she asked.

"No. Why?"

"I thought you looked—"

"Oh, no," he said. "It's nothing. Perhaps I am a little bothered," he admitted. "But it's only about business."

"Not about the 'Ornaby Four?'" she said, surprised. "I thought it was established as a tremendous success."

"Oh, it is," he assured her promptly. "It is. It's an extraordinary little car and nothing can stop it—except temporarily. It's bound to climb over any little temporary difficulties. We may have made mistakes, but they won't amount to anything in the long run."

"You say you have made mistakes?"

"Not until this year, and even then nothing we can't remedy. You see Dan's a great fellow for believing in almost anything that's new, and an inventor came along last summer with a new type of friction clutch; and we put it in our car. Then I'm afraid we built a

199

fairly enormous number of 'Fours' during the winter, but you see we were justified in that, because we knew there'd be a demand for them."

"And there wasn't?"

"Oh, yes; there was. But—" he paused; then went on: "Well, the people haven't seemed to like the new clutch, and that gives us rather a black eye for the time being. Of course we're going to do our best to straighten things out; we'll put our old clutch back on all the new cars, but—"

He paused uncomfortably again, and she inquired: "But won't that make everything all right again?"

"Oh, yes—after a time. The trouble is, I'm afraid it's stopped our sales rather flat—for the time being, that is. You see, there's a lot of money we expected would be pouring in on us about now—and it doesn't pour. I'm not really worried, but I'm a little afraid Dan might need it, because his inter-urban ventures appear to have been—well, rather hazardous. You told me once that his brother's description of him was 'dancing on the tight-rope' and in a way that's not so far wrong. Of course he'll pull through." George suddenly struck the stone railing beside him a light blow with his open hand, and jumped up. "Good gracious! What am I doing but talking business to a lady on a spring evening? I knew I was in my dotage!" And he went to the steps.

"Wait," Martha said hurriedly. "You don't really think—"

"That Dan Oliphant's affairs are in any real danger? No; of course not;—I don't know what made me run on like that. Men go through these little disturbances every day; it's a part of the game they play, and they don't think anything about it. You can be sure he isn't worrying. Did you ever know him to let such things stop him? He's been through a thousand of 'em and walked over 'em. He's absolutely all right."

"You're sure?" she said, as he went down the steps.

"He's absolutely all right, and I'd take my oath to it," George said; but he added: "That is, he is if the banks don't call him."

"If the banks don't what?"

He laughed reassuringly. "If the banks don't do something they have no reason to do and certainly won't do. Good-night. I'm going to stop in next door and see my sister a little while before she goes to bed."

His figure grew dimmer as he went toward the gate, and Martha, staring after him, began to be haunted by that mysterious phrase of his, "if the banks don't call him."

200

CHAPTER XXVII

THE next day, at lunch, she asked her father what it meant, though she did not mention Dan; and she brought out a crackling chuckle from that old bit of hickory, now brittle and almost sapless, but still serviceable.

"Means a bank wants its money back; that's all," he said. "There's plenty of reasons why a bank wants money—same as anybody else."

"But suppose I'd borrowed of a bank and was a good customer, and the bank knew I had plenty of property to cover the loan, would the First National, for instance, ever worry me to pay it, if they knew I only needed a little time to get all I owed it?"

"Not unless we thought you mightn't be as able to pay us as well later on as when we ask for it," the old man answered. "You'd be all right as long as the First stood by you. The First'll protect a customer long as anybody; and the others all follow our lead. What in time's the matter with you? You plannin' to borrow money? Geemunently! I should think you'd be able to put up with what you get out o' me!"

His voice cracked into falsetto, as it often did nowadays; but the vehemence that cracked it was not intended to be serious; he was in a jocular mood; and the conversation reassured her, for he was one of the directors of the "First"; and if Dan were really in difficulties and the bank meant to increase them, she thought her father would have seized upon the occasion to speak of it triumphantly. Indeed, he had once angrily instructed her to wait for such an occasion. "You just wait till the time comes!" he had said. "You sit there crowin' over me because I used to prophesy Dan Oliphant was never goin' to amount to anything, and you claim all this noise and gas proves he has! You just wait till the day comes when I get the chance to crow over you, miss! You'll hear me!"

She was convinced that he wouldn't have missed the chance to crow. Nevertheless a little of her uneasiness remained, and was still with her, two weeks later, when she went with Harlan to the concert of the new symphony orchestra, on an evening so drenched with rain that she inquired with some anxiety if his car was amphibious.

"If it can't swim I'm afraid we won't get there," she said, as they set off upon the splashing avenue. "Judging by the windows, we aren't in an automobile, but in one of those tanks that take pictures of ocean life for the movies. I'm not sure it's a tank though; the old avenue has turned into a river, and perhaps we're in a side-

201

wheel steamboat. I'm afraid this'll be bad for your attendance. You'll have a big deficit to make up in reward for your struggle to make us an artistic people."

There was to be no deficit, however, she discovered, as they went to their seats in the theatre Harlan's committee had taken for the concert;—interest in the new organization and in the coming of the renowned Venable had been stronger than the fear of a wetting. The place was being rapidly filled, and, glancing about her, Martha saw "almost everybody and a great many others," she said.

Not far away from where she and Harlan sat, Lena was in a box with George McMillan. The other seats in the box were vacant; and Lena, sitting close to the velvet rail, and wearing as a contrast to her own whiteness a Parisian interpretation of Spanish passion, in black jet and jet-black, was the most conspicuous figure in the theatre. She leaned back in her chair, her brilliant eyes upon the stage, though there was nothing there except a piano and a small forest of music stands; and Martha thought she looked excited— music was evidently a lively stimulant for her. Her brother, not quite so much within the public view, and possibly wishing his sister were less vividly offered to that view, appeared to the observing Martha as somewhat depressed and nervous. There was no conversation between the brother and sister, though he glanced at Lena from time to time, from the side of his eye.

Martha wondered where Dan was. He would prefer a concert by Sousa's Band to the French and Russian programme set for this evening, she knew; but the opening of "the Symphony" was in its way a civic occasion; one for which the credit was in some part due to his brother; and she had expected him to be there. "Isn't Dan coming?" she asked Harlan.

"I think so."

"Do you think he's worried about business lately, Harlan?"

"No, I don't think he ever worries about anything."

"Oh, but you're wrong!" she said quickly. "You don't know him; a man can't sacrifice everything to just one object in life, as he has, all these years, and not worry about it. I know your mother worries about him. She says he never takes any care of himself, and it's beginning to tell on him. But I mean are there any—any rumours around town that he's in some sort of business difficulty, or anything like that?"

"No; I think not. At least I haven't heard of anything like that being more prevalent with him than usual. He's always up and down, either up to his neck or riding on the crest—that's his way, and I don't believe he'd enjoy himself otherwise. The only thing he could talk about when I saw him yesterday at home was his new

202

house. It's finished at last; and they're going to move into it. Mother's sold our old place, you know, and the wrecking will begin next week. Pleasant for you!"

"Oh, I'm trying to get father to go, too," she said. "He's terribly obstinate, but with the house on the other side of us rebuilt into an apartment, and now your mother's to be torn down, he'll have to give in. We'll have to move out to northern Ornaby like everybody else. You'll have to come, too, Harlan."

"Thank you," he said. "I've been waiting a good many years for that invitation. May I make an appointment with your father for to-morrow morning?"

She laughed, blushed, and touched his coat sleeve with her folded fan of black feathers. "Hush! People will hear you!"

"You fear it may be suspected that I'm still serious in my intentions?"

"Hush!" she said again. "I mean we're about to hear some serious music, and it's no time for nonsense."

Harlan was obedient; he said no more, but brightened as he listened to the serious music;—her tone had been kind and he hoped that he was not mistaken in thinking he detected something a little self-conscious in it. He was no eager lover now; his bachelorhood was pleasant to him; and he could be content with it; but as Martha leaned forward to listen he looked sidelong at her and felt that he had been right and wise to wish for no other woman. They had been companions for so long, and understood each other so well, marriage would be no disturbing change for either of them. He was assured of happiness in it, if he could persuade her, and something in the way she had just spoken to him made him almost sure that he was about to persuade her at last.

After the first suite by the orchestra the great Venable appeared, making his way among the seated musicians and coming forward with an air of affability operatic in its sweeping expressiveness—a pale, handsome, black-haired man of grand dimensions. He needed no costume other than his black clothes and shapely ampleness of white front to make him seem, not an actual man, but a figure from romantic drama, a dweller in enchanted palaces and the master of heroic passions.

"I've always wanted to see one of those splendid, big, statuesque opera or concert people at home," Martha whispered to her escort. "I've never been near them except when they moved on the grand scale, like this. It would be an experience to see a man like that eat an egg—I can't imagine it at all. Do you suppose he could?"

A moment later, when he began to sing, she was sure he couldn't; and as the magnificent instrument in his throat continued

203

in operation, he carried her to such thrilling grandeurs of feeling that she could not even imagine herself eating an egg, or eating anything, or ever again doing anything commonplace—for while he sang she, too, dwelt in enchanted palaces, moved on the grand scale, and knew only heroic emotions.

But when he had finished the encore he was generous enough to add to this part of his programme, and had left the stage, she underwent a reaction not unusual after such stimulations. "It's a great voice and he's a great artist, if I'm equal to knowing either," she said. "But there's something about that man—I don't know what, except it all seems to end in being about himself. It's so personal, somehow. I'm positive he made every woman in the whole audience wish that he were singing just for her alone. I don't think music ought to be like that, unless perhaps sometimes when it's a love-song, and those things he sang weren't supposed to—" She broke off suddenly, as her glance wandered. "There's Dan. He got here, after all."

Dan was coming down the outer aisle to the box where Lena sat; and with him was the younger Sam Kohn, the two having just entered the theatre after the business conference that had detained them. Sam was talking hurriedly and earnestly in husky whispers, which he emphasized with many quick gestures; but he left his tall companion at the curtains of the latter's box.

"See you right after the show," he said, and then went slowly to the series of boxes occupied by his father and brother and their families, while Dan, who looked sallow and tired, Martha thought, stared after him for a moment, then moved forward and seated himself beside George McMillan. Lena gave her husband the greeting of a slightly lifted eyebrow, shown to him in profile; but McMillan leaned toward him and whispered an anxious question.

"It's all right," Dan said. "Sam Kohn's got his father's promise to hold out against 'em. They want every inch of Ornaby I've got left—that's what they've really been after a long time. I'd like to see anybody get Ornaby away from me! They want the Four, too, and they think they've got both; but they won't get either. The Kohns'll play it through on my—"

But Lena stopped this inappropriate talk of mere business. She made a slight gesture with her lovely little bare arm, her fingers flashing impatient sparks; and Dan was silent. He remained so throughout the rest of the concert, listening with an expression not unamiable, though at times his big face, lately grown flaccid and heavier, fell into the shapings that indicate drowsiness; and once or twice his glance was vaguely troubled, happening to rest upon the white contours of his wife's shoulders;—her glittering black scarf

204

had fallen as she leaned forward when the godlike baritone came out again.

"That fellow looks kind of soft-soapy, but he's got a crackin' good voice," was Dan's placid comment, at the conclusion of the last encore of the final number. Venable was withdrawing from the stage, and most of the audience were getting on their wraps; but an admiring and avaricious gallery demanded more of the charmer, and clapped on. He stopped, shook his head, smilingly; then made his last bow profoundly and obliquely, with a shift of his large eyes in the same direction. "Not bowin' to us, is he?" Dan inquired, surprised. "I don't know him."

"I do," Lena said, "I told you the other day I used to know him. I'm going around to speak to him."

"I can't wait, I'm afraid. Sam Kohn's lookin' for me in the lobby now, and he and I got to have a talk with his father. You take the car, Lena—I'll leave it in front for you, and I'll get Sam to drive me home from old man Kohn's. I'll have to hurry."

McMillan was looking at his sister darkly and steadily. "I'll see to Lena," he said. "I'll go with her wherever she wants to go, and then I'll take her home."

Lena laughed airily. "Why, no; it isn't necessary. You'd better go with Dan."

"No; I believe I'd better go with you, Lena."

"Can't wait for you to settle it," Dan said. "It's pretty important I don't miss Sam. I may be out fairly late, Lena. Good-night." And, leaving the brother and sister confronting each other, before they moved toward the stage door behind the boxes, he hurried out to the lobby, where Sam Kohn seized his arm.

"I'll take you over to papa's in my car, Dan," he said. "I been talkin' some more to the old man durin' the show. He'll stick, all right, as a favour to me, because I put it to him pretty stiff that you're my old friend, and what you've done for this town has made money for Kohn & Sons, and's bound to make more in the future, besides; and I told him anyhow, by golly, he just had to! Well, he says he'll stick, and he'll do it, Dan; but he ain't none too sure he can carry them old shellbacks with him. He ain't never been any pessimist about anything, Dan, but he thinks they see a chance to clean up if they call you. He's afraid he can't stop 'em from doin' it, Dan."

Dan frowned angrily. "Well—let 'em call! They can't break me! I'll make it, all right, Sam—I've been through these things before."

Sam's voice had shown some emotion, but now it became tremulous with sympathy and with anger. "That bunch of old shellbacks, they haven't got sense enough to see what a man like you

205

means to their own business in the long run. They haven't got any what you call vision, as it were. They belong to the old generation, the bunch of old back numbers! Honest, they make me sick as a cat, Dan."

He was still thus abusing the shellbacks when he and his friend passed out of the theatre, and were almost swept from their feet by squalls of chilling rain before they could get into his car. He did all the talking, an unusual thing for Dan to allow a companion to do. Always before, when misfortune had threatened, he had been jauntily voluble.

He did not come home until one o'clock, but there was a light in the library, and, going in, he found his mother reading "In Memoriam." She had begun to stoop after her husband's death, and her hair had lost its last touch of gray; it was all white now, so that even to the glamouring eyes of her son she had come to be a little, fragile old lady; but her good will to all the world still looked forth through the thick glass of her spectacles.

"Why, mother! You oughtn't to be up this late!"

"I just got to reading—" she explained. "I like to read on a rainy night. Did you lock the front door?"

"Yes. Isn't Lena in?"

"Yes. Mr. McMillan brought her home an hour ago. Yes; she's in."

Dan laughed, noting her emphasis. " 'She is?' " he repeated. "Well, then we're all in. Who else is left to come in?" He went to her and patted her shoulder. "I believe you were sitting up for me. Don't you know better?"

"I might be anxious about you, such a bad night, Dan," she said. "I don't like to pester you, but you ought to take some regular exercise. You never have taken any; and you eat your meals just anytime you happen to get a minute or two. I do think you've been looking pretty run-down lately; but I wasn't sitting up for you—not exactly, that is. I mean I was really sitting up for somebody else."

"Who?"

She smiled apologetically. "Of course I know young people are different nowadays, and it isn't a grandmother's place to interfere; but I am afraid it was a mistake, your getting Henry that car."

"You don't mean to tell me he's not in the house?"

"I'm afraid so. After the rest of you had gone he said he believed he'd go for a drive in his car. I said he mustn't think of it on such a night, but he laughed, and I couldn't get him to pay any attention. I was hoping to hear him come in before you did. Perhaps you'd better—"

"Yes," Dan said, as he strode into the hall. "I think I had."

206

CHAPTER XXVIII

HE FOUND Henry, but the search took two hours, and his clothes were sodden with the rain that drenched them as he got in and out of his car to make inquiries, or to investigate restaurants of lively all-night reputations. The red "speedster" he had bought for his son stood hub-deep in the running gutter before the last of these to be reached; and when the father brought his boy out of the place, and helped him into the Morgan limousine, Henry protested in a whimper somewhat incoherent that he wanted to drive his own car home;—he didn't like to leave it out all night in the rain he said.

"I guess it has stood where it is about long enough!" Dan told him grimly. "But we'll leave it there till I send a man for it in the morning—to sell it, Henry."

Henry whimpered again; then recovered enough presence of mind to say no more. When they reached home, he went upstairs as quickly as he could, although once he had to employ the assistance of the banister railing; and his father followed him.

A light still shone into the hall from the library door, and Dan, whose face was pallid and startled, made his voice cheerful as he called from the stairway: "It's all right, mother. The boy's home and everything's all right. Just a little foolishness with his car; and I've decided it'll be offered for sale to-morrow. You go to bed now."

Henry went to his room and Dan was following him, when Lena, wearing a bright kimono over her nightdress, made her appearance in the open doorway of her bedroom. "What is all this?" she asked petulantly.

"Never mind!"

"But I do mind! What are you saying about selling Henry's car? Didn't I hear you say—"

"Yes, you did." Dan closed the door of Henry's room and came to her. "I made a terrible mistake to give it to him. We've both made a mistake the way we've raised him. He's a good boy; he's got a fine nature and a noble soul. But he's got with bad companions. He's been—" He paused, and went on slowly, with difficulty: "He's been—he's been drinkin', Lena."

She said nothing, but stared at him blankly for a moment—then the stare became an angry one.

"We've got to change our whole way of treatin' Henry," her unhappy husband told her. "We've been all wrong. He—he got with bad companions—"

"Yes," she interrupted angrily. "I should think he might, in a town like this!"

207

"My Lord! It ain't the town's fault. For heaven's sake, don't go back to that old story at a time like this!"

"Yes, I will," she said. "The time's come when you've got to let me take Henry and go where I want to."

Dan looked dazed. "Go where you want to? Why, where do you want to go?"

"Anywhere I please!"

"But, my Lord! You were away seven months out of last year. You only got back from Europe last October! What do you—"

"I want to go and I want to take Henry with me! What's just happened proves that I'm right. This is the wrong place for him."

"But I tell you the place hasn't got anything on earth to do with it."

"Hasn't it?" she cried. "I tell you it has all to do with it, just as it's had all to do with me ever since I came here! I've hated it every instant of all these silly, wasted years I've been pent up here. And now it's ruining my child—yes, ruining him—and you want me still to stay here and let him stay here! You want me to waste the rest of my life, and ruin my child's life, but I tell you, Dan Oliphant, you can't make us do it—not either of us! Not either of us, do you hear?" She had become hysterical, and her voice was so wild and loud that Mrs. Oliphant had come into the hall, downstairs, and was calling up piteously to know what was the matter.

"What is the matter, Dan, dear?" she called. "What is the matter with Lena?"

But Lena, shrieking, "You can't make us—you can't make us!" ran into her room and locked the door. It was a thick old door, but she could still be heard, and it was not difficult to understand that she had thrown herself upon her bed, and was there convulsive, still shrieking: "You can't make us! You can't make us! You can't, you can't, you can't—"

CHAPTER XXIX

DAN reassured his mother as well as he could. "Only a fit of nerves;—too much music, I guess," he said; and, returning to his son's door, found it locked and Henry as unresponsive as the door. The father knocked repeatedly but not loudly, demanding admittance and obtaining the response of a profound silence. Then,

208

as he heard Mrs. Oliphant slowly ascending the stairs to her belated bed, he decided to keep out of her way until he had better composed himself, and, retiring to his own room, discovered that his teeth were chattering.

He removed his cold and sodden garments; but his bed seemed as cold as his clothes; so he got up, put a dressing-gown over his pajamas, and again tried to sleep. The bed still seemed cold—so cold that his teeth still showed the disposition to chatter. However, he told himself that he had "more to worry about than a little chill"; and, between the chill and his more important worries, slept but fitfully. He was warm when the drizzly morning came—too warm—and, again communing with himself on the subject of his physical annoyances, philosophically dismissed the fever as unworthy of his attention. "A little temperature's perfectly natural after a chill," he thought. "It'll pass off, and I've got other things to think about this day!"

So, descending early to the dining-room he had a cup of strong coffee, and left the house without having seen anybody except the cook and his chauffeur. The interview with his son was postponed until evening;—Dan felt he would be better fitted to speak with authority after he had beaten the shellbacks and had shown the First National, with the help of the Kohns and some others, that it wouldn't do to "call" him.

He had a hard day of it; the shells of the shellbacks were tough and seasoned casings, tough as old hickory, and about as penetrable to mere argument. The morning began ominously, and the afternoon came to a close, in the office of Sam Kohn, Junior, in something not far from complete disaster; though Sam insisted, when he and Dan were finally left alone together there, that it was not complete.

"No, sir!" he said. "The way you got a perfect right to look at it, it ain't near as bad as it might been. Maybe from one angle you can say you come out the little end of the horn, but from another angle, you certainly did come out, you might say. You got to look at it from this angle, Dan: you might been sittin' there stone cold broke right now. I tell you last night late, when I talked it over with the old man after you'd gone, I was mighty scared it was goin' to be bankruptcy—but it's a lot better than that. Ain't it better'n that, Dan?"

Dan looked up without altering the despondent attitude into which he had fallen, as he sat in one of his friend's mahogany office chairs. "Yes; I guess it could have been a good deal worse. The only trouble is—" He took a deep and laboured breath, then laughed plaintively. "The only trouble is, while it might have been worse, I wasn't hardly prepared for its bein' so bad!"

209

"But it ain't so blame bad, Dan."

"No; I thought when I showed 'em what I had to fall back on they'd see they couldn't afford to call. I thought I could show 'em it would be so profitable to tide me over and let me renew that they'd see it was the best policy. They ought to have seen it, too!"

Agreeing with this, Sam swore heartily, then he added, "Them old hardshells! The worst about 'em is they got their business training when everything was on the small scale, and they don't know what a liberal policy means. You take that old Shelby, for instance, he was raised on such a stingy scale he thinks everybody's a gambler that borrows a nickel on a million-dollar bond! He's got one foot in the grave and he's so shrunk it takes two people to see him, but, by golly, he wants to get his hands on everything! They're a tough bunch, Dan, and I'm glad you got away from 'em alive. Because you still are alive. Anyhow you're that much!"

Dan shook his head. "Just barely, I guess. If it had been that Broadwood hard luck by itself, I'd have pulled out o' the hole. If that hadn't come just at the same time our sales smashed with the Four—"

"That's exactly the way bad things do come, though," Sam interrupted, and went on to expound the philosophy of misfortune. "They come together, because that's what makes 'em bad. It's the comin' together of bad things that makes all the trouble there is. If they'd come one at a time a person wouldn't mind 'em so much. The angle I look at it, if a person goes along all right for a good while it's only because a whole lot of bad things are holdin' off on him. That makes 'em bound to come together when they do come. It never rains but it pours, Dan, as it were. That's why, when such things happen, we got to put up the best umbrella a feller can lay his hands on."

Dan did not seem to have heard him. "I could stand havin' to sign over the Four to 'em, Sam," he said. "I'd like to have kept it in my hands, but I could stand havin' 'em take it. But when I think I had to sit here and sign over Ornaby—" Suddenly he uttered a broken sound, like a groan; and his whole face became corrugated with a distortion that took more than a moment to conquer. "Why, I've just given my life's blood to Ornaby, and now—"

"Now?" Sam said testily. "Well, what's the matter with now? Didn't we force 'em to agree to turn you over some stock in it when they get the organization made? You ain't out of Ornaby, are you? Not entirely, by no means!"

"It's not mine," Dan said. "It's not mine any longer. Nothin's mine any longer!"

His friend affected an angry impatience. "Don't sit there and

210

talk like that to a person that knows something! If you'd had to make the kind of assignment you might had to, you'd be where it would be pretty hard for you to come back. Ain't you goin' to try to come back?"

"Don't you worry about that," Dan said. "I'm just as sure to come back as I am to go out of that door!" He laughed rather shakily, as he rose to go. "Why, a few years from now—less'n that!— why, by this time next year if I don't get Ornaby back I'll make a new Ornaby—I'll find it somewhere, and this town won't take long to grow out to it, the way it's started now. Don't you ever worry about my comin' back!"

"That's the ticket!" his friend cried. "That's the way you used to talk. You go home and get a good rest—you certainly been through a rough day, and you look like it!—and then you get up to-morrow morning and start to come back!"

"That's the programme I've mapped out, Sammy. I guess you're right about my gettin' on home, too. I don't feel just the freshest in the world."

"Wait a minute," the other said. "I want to make certain about one thing. You told me I mustn't go near your brother, and my tacklin' him the way I did this morning behind your back—well, I never liked the cold-blooded silk-stocking upstart, but he did show he's a gentleman. I been afraid—" He hesitated, somewhat confused. "Well, I know how it is in families, when one of a family don't want help from another of the same family, the last person on earth, and I been kind of afraid you might hold it some against me, my tacklin' him behind your back like that, after you told me not to."

"Bless you, no!" Dan said heartily. "You haven't done me anything except kindness."

"Well, and I've had many's the favour from you, both business and outside, Dan. That's why I persuaded the old man the city needs a man like you. You got many's the long year of good in you yet, Dan."

"I hope so; I hope so," Dan said, and held out his hand. "Good-night, and thank you."

But Sam almost jumped as he took the extended hand. "My goodness, man, you ought to be home in bed! You had too much excitement and you got a high fever. If I had a temperature like that, I wouldn't be here in my office; I'd be talkin' to my doctor."

"Oh, it'll pass off," Dan returned cheerfully. "It's only one of those up-and-down things—chilly a little while and too hot the next little while. Good-night, old man." And with that, he thanked this boyhood friend again, and descended to the busy street.

After a cloudy day the sky had cleared; a fair sunset was

perceptible as a gloomy fire in the heart of the western smoke; and Dan, having long since dismissed his chauffeur, decided to walk home, instead of taking either a trolley car or a taxicab. Before he had gone far, however, he regretted this decision, for his feet had assumed a peculiar independence, and seemed to be unfamiliar parts of him: it was only by concentrating his will upon them that he forced them to continue to be his carriers. "Strange!" he thought. "A man's own feet behavin' like that!"

Then he laughed to himself, not grimly, yet somewhat ruefully. Everything he had believed his own seemed to be behaving like that. Ornaby Addition had been as much a part of him as his feet were, but he was making his feet behave; and when he could get his breath, and start in again, he would make Ornaby behave once more. The shellbacks might get Ornaby away from him for a while, but they couldn't keep it!

When he reached the tall cast-iron Oliphant gateposts, white no longer, but oyster-coloured with the city grime, there was a taxicab waiting in the street before them; and by this time he was so lifelessly tired he wished the cab might carry him into the house, but exerting his will, made his erratic feet serve him that far. He found his brother-in-law in the library with Mrs. Oliphant, who was crying quietly.

George jumped up as Dan came into the room. "Dan, I'm glad you've come before I have to go. I've got to catch the six-fifteen for New York—"

"No," Dan said, and he sat heavily in one of the comfortable old easy-chairs. "No. I don't believe you better leave town just now. They've thrown me out of control, but I got 'em to promise they'll keep you on, George. If there's somebody there that's in my interest, maybe when I get on my feet again—" He turned to his mother, looking at her perplexedly: "For heaven's sake, don't cry, mother! I'm sorry you've heard about it, but don't you fret: I'll get back— after I've had a few days' rest, maybe I will. I don't believe you'd better go to New York just now, George."

"I've got to," George said. "Dan, I want—I want you to forgive me."

"For wanting to go to New York?"

"No. For ever introducing you to my sister. Your mother wasn't at home this afternoon, and at three o'clock Lena left for New York."

"She did?"

"Yes. Your chauffeur took her to the train. She told him—Dan, she told him to say she wouldn't be back, and she took Henry with her."

212

"Wait a minute!" Dan passed his hand over his forehead, and uttered a confused and plaintive sound of laughter. "Just a minute," he said apologetically. "There's a good deal kind of seems to've hit me all at once. I guess I'll have to go kind of slow takin' it in. You say Lena says she isn't comin' back home?"

"She had the kindness to tell the chauffeur to say so," George replied bitterly.

"And Henry—"

"Henry went with her."

"I guess then I better go after him," Dan said, and he rose; but immediately sank back in his chair. "I don't know if I'd be able to go on your train, though. I expect maybe I need a good night's sleep, first. I—"

"Will you leave it to me?" George asked sharply. "Will you just leave it to me?"

"You mean gettin' them to come home?"

" 'Them!' " George said. "I'm not sure that you need my sister here any longer. I don't think you ever needed her very much. But you do want your son, and if you'll leave it to me, I think I can bring him. Will you, Dan?"

"I guess I'll have to—just now," Dan answered, with a repetition of his apologetic laugh. "It's all seemed to've kind of hit me at once, as it were, George. I'm afraid what I need's a good night's sleep. I'm afraid I'll have to leave it to you."

"I'll bring him!" McMillan promised. "I'll have him back here with me four days from now."

CHAPTER XXX

HE MADE this promise with an angrily confident determination to fulfil it, but the next few days were to teach him that he had not yet learned all there was to know about his sister. When he forced his way to an interview with her in her rooms in the hotel to which she had gone in New York, she laughed at his fury.

"Why haven't I been a good wife to him?" she asked. "I've spent quite a number of years in purgatory, trying to stick to what I undertook when he married me! Oh, yes, I know you like the place, George; and I don't challenge your viewpoint. But I have my own,

213

and, whether it's right or not, it's mine and I can't get rid of it. I suffer by it, and I have to live by it—and to me the place has always been a purgatory. It's interesting to you, but it's hideous to me. You like the people;—to you they seem intelligent and friendly. To me they're intrusive barbarians with unbearable voices. I stood it at first because I had to; I didn't have anywhere else to go, and I did care for Dan. Then I kept on standing it because I'd got the habit, I suppose, and because it's hard to get the courage to break away. Well, thank Heaven, something's given me the courage at last. I was always just on the very verge of it, and the trouble about Henry pushed me over. I've perished for years because I couldn't get a breath of art; I haven't lived—"

"You could have!" he cried. "With such a man—"

"Dan? Good heavens! I might go on living with a man, even after I'd stopped caring for him, if he still cared for me; but it's years since I realized absolutely that neither of us cared for the other. I knew then I'd have to do this some day."

"And how beautifully you did do it!" her brother exclaimed. "His mother told me about your screaming and storming at Dan after he brought that miserable boy home. Do you think I didn't understand? You wanted a quarrel to justify your going, so that the real reason wouldn't be suspected. You'd seen that singing beef again, and you meant to see him again—oh, I kept near you that night, and I read you, every instant! You haven't fooled me about what gave you the 'courage,' Lena! It was indeed 'the breath of art,' old girl, and not 'the trouble about Henry!' You made that quarrel with Dan deliberately. It was to cover what you weren't thoroughbred enough to face. You weren't honest enough to—"

"At least I'm honest enough to tell you that you're wasting your breath," Lena said coolly. "You want to take Henry home with you, but he doesn't care to go. He behaved idiotically there—it isn't a good place for him—and of course, under the circumstances, he's embarrassed about going back. He wants to stay with me just now, and he'll do what I tell him. You can't take him back with you, but if you'll obtain a proper allowance for me, or a settlement, from my husband, I'll arrange later for Henry to spend a part of his time with his father. That's absolutely the best I'll do, and you'd better run back and make it quite clear to Dan. I bear him no ill will, and I'll be perfectly fair with him on the terms I've just mentioned."

Her brother's bitterness with her was not abated; but to effect his purpose he tried more reasonable persuasions, and when these were unavailing, raged again. All he did was useless; he could neither shake her nor exert the slightest influence upon Henry, though he continued the siege for three days over the four that he had promised. Then he returned, a defeated but fuming negotiator, to report his failure. His final instructions from his sister were to make it quite clear to Dan that she bore him no ill will and wished him well.

But when George reached the old house of the Oliphants, driving there directly from the train, he was told that he could not make her message clear to her husband; that he could not make anything clear to him.

Harlan took the dismayed traveller into the library. "The doctor says the trouble is there isn't anything to build up a resistance," Harlan said. "You see Dan's never taken any care of his health—'too busy,' of course—and he's exhausted his vitality. He caught a fearful cold going round in the rain hunting for that precious boy of his, and instead of staying in bed and nursing himself, he was hustling all over the place in a drizzle the next morning. He was all run-down to start with, and his system couldn't afford it. At least, that's what they told us after the consultation yesterday afternoon."

"Consultation?" McMillan repeated blankly, though Harlan's manner had already prepared him for words worse than this.

Harlan sighed audibly, and shook his head. "Both lungs are congested, they told us early this morning. He can't—" He went to the bay window and looked down at the slightly frayed upholstery of the easy-chair it had once been his wont to occupy there. "Well, at your age and mine we've had experience of sickness enough to know that nobody can stand that long."

"Yes," McMillan groaned. "I suppose so."

"I think we won't tell him you've got back," Harlan said. "He's asked about it every now and then—wants to know if you've brought Henry yet. It'll be better to let him keep on expecting him than to tell him you've come back alone. I telegraphed you after the consultation, but by that time you'd already left New York, of course."

"Yes; it didn't reach me."

Then, for a time, neither of them found more to say. Harlan, near the window, stared out into the smoke haze that a cloudy day held down upon the city; McMillan sat frowning at the floor, and the room was vaguely noisy with a confusion of sounds from outdoors: hammerings and clatterings of steel where buildings were going up; the rending of timbers and crashes and shoutings where they were going down; the uproar of ponderous trucks grinding by upon the brick-paved cross street to the south, so that the strong old house trembled with the subterranean communication of their

215

vibrations—all to the incessantly rasped accompaniment of motor signals on the avenue.

"Isn't this a hell to be sick in?" Harlan asked, turning abruptly to McMillan. "We couldn't raise the windows to give him air without giving him this infernal smoke that makes him cough harder. And the noise—there's hardly a respite from it all night long! When the workmen go home the joy-riders and the taxis keep it up till daylight. He was too sick to be taken to a hospital or—" He interrupted himself with a desperate laugh. "We almost had to! Yesterday morning the servants called me, and I found the house full of men; they'd brought trucks right across the lawn, and started to work. They'd come to wreck the house—to tear it down. I told the foreman my brother was very sick, and he said in that case we'd better take him to a hospital; he had his orders from the contractor, and he was going ahead! Some of his men were already on the roof, making a horrible noise and tearing away the slate—throwing it down into the yard under Dan's window. I had hard work to get rid of them; and they left a great hole in the roof when they went. My heaven! when such things happen how's anybody ever to see any meaning in life?"

"I don't know!" George groaned. "I don't see much meaning in anything—not after what you've told me about Dan's condition."

"McMillan, I don't see a bit of meaning to the whole miserable business. Here's my brother spent all his days and nights—and all his strength and health—just blindly building up a bigger confusion and uproar that smashes him; and then when he is smashed, it keeps on bothering him and disturbing him—yes, and choking him!—on his very deathbed! I know your theory that it all means power, and that power may be thought beautiful—but it can't last, because nothing can last. So what the deuce is the good of it?"

And when the other, groaning again, said that he didn't know, Harlan groaned, too—then crossed the room to where George sat in a crumpled attitude, touched him lightly on the shoulder, and turned away. "You're a good fellow, McMillan, and you haven't anything in the world to reproach yourself with. I don't think he's minded Lena's going away; he hasn't spoken of her at all, and I really believe he doesn't think of her. Your record with Dan is all right, but I've been realizing that mine isn't. I could have made success easier for him long ago; though I don't reproach myself so much with that, because he did get his success—for a while, and that's all anybody gets—and he enjoyed it all the more for having got it without help. What I'm thinking about this morning: I seem to have spent a great part of my life saying, 'What's the good of it?' as I did just now, and it's my brother's work I've been saying it about.

I've always been 'superior'—and I'll never be different. I was born so, I believe, and didn't see it in time. The most I've ever actually done was to help organize a dilettante musical club! And Dan—well, I hope it's as you intimated the other night on Martha's porch—I hope Dan's been too busy to be much bothered about my 'judgments!' I've been just nothing; but even if he falls, he's at least been a branch of the growing tree, though we don't know where it's growing to, or why."

"No," McMillan said. "We don't know anything."

Harlan had begun to pace up and down the room. "I didn't understand that Dan was in real trouble financially," he said. "He'd been on the edge so often—I talked about it, but I'd got to thinking of it as a permanent thing for him to be on the edge. I didn't realize he might actually fall off—not until that little Jew friend of his came to me the other morning and made me realize it. Well, there's one thing I can be thankful for: I can be grateful that all I thought of, for once in my life, was that I was Dan's brother!"

"Harlan?" Martha Shelby's voice called him softly from the stairway.

"Yes?" He turned to the door, explaining, "Dan may want me—he sends for me to come in sometimes. Perhaps you might—" He paused.

"Yes," George said, rising. "I'll go and wire her. She might want to come. At any rate she'll send Henry. Then I'll come back here. I'll be downstairs in this room, if there's anything—"

"I'll let you know," Harlan said, and he went upstairs to Martha.

"Your mother's been with him," she whispered. "She and the nurse said he seemed to be trying to ask for somebody, but he was so weak, and his cough troubled him so much—"

"I'll go in and see," he said; but he came back to her a few moments later, and told her it was for her that Dan was asking.

She went into his room, sat by his bed, and put her hand gently over his on the coverlet. "Why, you're better, Dan," she said, as he turned his head and looked at her with eyes that cleared and grew brighter, for he recognized her.

"Think so?" He spoke distinctly though his voice was weak. "Well, maybe—maybe. I did hope—"

"Yes, Dan?"

"I did hope I wouldn't have to be sick very long. I've got so much to do. I've done a good deal of work, but I haven't ever got anywhere with it, much. There's a mighty big lot I'll have to begin over, Martha. You don't"—he paused, and laughed faintly. "You

217

don't—you don't suppose God's used me and now He's goin' to throw me away, do you?"

"No, no, no!" she said, making her voice cheerful. "You've only got to go ahead with what you began long ago."

"No," he said reflectively. "No; it isn't exactly like that, Martha. Not exactly, that is. You see right now I'm a pretty complete failure—yes, I am. I'm a pretty bad failure."

"You? You're not!"

"Yes, I am," he returned feebly. "I better face it, Martha, or I'll never get anywhere. They've got Ornaby away from me—" His cough interrupted him; but he patiently let it have its way; and then, in a tone in which a wondering incredulity seemed to merge with resignation, he said, "Yes, sir; they did get Ornaby away from me!"

"But you'll get it back, Dan?"

"Think so? Well, maybe—maybe," he said indulgently. "But things do look like it came pretty close to a failure, Martha. It would have been one, too—it'd have been a bankruptcy, and I believe I just couldn't have stood that—but, well, anyhow it wasn't that bad, thanks to Harlan."

Martha's eyes widened. "Do you mean—do you mean Harlan helped you?"

"It was mighty good of him," Dan said. "My friends went to him and asked him if he wouldn't let us have some money on a second mortgage on the new house. Harlan dug out all the securities he could sell for ready cash and he brought the money to me down at Sam Kohn's office. I must make it up to him some day. If it hadn't been for that I'd have gone clean under!" He laughed huskily. "Everybody'd have known I was a failure for sure, if it hadn't been for that, Martha."

"But you're not!" she insisted. "You mustn't keep talking such nonsense, Dan."

"It isn't—it isn't exactly nonsense." The cough stopped him again; but he went on, while it still troubled him: "I'm a failure, Martha. I've been a failure in business—and a failure as a husband—and a failure as a father. George McMillan hasn't got here with Henry yet, has he?"

"No, dear; not yet."

Dan's hand moved restlessly under hers, and she released it. With a visible effort he rubbed his forehead, a gesture of perplexity that hurt her and made it difficult for her to retain her appearance of cheerfulness, because this characteristic gesture brought his boyhood so vividly to her memory. "I've just got to have Henry back," he said. "I've got to get him back so's to do right by him. It isn't—it isn't fair to a boy, Martha."

"What isn't?"

"Do you remember my grandmother Savage?"

"Of course. No one could forget her, Dan."

"No, I guess not. Well, she"—he shook his head, and half coughed, half laughed—"she was right about some things. My! but wouldn't she be sayin', 'Didn't I tell you so?' if she knew what's happened to my poor Henry! I've been a terrible failure with Henry, Martha." He looked patiently at her as she denied this; and then he said abruptly: "Why, I've even been a failure with you, Martha!"

"That's the absurdest thing you've said, dear!"

"No. I've been a failure as a friend, too. I let Lena fret me out of comin' in to see you when you'd been away that long stretch. I had no business to pay any attention to her. You see—why, you always really liked me better than she did, Martha!"

He spoke as if it were a discovery just made; and she assented to it, taking his hand again. "Yes, Dan. I've always liked you better than anybody."

"Have you?" he said inquiringly. "Well, I'm right glad to hear it. I'm right glad to hear it, Martha."

"Yes, dear. I always have."

He closed his eyes, but she felt a faint pressure upon her hand from his, and sat still for a time, looking at him with fond eyes that grew frightened as the pressure upon her fingers relaxed. She was not sure, for the moment, that he was still breathing; and she looked a terrified inquiry at the grave nurse who sat on the other side of the bed. The nurse shook her head, forming with her lips the word, "Sleeping"; but Dan opened his eyes again.

"It's curious," he said, "the way things are. A fellow goes along, and everything seems to run all right, year after year—he can hear a little kind of grindin' noise, maybe, sometimes, or something seems to slip, but he patches it up and doesn't let it scare him—he keeps goin' right along and everything seems to be workin' about as usual—and then one thing goes wrong—and then another—and then all of a sudden the whole works pile up on top of him, and he's down under the heap!" He took his hand again from Martha's, and again passed it tremulously over his forehead in the old familiar gesture. "Well—maybe I could start in again if I can get over what ails me. I expect I need a good night's rest first, though. Maybe I can sleep now."

Martha went tiptoeing out, and through the hall to the room that had been Lena's. Harlan was there, sitting close beside his mother. "He wants to sleep," Martha told them, but had no sooner spoken than Dan's renewed coughing was heard—a sound that

219

racked the sick man's mother. She shivered and gasped, and then, as the convulsion became fainter, went out trembling into the hall.

"Harlan," Martha said, "why didn't you tell me you tried to help Dan—at last?"

He rose, looking annoyed. "I didn't do anything that was in the slightest degree a sacrifice," he said. "I don't want you to misunderstand it. I never helped him when I thought it would be thrown away, and I didn't this time. He made over the new house to me, and I guess Lena'll sign the deed; she'll have to. In time it'll probably be worth all I gave for it. I wasn't going to see the name of Oliphant dragged through all the miserable notoriety of bankruptcy—and there was something besides."

"Yes?" she said. "What was that?"

"Well, a pack of old money-vultures were after him, and after all Dan's my brother."

"Yes, he is!" Martha said. She began to cry bitterly, but silently; then suddenly she put her arms about him. "He's still your brother, Harlan! We can say that yet;—he's just in that room down the hall there—he's not gone away—he's still your brother, Harlan!"

But even as Martha spoke, Mrs. Oliphant, looking through the door of the sick room, cried out in terror, then rushed to her son's bedside. Dan had unexpectedly lifted himself almost half upright; he seemed to struggle to rise; and in his eyes, wide-opened, but seeing neither his mother nor the nurse, there was a look of startled incredulity—the look of one who suddenly recognizes, to his utter astonishment, an old acquaintance long since disappeared but now abruptly returned.

A moment later the uncontrolled sobbing of his mother let Harlan know that he no longer had a brother in the room down the hall.

CHAPTER XXXI

THE war halted the wrecking of National Avenue, but not for long. Until the soldiers came home and the country could begin to get back into its great stride again, groups of the old, thick-walled, big-roomed houses were permitted to survive; and although it was a survival doomed, and the dignity of the dignified old things had begun to appear somewhat ridiculous, since they were smeared with

220

the smoke-fog and begirt with automobile warehouses and salesbuildings and noisy garages and repair shops, and every other kind of shop and office, yet here and there was the semblance—or, at least, the reminder—of a fine, ample, and mannerly old street that had once been the glory of its town.

But when the great heydays came, following the collapse of the war "expansion," and the country took up its dropped trades again, and renewed with furious and reckless energy its suppressed building, and, instead of getting back into its old great stride, set forth in a new stride gigantic beyond all its striding aforetime, then indeed the old avenue perished utterly, and nothing was left even to hint what it had been, or to tell its noble story. Old Hickory Shelby's house was the last to go;—the stone casing of his tall front doorway was the last of all the relics. Even when the rest of the house was flat, hauled away with the fountain swan and the cast-iron fence in dumping wagons and in the trucks of junk-dealers, the doorway was allowed to remain in place above the ruins of the veranda; and for several weeks stood forth against the setting sun like a fragment on the Roman Campagna. But in time it fell, too, as the Roman fragments will.

When it was gone the old hickory stick was gone, too. He had declined to the last to be an ornament of his daughter's fireside; and she never knew that she owed her husband's ownership of the "new house" to her father's insistence on a "conservative policy" for the bank of which he was one of the directors. Old Hickory's thoughts were his own, as his ways were his own; and what he knew about himself he kept to himself, as he once or twice with a dry crackling informed his daughter.

The new house was a white house, and it remained almost white; for the smoke reached it but thinly, and in northern Ornaby, where there were other large white houses among the groves Dan Oliphant had preserved, the people struggled successfully to keep the curse under. Shrubberies lived there, not suffocated; it was a place where faces stayed clean, children throve, and lilacs bloomed in transparent air.

Martha drove downtown, late one afternoon of a cool day at the end of a green May, to bring her husband home from a directors' meeting at the bank; for Harlan, in her interest, had inherited his father-in-law's position; and, as they rolled homeward, checked now and then in the jam of traffic that filled the whole length of National Avenue, she spoke of the prevalence of "Sheridans," those excellently serviceable cars.

"Rather!" Harlan said. "All that old rascal had to do when he got control of the 'Ornaby Four' was to put back the old clutch and change the name. They're all over the country. Dan would have made a great fortune if he'd lived and could have held on."

"I don't think he'd mind missing the fortune much," she said. "I wish he could know how many people are riding in his cars, though. He'd like to know about that."

They passed a "gas-station," a flamboyantly painted bit of carnival, with an automobile warehouse and salesroom, and then an apartment house built round a begrimed courtyard, for its neighbours; and Harlan sighed. "It's hard to imagine you and I once lived where these things are, isn't it?" he said.

"Yes, some of it's pretty ugly."

"It's all ugly. It's all hideous!" he said.

"No, not all." And when they had left the avenue behind them, and reached the district of the bungalows and small wooden houses, she showed him gardens that he was forced to admit were "pretty." But when they got beyond this, to where had been the broad stretches of woodland and meadow that Dan had planned for his "restricted residence district," she insisted on her husband's consent to the word "beautiful"; for the woodland was still there, so that one could hardly see the houses; and long hedges of bridal-wreath were flowering everywhere, as if snow had fallen upon the shrubberies.

"Hasn't beauty come, Harlan?" she said.

"Oh, it's well enough here," he grumbled, as they swept into their own deep-shaded driveway.

Then they descended at white stone steps that led them up and out upon a terrace, and there they found the other member of their household sitting placidly—"to enjoy the bridal-wreath," she said.

"Isn't it rather chilly for you outdoors, mother?" Harlan asked; for she was now so fragile that she seemed almost transparent. "Don't you want to go in?"

"No, not just yet," she said. "I was just sitting here thinking how your father would have enjoyed all this. The town was pleasant when he and I were young, but of course it was never anything like this."

"No," Harlan said, with satire. "I should say it wasn't!"

"It's a great change," the old lady continued. "I don't suppose my mother could have believed how beautiful it would come to be."

"No," Harlan said, with a short laugh. "I don't believe she could!"

She overlooked his sarcasm, or was unaware of it, for she went on: "I don't suppose I could believe how wonderful everything will be when my grandson gets to be as old as you are, Harlan." But this thought made her wander from the subject. "I wish Lena would let

222

him come home some day; I do want to see him;—I don't want to go till I've seen him again." Her voice became querulous, and then, with a habit she had formed in her old age, she began to talk more to herself than to her son and daughter-in-law, but for the most part in indistinct whispers. Her subject was still Henry, who had done well in the war, had been twice "decorated," and now lived in Paris with his mother. The old lady murmured of him and of Lena for a little time; then fell into a reverie.

Harlan joined his wife at the terrace wall. "Well, you've got a supporter in mother. She seems to think it's beautiful." He pointed upward to where an opening through the foliage of tall beech trees left a vista of the sky; and there, against the evening blue, the thinning end of a plume of smoke, miles long, was visible. "Do you, really? Even that?" he asked.

"Dan must have thought so," she said. "I think he felt something in it that neither you nor I can understand."

"I think maybe he did," Harlan agreed. "Then why couldn't he at least have lived to see the fruition of what he planted, since he loved it and it was beautiful to him? Why should he be 'dead and forgotten?'"

"Listen!" Martha said. She was still looking up at the smoke against the sky, so far above the long masses of flowering bridal-wreath that bordered the terrace where she and her husband stood. "Listen! That murmur of the city down yonder—why, it's almost his voice!"

THE END